THE INFERNAL DEVICES

· Book Two ·

Clockwork Prince

Also by Cassandra Clare

THE MORTAL INSTRUMENTS:

City of Bones

City of Ashes

City of Glass

City of Fallen Angels

City of Lost Souls

THE INFERNAL DEVICES:

Clockwork Angel

Clockwork Princess

THE INFERNAL DEVICES

· Book Two ·

Clockwork Prince

CASSANDRA CLARE

Margaret K. McElderry Books
NEW YORK LONDON TORONTO SYDNEY NEW DELHI

MARGARET K. McELDERRY BOOKS

An imprint of Simon & Schuster Children's Publishing Division

1230 Avenue of the Americas, New York, New York 10020

This book is a work of fiction. Any references to historical events, real people, or real places are used fictitiously. Other names, characters, places, and events are products of the author's imagination, and any resemblance to actual events or places or persons, living or dead, is entirely coincidental.

Copyright © 2011 by Cassandra Claire LLC

All rights reserved, including the right of reproduction in whole or in part in any form.

MARGARET K. McELDERRY BOOKS is a trademark of Simon & Schuster, Inc.

For information about special discounts for bulk purchases, please contact Simon & Schuster Special Sales at 1-866-506-1949 or business@simonandschuster.com.

The Simon & Schuster Speakers Bureau can bring authors to your live event. For more information or to book an event, contact the Simon & Schuster Speakers Bureau at 1-866-248-3049 or visit our website at www.simonspeakers.com.

Also available in a Margaret K. McElderry Books hardcover edition

Book design by Mike Rosamilia

The text for this book is set in Dolly.

Manufactured in the United States of America

First Margaret K. McElderry Books paperback edition March 2013

2 4 6 8 10 9 7 5 3 1

The Library of Congress has cataloged the hardcover edition as follows:

Clare, Cassandra.

Clockwork prince / Cassandra Clare.—1st ed.

p. cm.—(The infernal devices ; bk. 2)

Summary: As the Council attempts to strip Charlotte of her power, sixteen-year-old orphaned shapechanger Tessa Gray works with the London Shadowhunters to find the Magister and destroy his clockwork army, learning the secret of her own identity while investigating his past.

ISBN 978-1-4169-7588-5 (hardcover)

ISBN 978-1-4424-3134-8 (eBook)

[1. Supernatural—Fiction. 2. Demonology—Fiction. 3. Orphans—Fiction. 4. Secret societies—Fiction. 5. Identity—Fiction. 6. London (England)—History—19th century—Fiction. 7. Great Britain—History—Victoria, 1837–1901—Fiction.] I. Title.

PZ7.C5265Cp 2011

[Fic]—dc23

2011017869

ISBN 978-1-4169-7589-2 (pbk)

For Elka

Khalepa ta kala

"I wish you to know that you have been the last dream of my soul. . . . Since I knew you, I have been troubled by a remorse that I thought would never reproach me again, and have heard whispers from old voices impelling me upward, that I thought were silent for ever. I have had unformed ideas of striving afresh, beginning anew, shaking off sloth and sensuality, and fighting out the abandoned fight. A dream, all a dream, that ends in nothing. . . ."

—Charles Dickens, *A Tale of Two Cities*

THE INFERNAL DEVICES

· Book Two ·

Clockwork Prince

Prologue

The Outcast Dead

The fog was thick, muffling sound and sight. Where it parted, Will Herondale could see the street rising ahead of him, slick and wet and black with rain, and he could hear the voices of the dead.

Not all Shadowhunters could hear ghosts, unless the ghosts chose to be heard, but Will was one of those who could. As he approached the old cemetery, their voices rose in a ragged chorus—wails and pleading, cries and snarls. This was not a peaceful burial ground, but Will knew that; it was not his first visit to the Cross Bones Graveyard near London Bridge. He did his best to block out the noises, hunching his shoulders so that his collar covered his ears, head down, a fine mist of rain dampening his black hair.

The entrance to the cemetery was halfway down the block: a pair of wrought iron gates set into a high stone wall, though any mundane passing by would have observed nothing but a plot of overgrown land, part of an unnamed builder's yard. As Will neared the gates, something else no mundane would have seen materialized out of the fog: a great bronze knocker in the shape of a hand, the fingers bony and skeletal. With a grimace Will reached out one of his own gloved hands and lifted the knocker, letting it fall once, twice, three times, the hollow clank resounding through the night.

Beyond the gates mist rose like steam from the ground, obscuring the gleam of bone against the rough ground. Slowly the mist began to coalesce, taking on an eerie blue glow. Will put his hands to the bars of the gate; the cold of the metal seeped through his gloves, into his bones, and he shivered. It was a more than ordinary cold. When ghosts rose, they drew energy from their surroundings, depriving the air around them of heat. The hairs on the back of Will's neck prickled and stood up as the blue mist formed slowly into the shape of an old woman in a ragged dress and white apron, her head bent.

"Hallo, Mol," said Will. "You're looking particularly fine this evening, if I do say so."

The ghost raised her head. Old Molly was a strong spirit, one of the stronger Will had ever encountered. Even as moonlight speared through a gap in the clouds, she hardly looked transparent. Her body was solid, her hair twisted in a thick yellow-gray coil over one shoulder, her rough, red hands braced on her hips. Only her eyes were hollow, twin blue flames flickering in their depths.

"William 'erondale," she said. "Back again so soon?"

She moved toward the gate with that gliding motion peculiar to ghosts. Her feet were bare and filthy, despite the fact that they never touched the ground.

Will leaned against the gate. "You know I missed your pretty face."

She grinned, her eyes flickering, and he caught a glimpse of the skull beneath the half-transparent skin. Overhead the clouds had closed in on one another again, blocking out the moon. Idly, Will wondered what Old Molly had done to get herself buried here, far from consecrated ground. Most of the wailing voices of the dead belonged to prostitutes, suicides, and stillbirths—those outcast dead who could not be buried in a churchyard. Although Molly had managed to make the situation quite profitable for herself, so perhaps she didn't mind.

She chortled. "What d'you want, then, young Shadowhunter? Malphas venom? I 'ave the talon of a Morax demon, polished very fine, the poison at the tip entirely invisible—"

"No," Will said. "That's not what I need. I need Foraii demon powders, ground fine."

Molly turned her head to the side and spat a tendril of blue fire. "Now what's a fine young man like you want with stuff like that?"

Will just sighed inwardly; Molly's protests were part of the bargaining process. Magnus had already sent Will to Old Mol several times now, once for black stinking candles that stuck to his skin like tar, once for the bones of an unborn child, and once for a bag of faeries' eyes, which had dripped blood on his shirt. Foraii demon powder sounded pleasant by comparison.

"You think I'm a fool," Molly went on. "This is a trap, innit?

You Nephilim catch me selling that sort of stuff, an' it's the stick for Old Mol, it is."

"You're *already* dead." Will did his best not to sound irritable. "I don't know what you think the Clave could do to you now."

"Pah." Her hollow eyes flamed. "The prisons of the Silent Brothers, beneath the earth, can 'old either the living or the dead; you know that, Shadowhunter."

Will held up his hands. "No tricks, old one. Surely you must have heard the rumors running about in Downworld. The Clave has other things on its mind than tracking down ghosts who traffic in demon powders and faerie blood." He leaned forward. "I'll give you a good price." He drew a cambric bag from his pocket and dangled it in the air. It clinked like coins rattling together. "They all fit your description, Mol."

An eager look came over her dead face, and she solidified enough to take the bag from him. She plunged one hand into it and brought her palm out full of rings—gold wedding rings, each tied in a lovers' knot at the top. Old Mol, like many ghosts, was always looking for that talisman, that lost piece of her past that would finally allow her to die, the anchor that kept her trapped in the world. In her case it was her wedding ring. It was common belief, Magnus had told Will, that the ring was long gone, buried under the silty bed of the Thames, but in the meantime she'd take any bag of found rings in the hope one would turn out to be hers.

She dropped the rings back into the bag, which vanished somewhere on her undead person, and handed him a folded sachet of powder in return. He slipped it into his jacket pocket just as the ghost began to shimmer and fade. "Hold up, there, Mol. That isn't all I have come for tonight."

The spirit flickered while greed warred with impatience and the effort of remaining visible. Finally she grunted. "Very well. What else d'you want?"

Will hesitated. This was not something Magnus had sent him for; it was something he wanted to know for himself. "Love potions—"

Old Mol screeched with laughter. "*Love potions?* For Will 'erondale? 'Tain't my way to turn down payment, but any man who looks like you 'as got no need of love potions, and that's a fact."

"No," Will said, a little desperation in his voice. "I was looking for the opposite, really—something that might put an end to being in love."

"An 'atred potion?" Mol still sounded amused.

"I was hoping for something more akin to indifference? Tolerance?"

She made a snorting noise, astonishingly human for a ghost. "I 'ardly like to tell you this, Nephilim, but if you want a girl to 'ate you, there's easy enough ways of making it 'appen. You don't need *my* help with the poor thing."

And with that she vanished, spinning away into the mists among the graves. Will, looking after her, sighed. "Not for her," he said under his breath, though there was no one to hear him, "for *me* . . ." And he leaned his head against the cold iron gate.

1

The Council Chamber

Above, the fair hall-ceiling stately set
Many an arch high up did lift,
And angels rising and descending met
With interchange of gift.
–Alfred, Lord Tennyson, "The Palace of Art"

"Oh, yes. It really does look just as I imagined," Tessa said, and turned to smile at the boy who stood beside her. He had just helped her over a puddle, and his hand still rested politely on her arm, just above the crook of her elbow.

James Carstairs smiled back at her, elegant in his dark suit, his silver-fair hair whipped by the wind. His other hand rested on a jade-topped cane, and if any of the great crowd of people milling around them thought that it was odd that someone so young should need a walking stick, or found anything unusual about his coloring or the cast of his features, they didn't pause to stare.

"I shall count that as a blessing," said Jem. "I was beginning to worry, you know, that everything you encountered in London was going to be a disappointment."

A disappointment. Tessa's brother, Nate, had once promised her everything in London—a new beginning, a wonderful place to live, a city of soaring buildings and gorgeous parks. What Tessa had found instead was horror and betrayal, and danger beyond anything she could have imagined. And yet . . .

"Not everything has been." She smiled up at Jem.

"I am glad to hear it." His tone was serious, not teasing. She looked away from him up at the grand edifice that rose before them. Westminster Abbey, with its great Gothic spires nearly touching the sky. The sun had done its best to struggle out from behind the haze-tipped clouds, and the abbey was bathed in weak sunlight.

"This is really where it is?" she asked as Jem drew her forward, toward the abbey entrance. "It seems so . . ."

"Mundane?"

"I had meant to say crowded." The Abbey was open to tourists today, and groups of them swarmed busily in and out the enormous doors, most clutching Baedeker guidebooks in their hands. A group of American tourists—middle-aged women in unfashionable clothes, murmuring in accents that made Tessa briefly homesick—passed them as they went up the stairs, hurrying after a lecturer who was offering a guided tour of the Abbey. Jem and Tessa melted in effortlessly behind them.

The inside of the abbey smelled of cold stone and metal. Tessa looked up and around, marveling at the size of the place. It made the Institute look like a village church.

"Notice the triple division of the nave," a guide droned,

going on to explain that smaller chapels lined the eastern and western aisles of the Abbey. There was a hush over the place even though no services were going on. As Tessa let Jem lead her toward the eastern side of the church, she realized she was stepping over stones carved with dates and names. She had known that famous kings, queens, soldiers, and poets were buried in Westminster Abbey, but she hadn't quite expected she'd be standing on top of them.

She and Jem slowed finally at the southeastern corner of the church. Watery daylight poured through the rose window overhead. "I know we are in a hurry to get to the Council meeting," said Jem, "but I wanted you to see this." He gestured around them. "Poets' Corner."

Tessa had read of the place, of course, where the great writers of England were buried. There was the gray stone tomb of Chaucer, with its canopy, and other familiar names: "Edmund Spenser, oh, and Samuel Johnson," she gasped, "and Coleridge, and Robert Burns, and *Shakespeare*—"

"He isn't really buried here," said Jem quickly. "It's just a monument. Like Milton's."

"Oh, I know, but—" She looked at him, and felt herself flush. "I can't explain it. It's like being among friends, being among these names. Silly, I know . . ."

"Not silly at all."

She smiled at him. "How did you know just what I'd want to see?"

"How could I not?" he said. "When I think of you, and you are not there, I see you in my mind's eye always with a book in your hand." He looked away from her as he said it, but not before she caught the slight flush on his cheekbones. He was so pale, he could never hide even the least blush, she thought—and was surprised how affectionate the thought was.

She had become very fond of Jem over the past fortnight; Will had been studiously avoiding her, Charlotte and Henry were caught up in issues of Clave and Council and the running of the Institute—and even Jessamine seemed preoccupied. But Jem was always there. He seemed to take his role as her guide to London seriously. They had been to Hyde Park and Kew Gardens, the National Gallery and the British Museum, the Tower of London and Traitors' Gate. They had gone to see the cows being milked in St. James's Park, and the fruit and vegetable sellers hawking their wares in Covent Garden. They had watched the boats sailing on the sun-sparked Thames from the Embankment, and had eaten things called "door-stops," which sounded horrible but turned out to be butter, sugar, and bread. And as the days went on, Tessa felt herself unfolding slowly out of her quiet, huddled unhappiness over Nate and Will and the loss of her old life, like a flower climbing out of frozen ground. She had even found herself laughing. And she had Jem to thank for it.

"You *are* a good friend," she exclaimed. And when to her surprise he said nothing to that, she said, "At least, I hope we are good friends. You do think so too, don't you, Jem?"

He turned to look at her, but before he could reply, a sepulchral voice spoke out of the shadows,

"'Mortality, behold and fear!
What a change of flesh is here:
Think how many royal bones
Sleep within these heaps of stones.'"

A dark shape stepped out from between two monuments. As Tessa blinked in surprise, Jem said, in a tone of resigned amusement, "Will. Decided to grace us with your presence after all?"

"I never said I wasn't coming." Will moved forward, and the light from the rose windows fell on him, illuminating his face. Even now, Tessa never could look at him without a tightening in her chest, a painful stutter of her heart. Black hair, blue eyes, graceful cheekbones, thick dark lashes, full mouth—he would have been pretty if he had not been so tall and so muscular. She had run her hands over those arms. She knew what they felt like—iron, corded with hard muscles; his hands, when they cupped the back of her head, slim and flexible but rough with calluses . . .

She tore her mind away from the memories. Memories did one no good, not when one knew the truth in the present. Will was beautiful, but he was not hers; he was not anybody's. Something in him was broken, and through that break spilled a blind cruelty, a need to hurt and to push away.

"You're late for the Council meeting," said Jem good-naturedly. He was the only one Will's puckish malice never seemed to touch.

"I had an errand," said Will. Up close Tessa could see that he looked tired. His eyes were rimmed with red, the shadows beneath them nearly purple. His clothes looked crumpled, as if he had slept in them, and his hair wanted cutting. *But that has nothing to do with you,* she told herself sternly, looking away from the soft dark waves that curled around his ears, the back of his neck. *It does not matter what you think of how he looks or how he chooses to spend his time. He has made that very clear.* "And you are not exactly on the dot of the hour yourselves."

"I wanted to show Tessa Poets' Corner," said Jem. "I thought she would like it." He spoke so simply and plainly, no one could ever doubt him or imagine he said anything but the truth. In the face of his simple desire to please, even Will didn't seem to be able to think of anything unpleasant to say; he merely shrugged, and moved on ahead of them at a rapid pace through the abbey and out into the East Cloister.

There was a square garden here surrounded by cloister walls, and people were walking around the edges of it, murmuring in low voices as if they were still in the church. None of them took notice of Tessa and her companions as they approached a set of double oak doors set into one of the walls. Will, after glancing around, took his stele from his pocket and drew the tip across the wood. The door sparked with a brief blue light and swung open. Will stepped inside, Jem and Tessa following just behind. The door was heavy, and closed with a resounding bang behind Tessa, nearly trapping her skirts; she pulled them away only just in time, and stepped backward quickly, turning around in what was a near pitch-darkness. "Jem?"

Light blazed up; it was Will, holding his witchlight stone. They were in a large stone-bound room with vaulted ceilings. The floor appeared to be brick, and there was an altar at one end of the room. "We're in the Pyx Chamber," he said. "Used to be a treasury. Boxes of gold and silver all along the walls."

"A Shadowhunter treasury?" Tessa was thoroughly puzzled.

"No, the British royal treasury—thus the thick walls and doors," said Jem. "But we Shadowhunters have always had access." He smiled at her expression. "Monarchies down through the ages have tithed to the Nephilim, in secret, to keep their kingdoms safe from demons."

"Not in America," said Tessa with spirit. "We haven't got a monarchy—"

"You've got a branch of government that deals with Nephilim, never fear," said Will, crossing the floor to the altar. "It used to be the Department of War, but now there's a branch of the Department of Justice—"

He was cut off as the altar moved sideways with a groan, revealing a dark, empty hole behind it. Tessa could see faint flickers of light in among the shadows. Will ducked into the hole, his witchlight illuminating the darkness.

When Tessa followed, she found herself in a long downward-sloping stone corridor. The stone of the walls, floors, and ceiling was all the same, giving the impression that the passage had been hewed directly through the rock, though it was smooth instead of rough. Every few feet witchlight burned in a sconce shaped like a human hand pushing through the wall, fingers gripping a torch.

The altar slid shut behind them, and they set off. As they went, the passage began to slope more steeply downward. The torches burned with a blue-green glow, illuminating carvings in the rock—the same motif, repeated over and over, of an angel rising in burning fire from a lake, carrying a sword in one hand and a cup in the other.

At last they found themselves standing before two great silver doors. Each door was carved with a design Tessa had seen before—four interlocking *C*s. Jem pointed to them. "They stand for Clave and Council, Covenant and Consul," he said, before she could ask.

"The Consul. He's—the head of the Clave? Like a sort of king?"

"Not quite so inbred as your usual monarch," said Will. "He's elected, like the president or the prime minister."

"And the Council?"

"You'll see them soon enough." Will pushed the doors open.

Tessa's mouth fell open; she closed it quickly, but not before she caught an amused look from Jem, standing at her right side. The room beyond them was one of the biggest she had ever seen, a huge domed space, the ceiling of which was painted with a pattern of stars and constellations. A great chandelier in the shape of an angel holding blazing torches dangled from the highest point of the dome. The rest of the room was set up as an amphitheater, with long, curving benches. Will, Jem, and Tessa were standing at the top of a row of stairs that cut through the center of the seating area, which was three quarters full of people. Down at the bottom of the steps was a raised platform, and on that platform were several uncomfortable-looking high-backed wooden chairs.

In one of them sat Charlotte; beside her was Henry, looking wide-eyed and nervous. Charlotte sat calmly with her hands in her lap; only someone who knew her well would have seen the tension in her shoulders and the set of her mouth.

Before them, at a sort of speaker's lectern—it was broader and longer than the usual lectern—stood a tall man with long, fair hair and a thick beard; his shoulders were broad, and he wore long black robes over his clothes like a judge, the sleeves glimmering with woven runes. Beside him, in a low chair, sat an older man, his brown hair streaked with gray, his face clean-shaven but sunk into stern lines. His robe was dark blue, and gems glittered on his fingers when he moved his hand. Tessa recognized him: the ice-voiced, ice-eyed Inquisitor Whitelaw who questioned witnesses on behalf of the Clave.

"Mr. Herondale," said the blond man, looking up at Will, and his mouth quirked into a smile. "How kind of you to join us. And Mr. Carstairs as well. And your companion must be—"

"Miss Gray," Tessa said before he could finish. "Miss Theresa Gray of New York."

A little murmur ran around the room, like the sound of a wave receding. She felt Will, next to her, tense, and Jem draw a breath as if to speak. *Interrupting the Consul*, she thought she heard someone say. So this was Consul Wayland, the chief officer of the Clave. Glancing around the room, she saw a few familiar faces—Benedict Lightwood, with his sharp, beaky features and stiff carriage; and his son, tousle-haired Gabriel Lightwood, looking stonily straight ahead. Dark-eyed Lilian Highsmith. Friendly-looking George Penhallow; and even Charlotte's formidable aunt Callida, her hair piled on her head in thick gray waves. There were many other faces as well, ones she didn't know. It was like looking at a picture book meant to tell you about all the peoples of the world. There were blond Viking-looking Shadowhunters, and a darker-skinned man who looked like a caliph out of her illustrated *The Thousand and One Nights*, and an Indian woman in a beautiful sari trimmed with silver runes. She sat beside another woman, who had turned her head and was looking at them. She wore an elegant silk dress, and her face was like Jem's—the same delicately beautiful features, the same curves to her eyes and cheekbones, though where his hair and eyes were silver, hers were dark.

"Welcome, then, Miss Tessa Gray of New York," said the Consul, sounding amused. "We appreciate your joining us here today. I understand you have already answered quite a few questions for the London Enclave. I had hoped you would be willing to answer a few more."

Across the distance that separated them, Tessa's eyes met Charlotte's. *Should I?*

Charlotte dropped her a nearly imperceptible nod. *Please.*

Tessa squared her shoulders. "If that is your request, certainly."

"Approach the Council bench, then," said the Consul, and Tessa realized he must mean the long, narrow wooden bench that stood before the lectern. "And your gentleman friends may escort you," he added.

Will muttered something under his breath, but so quietly even Tessa couldn't hear it; flanked by Will on her left and Jem on her right, Tessa made her way down the steps and to the bench before the lectern. She stood behind it uncertainly. This close up, she could see that the Consul had friendly blue eyes, unlike the Inquisitor's, which were a bleak and stormy gray, like a rainy sea.

"Inquisitor Whitelaw," said the Consul to the gray-eyed man, "the Mortal Sword, if you please."

The Inquisitor stood, and from his robes drew a massive blade. Tessa recognized it instantly. It was long and dull silver, its hilt carved in the shape of outspread wings. It was the sword from the *Codex*, the one that the Angel Raziel had risen from the lake carrying, and had given to Jonathan Shadowhunter, the first of them all.

"Maellartach," she said, giving the Sword its name.

The Consul, taking the Sword, looked amused again. "You *have* been studying up," he said. "Which of you has been teaching her? William? James?"

"Tessa picks things up on her own, sir," Will's drawl was bland and cheerful, at odds with the grim feeling in the room. "She's very inquisitive."

"All the more reason she shouldn't be here." Tessa didn't have to turn; she knew the voice. Benedict Lightwood. "This is the Gard Council. We don't bring Downworlders to this place." His voice was tight. "The Mortal Sword cannot be used to make her tell the truth; she's not a Shadowhunter. What use is it, or her, here?"

"Patience, Benedict." Consul Wayland held the Sword lightly, as if it weighed nothing. His gaze on Tessa was heavier. She felt as if he were searching her face, reading the fear in her eyes. "We are not going to hurt you, little warlock," he said. "The Accords would forbid it."

"You should not call me warlock," Tessa said. "I bear no warlock's mark." It was strange, having to say this again, but when she had been questioned before, it had always been by members of the Clave, not the Consul himself. He was a tall, broad-shouldered man, exuding a sense of power and authority. Just that sort of power and authority that Benedict Lightwood so resented Charlotte laying claim to.

"Then, what are you?" he asked.

"She doesn't know." The Inquisitor's tone was dry. "Neither do the Silent Brothers."

"She may be allowed to sit," said the Consul. "And to give evidence, but her testimony will be counted only as half a Shadowhunter's." He turned to the Branwells. "In the meantime, Henry, you are dismissed from questioning for the moment. Charlotte, please remain."

Tessa swallowed back her resentment and went to sit in the front row of seats, where she was joined by a drawn-looking Henry, whose gingery hair was sticking up wildly. Jessamine was there, in a dress of pale brown alpaca, looking bored and annoyed. Tessa sat down next to her, with Will and Jem on her other side. Jem was directly beside her, and as the seats were narrow, she could feel the warmth of his shoulder against hers.

At first the Council proceeded much as had other meetings of the Enclave. Charlotte was called upon to give her recollections of the night when the Enclave attacked the stronghold of the vampire de Quincey, killing him and those of his followers who'd been present, while Tessa's brother, Nate, had betrayed their trust in him and allowed the Magister, Axel Mortmain, entry into the Institute, where he had murdered two of the servants and nearly kidnapped Tessa. When Tessa was called up, she said the same things she had said before, that she did not know where Nate was, that she had not suspected him, that she had known nothing of her powers until the Dark Sisters had shown them to her, and that she had always thought her parents were human.

"Richard and Elizabeth Gray have been thoroughly investigated," said the Inquisitor. "There is no evidence to suggest either was anything but human. The boy, the brother—human as well. It could well be that, as Mortmain hinted, the girl's father is a demon, but if so, there is the question of the missing warlock mark."

"Most curious, everything about you, including this power of yours," said the Consul, looking at Tessa with eyes that were steady and pale blue. "You have no idea what its limits, its constructs are? Have you been tested with an item of Mortmain's? To see if you can access his memories or thoughts?"

"Yes, I—tried. With a button he had left behind him. It should have worked."

"But?"

She shook her head. "I could not do it. There was no spark to it, no—no life. Nothing for me to connect with."

"Convenient," muttered Benedict, almost too low to be heard, but Tessa heard it, and flushed.

The Consul indicated that she might take her seat again. She caught sight of Benedict Lightwood's face as she did so; his lips were compressed into a thin, furious line. She wondered what she could possibly have said to anger him.

"And no one has seen hide nor hair of this Mortmain since Miss Gray's . . . altercation with him in the Sanctuary," the Consul went on as Tessa took her seat.

The Inquisitor flipped some of the papers that were stacked on the lectern. "His houses have been searched and found to be completely emptied of all his belongings. His warehouses were searched with the same result. Even our friends at Scotland Yard have investigated. The man has vanished. Quite literally, as our young friend William Herondale tells us."

Will smiled brilliantly as if complimented, though Tessa, seeing the malice under the smile, thought of light sparking off the cutting edge of a razor.

"My suggestion," said the Consul, "is that Charlotte and Henry Branwell be censured, and that for the next three months their official actions, undertaken on behalf of the Clave, be required to pass through me for approval before—"

"My lord Consul." A firm, clear voice spoke out from the crowd. Heads swiveled, staring; Tessa got the feeling that this—someone interrupting the Consul midspeech—didn't happen very often. "If I might speak."

The Consul's eyebrows went up. "Benedict Lightwood," he said. "You had your chance to speak earlier, during the testimonials."

"I hold no arguments with the testimonials given," said Benedict Lightwood. His beaky, sharp profile looked even sharper in the witchlight. "It is your sentence I take issue with."

The Consul leaned forward on the lectern. He was a big man, thick-necked and deep-chested, and his large hands looked as if he could span Benedict's throat easily with a single one. Tessa rather wished he would. From what she had seen of Benedict Lightwood, she did not like him. "And why is that?"

"I think you have let your long friendship with the Fairchild family blind you to Charlotte's shortcomings as head of the Institute," said Benedict, and there was an audible intake of breath in the room. "The blunders committed on the night of July the fifth did more than embarrass the Clave and lose us the Pyxis. We have damaged our relationship with London's Downworlders by futilely attacking de Quincy."

"There have already been a number of complaints lodged through Reparations," rumbled the Consul. "But those will be dealt with as the Law sees fit. Reparations isn't really your concern, Benedict—"

"*And*," Benedict went on, his voice rising, "worst of all, she has let a dangerous criminal with plans to harm and destroy Shadowhunters escape, and we have no idea where he might be. Nor is the responsibility for finding him being laid where it should be, on the shoulders of those who lost him!"

His voice rose. In fact, the whole room was in an uproar; Charlotte looked dismayed, Henry confused, and Will furious. The Consul, whose eyes had darkened alarmingly when Benedict had mentioned the Fairchilds—they must have been Charlotte's family, Tessa realized—remained silent as the noise died down. Then he said, "Your hostility toward the leader of your Enclave does not do you credit, Benedict."

"My apologies, Consul. I do not believe that keeping Charlotte Branwell as the head of the Institute—for we all know that Henry Branwell's involvement is nominal at most—is in the best interests of the Clave. I believe a woman cannot run an Institute; women do not think with logic and discretion but with the emotions of the heart. I have no doubt that Charlotte is a good and decent woman, but a *man* would not have been fooled by a flimsy spy like Nathaniel Gray—"

"*I* was fooled." Will had leaped to his feet and swung around, eyes blazing. "We all were. What insinuations are you making about myself and Jem and Henry, *Mr.* Lightwood?"

"You and Jem are children," said Benedict cuttingly. "And Henry never looks up from his worktable."

Will started to climb over the back of his chair; Jem tugged him back into his seat with main force, hissing under his breath. Jessamine clapped her hands together, her brown eyes bright.

"This is *finally* exciting," she exclaimed.

Tessa looked at her in disgust. "Are you hearing any of this? He's insulting Charlotte!" she whispered, but Jessamine brushed her off with a gesture.

"And who would you suggest run the Institute instead?" the Consul demanded of Benedict, his voice dripping sarcasm. "Yourself, perhaps?"

Benedict spread his hands wide self-deprecatingly. "If you say so, Consul . . ."

Before he could finish speaking, three other figures had risen of their own accord; two Tessa recognized as members of the London Enclave, though she did not know their names; the third was Lilian Highsmith.

Benedict smiled. Everyone was staring at him now; beside him sat his youngest son Gabriel, who was looking up at his father with unreadable green eyes. His slim fingers gripped the back of the chair in front of him.

"Three to support my claim," Benedict said. "That's what the Law requires for me to formally challenge Charlotte Branwell for the position of head of the London Enclave."

Charlotte gave a little gasp but sat motionless in her seat, refusing to turn around. Jem still had Will by the wrist. And Jessamine continued to look as if she were watching an exciting play.

"No," said the Consul.

"You cannot prevent me from challenging—"

"Benedict, you challenged my appointment of Charlotte the moment I made it. You've always wanted the Institute. Now, when the Enclave needs to work together more than ever, you bring division and contention to the proceedings of the Council."

"Change is not always accomplished peacefully, but that does not make it disadvantageous. My challenge stands." Benedict's hands gripped each other.

The Consul drummed his fingers on the lectern. Beside him the Inquisitor stood, cold-eyed. Finally the Consul said, "You suggest, Benedict, that the responsibility of finding Mortmain should be laid upon the shoulders of those who you claim 'lost him.' You would agree, I believe, that finding Mortmain is our first priority?"

Benedict nodded curtly.

"Then, my proposal is this: Let Charlotte and Henry Branwell have charge of the investigation into Mortmain's whereabouts. If by the end of two weeks they have not located him, or at least some strong evidence pointing to his location, then the challenge may go forward."

Charlotte shot forward in her seat. "Find Mortmain?" she said. "Alone, just Henry and I—with no help from the rest of the Enclave?"

The Consul's eyes when they rested on her were not unfriendly, but neither were they entirely forgiving. "You may call upon other members of the Clave if you have some specific need, and of course the Silent Brothers and Iron Sisters are at your disposal," he said. "But as for the investigation, yes, that is for you to accomplish on your own."

"I don't like this," complained Lilian Highsmith. "You're turning the search for a madman into a game of power—"

"Do you wish to withdraw your support for Benedict, then?" asked the Consul. "His challenge would be ended and there would be no need for the Branwells to prove themselves."

Lilian opened her mouth—and then, at a look from Benedict, closed it. She shook her head.

"We have just lost our servants," said Charlotte in a strained voice. "Without them—"

"New servants will be provided to you, as is standard," said the Consul. "Your late servant Thomas's brother, Cyril, is traveling here from Brighton to join your household, and the Dublin Institute has given up its second cook for you. Both are well-trained fighters—which, I must say, Charlotte, yours should have been as well."

"Both Thomas and Agatha *were* trained," Henry protested.

"But you have several in your house who are not," said Benedict. "Not only is Miss Lovelace woefully behind in her training, but your parlor girl, Sophie, and that Downworlder there—" He pointed at Tessa. "Well, since you seem bent on making her a permanent addition to your household, it would hardly hurt if she—and the maid—were trained in the basics of defense."

Tessa looked sideways at Jem in astonishment. "He means *me*?"

Jem nodded. His expression was somber.

"I can't— I'll chop off my own foot!"

"If you're going to chop off anyone's foot, chop off Benedict's," Will muttered.

"You'll be fine, Tessa. It's nothing you can't do," Jem began, but the rest of his words were drowned out by Benedict.

"In fact," Benedict said, "since the two of you will be so busy investigating Mortmain's whereabouts, I suggest I lend you my sons—Gabriel, and Gideon, who returns from Spain tonight—as trainers. Both are excellent fighters and could use the teaching experience."

"Father!" Gabriel protested. He looked horrified; clearly this was not something Benedict had discussed with him in advance.

"We can train our own servants," Charlotte snapped, but the Consul shook his head at her.

"Benedict Lightwood is offering you a generous gift. Accept it."

Charlotte was crimson in the face. After a long moment she bent her head, acknowledging the Consul's words. Tessa felt dizzy. She was going to be trained? Trained to fight, to throw knives and swing a sword? Of course, one of her favorite heroines had always been Capitola in *The Hidden Hand*, who could fight as well as a man—and dressed like one. But that didn't mean she wanted to *be* her.

"Very well," said the Consul. "This session of the Council is ended, to be reconvened here, in the same location, in a fortnight. You are all dismissed."

Of course, everyone did not depart immediately. There was a sudden clamor of voices as people began to rise from their seats and chatter eagerly with their neighbors. Charlotte sat still; Henry beside her, looked as if he wanted desperately to say something comforting but could think of nothing. His hand hovered uncertainly over his wife's shoulder. Will was glaring across the room at Gabriel Lightwood, who looked coldly in their direction.

Slowly Charlotte rose to her feet. Henry had his hand on her back now, murmuring. Jessamine was already standing, twirling her new white lace parasol. Henry had replaced the old one that had been destroyed in battle with Mortmain's automatons. Her hair was done up in tight bunches over her ears like grapes. Tessa got quickly to her feet, and the group of them headed up the center aisle of the Council room. Tessa caught whispers on each side of her, bits of the same words, over and over:

"Charlotte," "Benedict," "never find the Magister," "two weeks," "challenge," "Consul," "Mortmain," "Enclave," "humiliating."

Charlotte walked with her back straight, her cheeks red, and her eyes gazing straight ahead as if she couldn't hear the gossip. Will seemed about to lunge off toward the whisperers to administer rough justice, but Jem had a firm grip on the back of his *parabatai*'s coat. Being Jem, Tessa reflected, must be a great deal like being the owner of a thoroughbred dog that liked to bite your guests. You had to have a hand on his collar constantly. Jessamine merely looked bored again. She wasn't terribly interested in what the Enclave thought of her, or any of them.

By the time they had reached the doors of the Council chamber, they were nearly running. Charlotte paused a moment to let the rest of their group catch up. Most of the crowd was streaming off to the left, where Tessa, Jem, and Will had come from, but Charlotte turned right, marched several paces down the hall, spun around a corner, and abruptly stopped.

"Charlotte?" Henry, catching up to her, sounded worried. "Darling—"

Without warning Charlotte drew her foot back and kicked the wall, as hard as she could. As the wall was stone, this did little damage, though Charlotte let out a low shriek.

"Oh, my," said Jessamine, twirling her parasol.

"If I might make a suggestion," said Will. "About twenty paces behind us, in the Council room, is Benedict. If you'd like to go back in there and try kicking *him*, I recommend aiming upward and a bit to the left—"

"Charlotte." The deep, gravelly voice was instantly recognizable. Charlotte spun around, her brown eyes widening.

It was the Consul. The runes picked out in silver thread on the hem and sleeves of his cloak glittered as he moved toward the little group from the Institute, his gaze on Charlotte. One hand against the wall, she didn't move.

"Charlotte," Consul Wayland said again, "you know what your father always said about losing your temper."

"He did say that. He also said that he should have had a son," Charlotte replied bitterly. "If he had—if I were a man—would you have treated me as you just did?"

Henry put his hand on his wife's shoulder, murmuring something, but she shook it off. Her large, hurt brown eyes were on the Consul.

"And how did I just treat you?" he asked.

"As if I were a child, a little girl who needed scolding."

"Charlotte, I am the one who named you as head of the Institute and the Enclave." The Consul sounded exasperated. "I did it not just because I was fond of Granville Fairchild and knew he wanted his daughter to succeed him, but because I thought you would accomplish the job well."

"You named Henry, too," she said. "And you even told us when you did it that it was because the Enclave would accept a married couple as their leader, but not a woman alone."

"Well, congratulations, Charlotte. I do not think any members of the London Enclave are under the impression that they are in any way being led by Henry."

"It's true," Henry said, looking at his shoes. "They all know I'm rather useless. It's my fault all this happened, Consul—"

"It isn't," said Consul Wayland. "It is a combination of a generalized complacency on the part of the Clave, bad luck and bad timing, and some poor decisions on your part, Charlotte.

Yes, I am holding you accountable for them—"

"So you agree with Benedict!" Charlotte cried.

"Benedict Lightwood is a blackguard and a hypocrite," said the Consul wearily. "Everyone knows that. But he is politically powerful, and it is better to placate him with this show than it would be to antagonize him further by ignoring him."

"A show? Is that what you call this?" Charlotte demanded bitterly. "You have set me an impossible task."

"I have set you the task of locating the Magister," said Consul Wayland. "The man who broke into the Institute, killed your servants, took your Pyxis, and plans to build an army of clockwork monsters to destroy us all—in short, a man who must be stopped. As head of the Enclave, Charlotte, stopping him *is* your task. If you consider it impossible, then perhaps you should ask yourself why you want the job so badly in the first place."

2
Reparations

Then share thy pain, allow that sad relief;
Ah, more than share it! give me all thy grief.
—Alexander Pope, "Eloisa to Abelard"

The witchlight that illuminated the Great Library seemed to be flickering low, like a candle guttering down in its holder, though Tessa knew that was just her imagination. Witchlight, unlike fire or gas, never seemed to fade or burn away.

Her eyes, on the other hand, were beginning to tire, and from the looks of her companions, she wasn't the only one. They were all gathered around one of the long tables, Charlotte at its head, Henry at Tessa's right. Will and Jem sat farther down, beside each other; only Jessamine had retreated to the very far end of the table, separated from the others. The surface of the table was liberally covered with papers of all sorts—old newspaper articles, books, sheets of parchment covered with fine spidery writing. There were genealogies of various Mortmain families, histories of automatons, endless books of spells of summoning and binding, and every bit of research on the Pandemonium Club that the Silent Brothers had managed to scrape out of their archives.

Tessa had been tasked with the job of reading through the newspaper articles, looking for stories about Mortmain and his shipping company, and her eyes were beginning to blur, the words dancing on the pages. She was relieved when Jessamine at last broke the silence, pushing away the book she had been reading—*On the Engines of Sorcery*—and said, "Charlotte, I think we're wasting our time."

Charlotte looked up with a pained expression. "Jessamine, there is no need for you to remain if you do not wish to. I must say, I doubt any of us was expecting your help in this matter, and since you have never much applied yourself to your studies, I cannot help but wonder if you even know what it is you are looking for. Could you tell a binding spell from a summoning spell if I set the two before you?"

Tessa couldn't help being surprised. Charlotte was rarely so sharp with any of them. "I *want* to help," Jessie said sulkily. "Those mechanical *things* of Mortmain's nearly killed me. I want him caught and punished."

"No, you don't." Will, unrolling a parchment so old that it crackled, squinted down at the black symbols on the page. "You want Tessa's brother caught and punished, for making you think he was in love with you when he wasn't."

Jessamine flushed. "I do *not*. I mean, I did not. I mean—ugh! Charlotte, Will's being vexing."

"And the sun has come up in the east," said Jem, to no one in particular.

"I don't want to be thrown out of the Institute if we can't find the Magister," Jessamine went on. "Is that so difficult to understand?"

"You won't be thrown out of the Institute. Charlotte will. I'm sure the Lightwoods will let you stay. And Benedict has two marriageable sons. You ought to be delighted," said Will.

Jessamine made a face. "Shadowhunters. As if I'd want to marry one of them."

"Jessamine, you *are* one of them."

Before Jessamine could reply, the library door opened and Sophie came in, ducking her white-capped head. She spoke quietly to Charlotte, who rose to her feet. "Brother Enoch is here," Charlotte said to the assembled group. "I must speak with him. Will, Jessamine, do try not to kill each other while I am gone. Henry, if you could . . ."

Her voice trailed off. Henry was gazing down at a book—Al-Jazari's *Book of Knowledge of Ingenious Mechanical Devices*—and paying no attention whatsoever to anything else. Charlotte threw up her hands, and left the room with Sophie.

The moment the door closed behind Charlotte, Jessamine shot Will a poisonous look. "If you think I don't have the experience to help, then why is *she* here?" She indicated Tessa. "I don't mean to be rude, but do you think *she* can tell a binding spell from a summoning one?" She looked at Tessa. "Well, can you? And for that matter, Will, you pay so little attention at lessons, can *you* tell a binding spell from a soufflé recipe?"

Will leaned back in his chair and said dreamily, "'I am but mad north-north-west; when the wind is southerly I know a hawk from a handsaw.'"

"Jessamine, Tessa has kindly offered to help, and we need all the eyes we can get right now," said Jem severely. "Will, don't quote *Hamlet*. Henry . . ." He cleared his throat. "HENRY."

Henry looked up, blinking. "Yes, darling?" He blinked again, looking around. "Where's Charlotte?"

"She went to talk to the Silent Brothers," said Jem, who did not appear put out of temper to have been mistaken by Henry for his wife. "In the meantime I'm afraid . . . that I rather agree with Jessamine."

"And the sun comes up in the *west*," said Will, who had apparently heard Jem's earlier comment.

"But why?" Tessa demanded. "We can't give up now. It would be just like handing the Institute over to that awful Benedict Lightwood."

"I'm not suggesting we do nothing, you understand. But we're trying to decipher what it is that Mortmain is going to *do*. We're trying to predict the future instead of trying to understand the past."

"We know Mortmain's past, *and* his plans." Will waved his hand in the direction of the newspapers. "Born in Devon, was a ship's surgeon, became a wealthy trader, got himself mixed up in dark magic, and now plans to rule the world with his massive army of mechanical creatures by his side. A not atypical story for a determined young man—"

"I don't think he ever said anything about ruling the world," interrupted Tessa. "Just the British Empire."

"Admirably literal," said Will. "My point is, we do know

where Mortmain came from. It's hardly our fault that it isn't very interesting . . ." His voice trailed off. "Ah."

"Ah, what?" Jessamine demanded, looking from Will to Jem in a vexed manner. "I declare, the way you two seem to read each other's minds gives me the shudders."

"Ah," said Will. "Jem was just thinking, and I would tend to agree, that Mortmain's life story is, quite simply, balderdash. Some lies, some truth, but very likely there isn't anything in here that will help us. These are just stories he made up to give the newspapers something to print about him. Besides, we don't care how many ships he owns; we want to know where he learned dark magic, and from whom."

"And why he hates Shadowhunters," said Tessa.

Will's blue eyes slid lazily toward her. "Is it hatred?" he said. "I assumed it was a simple greed for domination. With us out of the way, and a clockwork army on his side, he could take power as he liked."

Tessa shook her head. "No, it is more than that. It is difficult to explain, but—he *hates* the Nephilim. It is something very personal for him. And it has something to do with that watch. It's—it's as if he desires recompense for some wrong or hurt they've done him."

"Reparations," said Jem very suddenly, setting down the pen he was holding.

Will looked at him in puzzlement. "Is this a game? We just blurt out whatever word comes next to mind? In that case mine's 'genuphobia.' It means an unreasonable fear of knees."

"What's the word for a perfectly reasonable fear of annoying idiots?" inquired Jessamine.

"The Reparations section of the archives," said Jem, ignoring them both. "The Consul mentioned it yesterday, and it's been in my head since. We haven't looked there."

"Reparations?" asked Tessa.

"When a Downworlder, or a mundane, alleges that a Shadowhunter has broken the Law in their dealings with them, the Downworlder lodges a complaint through Reparations. There will be a trial, and the Downworlder will be accorded some sort of payment, based on whether they can prove their case."

"Well, it seems a bit silly, looking there," said Will. "It's not like Mortmain's going to lodge a complaint against the Shadowhunters through official channels. 'Very upset Shadowhunters refused to all die when I wanted them to. Demand recompense. Please mail cheque to A. Mortmain, 18 Kensington Road—'"

"Enough persiflage," said Jem. "Maybe he hasn't always hated Shadowhunters. Maybe there was a time when he did attempt to gain compensation through the official system and it failed him. What's the harm in asking? The worst thing that could happen is that we turn up nothing, which is exactly what we're turning up right now." He rose to his feet, pushing his silvery hair back. "I'm off to catch Charlotte before Brother Enoch leaves and ask her to have the Silent Brothers check the archives."

Tessa rose to her feet. She did not relish the idea of being left alone in the library with Will and Jessamine, who were bound to bicker. Of course Henry was there, but he seemed to be taking a gentle nap on a pile of books, and was not much of a buffer in the best of cases. Being around Will was uncomfortable in most circumstances; only with Jem there was it bearable. Somehow Jem was able to whittle down Will's sharp edges and make him nearly human. "I'll go with you, Jem," she said. "There's—there was something I wished to speak to Charlotte about anyway."

Jem seemed surprised but pleased; Will looked from one of them to the other and pushed his chair back. "We've been among these moldering old books for ages," he announced. "Mine beautiful eyes are weary, and I have paper cuts. See?" He spread his fingers wide. "I'm going for a walk."

Tessa couldn't help herself. "Perhaps you could use an *iratze* to take care of them."

He glared at her. His eyes *were* beautiful. "Ever and always helpful, Tessa."

She matched his glare. "My only desire is to be of service."

Jem put his hand on her shoulder, his voice concerned. "Tessa, Will. I don't think—"

But Will was gone, snatching up his coat and banging his way out of the library, with enough force to make the door frame vibrate.

Jessamine sat back in her chair, narrowing her brown eyes. "How interesting."

Tessa's hands shook as she tucked a lock of hair behind her ear. She hated that Will had this effect on her. Hated it. She knew better. She knew what he thought of her. That she was nothing, worth nothing. And still a look from him could make her tremble with mingled hatred and longing. It was like a poison in her blood, to which Jem was the only antidote. Only with him did she feel on steady ground.

"Come." Jem took her arm lightly. A gentleman would not normally touch a lady in public, but here in the Institute the

Shadowhunters were more familiar with one another than were the mundanes outside. When she turned to look at him, he smiled at her. Jem put the full force of himself into each smile, so that he seemed to be smiling with his eyes, his heart, his whole being. "We'll find Charlotte."

"And what am I supposed to do while you're gone?" Jessamine said crossly as they made their way to the door.

Jem glanced back over his shoulder. "You could always wake up Henry. It looks like he's eating paper in his sleep again, and you know how Charlotte hates that."

"Oh, *bother*," said Jessamine with an exasperated sigh. "Why do I always get the silly tasks?"

"Because you don't want the serious ones," said Jem, sounding as close to exasperated as Tessa had ever heard him. Neither of them noticed the icy look she shot them as they left the library behind and headed down the corridor.

"Mr. Bane has been awaiting your arrival, sir," the footman said, and stepped aside to let Will enter. The footman's name was Archer—or Walker, or something like that, Will thought—and he was one of Camille's human subjugates. Like all those enslaved to a vampire's will, he was sickly-looking, with parchment pale skin and thin, stringy hair. He looked about as happy to see Will as a dinner party guest might be to see a slug crawling out from under his lettuce.

The moment Will entered the house, the smell hit him. It was the smell of dark magic, like sulfur mixed with the Thames on a hot day. Will wrinkled his nose. The footman looked at him with even more loathing. "Mr. Bane is in the drawing room." His voice indicated that there was no chance whatsoever that he was going to accompany Will there. "Shall I take your coat?"

"That won't be necessary." Coat still on, Will followed the scent of magic down the corridor. It intensified as he drew nearer to the door of the drawing room, which was firmly closed. Tendrils of smoke threaded out from the gap beneath the door. Will took a deep breath of sour air, and pushed the door open.

The inside of the drawing room looked peculiarly bare. After a moment Will realized that this was because Magnus had taken all the heavy teak furniture, even the piano, and pushed it up against the walls. An ornate gasolier hung from the ceiling, but the light in the room was provided by dozens of thick black candles arranged in a circle in the center of the room. Magnus stood beside the circle, a book open in his hands; his old-fashioned cravat was loosened, and his black hair stood up wildly about his face as if charged with electricity. He looked up when Will came in, and smiled. "Just in time!" he cried. "I really think we may have him this round. Will, meet Thammuz, a minor demon from the eighth dimension. Thammuz, meet Will, a minor Shadowhunter from—Wales, was it?"

"I will rip out your eyes," hissed the creature sitting in the center of the burning circle. It was certainly a demon, no more than three feet high, with pale blue skin, three coal black, burning eyes, and long blood-red talons on its eight-fingered hands. *"I will tear the skin from your face."*

"Don't be rude, Thammuz," said Magnus, and although his tone was light, the circle of candles blazed suddenly, brightly upward, causing the demon to shrink in on itself with a scream. "Will has questions. You will answer them."

Will shook his head. "I don't know, Magnus," he said. "He doesn't look like the right one to me."

"You *said* he was blue. This one's blue."

"He is blue," Will acknowledged, stepping closer to the circle of flame. "But the demon I need—well, he was really a cobalt blue. This one's more . . . periwinkle."

"What did you call me?" The demon roared with rage. *"Come closer, little Shadowhunter, and let me feast upon your liver! I will tear it from your body while you scream."*

Will turned to Magnus. "He doesn't *sound* right either. The voice is different. And the number of eyes."

"Are you sure—"

"I'm absolutely sure," said Will in a voice that brooked no contradiction. "It's not something I would ever—could ever—forget."

Magnus sighed and turned back to the demon. "Thammuz," he said, reading aloud from the book. "I charge you, by the power of bell and book and candle, and by the great names of Sammael and Abbadon and Moloch, to speak the truth. Have you ever encountered the Shadowhunter Will Herondale before this day, or any of his blood or lineage?"

"I don't know," said the demon petulantly. *"Humans all look alike to me."*

Magnus's voice rose, sharp and commanding. "Answer me!"

"Oh, very well. No, I've never seen him before in my life. I'd remember. He looks as if he'd taste good." The demon grinned, showing razor-sharp teeth. *"I haven't even been to this world for, oh, a hundred years, possibly more. I can never remember the difference between a hundred and a thousand. Anyway, the last time I was here, everyone was living in mud huts and eating bugs. So I doubt*

he *was around*"—he pointed a many-jointed finger at Will—"*unless Earthkind lives much longer than I was led to believe.*"

Magnus rolled his eyes. "You're just determined not to be any help at all, aren't you?"

The demon shrugged, a peculiarly human gesture. "*You forced me to tell the truth. I told it.*"

"Well, then, have you ever *heard* of a demon like the one I was describing?" Will broke in, a tinge of desperation in his voice. "Dark blue, with a raspy sort of voice, like sandpaper—and he had a long, barbed tail."

The demon regarded him with a bored expression. "*Do you have any idea how many kinds of demons there are in the Void, Nephilim? Hundreds upon hundreds of millions. The great demon city of Pandemonium makes your London look like a village. Demons of all shapes and sizes and colors. Some can change their appearance at will—*"

"Oh, be quiet, then, if you're not going to be of any use," Magnus said, and slammed the book shut. Instantly the candles went out, the demon vanishing with a startled cry, leaving behind only a wisp of foul-smelling smoke.

The warlock turned to Will. "I was so sure I had the right one this time."

"It's not your fault." Will flung himself onto one of the divans shoved up against the wall. He felt hot and cold at the same time, his nerves prickling with a disappointment he was trying to force back without much success. He pulled his gloves off restlessly and shoved them into the pockets of his still buttoned coat. "You're trying. Thammuz was right. I haven't given you very much to go on."

"I assume," Magnus said quietly, "that you have told me all you remember. You opened a Pyxis and released a demon. It cursed you. You want me to find that demon and see if it will remove the curse. And that is all you can tell me?"

"It is all I can tell you," said Will. "It would hardly benefit me to hold anything back unnecessarily, when I know what I'm asking. For you to find a needle in—God, not even a haystack. A needle in a tower full of other needles."

"Plunge your hand into a tower of needles," said Magnus, "and you are likely to cut yourself badly. Are you really sure this is what you want?"

"I am sure that the alternative is worse," said Will, staring at the blackened place on the floor where the demon had crouched. He was exhausted. The energy rune he'd given himself that morning before leaving for the Council meeting had worn off by noon, and his head throbbed. "I have had five years to live with it. The idea of living with it for even one more frightens me more than the idea of death."

"You are a Shadowhunter; you are not afraid of death."

"Of course I am," said Will. "Everyone is afraid of death. We may be born of angels, but we have no more knowledge of what comes after death than you do."

Magnus moved closer to him and sat down on the opposite side of the divan. His green-gold eyes shone like a cat's in the dimness. "You don't know that there is only oblivion after death."

"You don't know that there isn't, do you? Jem believes we are all reborn, that life is a wheel. We die, we turn, we are reborn as we deserve to be reborn, based on our doings in this world." Will looked down at his bitten nails. "I will probably be reborn as a slug that someone salts."

"The Wheel of Transmigration," said Magnus. His lips twitched into a smile. "Well, think of it this way. You must have done something right in your last life, to be reborn as you were. Nephilim."

"Oh, yes," said Will in a dead tone. "I've been very lucky." He leaned his head back against the divan, exhausted. "I take it you'll be needing more . . . ingredients? I think Old Mol over at Cross Bones is getting sick of the sight of me."

"I have other connections," said Magnus, clearly taking pity on him, "and I need to do more research first. If you could tell me the nature of the curse—"

"No." Will sat up. "I can't. I told you before, I took a great risk even in telling you of its existence. If I told you any more—"

"Then what? Let me guess. You don't know, but you're sure it would be bad."

"Don't start making me think coming to you was a mistake—"

"This has something to do with Tessa, doesn't it?"

Over the past five years Will had trained himself well not to show emotion—surprise, affection, hopefulness, joy. He was fairly sure his expression didn't change, but he heard the strain in his voice when he said, "Tessa?"

"It's been five years," said Magnus. "Yet somehow you have managed all this time, telling no one. What desperation drove you to me, in the middle of the night, in a rainstorm? What has changed at the Institute? I can think of only one thing—and quite a pretty one, with big gray eyes—"

Will got to his feet so abruptly, he nearly tipped the divan over. "There are other things," he said, struggling to keep his voice even. "Jem is dying."

Magnus looked at him, a cool, even stare. "He has been dying for years," he said. "No curse laid on you could cause or repair his condition."

Will realized his hands were shaking; he tightened them into fists. "You don't understand—"

"I know you are *parabatai*," said Magnus. "I know that his death will be a great loss for you. But what I don't know—"

"You know what you need to know." Will felt cold all over, though the room was warm and he still wore his coat. "I can pay you more, if it will make you stop asking me questions."

Magnus put his feet up on the divan. "Nothing will make me stop asking you questions," he said. "But I will do my best to respect your reticence."

Relief loosened Will's hands. "Then, you will still help me."

"I will still help you." Magnus put his hands behind his head and leaned back, looking at Will through half-lowered lids. "Though I could help you better if you told me the truth, I will do what I can. You interest me oddly, Will Herondale."

Will shrugged. "That will do well enough as a reason. When do you plan to try again?"

Magnus yawned. "Probably this weekend. I shall send you a message by Saturday if there are . . . developments."

Developments. Curse. Truth. Jem. Dying. Tessa. Tessa, Tessa, Tessa. Her name rang in Will's mind like the chime of a bell; he wondered if any other name on earth had such an inescapable resonance to it. She couldn't have been named something awful, could she, like Mildred. He couldn't imagine lying awake at night, staring up at the ceiling while invisible voices whispered "Mildred" in his ears. But *Tessa*—

"Thank you," he said abruptly. He had gone from being too cold to being too warm; it was stifling in the room, still smelling of burned candle wax. "I will look forward to hearing from you, then."

"Yes, do," said Magnus, and he closed his eyes. Will couldn't tell whether he was actually asleep or simply waiting for Will to leave; either way, it was clearly a hint that he expected Will to depart. Will, not entirely without relief, took it.

Sophie was on her way to Miss Jessamine's room, to sweep the ashes and clean the grate of the fireplace, when she heard voices in the hall. In her old place of employment she had been taught to "give room"—to turn and look at the walls while her employers passed by, and do her best to resemble a piece of furniture, something inanimate that they could ignore.

She had been shocked on coming to the Institute to find that things were not managed that way here. First, for such a large house to have so few servants had surprised her. She had not realized at first that the Shadowhunters did much for themselves that a typical family of good breeding would find beneath them—started their own fires, did some of their own shopping, kept rooms like the training area and the weapons room cleaned and neat. She had been shocked at the familiarity with which Agatha and Thomas had treated their employers, not realizing that her fellow servants had come from families that had served Shadowhunters through the generations—or that they'd had magic of their own.

She herself had come from a poor family, and had been called "stupid" and been slapped often when she'd first begun working as a maid—because she hadn't been used to delicate furniture or real silver, or china so thin you could see the darkness of the tea through the sides. But she had learned, and when it had become clear that she was going to be very pretty, she had been promoted to parlor maid.

A parlor maid's lot was a precarious one. She was meant to look beautiful for the household, and therefore her salary had begun to go down each year that she'd aged, once she had turned eighteen.

It had been such a relief, coming to work at the Institute—where no one minded that she was nearly twenty, or demanded that she stare at the walls, or cared whether she spoke before she was spoken to—that she had almost thought it worth the mutilation of her pretty face at the hands of her last employer. She still avoided looking at herself in mirrors if she could, but the dreadful horror of loss had faded. Jessamine mocked her for the long scar that disfigured her cheek, but the others seemed not to notice, save Will, who occasionally said something unpleasant, but in an almost perfunctory way, as if it were expected of him but his heart were not in it.

But that was all before she had fallen in love with Jem.

She recognized his voice now as he came down the hall, raised in laughter, and answering him was Miss Tessa. Sophie felt an odd little pressure against her chest. Jealousy. She despised herself for it, but it could not be stopped. Miss Tessa was always kind to her, and there was such enormous vulnerability in her wide gray eyes—such a need for a friend—that it was impossible to dislike her. And yet, the way Master Jem looked at her . . . and Tessa did not even seem to notice.

No. Sophie just couldn't bear to encounter the two of them in the hall, with Jem looking at Tessa the way he had been lately. Clutching the sweeping brush and bucket to her chest, Sophie opened the nearest door and ducked inside, closing it most of the way behind her. It was, like most of the rooms in the Institute, an unused bedroom, meant for visiting Shadowhunters. She would give the rooms a turn once a fortnight or so, unless someone was using them; otherwise they stood undisturbed. This one was quite dusty; motes danced in the light from the windows, and Sophie fought the urge to sneeze as she pressed her eye to the crack in the door.

She had been right. It was Jem and Tessa, coming toward her down the hall. They appeared entirely engaged with each other. Jem was carrying something—folded gear, it looked like—and Tessa was laughing at something he had said. She was looking a little down and away from him, and he was gazing at her, the way one did when one felt one was unobserved. He had that look on his face, that look he usually got only when he was playing the violin, as if he were completely caught up and entranced.

Her heart hurt. He was so beautiful. She had always thought so. Most people went on about Will, how handsome he was, but she thought that Jem was a thousand times better-looking. He had the ethereal look of angels in paintings, and though she knew that the silvery color of his hair and skin was a result of the medicine he took for his illness, she couldn't help finding it lovely too. And he was gentle, firm, and kind. The thought of his hands in her hair, stroking it back from her face, made her feel comforted, whereas usually the thought of a man, even a boy, touching her made her feel vulnerable and ill. He had the most careful, beautifully constructed hands. . . .

"I can't quite believe they're coming tomorrow," Tessa was saying, turning her gaze back to Jem. "I feel as if Sophie and I are being tossed to Benedict Lightwood to appease him, like a dog with a bone. He can't *really* mind if we're trained or not. He just wants his sons in the house to bother Charlotte."

"That's true," Jem acknowledged. "But why not take advantage of the training when it's offered? That's why Charlotte is trying to encourage Jessamine to take part. As for you, given your talent, even if—I should say, when—Mortmain is no longer a threat, there will be others attracted to your power. You might do well to learn how to fend them off."

Tessa's hand went to the angel necklace at her throat, a habitual gesture Sophie suspected she was not even aware of. "I know what Jessie will say. She'll say the only thing she needs assistance fending off is handsome suitors."

"Wouldn't she rather have help fending off the unattractive ones?"

"Not if they're mundanes." Tessa grinned. "She'd rather an ugly mundane than a handsome Shadowhunter any day."

"That does put me right out of the running, doesn't it?" said Jem with mock chagrin, and Tessa laughed again.

"It is too bad," she said. "Someone as pretty as Jessamine ought to have her pick, but she's so determined that a Shadowhunter won't do—"

"You are much prettier," said Jem.

Tessa looked at him in surprise, her cheeks coloring. Sophie felt the twist of jealousy in her chest again, though she agreed with Jem. Jessamine was quite traditionally pretty, a pocket Venus if ever there was one, but her habitual sour expression spoiled her charms. Tessa, though, had a warm appeal, with her rich, dark, waving hair and sea gray eyes, that grew on you the longer you knew her. There was intelligence in her face, and humor, which Jessamine did not have, or at least did not display.

Jem paused in front of Miss Jessamine's door, and knocked upon it. When there was no answer, he shrugged, bent down, and placed a stack of dark fabric—gear—in front of the door.

"She'll never wear it." Tessa's face dimpled.

Jem straightened up. "I never agreed to wrestle her into the clothes, just deliver them."

He started off down the hallway again, Tessa beside him. "I don't know how Charlotte can bear to talk to Brother Enoch so often. He gives me the horrors," she said.

"Oh, I don't know. I prefer to think that when they're at home, the Silent Brothers are much like us. Playing practical jokes in the Silent City, making toasted cheese—"

"I hope they play charades," said Tessa dryly. "It would seem to take advantage of their natural talents."

Jem burst out laughing, and then they were around the corner and out of sight. Sophie sagged against the door frame. She did not think she had ever made Jem laugh like that; she didn't think anyone had, except for Will. You had to know someone very well to make them laugh like that. She had loved him for such a long time, she thought. How was it that she did not know him at all?

With a sigh of resignation she made ready to depart her hiding place—when the door to Miss Jessamine's room opened, and its resident emerged. Sophie shrank bank into the dimness. Miss Jessamine was dressed in a long velvet traveling cloak that concealed most of her body, from her neck to her feet. Her hair was bound tightly behind her head, and she carried a gentleman's hat in one hand. Sophie froze in surprise as Jessamine looked down, saw the gear at her feet, and made a face. She kicked it swiftly into the room—giving Sophie a view of her foot, which seemed to be clad in a man's boot—and closed the door soundlessly behind her. Glancing up and down the corridor, she placed the hat on her head, dropped her chin low into the cloak, and slunk off into the shadows, leaving Sophie staring, mystified, after her.

3
Unjustifiable Death

Alas! they had been friends in youth;
But whispering tongues can poison truth;
And constancy lives in realms above;
And life is thorny; and youth is vain;
And to be wroth with one we love
Doth work like madness in the brain.
—Samuel Taylor Coleridge, "Christabel"

After breakfast the next day Charlotte instructed Tessa and Sophie to return to their rooms, dress in their newly acquired gear, and meet Jem in the training room, where they would wait for the Lightwood brothers. Jessamine had not come to breakfast, claiming a headache, and Will, likewise, was nowhere to be found. Tessa suspected he was hiding, in an attempt to avoid being forced to be polite to Gabriel Lightwood and his brother. She could only partly blame him.

Back in her room, picking up the gear, she felt a flutter of nerves in her stomach; it was so very much unlike anything she'd ever worn before. Sophie was not there to help her with the new clothes. Part of the training, of course, was being able to dress and to familiarize oneself with the gear: flat-soled shoes; a loose pair of trousers made of thick black material; and a long, belted tunic that reached nearly to her knees. They were the same clothes she had seen Charlotte fight in before, and had seen illustrated in the *Codex*; she had thought them strange then, but the act of actually wearing them was even stranger. If Aunt Harriet could have seen her now, Tessa thought, she would likely have fainted.

She met Sophie at the foot of the steps that led up to the Institute's training room. Neither she nor the other girl exchanged a word, just encouraging smiles. After a moment Tessa went first up the steps, a narrow wooden flight with banisters so old that the wood had begun to splinter. It was strange, Tessa thought, going up a flight of stairs and *not* having to worry about pulling in your skirts or tripping on the hem. Though her body was completely covered, she felt peculiarly naked in her training gear.

It helped to have Sophie with her, obviously equally uncomfortable in her own Shadowhunter gear. When they reached the top of the stairs, Sophie swung the door open and they made their way into the training room in silence, together.

They were obviously at the top of the Institute, in a room adjacent to the attic, Tessa thought, and nearly twice the size. The floor was polished wood with various patterns drawn here and there in black ink—circles and squares, some of them numbered. Long, flexible ropes hung from great raftered beams overhead, half-invisible in the shadows. Witchlight torches burned along the walls, interspersed with hanging weapons—maces and axes and all sorts of other deadly-looking objects.

"Ugh," said Sophie, looking at them with a shudder. "Don't they look too horrible by half?"

"I actually recognize a few from the *Codex*," said Tessa, pointing. "That one there's a longsword, and there's a rapier, and a fencing foil, and that one that looks like you'd need two hands to hold it is a claymore, I think."

"Close," came a voice, very disconcertingly, from above their heads. "It's an executioner's sword. Mostly for decapitations. You can tell because it doesn't have a sharp point."

Sophie gave a little yelp of surprise and backed up as one of the dangling ropes began to sway and a dark shape appeared over their heads. It was Jem, clambering down the rope with the graceful agility of a bird. He landed lightly in front of them, and smiled. "My apologies. I didn't mean to startle you."

He was dressed in gear as well, though instead of a tunic he wore a shirt that reached only to his waist. A single leather strap went across his chest, and the hilt of a sword protruded from behind one shoulder. The darkness of the gear made his skin look even paler, his hair and eyes more silver than ever.

"Yes, you did," said Tessa with a little smile, "but it's all right. I was beginning to worry Sophie and I were going to be left here to train each other."

"Oh, the Lightwoods will be here," said Jem. "They're simply being late to make a point. They don't have to do what we say, or what their father says either."

"I wish you were the one training us," Tessa said impulsively.

Jem looked surprised. "I couldn't—I haven't completed my

own training yet." But their eyes met, and in another moment of wordless communication, Tessa heard what he was really saying: *I'm not well enough often enough to train you reliably.* Her throat hurt suddenly, and she locked eyes with Jem, hoping he could read her silent sympathy in them. She did not want to look away, and found herself wondering if the way that she had scraped her hair back, carefully pinning it into a bun from which no stray strands escaped, looked horribly unflattering. Not that it mattered, of course. It was just *Jem*, after all.

"We won't be going through a *full* course of training, will we?" Sophie said, her worried voice breaking into Tessa's thoughts. "The Council only said that we needed to know how to defend ourselves a bit. . . ."

Jem looked away from Tessa; the connection broke with a snap. "There's nothing to be frightened of, Sophie," he said in his gentle voice. "And you'll be glad of it; it's always useful for a beautiful girl to be able to fend off the unwanted attentions of gentlemen."

Sophie's face tightened, the livid scar on her cheek standing out as red as if it had been painted there. "Don't make fun," she said. "It isn't kind."

Jem looked startled. "Sophie, I wasn't—"

The door to the training room opened. Tessa turned as Gabriel Lightwood strode into the room, followed by a boy she didn't know. Where Gabriel was slender and dark-haired, the other boy was muscular, with thick sandy-blond hair. They were both dressed in gear, with expensive-looking dark gloves studded with metal across the knuckles. Each wore silver bands around each wrist—knife sheaths, Tessa knew—and had the same elaborate white pattern of runes woven into their sleeves. It was clear not just from the similarity of their clothes but from the shape of their faces and the pale, luminous green of their eyes that they were related, so Tessa was not in the least surprised when Gabriel said, in his abrupt manner:

"Well, we're here as we said we would be. James, I assume you remember my brother, Gideon. Miss Gray, Miss Collins—"

"Pleased to make your acquaintance," Gideon muttered, meeting neither of their eyes with his. Bad moods seemed to run in the family, Tessa thought, remembering that Will had said that next to his brother, Gabriel seemed a sweetheart.

"Don't worry. Will's not here," Jem said to Gabriel, who was glancing around the room. Gabriel frowned at him, but Jem had already turned to Gideon. "When did you get back from Madrid?" he asked politely.

"Father called me back home a short while ago." Gideon's tone was neutral. "Family business."

"I do hope everything's all right—"

"Everything is quite all right, thank you, James," said Gabriel, his tone clipped. "Now, before we move to the training portion of this visit, there are two people you should probably meet." He turned his head and called out, "Mr. Tanner, Miss Daly! Please come up."

There were footfalls on the steps, and two strangers entered, neither in gear. Both wore servants' clothes. One was a young woman who was the very definition of "rawboned"—her bones seemed too big for her skinny, awkward frame. Her hair was a bright scarlet, drawn back into a chignon under a modest hat. Her bare hands were red and scrubbed-looking. Tessa guessed she was about twenty. Beside her stood a young man with dark brown curling hair, tall and muscular—

Sophie took a sharp indrawn breath. She had gone pale. "Thomas . . ."

The young man looked terribly awkward. "I'm Thomas's brother, miss. Cyril. Cyril Tanner."

"These are the replacements the Council promised you for your lost servants," said Gabriel. "Cyril Tanner and Bridget Daly. The Consul asked us if we would bring them from Kings Cross here, and naturally we obliged. Cyril will replace Thomas, and Bridget will replace your lost cook, Agatha. They were both trained in fine Shadowhunter households and come soundly recommended."

Red spots had begun to burn on Sophie's cheeks. Before she could say anything, Jem said quickly, "No one could replace Agatha or Thomas for us, Gabriel. They were friends as well as servants." He nodded toward Bridget and Cyril. "No offense intended."

Bridget only blinked her brown eyes, but, "None taken," said Cyril. Even his voice was like Thomas's, almost eerily so. "Thomas was my brother. No one can replace him for me, either."

An awkward silence descended on the room. Gideon leaned back against one of the walls, his arms crossed, a slight scowl on his face. He was quite good-looking, like his brother, Tessa thought, but the scowl rather spoiled it.

"Very well," Gabriel said finally into the silence. "Charlotte had asked us to bring them up so you could meet them. Jem, if you'd like to escort them back to the drawing room, Charlotte's waiting with instructions—"

"So neither of them needs any extra training?" Jem said.

"Since you'll be training Tessa and Sophie regardless, if Bridget or Cyril—"

"As the Consul said, they have been quite effectively trained in their previous households," said Gideon. "Would you like a demonstration?"

"I don't think that's necessary," Jem said.

Gabriel grinned. "Come along, Carstairs. The girls might as well see that a mundane can fight almost like a Shadowhunter, with the *right* kind of instruction. Cyril?" He stalked over to the wall, selected two longswords, and threw one toward Cyril, who caught it out of the air handily and advanced toward the center of the room, where a circle was painted on the floorboards.

"We already know that," muttered Sophie, in a voice low enough that only Tessa could hear. "Thomas and Agatha were both trained."

"Gabriel is only trying to annoy you," said Tessa, also in a whisper. "Do not let him see that he bothers you."

Sophie set her jaw as Gabriel and Cyril met in the center of the room, swords flashing.

Tessa had to admit there was something rather beautiful about it, the way they circled each other, blades singing through the air, a blur of black and silver. The ringing sound of metal on metal, the way they moved, so fast her vision could barely follow. And yet, Gabriel was better; that was clear even to the untrained eye. His reflexes were faster, his movements more graceful. It was not a fair fight; Cyril, his hair pasted to his forehead with sweat, was clearly giving everything he had, while Gabriel was simply marking time. In the end, when Gabriel swiftly disarmed Cyril with a neat flicking motion of his wrist, sending the other boy's sword rattling to the floor, Tessa couldn't help but feel almost indignant on Cyril's behalf. No human could best a Shadowhunter. Wasn't that the point?

The point of Gabriel's blade rested an inch from Cyril's throat. Cyril raised his hands in surrender, a smile, much like his brother's easy grin, spreading across his face. "I yield—"

There was a blur of movement. Gabriel yelped and went down, his sword skittering from his hand. His body hit the ground, Bridget kneeling atop his chest, her teeth bared. She had slipped up behind him and tripped him while no one was looking. Now she whipped a small dagger from the inside of her bodice and held it against his throat. Gabriel looked up at her for a moment, dazed, blinking his green eyes. Then he began to laugh.

Tessa liked him more in that moment than she ever had before. Not that that was saying much.

"Very impressive," drawled a familiar voice from the doorway. Tessa turned. It was Will, looking, as her aunt would have said, as if he'd been dragged through a hedge backward. His shirt was torn, his hair was mussed, and his blue eyes were rimmed with red. He bent down, picked up Gabriel's fallen sword, and leveled it in Bridget's direction with an amused expression. "But can she *cook*?"

Bridget scrambled to her feet, her cheeks flushing dark red. She was looking at Will the way girls always did—a little openmouthed, as if she couldn't quite believe the vision that had materialized in front of her. Tessa wanted to tell her that Will looked better when less bedraggled, and that being fascinated by his beauty was like being fascinated by a razor-sharp piece of steel—dangerous and unwise. But what was the point? She'd learn it herself soon enough. "I am a fine cook, sir," she said in a lilting Irish accent. "My previous employers had no complaints."

"Lord, you're Irish," said Will. "Can you make things that don't have potatoes in them? We had an Irish cook once when I was a boy. Potato pie, potato custard, potatoes with potato sauce . . ."

Bridget looked baffled. Meanwhile, somehow Jem had crossed the room and seized Will's arm. "Charlotte wants to see Cyril and Bridget in the drawing room. Shall we show them where it is?"

Will wavered. He was looking at Tessa now. She swallowed against her dry throat. He looked as if there were something he wanted to say to her. Gabriel, glancing between them, smirked. Will's eyes darkened, and he turned, Jem's hand guiding him toward the stairway, and stalked out. After a startled moment Bridget and Cyril followed.

When Tessa turned back to the center of the room, she saw that Gabriel had taken one of the blades and handed it to his brother. "Now," he said. "It's about time to start training, wouldn't you say, ladies?"

Gideon took the blade. *"Esta es la idea más estúpida que nuestro padre ha tenido,"* he said. *"Nunca."*

Sophie and Tessa exchanged a look. Tessa wasn't sure *exactly* what Gideon had said, but "*estúpida*" sounded familiar enough. It was going to be a long remainder of the day.

They spent the next few hours performing balancing and blocking exercises. Gabriel took it upon himself to oversee

Tessa's instruction, while Gideon was assigned to Sophie. Tessa couldn't help but feel that Gabriel had chosen her to annoy Will in some obscure way, whether Will knew about it or not. He wasn't a bad teacher, actually—fairly patient, willing to pick up weapons again and again as she dropped them, until he could show her how to get the grip correct, even praising when she did something right. She was concentrating too fiercely to notice whether Gideon was as adept at training Sophie, though Tessa heard him muttering in Spanish from time to time.

By the time the training was over and Tessa had bathed and dressed for dinner, she was starving in a most unladylike manner. Fortunately, despite Will's fears, Bridget *could* cook, and very well. She served a hot roast with vegetables, and a jam tart with custard, to Henry, Will, Tessa, and Jem for dinner. Jessamine was still in her room with a headache, and Charlotte had gone to the Bone City to look directly through the Reparations archives herself.

It was odd, having Sophie and Cyril coming in and out of the dining room with platters of food, Cyril carving the roast just as Thomas would have, Sophie helping him silently. Tessa could hardly help but think how difficult it had to be for Sophie, whose closest companions in the Institute had been Agatha and Thomas, but every time Tessa tried to catch the other girl's eye, Sophie looked away.

Tessa remembered the look on Sophie's face the last time Jem had been ill, the way she'd twisted her cap in her hands, begging for news of him. Tessa had ached to talk to Sophie about it afterward, but knew she never could. Romances between mundanes and Shadowhunters were forbidden; Will's mother was a mundane, and his father had been forced to leave the Shadowhunters to be with her. He must have been terribly in love to be willing to do it—and Tessa had never had the sense that Jem was fond of Sophie in that way at all. And then there was the matter of his illness. . . .

"Tessa," Jem said in a low voice, "are you all right? You look a million miles away."

She smiled at him. "Just tired. The training—I'm not used to it." It was the truth. Her arms were sore from holding the heavy practice sword, and though she and Sophie had done little beyond balancing and blocking exercises, her legs ached too.

"There's a salve the Silent Brothers make, for sore muscles. Knock on the door of my room before you go to sleep, and I'll give you some."

Tessa flushed slightly, then wondered why she had flushed. The Shadowhunters had their odd ways. She had been in Jem's room before, even alone with him, even alone with him in her night attire, and no fuss had been made over it. All he was doing now was offering her a bit of medicine, and yet she could feel the heat rise in her face—and he seemed to see it, and flushed himself, the color very visible against his pale skin. Tessa looked away hastily and caught Will watching them both, his blue eyes level and dark. Only Henry, chasing mushy peas around his plate with a fork, seemed oblivious.

"Much obliged," she said. "I will—"

Charlotte burst into the room, her dark hair escaping from its pins in a whirl of curls, a long scroll of paper clutched in her hand. "I've found it!" she cried. She collapsed breathlessly into the seat beside Henry, her normally pale face rosy with exertion. She smiled at Jem. "You were quite right—the

Reparations archives—I found it after only a few hours of looking."

"Let me see," said Will, setting down his fork. He had eaten only a very little of his food, Tessa couldn't help noticing. The bird design ring flashed on his fingers as he reached for the scroll in Charlotte's hand.

She swatted his hand away good-naturedly. "No. We shall all look at them at the same time. It was Jem's idea, anyway, wasn't it?"

Will frowned, but said nothing; Charlotte spread the scroll out over the table, pushing aside teacups and empty plates to make room, and the others rose and crowded around her, gazing down at the document. The paper was really more like thick parchment, with dark red ink, like the color of the runes on the Silent Brothers' robes. The handwriting was in English, but cramped and full of abbreviations; Tessa could make neither head nor tail of what she was looking at.

Jem leaned in close to her, his arm brushing hers, reading over her shoulder. His expression was thoughtful.

She turned her head toward him; a lock of his pale hair tickled her face. "What does it say?" she whispered.

"It's a request for recompense," said Will, ignoring the fact that she had addressed her question to Jem. "Sent to the York Institute in 1825 in the name of Axel Hollingworth Mortmain, seeking reparations for the unjustified death of his parents, John Thaddeus and Anne Evelyn Shade, almost a decade before."

"John Thaddeus Shade," said Tessa. "*JTS*, the initials on Mortmain's watch. But if he was their son, why doesn't he have the same surname?"

"The Shades were warlocks," said Jem, reading farther down the page. "Both of them. He couldn't have been their blood son; they must have adopted him, and let him keep his mundane name. It does happen, from time to time." His eyes flicked toward Tessa, and then away; she wondered if he was remembering, as she was, their conversation in the music room about the fact that warlocks could not have children.

"He said he began to learn about the dark arts during his travels," said Charlotte. "But if his parents were warlocks—"

"Adoptive parents," said Will. "Yes, I'm sure he knew just who in Downworld to contact to learn the darker arts."

"Unjustifiable death," Tessa said in a small voice. "What does that mean, exactly?"

"It *means* he believes that Shadowhunters killed his parents despite the fact that they had broken no Laws," said Charlotte.

"What Law were they meant to have broken?"

Charlotte frowned. "It says something here about unnatural and illegal dealings with demons—that could be nearly anything—and that they stood accused of creating a weapon that could destroy Shadowhunters. The sentence for that would have been death. This was before the Accords, though, you must remember. Shadowhunters could kill Downworlders on the mere suspicion of wrongdoing. That's probably why there's nothing more substantive or detailed in the paperwork here. Mortmain filed for recompense through the York Institute, under the aegis of Aloysius Starkweather. He was asking not for money but for the guilty parties—Shadowhunters—to be tried and punished. But the trial was refused here in London on the grounds that the Shades were 'beyond a doubt' guilty. And that's really all there is. This is simply a short record of the event, not the full papers. Those would still be in the York Institute." Charlotte pushed her damp hair back from her forehead. "And yet. It *would* explain Mortmain's hatred of Shadowhunters. You were correct, Tessa. It was—it *is*—personal."

"And it gives us a starting point. The York Institute," said Henry, looking up from his plate. "The Starkweathers run it, don't they? They'll have the full letters, papers—"

"And Aloysius Starkweather is eighty-nine," said Charlotte. "He would have been a young man when the Shades were killed. He may remember something of what transpired." She sighed. "I'd better send him a message. Oh, dear. This will be awkward."

"Why is that, darling?" Henry asked in his gentle, absent way.

"He and my father were friends once, but then they had a falling-out—some dreadful thing, absolutely ages ago, but they never spoke again."

"What's that poem again?" Will, who had been twirling his empty teacup around his fingers, stood up straight and declaimed:

"Each spake words of high disdain,
And insult to his heart's best brother—"

"Oh, by the Angel, Will, do be quiet," said Charlotte, standing up. "I must go and write a letter to Aloysius Starkweather that drips remorse and pleading. I don't need you distracting me." And, gathering up her skirts, she hurried from the room.

"No appreciation for the arts," Will murmured, setting his

teacup down. He looked up, and Tessa realized she had been staring at him. She knew the poem, of course. It was Coleridge, one of her favorites. There was more to it as well, about love and death and madness, but she could not bring the lines to mind; not now, with Will's blue eyes on hers.

"And of course, Charlotte hasn't eaten a bit of dinner," Henry said, getting up. "I'll go see if Bridget can't make her up a plate of cold chicken. As for the rest of you—" He paused for a moment, as if he were about to give them an order—send them to bed, perhaps, or back to the library to do more research. The moment passed, and a look of puzzlement crossed his face. "Blast it, I can't remember what I was going to say," he announced, and vanished into the kitchen.

The moment Henry left, Will and Jem fell into an earnest discussion of reparations, Downworlders, Accords, covenants, and laws that left Tessa's head spinning. Quietly she rose and left the table, making her way to the library.

Despite its immense size, and the fact that barely any of the books that lined its walls were in English, it was her favorite room in the Institute. There was something about the smell of books, the ink-and-paper-and-leather scent, the way dust in a library seemed to behave differently from the dust in any other room—it was golden in the light of the witchlight tapers, settling like pollen across the polished surfaces of the long tables. Church the cat was asleep on a high book stand, his tail curled round above his head; Tessa gave him a wide berth as she moved toward the small poetry section along the lower right-hand wall. Church adored Jem but had been known to bite others, often with very little warning.

She found the book she was looking for and knelt down beside the bookcase, flipping until she found the right page, the scene where the old man in "Christabel" realizes that the girl standing before him is the daughter of his once best friend and now most hated enemy, the man he can never forget.

Alas! they had been friends in youth;
But whispering tongues can poison truth;
And constancy lives in realms above;
And life is thorny; and youth is vain;
And to be wroth with one we love,
Doth work like madness in the brain.

. . .

Each spake words of high disdain
And insult to his heart's best brother:
They parted—ne'er to meet again!

The voice that spoke above her head was as light as it was drawling—instantly familiar. "Checking my quotation for accuracy?"

The book slid out of Tessa's hands and hit the floor. She rose to her feet and watched, frozen, as Will bent to pick it up, and held it out to her, his manner one of utmost politeness.

"I assure you," he told her, "my recall is perfect."

So is mine, she thought. This was the first time she had been alone with him in weeks. Not since that awful scene on the roof when he had intimated that he thought her little better than a prostitute, and a barren one at that. They had never mentioned the moment to each other again. They had gone on as if everything were normal, polite to each other in company, never alone together. Somehow, when they were with other people, she was able to push it to the back of her mind, forget it. But faced with Will, just Will—beautiful as always, the collar of his shirt open to show the black Marks twining his collarbone and rising up the white skin of his throat, the flickering taper light glancing off the elegant planes and angles of his face—the memory of her shame and anger rose up in her throat, choking off her words.

He glanced down at his hand, still holding the little green leather-bound volume. "Are you going to take Coleridge back from me, or shall I just stand here forever in this rather foolish position?"

Silently Tessa reached out and took the book from him. "If you wish to use the library," she said, preparing to depart, "you most certainly may. I found what I was looking for, and as it grows late—"

"Tessa," he said, holding out a hand to stop her.

She looked at him, wishing she could ask him to go back to calling her Miss Gray. Just the way he said her name undid her, loosened something tight and knotted underneath her rib cage, making her breathless. She wished he wouldn't use her Christian name, but knew how ridiculous it would sound if she made the request. It would certainly spoil all her work training herself to be indifferent to him.

"Yes?" she asked.

There was a little wistfulness in his expression as he looked at her. It was all she could do not to stare. Will, wistful? He had to be playacting. "Nothing. I—" He shook his head; a lock of dark hair fell over his forehead, and he pushed it out of his eyes impatiently. "Nothing," he said again. "The first time I showed you the library, you told me your favorite book was *The Wide, Wide World.* I thought you might want to know that I . . . read it." His head was down, his blue eyes looking up at her through those thick dark lashes; she wondered how many times he'd gotten whatever he wanted just by doing that.

She made her voice polite and distant. "And did you find it to your liking?"

"Not at all," said Will. "Drivelly and sentimental, I thought."

"Well, there's no accounting for taste," Tessa said sweetly, knowing he was trying to goad her, and refusing to take the bait. "What is one person's pleasure is another's poison, don't you find?"

Was it her imagination, or did he look disappointed? "Have you any other American recommendations for me?"

"Why would you want one, when you scorn my taste? I think you may have to accept that we are quite far apart on the matter of reading material, as we are on so many things, and find your recommendations elsewhere, Mr. Herondale." She bit her tongue almost as soon as the words were out of her mouth. That had been too much, she knew.

And indeed Will was on it, like a spider leaping onto a particularly tasty fly. "*Mr. Herondale?*" he demanded. "Tessa, I thought . . . ?"

"You thought what?" Her tone was glacial.

"That we could at least talk about books."

"We did," she said. "You insulted my taste. And you should know, *The Wide, Wide World* is not my *favorite* book. It is simply a story I enjoyed, like *The Hidden Hand*, or— You know, perhaps you should suggest something to me, so I can judge *your* taste. It's hardly fair otherwise."

Will hopped up onto the nearest table and sat, swinging his legs, obviously giving the question some thought. "*The Castle of Otranto*—"

"Isn't that the book in which the hero's son is crushed to death by a gigantic helmet that falls from the sky? And you said *A Tale of Two Cities* was silly!" said Tessa, who would have died rather than admit she had read *Otranto* and loved it.

"*A Tale of Two Cities*," echoed Will. "I read it again, you know, because we had talked about it. You were right. It isn't silly at all."

"No?"

"No," he said. "There is too much of despair in it."

She met his gaze. His eyes were as blue as lakes; she felt as if she were falling into them. "Despair?"

Steadily he said, "There is no future for Sydney, is there, with or without love? He knows he cannot save himself without Lucie, but to let her near him would be to degrade her."

She shook her head. "That is not how I recall it. His sacrifice is noble—"

"It is what is left to him," said Will. "Do you not recall what he says to Lucie? 'If it had been possible . . . that you could have returned the love of the man you see before yourself—flung away, wasted, drunken, poor creature of misuse as you know him to be—he would have been conscious this day and hour, in spite of his happiness, that he would bring you to misery, bring you to sorrow and repentance, blight you, disgrace you, pull you down with him—'"

A log fell in the fireplace, sending up a shower of sparks and startling them both and silencing Will; Tessa's heart leaped, and she tore her eyes away from Will. Stupid, she told herself angrily. So stupid. She remembered how he had treated her, the things he had said, and now she was letting her knees turn to jelly at the drop of a line from Dickens.

"Well," she said. "You have certainly memorized a great deal of it. That was impressive."

Will pulled aside the neck of his shirt, revealing the graceful curve of his collarbone. It took her a moment to realize he was showing her a Mark a few inches above his heart. "*Mnemosyne*," he said. "The Memory rune. It's permanent."

Tessa looked away quickly. "It is late. I must retire—I am exhausted." She stepped past him, and moved toward the door. She wondered if he looked hurt, then pushed the thought from her mind. This was Will; however mercurial and passing his moods, however charming he was when he was in a good one, he was poison for her, for anyone.

"*Vathek,*" he said, sliding off the table.

She paused in the doorway, realizing she was still clutching the Coleridge book, but then decided she might as well take it. It would be a pleasant diversion from the *Codex*. "What was that?"

"*Vathek,*" he said again. "By William Beckford. If you found *Otranto* to your liking"—though, she thought, she had not admitted she did—"I think you will enjoy it."

"Oh," she said. "Well. Thank you. I will remember that."

He did not answer; he was still standing where she had left him, near the table. He was looking at the ground, his dark hair hiding his face. A little bit of her heart softened, and before she could stop herself, she said, "And good night, Will."

He looked up. "Good night, Tessa." He sounded wistful again, but not as bleak as he had before. He reached out to stroke Church, who had slept through their entire conversation and the sound of the falling log in the fireplace, and was still stretched out on the book stand, paws in the air.

"Will—," Tessa began, but it was too late. Church made a yowling noise at being woken, and lashed out with his claws. Will began to swear. Tessa left, unable to hide the slightest of smiles as she went.

4
A Journey

Friendship is one mind in two bodies.
—Meng-tzu

Charlotte slammed the paper down onto her desk with an exclamation of rage. "Aloysius Starkweather is the most stubborn, hypocritical, obstinate, degenerate—" She broke off, clearly fighting for control of her temper. Tessa had never seen Charlotte's mouth so firmly set into a hard line.

"Would you like a thesaurus?" Will inquired. He was sprawled in one of the wing-back armchairs near the fireplace in the drawing room, his boots up on the ottoman. They were caked with mud, and now so was the ottoman. Normally Charlotte would have been taking him to task for it, but the letter from Aloysius that she had received that morning, and that she had called them all into the drawing room to discuss, seemed to have absorbed all her attention. "You seem to be running out of words."

"And is he really *degenerate?*" Jem asked equably from the depths of the other armchair. "I mean, the old codger's almost ninety—surely past real deviancy."

"I don't know," said Will. "You'd be surprised at what some of the old fellows over at the Devil Tavern get up to."

"Nothing anyone *you* know might get up to would surprise us, Will," said Jessamine, who was lying on the chaise longue, a damp cloth over her forehead. She still had not gotten over her headache.

"Darling," said Henry anxiously, coming around the desk to where his wife was sitting, "are you quite all right? You look a bit—splotchy."

He wasn't wrong. Red patches of rage had broken out over Charlotte's face and throat.

"I think it's charming," said Will. "I've heard polka dots are the last word in fashion this season."

Henry patted Charlotte's shoulder anxiously. "Would you like a cool cloth? What can I do to help?"

"You could ride up to Yorkshire and chop that old goat's head off." Charlotte sounded mutinous.

"Won't that make things rather awkward with the Clave?" asked Henry. "They're not generally very receptive about, you know, beheadings and things."

"Oh!" said Charlotte in despair. "It's all my fault, isn't it? I don't know why I thought I could win him over. The man's a nightmare."

"What did he say *exactly?*" said Will. "In the letter, I mean."

"He refuses to see me, or Henry," said Charlotte. "He says he'll never forgive my family for what my father did. My father . . ." She sighed. "He was a difficult man. Absolutely faithful to the letter of the Law, and the Starkweathers have always interpreted the Law more loosely. My father thought they lived wild up there in the north, like savages, and he wasn't shy about saying so. I don't know what else he did, but old Aloysius seems personally insulted still. Not to mention that he also said if I really cared what he thought about anything, I would have invited him to the last Council meeting. As if I'm in charge of that sort of thing!"

"Why *wasn't* he invited?" inquired Jem.

"He's too old—not meant to be running an Institute at all. He just refuses to step down, and so far Consul Wayland hasn't made him, but the Consul won't invite him to Councils either. I think he hopes Aloysius will either take the hint or simply die of old age. But Aloysius's father lived to be a hundred and four. We could be in for another fifteen years of him." Charlotte shook her head in despair.

"Well, if he won't see you or Henry, can't you send someone else?" asked Jessamine in a bored voice. "You run the Institute; the Enclave members are supposed to do whatever you say."

"But so many of them are on Benedict's side," said Charlotte. "They *want* to see me fail. I just don't know who I can trust."

"You can trust us," said Will. "Send me. And Jem."

"What about me?" said Jessamine indignantly.

"What *about* you? You don't really want to go, do you?"

Jessamine lifted a corner of the damp cloth off her eyes to glare. "On some smelly train all the way up to deadly dull

Yorkshire? No, of course not. I just wanted Charlotte to say she could trust me."

"I can trust you, Jessie, but you're clearly not well enough to go. Which is unfortunate, since Aloysius always had a weakness for a pretty face."

"Even more reason why I should go," said Will.

"Will, Jem . . ." Charlotte bit her lip. "Are you sure? The Council was hardly best pleased by the independent actions you took in the matter of Mrs. Dark."

"Well, they ought to be. We killed a dangerous demon!" Will protested.

"And we saved Church," said Jem.

"Somehow I doubt that counts in our favor," said Will. "That cat bit me three times the other night."

"That probably does count in your favor," said Tessa. "Or Jem's, at least."

Will made a face at her, but didn't seem angry; it was the sort of face he might have made at Jem had the other boy mock insulted him. Perhaps they really could be civil to each other, Tessa thought. He had been quite kind to her in the library the night before last.

"It seems a fool's errand," said Charlotte. The red splotches on her skin were beginning to fade, but she looked miserable. "He isn't likely to tell you anything if he knows I sent you. If only—"

"Charlotte," Tessa said, "there *is* a way we could make him tell us."

Charlotte looked at her in puzzlement. "Tessa, what do you—" She broke off then, light dawning in her eyes. "Oh, I see. Tessa, what an excellent idea."

"Oh, *what?*" demanded Jessamine from the chaise. "What idea?"

"If something of his could be retrieved," said Tessa, "and given to me, I could use it to Change into him. And perhaps access his memories. I could tell you what he recollects about Mortmain and the Shades, if anything at all."

"Then, you'll come with us to Yorkshire," said Jem.

Suddenly all eyes in the room were on Tessa. Thoroughly startled, for a moment she said nothing.

"She hardly needs to accompany us," said Will. "We can retrieve an object and bring it back to her here."

"But Tessa's said before that she needs to use something that has strong associations for the wearer," said Jem. "If what we select turns out to be insufficient—"

"She also said she can use a nail clipping, or a strand of hair—"

"So you're suggesting we take the train up to York, meet a ninety-year-old man, leap on him, and yank out his hair? I'm sure the Clave will be ecstatic."

"They'll just say you're mad," said Jessamine. "They already think it, so what's the difference, really?"

"It's up to Tessa," said Charlotte. "It's her power you're asking to use; it should be her decision."

"Did you say we'd be taking the train?" Tessa asked, looking over at Jem.

He nodded, his silver eyes dancing. "The Great Northern runs trains out of Kings Cross all day long," he said. "It's only a matter of hours."

"Then, I'll come," said Tessa. "I've never been on a train."

Will threw up his hands. "That's it? You're coming because you've never been on a train before?"

"Yes," she said, knowing how much her calm demeanor drove him mad. "I should like to ride in one, very much."

"Trains are great dirty smoky things," said Will. "You won't like it."

Tessa was unmoved. "I won't know if I like it until I try it, will I?"

"I've never swum naked in the Thames, but I know I wouldn't like it."

"But think how entertaining for sightseers," said Tessa, and she saw Jem duck his head to hide the quick flash of his grin. "Anyway, it doesn't matter. I wish to go, and I shall. When do we leave?"

Will rolled his eyes, but Jem was still grinning. "Tomorrow morning. That way we'll arrive well before dark."

"I'll have to send Aloysius a message saying to expect you," said Charlotte, picking up her pen. She paused, and looked up at them all. "Is this a dreadful idea? I—I feel as if I cannot be sure."

Tessa looked at her worriedly—seeing Charlotte like this, doubting her own instincts, made her hate Benedict Lightwood and his cohorts even more than she already did.

It was Henry who stepped up and put a gentle hand on his wife's shoulder. "The only alternative seems to be doing nothing, dearest Charlotte," he said. "And doing nothing, I find, rarely accomplishes anything. Besides, what could go wrong?"

"Oh, by the Angel, I wish you hadn't asked that," replied Charlotte with fervor, but she bent over the paper and began to write.

That afternoon was Tessa's and Sophie's second training session with the Lightwoods. Having changed into her gear,

Tessa left her room to find Sophie waiting for her in the corridor. She was dressed to train as well, her hair knotted up expertly behind her head, and a dark expression on her face.

"Sophie, what is it?" Tessa inquired, falling into step beside the other girl. "You look quite out of countenance."

"Well, if you must know . . ." Sophie dropped her voice. "It's Bridget."

"Bridget?" The Irish girl had been nearly invisible in the kitchen since she'd arrived, unlike Cyril, who had been here and there about the house, doing errands like Sophie. The last memory Tessa had of Bridget involved her sitting atop Gabriel Lightwood with a knife. She let herself dwell on it pleasantly for a moment. "What's she done?"

"She just . . ." Sophie let out a gusty sigh. "She isn't very amiable. Agatha was my friend, but Bridget—well, we have a way of talking, among us servants, you know, usually, but Bridget just won't. Cyril's friendly enough, but Bridget just keeps to herself in the kitchen, singing those awful Irish ballads of hers. I'd wager she's singing one now."

They were passing not far from the scullery door; Sophie gestured for Tessa to follow her, and together they crept close and peered inside. The scullery was quite large, with doors leading off to the kitchen and pantry. The sideboard was piled with food meant for dinner—fish and vegetables, lately cleaned and prepared. Bridget stood at the sink, her hair standing out around her head in wild red curls, made frizzy by the humidity of the water. She was singing too; Sophie had been quite right about that. Her voice drifting over the sound of the water was high and sweet.

"Oh, her father led her down the stair,
Her mother combed her yellow hair.
Her sister Ann led her to the cross,
And her brother John set her on her horse.
'Now you are high and I am low,
Give me a kiss before ye go.'
She leaned down to give him a kiss,
He gave her a deep wound and did not miss.
And with a knife as sharp as a dart,
Her brother stabbed her to the heart."

Nate's face flashed in front of Tessa's eyes, and she shuddered. Sophie, looking past her, didn't seem to notice. "That's all she sings about," she whispered. "Murder and betrayal. Blood and pain. It's horrid."

Mercifully Sophie's voice covered the end of the song. Bridget had begun drying dishes and started up with a new ballad, the tune even more melancholy than the first.

"Why does your sword so drip with blood,
Edward, Edward?
Why does your sword so drip with blood?
And why so sad are ye?"

"Enough of this." Sophie turned and began hurrying down the hall; Tessa followed. "You do see what I meant, though? She's so dreadfully morbid, and it's awful sharing a room with her. She never says a word in the morning or at night, just moans—"

"You share a room with her?" Tessa was astonished. "But the Institute has so many rooms—"

"For visiting Shadowhunters," Sophie said. "Not for servants." She spoke matter-of-factly, as if it would never have occurred to her to question or complain about the fact that dozens of grand rooms stood empty while she shared a room with Bridget, singer of murderous ballads.

"I could talk to Charlotte—," Tessa began.

"Oh, no. Please don't." They had reached the door to the training room. Sophie turned to her, all distress. "I wouldn't want her to think I'd been complaining about the other servants. I really wouldn't, Miss Tessa."

Tessa was about to assure the other girl that she would say nothing to Charlotte if that was what Sophie really wanted, when she heard raised voices from the other side of the training room door. Gesturing at Sophie to be quiet, she leaned in and listened.

The voices were quite clearly those of the Lightwood brothers. She recognized Gideon's lower, rougher tones as he said, "There will be a moment of reckoning, Gabriel. You can depend upon it. What will matter is where we stand when it comes."

Gabriel replied, his voice tense, "We will stand with Father, of course. Where else?"

There was a pause. Then, "You don't know everything about him, Gabriel. You don't know all that he has done."

"I know that we are Lightwoods and that he is our father. I know he fully expected to be named head of the Institute when Granville Fairchild died—"

"Maybe the Consul knows more about him than you do. And more about Charlotte Branwell. She isn't the fool you think she is."

"Really?" Gabriel's voice was a sneer. "Letting us come

here to train her precious girls, doesn't that make her a fool? Shouldn't she have assumed we'd be spying for our father?"

Sophie and Tessa looked at each other with round eyes.

"She agreed to it because the Consul forced her hand. And besides, we are met at the door here, escorted to this room, and escorted out. And Miss Collins and Miss Gray know nothing of import. What damage is our presence here really doing her, would you say?"

There was a silence through which Tessa could almost hear Gabriel sulking. At last he said, "If you despise Father so much, why did you ever come back from Spain?"

Gideon replied, sounding exasperated, "I came back for *you*—"

Sophie and Tessa had been leaning against the door, ears pressed to the wood. At that moment the door gave way and swung open. Both straightened hastily, Tessa hoping that no evidence of their eavesdropping appeared on their faces.

Gabriel and Gideon were standing in a patch of light at the center of the room, facing off against each other. Tessa noticed something she had not noticed before: Gabriel, despite being the younger brother, was lankily taller than Gideon by some inches. Gideon was more muscular, broader through the shoulders. He swept a hand through his sandy hair, nodding curtly to the girls as they appeared in the doorway. "Good day."

Gabriel Lightwood strode across the room to meet them. He really was quite tall, Tessa thought, craning her neck to look up at him. As a tall girl herself, she didn't often find herself bending her head back to look up at men, though both Will and Jem were taller than she was.

"Miss Lovelace still regrettably absent?" he inquired without bothering to greet them. His face was calm, the only sign of his earlier agitation a pulse hammering just beneath a Courage in Combat rune inked upon his throat.

"She continues to have the headache," said Tessa, following him into the training room. "We don't know how long she'll be indisposed."

"Until these training sessions are over, I suspect," said Gideon, so dryly that Tessa was surprised when Sophie laughed. Sophie immediately composed her features again, but not before Gideon had given her a surprised, almost appreciative glance, as if he weren't used to having his jokes laughed at.

With a sigh Gabriel reached up and freed two long sticks from their holsters on the wall. He handed one to Tessa. "Today," he began, "we shall be working on parrying and blocking . . ."

As usual, Tessa lay awake a long time that night before sleep began to come. Nightmares had plagued her recently—usually of Mortmain, his cold gray eyes, and his colder voice saying measuredly that he had made her, that *There is no Tessa Gray.*

She had come face-to-face with him, the man they sought, and still she did not really know what he wanted from her. To marry her, but why? To claim her power, but to what end? The thought of his cold lizardlike eyes on her made her shiver; the thought that he might have had something to do with her birth was even worse. She did not think anyone—not even Jem, wonderful understanding Jem—quite understood her burning need to know what she *was*, or the fear that she was some sort of monster, a fear that woke her in the middle of the night, leaving her gasping and clawing at her own skin, as if she could peel it away to reveal a devil's hide beneath.

Just then she heard a rustle at her door, and the faint scratch of something being gently pushed against it. After a moment's pause she slid off the bed and padded across the room.

She eased the door open to find an empty corridor, the faint sound of violin music drifting from Jem's room across the hall. At her feet was a small green book. She picked it up and gazed at the words stamped in gold on its spine: "*Vathek*, by William Beckford."

She shut the door behind her and carried the book over to her bed, sitting down so she could examine it. Will must have left it for her. Obviously it could have been no one else. But *why*? Why these odd, small kindnesses in the dark, the talk about books, and the coldness the rest of the time?

She opened the book to its title page. Will had scrawled a note for her there—not just a note, in fact. A poem.

For Tessa Gray, on the occasion of being given
a copy of Vathek *to read:*

Caliph Vathek and his dark horde
Are bound for Hell, you won't be bored!
Your faith in me will be restored–
Unless this token you find untoward
And my poor gift you have ignored.

–Will

Tessa burst out laughing, then clapped a hand over her mouth. *Drat* Will, for always being able to make her laugh, even when she didn't want to, even when she knew that opening her heart to him even an inch was like taking a pinch of some deadly addictive drug. She dropped the copy of *Vathek*, complete with Will's deliberately terrible poem, onto her nightstand and rolled onto the bed, burying her face in the pillows. She could still hear Jem's violin music, sweetly sad, drifting beneath her door. As hard as she could, she tried to push thoughts of Will out of her mind; and indeed, when she fell asleep at last and dreamed, for once he made no appearance.

It rained the next day, and despite her umbrella Tessa could feel the fine hat she had borrowed from Jessamine beginning to sag like a waterlogged bird around her ears as they—she, Jem, Will, and Cyril, carrying their luggage—hurried from the coach into Kings Cross Station. Through the sheets of gray rain she was conscious only of a tall, imposing building, a great clock tower rising from the front. It was topped with a weathercock that showed that the wind was blowing due north—and not gently, spattering drops of cold rain into her face.

Inside, the station was chaos: people hurrying hither and thither, newspaper boys hawking their wares, men striding up and down with sandwich boards strapped to their chests, advertising everything from hair tonic to soap. A little boy in a Norfolk jacket dashed to and fro, his mother in hot pursuit. With a word to Jem, Will vanished immediately into the crowd.

"Gone off and left us, has he?" said Tessa, struggling with her umbrella, which was refusing to close.

"Let me do that." Deftly Jem reached over and flicked at the mechanism; the umbrella shut with a decided snap. Pushing her damp hair out of her eyes, Tessa smiled at him, just as Will returned with an aggrieved-looking porter who relieved Cyril of the baggage and snapped at them to hurry up, the train wouldn't wait all day.

Will looked from the porter to Jem's cane, and back. His blue eyes narrowed. "It will wait for *us*," Will said with a deadly smile.

The porter looked bewildered but said "Sir" in a decidedly less aggressive tone and proceeded to lead them toward the departure platform. People—so many people!—streamed about Tessa as she made her way through the crowd, clutching at Jem with one hand and Jessamine's hat with the other. Far at the end of the station, where the tracks ran out into open ground, she could see the steel gray sky, smudged with soot.

Jem helped her up into their compartment; there was much bustling about the luggage, and Will tipping the porter in among shouts and whistling as the train prepared to depart. The door swung shut behind them just as the train pulled forward, steam rushing past the windows in white drifts, wheels clacking merrily.

"Did you bring anything to read on the journey?" asked Will, settling into the seat opposite Tessa; Jem was beside her, his cane leaning up against the wall.

She thought of the copy of *Vathek* and his poem in it; she had left it at the Institute to avoid temptation, the way you might leave behind a box of candies if you were banting and didn't want to put on weight. "No," she said. "I haven't come across anything I particularly wanted to read lately."

Will's jaw set, but he said nothing.

"There is always something so exciting about the start of a

journey, don't you think?" Tessa went on, nose to the window, though she could see little but smoke and soot and hurtling gray rain; London was a dim shadow in the mist.

"No," said Will as he sat back and pulled his hat down over his eyes.

Tessa kept her face against the glass as the gray of London began to fall away behind them, and with it the rain. Soon they were rolling through green fields dotted with white sheep, with here and there the point of a village steeple in the distance. The sky had turned from steel to a damp, misty blue, and small black clouds scudded overhead. Tessa watched it all with fascination.

"Haven't you ever been in the countryside before?" asked Jem, though unlike Will's, his question had the flavor of actual curiosity.

Tessa shook her head. "I don't remember ever leaving New York, except to go to Coney Island, and that isn't really countryside. I suppose I must have passed through some of it when I came from Southampton with the Dark Sisters, but it was dark, and they kept the curtains across the windows, besides." She took off her hat, which was dripping water, and laid it on the seat between them to dry. "But I feel as if I have seen it before. In books. I keep imagining I'll see Thornfield Hall rising up beyond the trees, or Wuthering Heights perched on a stony crag—"

"Wuthering Heights is in Yorkshire," said Will, from under his hat, "and we're nowhere near Yorkshire yet. We haven't even reached Grantham. And there's nothing that impressive about Yorkshire. Hills and dales, no proper mountains like we have in Wales."

“Do you miss Wales?” Tessa inquired. She wasn’t sure why she did it; she knew asking Will about his past was like poking a dog with a sore tail, but she couldn’t seem to help it.

Will shrugged lightly. “What’s to miss? Sheep and singing,” he said. “And the ridiculous language. *Fe hoffwn i fod mor feddw, fyddai ddim yn cofio fy enw.*”

“What does that mean?”

“It means ‘I wish to get so drunk I no longer remember my own name,’ Quite useful.”

“You don’t sound very patriotic,” observed Tessa. “Weren’t you just reminiscing about the mountains?”

“Patriotic?” Will looked smug. “I’ll tell you what’s patriotic,” he said. “In honor of my birthplace, I’ve the dragon of Wales tattooed on my—”

“You’re in a *charming* temper, aren’t you, William?” interrupted Jem, though there was no edge to his voice. Still, having observed them now for some time, together and apart, Tessa knew it meant something when they called each other by their full first names instead of the familiar shortened forms. “Remember, Starkweather can’t stand Charlotte, so if this is the mood you’re in—”

“I promise to charm the dickens out of him,” said Will, sitting up and readjusting his crushed hat. “I shall charm him with such force that when I am done, he will be left lying limply on the ground, trying to remember his own name.”

“The man’s eighty-nine,” muttered Jem. “He may well have that problem anyway.”

“I suppose you’re storing up all that charm now?” Tessa inquired. “Wouldn’t want to waste any of it on us?”

“That’s it exactly.” Will sounded pleased. “And it isn’t

Charlotte the Starkweathers can't stand, Jem. It's her father."

"Sins of the fathers," said Jem. "They're not inclined to like any Fairchild, or anyone associated with one. Charlotte wouldn't even let Henry come up—"

"That is because every time one lets Henry out of the house on his own, one risks an international incident," said Will. "But yes, to answer your unasked question, I do understand the trust Charlotte has placed in us, and I do intend to behave myself. I don't want to see that squinty-eyed Benedict Lightwood and his hideous sons in charge of the Institute any more than anyone else does."

"They're not hideous," said Tessa.

Will blinked at her. "What?"

"Gideon and Gabriel," said Tessa. "They're really quite good-looking, not hideous at all."

"I spoke," said Will in sepulchral tones, "of the pitch-black inner depths of their souls."

Tessa snorted. "And what color do you suppose the inner depths of *your* soul are, Will Herondale?"

"Mauve," said Will.

Tessa looked over at Jem for help, but he only smiled. "Perhaps we should discuss strategy," he said. "Starkweather hates Charlotte but knows that she sent us. So how to worm our way into his good graces?"

"Tessa can utilize her feminine wiles," said Will. "Charlotte said he enjoys a pretty face."

"How did Charlotte explain my presence?" Tessa inquired, realizing belatedly that she should have asked this earlier.

"She didn't really; she just gave our names. She was quite

curt," said Will. "I think it falls to us to concoct a plausible story."

"We can't say I'm a Shadowhunter; he'll know immediately that I'm not. No Marks."

"And no warlock mark. He'll think she's a mundane," said Jem. "She could Change, but . . ."

Will eyed her speculatively. Though Tessa knew it meant nothing—worse than nothing, really—she still felt his gaze on her like the brush of a finger across the back of her neck, making her shiver. She forced herself to return his look stonily. "Perhaps we could say she's a mad maiden aunt who insists on chaperoning us everywhere."

"My aunt or yours?" Jem inquired.

"Yes, she doesn't really look like either of us, does she? Perhaps she's a girl who's fallen madly in love with me and persists in following me wherever I go."

"My talent is shape-shifting, Will, not acting," said Tessa, and at that, Jem laughed out loud. Will glared at him.

"She had the better of you there, Will," he said. "It does happen sometimes, doesn't it? Perhaps I should introduce Tessa as my fiancée. We can tell mad old Aloysius that her Ascension is underway."

"Ascension?" Tessa remembered nothing of the term from the *Codex*.

Jem said, "When a Shadowhunter wishes to marry a mundane—"

"But I thought that was forbidden?" Tessa asked, as the train slid into a tunnel. It was dark suddenly in their compartment, though she had the feeling nevertheless that Will was looking at her, that shivering sense that his gaze was on her somehow.

"It is. *Unless* the Mortal Cup is used to turn that mundane into a Shadowhunter. It is not a common result, but it does happen. If the Shadowhunter in question applies to the Clave for an Ascension for their partner, the Clave is required to consider it for at least three months. Meanwhile, the mundane embarks on a course of study to learn about Shadowhunter culture—"

Jem's voice was drowned out by the train whistle as the locomotive emerged from the tunnel. Tessa looked at Will, but he was staring fixedly out the window, not looking at her at all. She must have imagined it.

"It's not a bad idea, I suppose," said Tessa. "I do know rather a lot; I've finished nearly all of the *Codex*."

"It would seem reasonable that I brought you with me," said Jem. "As a possible Ascender, you might want to learn about Institutes other than the one in London." He turned to Will. "What do you think?"

"It seems as fine an idea as any." Will was still looking out the window; the countryside had grown less green, more stark. There were no villages visible, only long swathes of gray-green grass and outcroppings of black rock.

"How many Institutes are there, other than the one in London?" Tessa asked.

Jem ticked them off on his hands. "In Britain? London, York, one in Cornwall—near Tintagel—one in Cardiff, and one in Edinburgh. They're all smaller, though, and report to the London Institute, which in turn reports to Idris."

"Gideon Lightwood said he was at the Institute in Madrid. What on earth was he doing there?"

"Faffing about, most likely," said Will.

"Once we finish our training, at eighteen," said Jem, as if Will hadn't spoken, "we're encouraged to travel, to spend time at other Institutes, to experience something of Shadowhunter culture in new places. There are always different techniques, local tricks to be learned. Gideon was away for only a few months. If Benedict called him back so soon, he must think that his acquisition of the Institute is assured." Jem looked troubled.

"But he's wrong," Tessa said firmly, and when the troubled look didn't leave Jem's gray eyes, she cast about for something to change the subject. "Where is the Institute in New York?"

"We haven't memorized all their addresses, Tessa." There was something in Will's voice, a dangerous undercurrent. Jem looked at him narrowly, and said:

"Is everything all right?"

Will took his hat off and laid it on the seat next to him. He looked at them both steadily for a moment, his gaze level. He was beautiful to look at as always, Tessa thought, but there seemed something *gray* about him, almost faded. For someone who so often seemed to burn very brightly, that light in him seemed exhausted now, as if he had been rolling a rock up a hill like Sisyphus. "Too much to drink last night," he said finally.

Really, why do you bother, Will? Don't you realize we both know you're lying? Tessa almost said, but one look at Jem stopped her. His gaze as he regarded Will was worried—very worried indeed, though Tessa knew he did not believe Will about the drinking, any more than she did. But, "Well," was all he said, lightly, "if only there were a Rune of Sobriety."

"Yes." Will looked back at him, and the strain in his expression relaxed slightly. "If we might return to discussing your plan, James. It's a good one, save one thing." He leaned forward. "If she is meant to be affianced to you, Tessa will need a ring."

"I had thought of that," said Jem, startling Tessa, who had imagined he had come up with this Ascendant idea on the spot. He slipped his hand into his waistcoat pocket and drew out a silver ring, which he held out to Tessa on his palm. It was not unlike the silver ring Will often wore, though where Will's had a design of birds in flight, this one had a careful etching of the crenellations of a castle tower around it. "The Carstairs family ring," he said. "If you would . . ."

She took it from him and slipped it onto her left ring finger, where it seemed to magically fit itself. She felt as if she ought to say something like *It's lovely*, or *Thank you*, but of course this wasn't a proposal, or even a gift. It was simply an acting prop. "Charlotte doesn't wear a wedding ring," she said. "I hadn't realized Shadowhunters did."

"We don't," said Will. "It is customary to give a girl your family ring when you become engaged, but the actual wedding ceremony involves exchanging runes instead of rings. One on the arm, and one over the heart."

"'Set me as a seal upon thine heart, as a seal upon thine arm: for love is strong as death; jealousy is cruel as the grave,'" said Jem. "Song of Solomon."

"'Jealousy is cruel as the grave'?" Tessa raised her eyebrows. "That's not . . . very romantic."

"'The coals thereof are coals of fire, which hath a most vehement flame,'" said Will, quirking his eyebrows up. "I always thought females found the idea of jealousy romantic. Men, fighting over you . . ."

"Well, there aren't any *graves* in mundane wedding ceremonies," said Tessa. "Though your ability to quote the Bible is impressive. Better than my aunt Harriet's."

"Did you hear that, James? She just compared us to her aunt Harriet."

Jem, as always, was unruffled. "We must be on familiar terms with all religious texts," he said. "To us they are instruction manuals."

"So you memorize them all in school?" She realized she had seen neither Will nor Jem at their studies since she had been at the Institute. "Or rather, when you are tutored?"

"Yes, though Charlotte's rather fallen off in tutoring us lately, as you might imagine," said Will. "One either has a tutor or one is schooled in Idris—that is, until you attain your majority at eighteen. Which will be soon, thankfully, for the both of us."

"Which one of you is older?"

"Jem," said Will, and "I am," said Jem, at the same time. They laughed in unison as well, and Will added, "Only by three months, though."

"I knew you'd feel compelled to point that out," said Jem with a grin.

Tessa looked from one of them to the other. There could not be two boys who looked more different, or who had more different dispositions. And yet. "Is that what it means to be *parabatai?*" she said. "Finishing each other's sentences and the like? Because there isn't much on it in the *Codex.*"

Will and Jem looked at each other. Will shrugged first,

casually. "It is rather difficult to explain," he said loftily. "If you haven't experienced it—"

"I meant," Tessa said, "you cannot—I don't know—read each other's minds, or the like?"

Jem made a spluttering noise. Will's lambent blue eyes widened. "Read each other's minds? Horrors, no."

"Then, what's the point? You swear to guard each other, I understand that, but aren't all Shadowhunters meant to do that for each other?"

"It's more than that," said Jem, who had stopped spluttering and spoke somberly. "The idea of *parabatai* comes from an old tale, the story of Jonathan and David. 'And it came to pass . . . that the soul of Jonathan was knit with the soul of David, and Jonathan loved him as his own soul. . . . Then Jonathan and David made a covenant, because he loved him as his own soul.' They were two warriors, and their souls were knit together by Heaven, and out of that Jonathan Shadowhunter took the idea of *parabatai*, and encoded the ceremony into the Law."

"But it doesn't just have to be two men. It can be a man and a woman, or two women?"

"Of course." Jem nodded. "You have only eighteen years to find and choose a *parabatai.* Once you are older than that, the ritual is no longer open to you. And it is not merely a matter of promising to guard each other. You must stand before the Council and swear to lay down your life for your *parabatai.* To go where they go, to be buried where they are buried. If there were an arrow speeding toward Will, I would be bound by oath to step in front of it."

"Handy, that," said Will.

"And he, of course, is bound to do the same for me," said Jem. "Whatever he may say to the contrary, Will does not break oaths, or the Law." He looked hard at Will, who smiled faintly and stared out the window.

"Goodness," said Tessa. "That's all very touching, but I don't see exactly how it confers any advantages."

"Not everyone has a *parabatai*," said Jem. "Very few of us, actually, find one in the allotted time. But those who do can draw on the strength of their *parabatai* in battle. A rune put on you by your *parabatai* is always more potent than one you put on yourself, or one put on by another. And there are some runes we can utilize that no other Shadowhunter can, because they draw on our doubled power."

"But what if you decide that you don't want to be *parabatai* anymore?" Tessa asked curiously. "Can the ritual be broken?"

"Dear God, woman," said Will. "Are there any questions you *don't* want to know the answer to?"

"I don't see the harm in telling her." Jem's hands were folded atop his cane. "The more she knows, the better she will be able to pretend she plans to Ascend." He turned to Tessa. "The ritual cannot be broken save in a few situations. If one of us were to become a Downworlder or a mundane, then the binding is cut. And of course, if one of us were to die, the other would be free. But not to choose another *parabatai*. A single Shadowhunter cannot take part in the ritual more than once."

"It is like being married, isn't it," said Tessa placidly, "in the Catholic church. Like Henry the Eighth; he had to create a new religion just so he could escape from his vows."

"Till death do us part," said Will, his gaze still fixed on the countryside speeding past outside the window.

"Well, Will won't need to create a new religion just to be rid of me," said Jem. "He'll be free soon enough."

Will looked over sharply, but it was Tessa who spoke. "Don't say that," she admonished Jem. "A cure could still be found. I don't see any reason to abandon all hope."

She almost shrank back at the look Will bent on her: blue, blazing, and furious. Jem seemed not to notice as he replied, calmly and unaffectedly. "I haven't abandoned hope," he said. "I just hope for different things than you do, Tessa Gray."

Hours went by after that, hours during which Tessa nodded off, her head propped against her hand, the dull sound of the train's wheels winding its way into her dreams. She woke at last with Jem shaking her gently by the shoulders, the train whistle blowing, and the guard shouting out the name of York station. In a flurry of bags and hats and porters they descended to the platform. It was nowhere near as crowded as Kings Cross, and covered by a far more impressive arched glass and iron roof, through which could be glimpsed the gray-black sky.

Platforms stretched as far as the eye could see; Tessa, Jem, and Will stood on the one closest to the main body of the station, where great gold-faced railway clocks proclaimed the time to be six o'clock. They were farther north now, and the sky had already begun to darken to twilight.

They had only just gathered beneath one of the clocks when a man stepped out of the shadows. Tessa barely suppressed a start at the sight of him. He was heavily cloaked, wearing a black oilskin-looking hat, and boots like an old sailor. His beard was long and white, his eyes crested with thick white eyebrows. He reached out and laid a hand on Will's shoulder. "Nephilim?" he said, his voice gruff and thickly accented. "Is it you?"

"Dear God," said Will, putting his hand over his heart in a theatrical gesture. "It's the Ancient Mariner who stoppeth one of three."

"Ah'm 'ere at t'bequest of Aloysius Starkweather. Art t'lads he wants or not? Ah've not got all night to stand about."

"Important appointment with an albatross?" Will inquired. "Don't let us keep you."

"What my mad friend means to say," said Jem, "is that we are indeed Shadowhunters of the London Institute. Charlotte Branwell sent us. And you are . . . ?"

"Gottshall," the man said gruffly. "Me family's been serving the Shadowhunters of the York Institute for nigh on three centuries now. I can see through tha' glamours, young ones. Save for this one," he added, and turned his eyes on Tessa. "If there's a glamour on the girl, it's summat I've never seen before."

"She's a mundane—an Ascendant," Jem said quickly. "Soon to be my wife." He took Tessa's hand protectively, and turned it so that Gottshall could see the ring on her finger. "The Council thought it would be beneficial for her to see another Institute besides London's."

"Has Mr. Starkweather been told aught about this?" Gottshall asked, black eyes keen beneath the rim of his hat.

"It depends what Mrs. Branwell told him,"said Jem.

"Well, I hope she told him something, for yer sakes," said the old servant, raising his eyebrows. "If there's a man in t' world who hates surprises more than Aloysius Starkweather, Ah've yet to meet the bast— beggar. Begging your pardon, miss."

Tessa smiled and inclined her head, but inside, her stomach

was churning. She looked from Jem to Will, but both boys were calm and smiling. They were used to this sort of subterfuge, she thought, and she was not. She had played parts before, but never as herself, never wearing her own face and not someone else's. For some reason the thought of lying without a false image to hide behind terrified her. She could only hope that Gottshall was exaggerating, though something—the glint in his eye as he regarded her, perhaps—told her that he wasn't.

5
Shades of the Past

But evil things, in robes of sorrow,
Assailed the monarch's high estate;
(Ah, let us mourn, for never morrow
Shall dawn upon him desolate!)
And round about his home the glory
That blushed and bloomed,
Is but a dim-remembered story
Of the old time entombed.
—Edgar Allan Poe, "The Haunted Palace"

Tessa barely noticed the interior of the station as they followed Starkweather's servant through its crowded entry hall. Hustle and bustle, people bumping into her, the smell of coal smoke and cooking food, blurring signs for the Great Northern Railway company and the York and North Midland lines. Soon enough they were outside the station, under a graying sky that arched overhead, threatening rain. A grand hotel reared up against the twilit sky at one end of the station; Gottshall hurried them toward it, where a black carriage with the four *C*s of the Clave painted on the door waited near the entrance. After settling the luggage and clambering inside, they were off, the carriage surging into Tanner Row to join the flow of traffic.

Will was silent most of the way, drumming his slim fingers on his black-trousered knees, his blue eyes distant and thoughtful. It was Jem who did the talking, leaning across Tessa to draw the curtains back on her side of the carriage. He pointed out items of interest—the graveyard where the victims of a cholera epidemic had been interred, and the ancient gray walls of the city rising up in front of them, crenellated across the top like the pattern on his ring. Once they were through the walls, the streets narrowed. It was like London, Tessa thought, but on a reduced scale; even the stores they passed—a butcher's, a draper's—seemed smaller. The pedestrians, mostly men, who hurried by, chins dug into their collars to block the light rain that had begun to fall, were not as fashionably dressed; they looked "country," like the farmers who came into Manhattan on occasion, recognizable by the redness of their big hands, the tough, sunburned skin of their faces.

The carriage swung out of a narrow street and into a huge square; Tessa drew in a breath. Before them rose a magnificent cathedral, its Gothic turrets piercing the gray sky like Saint Sebastian stuck through with arrows. A massive limestone tower surmounted the structure, and niches along the front of the building held sculpted statues, each one different. "Is that the Institute? Goodness, it's so much grander than London's—"

Will laughed. "Sometimes a church is only a church, Tess."

"That's York Minster," said Jem. "Pride of the city. *Not* the Institute. The Institute's in Goodramgate Street." His words were confirmed as the carriage swung away from the cathedral, down Deangate, and onto the narrow, cobbled lane of Goodramgate, where they rattled beneath a small iron gate between two leaning Tudor buildings.

When they emerged on the other side of the gate, Tessa saw why Will had laughed. What rose before them was a pleasant-enough-looking church, surrounded by enclosing walls and smooth grass, but it had none of the grandeur of York Minster. When Gottshall came around to swing the door of the carriage open and help Tessa down to the ground, she saw that occasional headstones rose from the rain-dampened grass, as if someone had intended to begin a cemetery here and had lost interest halfway through the proceedings.

The sky was nearly black now, silvered here and there with clouds made near-transparent by starlight. Behind her, Jem's and Will's familiar voices murmured; before her, the doors of the church stood open, and through them she could see flickering candles. She felt suddenly bodiless, as if she were the ghost of Tessa, haunting this odd place so far from the life she had known in New York. She shivered, and not just from the cold.

She felt the brush of a hand against her arm, and warm breath stirred her hair. She knew who it was without turning. "Shall we go in, my betrothed?" Jem said softly in her ear. She could feel the laughter in him, vibrating through his bones, communicating itself to her. She almost smiled. "Let us beard the lion in his den together."

She put her hand through his arm. They made their way up the steps of the church; she looked back at the top, and saw Will gazing up after them, apparently unheeding as Gottshall tapped him on the shoulder, saying something into his ear. Her eyes met his, but she looked quickly away; entangling gazes with Will was confusing at best, dizzying at worst.

The inside of the church was small and dark compared to the London Institute's. Pews dark with age ran the length of the walls, and above them witchlight tapers burned in holders made of blackened iron. At the front of the church, in front of a veritable cascade of burning candles, stood an old man dressed all in Shadowhunter black. His hair and beard were thick and gray, standing out wildly around his head, his gray-black eyes half-hidden beneath massive eyebrows, his skin scored with the marks of age. Tessa knew him to be almost ninety, but his back was still straight, his chest as thick around as the trunk of a tree.

"Young Herondale, are you?" he barked as Will stepped forward to introduce himself. "Half-mundane, half-Welsh, and the worst traits of both, I've heard."

Will smiled politely. "*Diolch*."

Starkweather bristled. "Mongrel tongue," he muttered, and turned his gaze to Jem. "James Carstairs," he said. "Another Institute brat. I've half a mind to tell the lot of you to go to blazes. That upstart bit of a girl, that Charlotte Fairchild, foisting you all on me with nary a by-your-leave." He had a little of the Yorkshire accent that his servant had, though much fainter; still, the way he pronounced "I" did sound a bit like "Ah." "None of that family ever had a bit o' manners. I could do without her father, and I can do without—"

His flashing eyes came to rest on Tessa then, and he stopped abruptly, his mouth open, as if he had been slapped in the face midsentence. Tessa glanced at Jem; he looked as startled as she did at Starkweather's sudden silence. But there, in the breach, was Will.

"This is Tessa Gray, sir," he said. "She is a mundane girl, but she is the betrothed of Carstairs here, and an Ascendant."

"A *mundane*, you say?" demanded Starkweather, his eyes wide.

"An Ascendant," said Will in his most soothing, silken voice. "She has been a faithful friend to the Institute in London, and we hope to welcome her into our ranks soon."

"A mundane," the old man repeated, and broke into a fit of coughing. "Well, times have— Yes, I suppose then—" His eyes skipped across Tessa's face again, and he turned to Gottshall, who was looking martyred among the luggage. "Get Cedric and Andrew to help you bring our guests' belongings up to their rooms," he said. "And do tell Ellen to instruct Cook to set three extra places for dinner tonight. I may have forgotten to remind her that we would have guests."

The servant gaped at his master before nodding in a seeming daze; Tessa couldn't blame him. It was clear that Starkweather had meant to send them packing and had changed his mind at the last moment. She glanced at Jem, who looked just as mystified as she felt; only Will, blue eyes wide and face as innocent as a choirboy's, seemed as if he had expected nothing else.

"Well, come along, then," said Starkweather gruffly without looking at Tessa. "You needn't stand there. Follow me and I'll show you to your rooms."

"By the Angel," Will said, scraping his fork through the brownish mess on his plate. "What *is* this stuff?"

Tessa had to admit, it was difficult to tell. Starkweather's servants—mostly bent old men and women and a sour-faced female housekeeper—had done as he'd asked and had set three extra places for supper, which consisted of a dark, lumpy stew ladled out of a silver tureen by a woman in a black dress and white cap, so bent and old that Tessa had to physically prevent herself from leaping up to assist her with the serving. When the woman was done, she turned and shuffled off, leaving Jem, Tessa, and Will alone in the dining room to stare at one another across the table.

A place had been set for Starkweather as well, but he wasn't at it. Tessa had to admit that if she were him, she wouldn't be rushing to eat the stew either. Heavy with overcooked vegetables and tough meat, it was even more unappetizing-looking in the dim light of the dining room. Only a few tapers lit the cramped space; the wallpaper was dark brown, the mirror over the unlit hearth stained and discolored. Tessa felt dreadfully uncomfortable in her evening dress, a stiff blue taffeta borrowed from Jessamine and let out by Sophie, which had turned to the color of a bruise in the unhealthy light.

Still, it was awfully peculiar behavior for a host, to be so insistent that they join him for supper and then not to appear. A servant just as frail and ancient as the one who'd ladled out the stew had led Tessa to her room earlier, a great dim cavern full of heavy carved furniture. It too was dimly lit, as if Starkweather were trying to save money on oil or tapers, though as far as Tessa knew, witchlight cost nothing. Perhaps he simply liked the dark.

She had found her room chilly, dark, and more than slightly ominous. The low fire burning in the grate had done little to warm the room. On either side of the hearth was carved a jagged lightning bolt. The same symbol was on the white pitcher full of chilly water that Tessa had used to wash her hands and face. She had dried off quickly, wondering why she couldn't remember the symbol from the *Codex*. It must mean something important. The whole of the London Institute was decorated with Clave symbols like the Angel rising from the lake, or the interlocked Cs of Council, Covenant, Clave, and Consul.

Heavy old portraits were everywhere as well—in her bedroom, in the corridors, lining the staircase. After changing into evening dress and hearing the dinner bell ring, Tessa had made her way down the staircase, a great carved Jacobean monstrosity, only to pause on the landing to gaze at the portrait of a very young girl with long, fair hair, dressed in an old-fashioned child's dress, a great ribbon surmounting her small head. Her face was thin and pale and sickly, but her eyes were bright—the only bright thing in this dark place, Tessa had thought.

"Adele Starkweather," had come a voice at her elbow, reading off the placard on the portrait's frame. "1842."

She had turned to look at Will, who'd stood with his feet apart, his hands behind his back, gazing at the portrait and frowning.

"What is it? You look as if you don't like her, but I rather do. She must be Starkweather's daughter—no, granddaughter, I think."

Will had shaken his head, looking from the portrait to Tessa. "No doubt. This place is decorated like a family home. It is clear there have been Starkweathers in the York Institute for generations. You've seen the lightning bolts everywhere?"

Tessa had nodded.

"That is the Starkweather family symbol. There is as much of the Starkweathers here as there is of the Clave. It is bad form to behave as if one owns a place like this. One cannot inherit an Institute. The guardian of an Institute is appointed by the Consul. The place itself belongs to the Clave."

"Charlotte's parents ran the London Institute before she did."

"Part of the reason old Lightwood is so tinder-tempered about the whole business," Will had replied. "Institutes aren't necessarily meant to stay in families. But the Consul wouldn't have given Charlotte the post if he hadn't thought she was the right person for it. And it's only one generation. This—" He swept his arm about as if to encompass the portraits, the landing, and odd, lonely Aloysius Starkweather, all in one gesture. "Well, no wonder the old man thinks he has the right to throw us out of the place."

"Mad as hops, my aunt would have said. Shall we go down to dinner?"

In a rare show of gentility, Will had offered his arm. Tessa hadn't looked at him as she'd taken it. Will dressed for dinner was handsome enough to take away her breath, and she'd had the feeling she'd need her wits about her.

Jem had already been waiting in the dining room when they'd arrived, and Tessa had settled herself beside him to await their host. His place had been set, his plate filled with stew, even his wineglass filled with dark red wine, but there had been no sign of him. It was Will who had shrugged first and begun to eat, though he'd soon looked as if he wished he hadn't.

"What *is* this?" he went on now, spearing an unfortunate object on a fork and raising it to eye level. "This . . . this . . . *thing*?"

"A parsnip?" Jem suggested.

"A parsnip planted in Satan's own garden," said Will. He

glanced about. "I don't suppose there's a dog I could feed it to."

"There don't seem to be any pets about," Jem—who loved all animals, even the inglorious and ill-tempered Church—observed.

"Probably all poisoned by parsnips," said Will.

"Oh, dear," Tessa said sadly, laying her fork down. "And I was so hungry too."

"There's always the dinner rolls," said Will, pointing to a covered basket. "Though I warn you, they're as hard as stones. You could use them to kill black beetles, if any beetles bother you in the middle of the night."

Tessa made a face and took a swig of her wine. It was as sour as vinegar.

Will set his fork down and began cheerfully, in the manner of Edward Lear's *Book of Nonsense*:

> *"There once was a lass from New York*
> *Who found herself hungry in York.*
> *But the bread was like rocks,*
> *The parsnips shaped like—"*

"You can't rhyme 'York' with 'York,'" interrupted Tessa. "It's cheating."

"She's right, you know," said Jem, his delicate fingers playing with the stem of his wineglass. "Especially with 'fork' being so obviously the correct choice—"

"Good evening." The hulking shadow of Aloysius Starkweather loomed up suddenly in the doorway; Tessa wondered with a flush of embarrassment how long he'd been standing there. "Mr. Herondale, Mr. Carstairs, Miss, ah—"

"Gray," Tessa said. "Theresa Gray."

"Indeed." Starkweather made no apologies, just settled himself heavily at the head of the table. He was carrying a square, flat box, the sort bankers used to keep their papers in, which he set down beside his plate. With a flash of excitement Tessa saw that there was a year marked on it—1825—and even better, three sets of initials. *JTS, AES, AHM.*

"No doubt your young miss will be pleased to know I've buckled to her demands and searched the archives all day and half last night besides," Starkweather began in an aggrieved tone. It took Tessa a moment to realize that in this case, "young miss" meant Charlotte. "It's lucky, she is, that my father never threw anything out. And the moment I saw the papers, I remembered." He tapped his temple. "Eighty-nine years, and I never forget a thing. You tell old Wayland that when he talks about replacing me."

"We surely will, sir," said Jem, his eyes dancing.

Starkweather took a hearty gulp of his wine and made a face. "By the Angel, this stuff's disgusting." He set the glass down and began pulling papers from the box. "What we have here is an application for Reparations on behalf of two warlocks. John and Anne Shade. A married couple.

"Now, here's the odd bit," the old man went on. "The filing was done by their son, Axel Hollingworth Mortmain, twenty-two years old. Now, of course warlocks are barren—"

Will shifted uncomfortably in his seat, his eyes slanting away from Tessa's.

"This son was adopted," said Jem.

"Shouldn't be allowed, that," said Starkweather, taking another slug of the wine he had pronounced disgusting. His cheeks were beginning to redden. "Like giving a human child to wolves to raise. Before the Accords—"

"If there are any clues to his whereabouts," said Jem, gently trying to steer the conversation back onto its track. "We have very little time—"

"Very well, very well," snapped Starkweather. "There's little information about your precious Mortmain in here. More about the parents. It seems suspicion fell on them when it was discovered that the male warlock, John Shade, was in possession of the Book of the White. Quite a powerful spell book, you understand; disappeared from the London Institute's library under suspicious circumstances back in 1752. The book specializes in binding and unbinding spells—tying the soul to the body, or untying it, as the case may be. Turned out the warlock was trying to animate things. He was digging up corpses or buying them off medical students and replacing the more damaged bits with mechanisms. Then trying to bring them to life. Necromancy—very much against the Law. And we didn't have the Accords in those days. An Enclave group swept in and slaughtered both warlocks."

"And the child?" said Will. "Mortmain?"

"No hide nor hair of him," said Starkweather. "We searched, but nothing. Assumed he was dead, till this turned up, cheeky as you please, demanding reparations. Even his address—"

"His *address*?" Will demanded. That information had *not* been included in the scroll they had seen at the Institute. "In London?"

"Nay. Right here in Yorkshire." Starkweather tapped the page with a wrinkled finger. "Ravenscar Manor. A massive old pile up north from here. Been abandoned now, I think, for decades. Now that I think about it, can't figure how he could've afforded it in the first place. It's not where the Shades lived."

"Still," said Jem. "An excellent starting point for us to go looking. If it's been abandoned since his tenancy, there may be things he left behind. In fact, he may well still be using the place."

"I suppose." Starkweather sounded unenthusiastic about the whole business. "Most of the Shades' belongings were taken for spoils."

"Spoils," Tessa echoed faintly. She remembered the term from the *Codex*. Anything a Shadowhunter took from a Downworlder who had been caught breaking the Law belonged to him. Those were the spoils of war. She looked across the table at Jem and Will; Jem's gentle eyes resting on her with concern, Will's haunted blue ones holding all their secrets. Did she really belong to a race of creatures that was at war with what Jem and Will were?

"Spoils," Starkweather rumbled. He had polished off his wine and started on Will's untouched glass. "Do those interest you, girl? We've quite a collection here in the Institute. Puts the London collection to shame, or so I'm told." He stood up, nearly knocking over his chair. "Come along. I'll show them to you, and tell you the rest of this sorry tale, though there's not that much more to it."

Tessa looked quickly to Will and Jem for a cue, but they were already on their feet, following the old man out of the room. Starkweather spoke as he walked, his voice drifting back over his shoulder, making the rest of them hurry to match his long strides.

"Never thought much of this Reparations business myself,"

he said as they passed down another dimly lit, interminably long stone corridor. "Makes Downworlders uppity, thinking they have a right to get something out of us. All the work we do and no thanks, just hands held out for more, more, more. Don't you think so, gentlemen?"

"Bastards, all of them," said Will, who seemed as if his mind were a thousand miles away. Jem looked at him sideways.

"Absolutely!" barked Starkweather, clearly pleased. "Not that one should use such language in front of a lady, of course. As I was saying, this Mortmain was protesting the death of Anne Shade, the male warlock's wife—said she'd had nothing to do with her husband's projects, hadn't known about them, he claimed. Her death was undeserved. Wanted a trial of those guilty of what he called her 'murder,' and his parents' belongings back."

"Was the Book of the White among what he asked for?" Jem inquired. "I know it's a crime for a warlock to own such a volume . . ."

"It was. It was retrieved and placed in the London Institute library, where no doubt it remains still. Certainly no one was going to give it to *him*."

Tessa did a quick mental calculation in her head. If he was eighty-nine now, Starkweather would have been twenty-six at the time of the Shades' deaths. "Were you there?"

His bloodshot eyes danced over her; she noticed that even now, a little drunk, he didn't seem to want to look at her too directly. "Was I where?"

"You said an Enclave group was sent out to deal with the Shades. Were you among them?"

He hesitated, then shrugged. "Aye," he said, his Yorkshire

accent thickening for a moment. "Dinna take long to get the both of them. They weren't prepared. Not a bit. I remember them lying there in their blood. The first time I saw dead warlocks, I was surprised they bled red. I could have sworn it'd be another color, blue or green or some such." He shrugged. "We took the cloaks off them, like skins off a tiger. I was given the keeping of them, or more rightly, my father was. Glory, glory. Those were the days." He grinned like a skull, and Tessa thought of Bluebeard's chamber where he kept the remains of the wives he had killed. She felt both very hot and very cold all over.

"Mortmain never had a chance, did he," she said quietly. "Filing his complaint like that. He was never going to get his reparations."

"Of course not!" barked Starkweather. "Rubbish, all of it—claiming the wife wasn't involved. What wife isn't neck-deep in her husband's business? Besides, he wasn't even their blood son, couldn't have been. Probably more of a pet to them than anything else. I'd wager the father'd have used him for spare parts if it came down to it. He was better off without them. He should have been thanking us, not asking for a trial—"

The old man broke off as he reached a heavy door at the end of the corridor and put his shoulder to it, grinning down at them from beneath beetling brows. "Ever been to the Crystal Palace? Well, this is even better."

He shouldered the door open, and light blazed up around them as they passed through into the room beyond. Clearly it was the only well-lit room in the place.

The room was full of glass-fronted cabinets, and over each cabinet was mounted a lamp of witchlight, illuminating the contents within. Tessa saw Will's back stiffen, and Jem reached for her, his hand tightening on her arm with an almost bruising grip. "Don't—," he began, but she had pushed forward, and was staring at the contents of the cabinets.

Spoils. A gold locket, open to a daguerreotype of a laughing child. The locket was splattered with dried blood. Behind her Starkweather was talking about digging the silver bullets out of the bodies of freshly killed werewolves and melting them down to recast. There was a dish of such bullets, in fact, in one of the cabinets, filling a bloodstained bowl. Sets of vampire fangs, row on row of them. What looked like sheets of gossamer or delicate fabric, pressed under glass. Only on closer inspection did Tessa realize they were the wings of faeries. A goblin, like the one she had seen with Jessamine in Hyde Park, floating open-eyed in a large jar of preservative fluid.

And the remains of warlocks. Mummified taloned hands, like Mrs. Black's. A stripped skull, utterly de-fleshed, human-looking save that it had tusks instead of teeth. Vials of sludgy-looking blood. Starkweather was now talking about how much warlock parts, especially a warlock's "mark," could be sold for on the Downworld market. Tessa felt dizzy and hot, her eyes burning.

Tessa turned around, her hands shaking. Jem and Will stood, looking at Starkweather with mute expressions of horror; the old man was holding up another hunting trophy—a human-looking head mounted to a backing. The skin had shriveled and gone gray, drawn back against the bones. Fleshless spiral horns protruded from the top of its skull. "Got this off a warlock I killed down by Leeds way," he said. "You wouldn't believe the fight he put up—"

Starkweather's voice hollowed out, and Tessa felt herself suddenly cut free and floating. Darkness rushed up, and then there were arms around her, and Jem's voice. Words floated by her in ragged scraps. "My fiancée—never seen spoils before—can't stand blood—very delicate—"

Tessa wanted to fight free of Jem, wanted to rush at Starkweather and strike the old man, but she knew it would ruin everything if she did. She clenched her eyes shut and pressed her face against Jem's chest, breathing him in. He smelled of soap and sandalwood. Then there were other hands on her, drawing her away from Jem. Starkweather's maidservants. She heard Starkweather telling them to take her upstairs and help her to bed. She opened her eyes to see Jem's troubled face as he looked after her, until the door of the spoils room closed between them.

It took Tessa a long time to fall asleep that night, and when she did, she had a nightmare. In the dream she lay manacled to the brass bed in the house of the Dark Sisters . . .

Light like thin gray soup seeped through the windows. The door opened and Mrs. Dark came in, followed by her sister, who had no head, only the white bone of her spine protruding from her raggedly severed neck.

"Here she is, the pretty, pretty princess," said Mrs. Dark, clapping her hands together. "Just think of what we will get for all the parts of her. A hundred each for her little white hands, and a thousand for the pair of her eyes. We'd get more if they were blue, of course, but one can't have everything."

She chuckled, and the bed began to spin as Tessa screamed and thrashed in the darkness. Faces appeared above her: Mortmain, his narrow features screwed up in amusement. "And they say the worth of a good woman is far above rubies," he said. "What of the worth of a warlock?"

"Put her in a cage, I say, and let the groundlings stare at her for pennies," said Nate, and suddenly the bars of a cage sprang up around her and he was laughing at her from the other side, his pretty face twisted up in scorn. Henry was there too, shaking his head. "I've taken her all apart," he said, "and I can't see what makes that heart of hers beat. Still, it's quite a curiosity, isn't it?" He opened his hand, and there was something red and fleshy on his palm, pulsing and contracting like a fish flipped out of water, gasping for air. "See how it's divided into two quite equal parts—"

"Tess," a voice came, urgently, in her ear. "Tess, you're dreaming. Wake up. Wake up." Hands were on her shoulders, shaking her; her eyes flew open, and she was gasping in her ugly gray dimly lit bedroom at the York Institute. The covers were tangled around her, and her nightgown stuck to her back with sweat. Her skin felt as if it were burning. She still saw the Dark Sisters, saw Nate laughing at her, Henry dissecting her heart.

"It was a dream?" she said. "It felt so real, so utterly real—" She broke off.

"Will," she whispered. He still wore his dinner clothes, though they were rumpled, his black hair tangled, as if he had fallen asleep without changing for bed. His hands remained on her shoulders, warming her cold skin through the material of her nightgown.

"What did you dream?" he said. His tone was calm and ordinary, as if there were nothing unusual about her waking up and finding him sitting on the edge of her bed.

She shuddered at the memory. "I dreamed I was being taken apart—that bits of me were being put on display for Shadowhunters to laugh at—"

"Tess." He touched her hair gently, pushing the tangled locks behind her ears. She felt pulled to him, like iron filings to a magnet. Her arms ached to go around him, her head to rest in the crook of his shoulder. "God damn that devil Starkweather for showing you what he did, but you must know it's not like that anymore. The Accords have forbidden spoils. It was just a dream."

But no, she thought. *This* is the dream. Her eyes had adjusted to the dark; the gray light in the room made his eyes glow an almost unearthly blue, like a cat's. When she drew a shuddering breath, her lungs felt filled with the scent of him, Will and salt and trains and smoke and rain, and she wondered if he had been out, walking the streets of York as he did in London. "Where have you been?" she whispered. "You smell like nighttime."

"Out kicking over the traces. As usual." He touched her cheek with warm, callused fingers. "Can you sleep now? We're meant to rise early tomorrow. Starkweather is lending us his carriage so that we might investigate Ravenscar Manor. You, of course, are welcome to remain here. You need not accompany us."

She shuddered. "Stay here without you? In this big, gloomy place? I would prefer not to."

"Tess." His voice was ever so gentle. "That must have been quite a nightmare, to have taken the spirit out of you so. Usually you are not afraid of much."

"It was awful. Even Henry was in my dream. He was taking apart my heart as if it were made of clockwork."

"Well, that settles it," Will said. "Pure fantasy. As if Henry is a danger to anyone except himself." When she didn't smile, he added, fiercely, "I would never let anyone touch a hair on your head. You know that, don't you, Tess?"

Their gazes caught and locked. She thought of the wave that seemed to catch at her whenever she was near Will, how she had felt herself drawn over and under, pulled to him by forces that seemed beyond her control—in the attic, on the roof of the Institute. As if he felt the same pull, he bent toward her now. It felt natural, as right as breathing, to lift her head, to meet his lips with hers. She felt his soft exhalation against her mouth; relief, as if a great weight had been taken from him. His hands rose to cup her face. Even as her eyes fluttered shut, she heard his voice in her head, again, unbidden:

There is no future for a Shadowhunter who dallies with warlocks.

She turned her face quickly, and his lips brushed her cheek instead of her mouth. He drew back, and she saw his blue eyes open, startled—and hurt. "No," she said. "No, I don't know that, Will." She dropped her voice. "You have made it very clear," she said, "what kind of use you have for me. You think I am a toy for your amusements. You should not have come in here; it is not proper."

He dropped his hands. "You called out—"

"Not for you."

He was silent except for his ragged breathing.

"Do you regret what you said to me that night on the roof, Will? The night of Thomas's and Agatha's funeral?" It was the first time either of them had made reference to the incident since it had happened. "Can you tell me you did not mean what you said?"

He bent his head; his hair fell forward, hiding his face. She clenched her own hands into fists at her sides to stop herself from reaching out and pushing it back. "No," he said, very low. "No, the Angel forgive me, I can't say that."

Tessa withdrew, curling in on herself, turning her face away. "Please go away, Will."

"Tessa—"

"Please."

There was a long silence. He stood up then, the bed creaking beneath him as he moved. She heard his light tread on the floorboards, and then the door of the bedroom shutting behind him. As if the sound had snapped some cord that held her upright, she fell back against the pillows. She stared up at the ceiling a long time, fighting back in vain against the questions that crowded her mind— What had Will meant, coming to her room like that? Why had he shown her such sweetness when she knew that he despised her? And why, when she knew that he was the worst thing in the world for her, did sending him away seem like such a terrible mistake?

The next morning dawned unexpectedly blue and beautiful, a balm to Tessa's aching head and exhausted body. After dragging herself from the bed, where she had spent most of the night tossing and turning, she dressed herself, unable to bear the thought of assistance from one of the ancient, half-blind maidservants. As she did up the buttons on her jacket, she caught sight of herself in the room's old, splotched mirror.

There were half-moons of shadow under her eyes, as if they had been smudged there with chalk.

Will and Jem had already gathered in the morning room for a breakfast of half-burned toast, weak tea, jam, and no butter. By the time Tessa arrived, Jem had already eaten, and Will was busy cutting his toast into thin strips and forming rude pictographs out of them.

"What *is* that supposed to be?" Jem asked curiously. "It looks almost like a—" He glanced up, saw Tessa, and broke off with a grin. "Good morning."

"Good morning." She slid into the seat across from Will; he glanced up at her once as she sat, but there was nothing in his eyes or expression to indicate that he recalled that anything had passed between them the night before.

Jem looked at her with concern. "Tessa, how are you feeling? After last night—" He broke off then, his voice rising, "Good morning, Mr. Starkweather," he said hastily, jostling Will's shoulder hard so that Will dropped his fork, and the toast bits slid all over his plate.

Mr. Starkweather, who had swept into the room, still wrapped in the dark cloak he had worn the night before, regarded him balefully. "The carriage is waiting for you in the courtyard," he said, his clipped diction as tight as ever. "You'd better cut a stick if you want to get back before dinnertime; I'll be needing the carriage this evening. I've told Gottshall to drop you straight at the station on your return, no need for lingering. I trust you've gotten everything you need."

It wasn't a question. Jem nodded. "Yes, sir. You've been very gracious."

Starkweather's eyes swept over Tessa again, one last time,

before he turned and stalked out of the room, his cloak flapping behind him. Tessa couldn't get the image of a great black bird of prey—a vulture, perhaps—out of her mind. She thought of the trophy cases full of "spoils," and shuddered.

"Eat quickly, Tessa, before he changes his mind about the carriage," Will advised her, but Tessa shook her head.

"I'm not hungry."

"At least have tea." Will poured it out for her, and ladled milk and sugar into it; it was much sweeter than Tessa would have liked, but it was so rare that Will made a kind gesture like that—even if it was just to hurry her along—that she drank it down anyway, and managed a few bites of toast. The boys went for their coats and the baggage; Tessa's traveling cloak, hat, and gloves were located, and they soon found themselves on the front steps of the York Institute, blinking in the watery sunlight.

Starkweather had been as good as his word. His carriage was there, waiting for them, the four *C*s of the Clave painted across the door. The old coachman with the long white beard and hair was already in the driver's seat, smoking a cheroot; he tossed it aside when he saw the three of them, and sank down farther in his seat, his black eyes glaring out from beneath his drooping eyelids.

"Bloody hell, it's the Ancient Mariner again," said Will, though he seemed more entertained than anything else. He swung himself up into the carriage and helped Tessa in after him; Jem was last, shutting the door behind him and leaning out the window to call to the coachman to drive on. Tessa, settling herself in beside Will on the narrow seat, felt her shoulder brush his; he tensed immediately, and she moved away, biting her lip. It was as if last night had never happened and he were back to behaving as if she were poison.

The carriage began moving with a jerk that nearly flung Tessa into Will again, but she braced herself against the window and stayed where she was. The three of them were silent as the carriage rolled down narrow, cobbled Stonegate Street, under a wide sign advertising the Old Star Inn. Both Jem and Will were quiet, Will reviving only to tell her with a ghoulish glee that they were passing through the old walls, under the city entrance where once traitors' heads had been displayed on spikes. Tessa made a face at him but gave no reply.

Once they had passed the walls, the city quickly gave way to countryside. The landscape was not gentle and rolling, but harsh and forbidding. Green hills dotted with gray gorse swept up into crags of dark rock. Long lines of mortarless stone walls, meant for keeping in sheep, crisscrossed the green; here and there was dotted the occasional lonely cottage. The sky seemed an endless expanse of blue, brushed with the strokes of long gray clouds.

Tessa could not have said how long they had been traveling when the stone chimneys of a large manor house rose in the distance. Jem stuck his head out the window again and called to the driver; the carriage came to a rolling stop.

"But we're not there yet," said Tessa, puzzled. "If that's Ravenscar Manor—"

"We can't just roll right up to the front door; be sensible, Tess," said Will as Jem leaped out of the carriage and reached up to help Tessa down. Her boots plashed into the wet, muddy ground as she landed; Will dropped down lightly beside her. "We need to get a look at the place. Use Henry's device to register demonic presence. Make sure we're not walking into a trap."

"Does Henry's device actually *work?*" Tessa lifted her skirts to keep them out of the mud as the three of them started down the road. Glancing back, she saw the coachman apparently already asleep, leaning back in the driver's seat with his hat tipped forward over his face. All around them the countryside was a patchwork of gray and green—hills rising starkly; their sides pitted with gray shale; flat sheep-cropped grass; and here and there copses of gnarled, entwined trees. There was a severe beauty to it all, but Tessa shuddered at the idea of living here, so far away from anything.

Jem, seeing her shudder, gave a sideways smile. "City lass."

Tessa laughed. "I *was* thinking how odd it would be to grow up in a place like this, so far from any people."

"Where I grew up was not so different from this," said Will unexpectedly, startling them both. "It's not so lonely as you might think. Out in the countryside, you can be assured, people visit one another a great deal. They just have a greater distance to traverse than they might in London. And once they arrive, they often make a lengthy stay. After all, why make the trip just to stay a night or two? We'd often have house guests who'd remain for weeks."

Tessa goggled at Will silently. It was so rare that he ever referred to anything regarding his early life that she sometimes thought of him as someone with no past at all. Jem seemed to be doing the same thing, though he recovered first.

"I share Tessa's view. I have never lived in anything but a city. I don't know how I could sleep at night, not knowing I was surrounded by a thousand other sleeping, dreaming souls."

"And filth everywhere, and everyone breathing down one another's necks," countered Will. "When I first arrived in London, I so quickly tired of being surrounded by so many people that it was only with great difficulty that I refrained from seizing the next unfortunate who crossed my path and committing violent acts upon their person."

"Some might say you retain that problem," said Tessa, but Will just laughed—a short, nearly surprised sound of amusement—and then stopped, looking ahead of them to Ravenscar Manor.

Jem whistled as Tessa realized why she had been able to see only the tops of the chimneys before. The manor was built in the center of a deep declivity between three hills; their slanting sides rose about it, cradling it as if in the palm of a hand. Tessa, Jem, and Will were poised on the edge of one of the hills, looking down at the manor. The building itself was very grand, a great gray stone pile that gave the impression it had been there for centuries. A large circular drive curved in front of the enormous front doors. Nothing about the place hinted at abandonment or disrepair—no weeds grew over the drive or the paths that led to the stone outbuildings, and no glass was missing from the mullioned windows.

"*Someone's* living here," said Jem, echoing Tessa's thoughts. He began to start down the hill. The grass here was longer, waving almost waist-high. "Perhaps if—"

He broke off as the rattle of wheels became audible; for a moment Tessa thought the carriage driver had come after them, but no, this was quite a different carriage—a sturdy-looking coach that turned into the gate and began rolling toward the manor. Jem crouched down immediately in the grass, and Will and Tessa dropped beside him. They watched as the carriage came to a stop before the manor, and the driver leaped down to open the carriage door.

A young girl stepped out, fourteen or fifteen years old, Tessa guessed—not old enough to have put her hair up, for it blew around her in a curtain of black silk. She wore a blue dress, plain but fashionable. She nodded to the driver, and then, as she started up the manor steps, she paused—paused and looked toward where Jem, Will, and Tessa crouched, almost as if she could see them, though Tessa was sure that they were well hidden by the grass.

The distance was too great for Tessa to make out her features, really—just the pale oval of her face below the dark hair. She was about to ask Jem if he had a telescope with him, when Will made a noise—a noise she had never heard anyone make before, a sick, terrible gasp, as if the air had been punched out of him by a tremendous blow.

But it was not just a gasp, she realized. It was a word; and not just a word, a name; and not just a name, but one she had heard him say before.

"Cecily."

6

In Silence Sealed

The human heart has hidden treasures,
In secret kept, in silence sealed;
The thoughts, the hopes, the dreams, the pleasures,
Whose charms were broken if revealed
—Charlotte Brontë, "Evening Solace"

The door of the great house swung open; the girl disappeared inside. The coach rattled off around the side of the manor to the coach house as Will staggered to his feet. He had gone a sickly gray color, like the ashes of a dead fire.

"Cecily," he said again. His voice held wonderment, and horror.

"Who on earth is Cecily?" Tessa scrambled into a standing position, brushing grass and thistles from her dress. "Will—"

Jem was already beside Will, his hand on his friend's shoulder. "Will, you must speak to us. You look as if you've seen a ghost."

Will dragged in a long breath. "Cecily—"

"Yes, you've said that already," said Tessa. She heard the sharpness in her own voice, and softened it with an effort. It was unkind to speak so to someone so obviously distraught, even if he did insist on staring into space and muttering "Cecily" at intervals.

It hardly mattered; Will seemed not to have heard her. "My sister," he said. "Cecily. She was— Christ, she was nine years old when I left."

"Your sister," said Jem, and Tessa felt a loosening of something tight around her heart, and cursed herself inwardly for it. What did it matter whether Cecily was Will's sister or someone he was in love with? It had nothing to do with her.

Will started down the hill, not looking for a path, just tramping blindly among the heather and furze. After a moment Jem went after him, catching at his sleeve. "Will, don't—"

Will tried to pull his arm away. "If Cecily's there, then the rest of them—my family—they must be there as well."

Tessa hurried to catch up with them, wincing as she nearly turned an ankle on a loose rock. "But it doesn't make any sense that your family would be here, Will. This was Mortmain's house. Starkweather said so. It was in the papers—"

"I *know* that," Will half-shouted.

"Cecily could be visiting someone here—"

Will gave her an incredulous look. "In the middle of Yorkshire, by herself? And that was our carriage. I recognized it. There's no other carriage in the carriage house. No, my family's in this somehow. They've been dragged into this bloody business and I—I have to warn them." He started down the hill again.

"Will!" Jem shouted, and went after him, catching at the

back of his coat; Will swung around and shoved Jem, not very hard; Tessa heard Jem say something about Will having held back all these years and not wasting it now, and then it all blurred together—Will swearing, and Jem yanking him backward, and Will slipping on the wet ground, and the both of them going over together, a rolling tangle of arms and legs, until they fetched up against a large rock, Jem pinning Will to the ground, his elbow against the other boy's throat.

"Get off me." Will shoved at him. "You don't understand. *Your* family's dead—"

"*Will.*" Jem took his friend by the shirtfront and shook him. "I *do* understand. And unless you want your family dead too, you'll listen to me."

Will went very still. In a choked voice he said, "James, you can't possibly— I've never—"

"Look." Jem raised the hand that wasn't gripping Will's shirt, and pointed. "There. Look."

Tessa looked where he was pointing—and felt her insides freeze. They were nearly halfway down the hill above the manor house, and there, above them, standing like a sort of sentry on the ridge at the hill's top, was an automaton. She knew immediately what it was, though it did not look like the automatons that Mortmain had sent against them before. Those had made some surface pretense of being human. This was a tall, spindly metal creature, with long hinged legs, a twisted metallic torso, and sawlike arms.

It was utterly still, not moving, somehow more frightening for its stillness and silence. Tessa could not even tell if it was watching them. It seemed to be turned toward them, but though it had a head, that head was featureless but for the slash of a mouth; metal teeth gleamed within. It seemed to have no eyes.

Tessa quelled the scream rising in her throat. It was an automaton. She had faced them before. She would *not* scream. Will, propped on his elbow, was staring. "By the Angel—"

"That thing's been following us; I'm sure of it," said Jem in a low, urgent voice. "I saw a flash of metal earlier, from the carriage, but I wasn't sure. Now I am. If you go tearing off down the hill, you risk leading that thing right to your family's door."

"I see," Will said. The half-hysterical tone had gone from his voice. "I won't go near the house. Let me up."

Jem hesitated.

"I swear on Raziel's name," Will ground out, between his teeth. "Now let me up."

Jem rolled away and onto his feet; Will leaped up, pushing Jem aside, and, without a glance at Tessa, took off running—not toward the house but away from it, toward the mechanical creature on the ridge. Jem staggered for a moment, open-mouthed, swore, and darted after him.

"Jem!" Tessa cried. But he was nearly out of earshot already, racing after Will. The automaton had vanished from view. Tessa said an unladylike word, hiked up her skirts, and gave chase.

It was not easy, running up a wet Yorkshire hill in heavy skirts, brambles tearing at her as she went. Practicing in her training clothes had given Tessa a new appreciation for why it was that men could move so quickly and cleanly, and could run so fast. The material of her dress weighed a ton, the heels on her boots caught on rocks as she ran, and her corset left her uncomfortably short of breath.

By the time she reached the top of the ridge, she was only

just in time to see Jem, far ahead of her, disappear into a dark copse of trees. She looked around wildly but could see neither the road nor the Starkweathers' carriage. With her heart pounding, she dashed after him.

The copse was wide, spreading along the ridgeline. The moment Tessa ducked in among the trees, the light vanished; thick tree branches interweaving above her blocked out the sun. Feeling like Snow White fleeing into the forest, she looked around helplessly for a sign of where the boys had gone—broken branches, trodden leaves—and caught a shimmer of light on metal as the automaton surged out of the dark space between two trees and lunged for her.

She screamed, leaping away, and promptly tripped on her skirts. She went over backward, thumping painfully into the muddy earth. The creature stabbed one of its long insectile arms toward her. She rolled aside and the metal arm sliced into the ground beside her. There was a fallen tree branch near her; her fingers scrabbled at it, closed around it, and lifted it just as the creature's other arm swung toward her. She swept the branch between them, concentrating on the parrying and blocking lessons she'd gotten from Gabriel.

But it was only a branch. The automaton's metal arm sheared it in half. The end of the arm sprang open into a multi-fingered metal claw and reached for her throat. But before it could touch her, Tessa felt a violent fluttering against her collarbone. Her angel. She lay frozen as the creature jerked its claw back, one of its "fingers" leaking black fluid. A moment later it gave a high-pitched whine and collapsed backward, a freshet of more black liquid pouring from the hole that had been sliced clean through its chest.

Tessa sat up and stared.

Will stood with a sword in his hand, its hilt smeared with black. He was bareheaded, his thick dark hair tousled and tangled with leaves and bits of grass. Jem stood beside him, a witchlight stone blazing through his fingers. As Tessa watched, Will slashed out with the sword again, cutting the automaton nearly in half. It crumpled to the muddy ground. Its insides were an ugly, horribly biological-looking mess of tubes and wires.

Jem looked up. His gaze met Tessa's. His eyes were as silver as mirrors. Will, despite having saved her, did not appear to notice she was there at all; he drew back his foot and delivered a savage kick to the metal creature's side. His boot rang against metal.

"Tell us," he said through gritted teeth. "What are you doing here? Why are you following us?"

The automaton's razor-lined mouth opened. Its voice when it spoke sounded like the buzzing and grinding of faulty machinery. "*I . . . am . . . a . . . warning . . . from the Magister.*"

"A warning to who? To the family in the manor? Tell me!" Will looked as if he were going to kick the creature again; Jem laid a hand on his shoulder.

"It doesn't feel pain, Will," he said in a low voice. "And it says it has a message. Let it deliver it."

"*A warning . . . to you, Will Herondale . . . and to all Nephilim . . .*" The creature's broken voice ground out, "*The Magister says . . . you must cease your investigation. The past . . . is the past. Leave Mortmain's buried, or your family will pay the price. Do not dare approach or warn them. If you do, they will be destroyed.*"

Jem was looking at Will; Will was still ashy-pale, but his

cheeks were burning with rage. "How did Mortmain bring my family here? Did he threaten them? What has he done?"

The creature whirred and clicked, then began to speak again. "*I . . . am . . . a . . . warning . . . from . . .*"

Will snarled like an animal and slashed down with the sword. Tessa remembered Jessamine, in Hyde Park, tearing a faerie creature to ribbons with her delicate parasol. Will cut at the automaton until it was little more than ribbons of metal; Jem, throwing his arms around his friend and yanking him bodily backward, finally stopped him.

"Will," he said. "Will, enough." He glanced up, and the other two followed his gaze. In the distance, through the trees, other shapes moved—more automatons, like this one. "We must go," Jem said. "If we want to draw them off, away from your family, we must leave."

Will hesitated.

"Will, you know you cannot go near them," Jem said desperately. "If nothing else, it is the Law. If we bring danger to them, the Clave will not move to help them in any way. They are not Shadowhunters anymore. *Will.*"

Slowly Will lowered his arm to his side. He stood, with one of Jem's arms still around his shoulders, staring down at the pile of scrap metal at his feet. Black liquid dripped from the blade of the sword that dangled in his hand, and scorched the grass below.

Tessa exhaled. She hadn't realized she'd been holding her breath until that moment. Will must have heard her, for he raised his head and his gaze met hers across the clearing. Something in it made her look away. Agony stripped so raw was not meant for her eyes.

***

In the end they hid the remains of the destroyed automaton as swiftly as possible, by burying them in the soft earth beneath a rotting log. Tessa helped as best she could, hampered by her skirts. By the end of it her hands were as black with dirt and mud as Will's and Jem's were.

None of them spoke; they worked in an eerie silence. When they were done, Will led the way out of the copse, guided by the light of Jem's witchlight rune-stone. They emerged from the woods nearly at the road, where the Starkweather carriage waited, Gottshall dozing in the driver's seat as if only a few moments had passed since they had arrived.

If their appearances—filthy, smeared with mud, and with leaves caught in their hair—surprised the old man at all, he didn't show it, nor did he ask them if they had found what they had come looking for. He only grunted a hello and waited for them to climb up into the carriage before he signaled the horses with a click of his tongue to turn around and begin the long journey back to York.

The curtains inside the carriage were drawn back; the sky was heavy with blackish clouds, pressing down on the horizon. "It's going to rain," Jem said, pushing damp silvery hair out of his eyes.

Will said nothing. He was staring out the window. His eyes were the color of the Arctic sea at night.

"Cecily," said Tessa in a much gentler voice than she was used to using with Will these days. He looked so miserable—as bleak and stark as the moors they were passing through. "Your sister—she looks like you."

Will remained silent. Tessa, seated next to Jem on the hard seat, shivered a little. Her clothes were damp from the wet earth and branches, and the inside of the carriage was cold. Jem reached down and, finding a slightly ragged lap rug, settled it over the both of them. She could feel the heat that radiated off his body, as if he were feverish, and fought the urge to move closer to him to get warm.

"Are you cold, Will?" she asked, but he only shook his head, his eyes still staring, unseeing, at the passing countryside. She looked at Jem in desperation.

Jem spoke, his voice clear and direct. "Will," he said. "I thought . . . I thought that your sister was dead."

Will drew his gaze from the window and looked at them both. When he smiled, it was ghastly. "My sister *is* dead," he said.

And that was all he would say. They rode the rest of the way back to the city of York in silence.

Having barely slept the night before, Tessa fell in and out of a fitful doze that lasted until they reached the York train station. In a fog she dismounted from the carriage and followed the others to the London platform; they were late for the train, and nearly missed it, and Jem held the door open for her, for her and Will, as both of them stumbled up the steps and into the compartment after him. Later she would remember the way he looked, hanging on to the door, hatless, calling to both of them, and recall staring out the window of the train as it pulled away, seeing Gottshall standing on the platform looking after them with his unsettling dark eyes, his hat pulled low. Everything else was a blur.

There was no conversation this time as the train puffed its way through countryside increasingly darkened by clouds, only silence. Tessa rested her chin on her palm, cradling her head against the hard glass of the window. Green hills flew by, and small towns and villages, each with their own neat small station, the name of it picked out in gold on a red sign. Church spires rose in the distance; cities swelled and vanished, and Tessa was aware of Jem whispering to Will, in Latin, she thought—"*Me specta, me specta,*" and Will not answering. Later she was aware that Jem had left the compartment, and she looked at Will across the small dimming space between them. The sun had begun to go down, and it lent a rosy flush to his skin, belying the blank look in his eyes.

"Will," she said softly, sleepily. "Last night—" *You were kind to me,* she was going to say. *Thank you.*

The glare from his blue eyes stabbed through her. "There was no last night," he said through his teeth.

At that, she sat up straight, almost awake. "Oh, truly? We just went right from one afternoon on through till the next morning? How odd no one else has remarked on it. I should think it some sort of miracle, a day with no night—"

"Don't test me, Tessa." Will's hands were clenched on his knees, his fingernails, half-moons of dirt under them, digging into the fabric of his trousers.

"Your sister's alive," she said, knowing perfectly well that she was provoking him. "Oughtn't you be glad?"

He whitened. "*Tessa—*," he began, and leaned forward as if he meant to do she knew not what—strike the window and break it, shake her by the shoulders, or hold her as if he never meant to let her go. It was all one great bewilderment with him, wasn't it? Then the compartment door opened and Jem came in, carrying a damp cloth.

He looked from Will to Tessa and raised his silvery eyebrows. "A miracle," he said. "You got him to speak."

"Just to shout at me, really," said Tessa. "Not quite loaves and fishes."

Will had gone back to staring out the window, and looked at neither of them as they spoke.

"It's a start," said Jem, and he sat down beside her. "Here. Give me your hands."

Surprised, Tessa held her hands out to him—and was horrified. They were filthy, the nails cracked and broken and thick with half-moons of dirt where she had clawed at the Yorkshire earth. There was even a bloody scratch across her knuckles, though she had no memory of having gotten it.

Not a lady's hands. She thought of Jessamine's perfect pink and white paws. "Jessie would be horrified," she said mournfully. "She'd tell me I had charwoman's hands."

"And what, pray tell, is dishonorable about that?" said Jem as he gently cleaned the dirt from her scratches. "I saw you chase after us, and that automaton creature. If Jessamine does not know by now that there is honor in blood and dirt, she never will."

The cool cloth felt good on her fingers. She looked up at Jem, who was intent on his task, his lashes a fringe of lowered silver. "Thank you," she said. "I doubt I was any help at all, and probably a hindrance, but thank you all the same."

He smiled at her, the sun coming out from behind clouds. "That's what we're training you for, isn't it?"

She lowered her voice. "Have you any idea what could have happened? Why Will's family would be living in a house Mortmain once owned?"

Jem glanced over at Will, who was still staring bitterly out the window. They had entered London, and gray buildings were beginning to rise up around them on either side. The look Jem gave Will was a tired, loving sort of look, a familial look, and Tessa realized that, though when she had imagined them as brothers, she had always imagined Will as the older, the caretaker, and Jem as the younger, the reality was far more complicated than that. "I do not," he said, "though it makes me think that the game Mortmain is playing is a long one. Somehow he knew exactly where our investigations would lead us, and he arranged for this—encounter—to shock us as much as possible. He wishes us to be reminded who it is who has the power."

Tessa shuddered. "I don't know what he wants from me, Jem," she said in a low voice. "When he said to me that he made me, it was as if he were saying he could unmake me just as easily."

Jem's warm arm touched hers. "You cannot be unmade," he said just as softly. "And Mortmain underestimates you. I saw how you used that branch against the automaton—"

"It was not enough. If it had not been for my angel—" Tessa touched the pendant at her throat. "The automaton touched it and recoiled. Another mystery I do not understand. It protected me before, and again this time, but in other situations lies dormant. It is as much a mystery as my talent."

"Which, fortunately, you did not need to use to Change into Starkweather. He seemed quite happy simply to give us the Shade files."

"Thank goodness," said Tessa. "I wasn't looking forward to it. He seems such an unpleasant, bitter man. But if it ever turns out to be necessary . . ." She took something from her pocket and held it up, something that glinted in the carriage's dim light. "A button," she said smugly. "It fell from the cuff of his jacket this morning, and I picked it up."

Jem smiled. "Very clever, Tessa. I knew we'd be glad we brought you with us—"

He broke off with a cough. Tessa looked at him in alarm, and even Will was roused out of his silent despondency, turning to look at Jem with narrowed eyes. Jem coughed again, his hand pressed to his mouth, but when he took it away, there was no blood visible. Tessa saw Will's shoulders relax.

"Just some dust in my throat," Jem reassured them. He looked not ill but very tired, though his exhaustion only served to point up the delicacy of his features. His beauty did not blaze like Will's did in fierce colors and repressed fire, but it had its own muted perfection, the loveliness of snow falling against a silver-gray sky.

"Your ring!" She started up suddenly as she remembered that she was still wearing it. She put the button back into her pocket, then reached to draw the Carstairs ring off her hand. "I had meant to give it back to you earlier," she said, placing the silver circlet in his palm. "I forgot . . ."

He curled his fingers around hers. Despite her thoughts of snow and gray skies, his hand was surprisingly warm. "That's all right," he said in a low voice. "I like the way it looks on you."

She felt her cheeks warm. Before she could answer, the train whistle sounded. Voices cried out that they were in London, Kings Cross Station. The train began to slow as the platform came into view. The hubbub of the station rose to assault Tessa's ears, along with the sound of the train braking. Jem said something, but his words were lost in the noise; it sounded like a warning, but Will was already on his feet, his hand reaching for the compartment door latch. He swung it open and leaped out and down. If he were not a Shadowhunter, Tessa thought, he would have fallen, and badly, but as it was, he simply landed lightly on his feet and began to run, pushing his way among the crowding porters, the commuters, the gentility traveling north for the weekend with their massive trunks and hunting hounds on leashes, the newspaper boys and pickpockets and costermongers and all the other human traffic of the grand station.

Jem was on his feet, hand reaching for the door—but he turned back and looked at Tessa, and she saw an expression cross his face, an expression that said that he realized that if he fled after Will, she could not follow. With another long look at her, he latched the door shut and sank into the seat opposite her as the train came to a stop.

"But Will—," she began.

"He will be all right," said Jem with conviction. "You know how he is. Sometimes he just wants to be alone. And I doubt he wishes to take part in recounting today's experiences to Charlotte and the others." When she didn't move her eyes from his, he repeated, gently, "Will can take care of himself, Tessa."

She thought of the bleak look in Will's eyes when he had spoken to her, starker than the Yorkshire moors they had just left behind them. She hoped Jem was right.

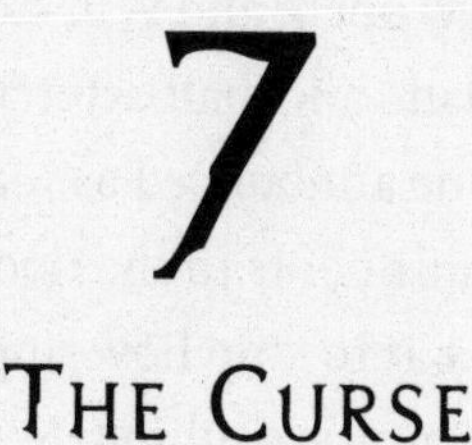

The Curse

An orphan's curse would drag to hell
A spirit from on high;
But oh! more horrible than that
Is the curse in a dead man's eye!
Seven days, seven nights, I saw that curse,
And yet I could not die.
—Samuel Taylor Coleridge,
"The Rime of the Ancient Mariner"

Magnus heard the sound of the front door opening and the following clatter of raised voices, and thought immediately, *Will.* And then was amused that he had thought it. The Shadowhunter boy was becoming like an annoying relative, he thought as he folded down a page of the book he was reading—Lucian's *Dialogues of the Gods*; Camille would be furious he had dog-eared her volume—someone whose habits you knew well but could not change. Someone whose presence you could recognize by the sound of their boots in the hallway. Someone who felt free to argue with the footman when he'd been given orders to tell everyone that you were not at home.

The parlor door flew open, and Will stood on the threshold, looking half-triumphant and half-wretched—quite a feat. "I *knew* you were here," he announced as Magnus sat up straight on the sofa, swinging his boots to the floor. "Now, will you tell this—this overgrown bat to stop hovering over my shoulder?" He indicated Archer, Camille's subjugate and Magnus's temporary footman, who was indeed lurking at Will's side. His face was set in a look of disapproval, but then it was always set in a look of disapproval. "Tell him you want to see me."

Magnus set his book down on the table beside him. "But maybe I don't want to see you," he said reasonably. "I told Archer to let no one in, not to let no one in but you."

"He threatened me," Archer said in his hissing not-quite-human voice. "I shall tell my mistress."

"You do that," said Will, but his eyes were on Magnus, blue and anxious. "Please. I *have* to talk to you."

Drat the boy, Magnus thought. After an exhausting day spent clearing a memory-blocking spell for a member of the Penhallow family, he had wanted only to rest. He had stopped listening for Camille's step in the hall, or waiting for her message, but he still preferred this room to others—this room, where her personal touch seemed to cling to the thorned roses on the wallpaper, the faint perfume that rose from the draperies. He had looked forward to an evening spent by the fire here—a glass of wine, a book, and being left strictly alone.

But now here was Will Herondale, his expression a study in pain and desperation, wanting Magnus's help. He was really going to have to do something about this annoying softhearted impulse to assist the desperate, Magnus thought. That, and his weakness for blue eyes.

"Very well," he said with a martyred sigh. "You may stay and talk to me. But I warn you, I'm not raising a demon. Not before I've had my supper. Unless you have turned up some sort of hard proof . . ."

"No." Will came eagerly into the room, shutting the door in Archer's face. He reached around and locked it, for good measure, and then strode over to the fire. It *was* chilly out. The visible bit of window not blocked by drapes showed the square outside darkening to a blackish twilight, leaves blown rattling across the pavement by a brisk-looking wind. Will drew off his gloves, laid them on the mantel, and stretched his hands out to the flames. "I don't want you to raise a demon."

"Huh." Magnus put his booted feet up on the small rosewood table before the sofa, another gesture that would have infuriated Camille, had she been there. "That's good news, I suppose—"

"I want you to send me through. To the demon realms."

Magnus choked. "You want me to do *what*?"

Will's profile was black against the flickering fire. "Create a portal to the demon worlds and send me through. You can do that, can't you?"

"That's black magic," said Magnus. "Not quite necromancy, but—"

"No one need know."

"Really." Magnus's tone was acid. "These things have a way of getting out. And if the Clave found out I'd sent one of their own, their most promising, to be rent apart by demons in another dimension—"

"The Clave does not consider me promising." Will's voice was cold. "I am not promising. I am not anything, nor will I ever be. Not without your help."

"I am beginning to wonder if you've been sent to test me, Will Herondale."

Will gave a harsh little bark of laughter. "By God?"

"By the Clave. Who might as well be God. Perhaps they simply seek to find out whether I am willing to break the Law."

Will swung around and stared at him. "I am deadly earnest," he said. "This is not some sort of test. I cannot go on like this, summoning up demons at random, never having them be the correct one, endless hope, endless disappointment. Every day dawns blacker and blacker, and I will lose her forever if you—"

"Lose *her*?" Magnus's mind fastened on the word; he sat up straight, narrowing his eyes. "This *is* about Tessa. I knew it was."

Will flushed, a wash of color across the pallor of his face. "Not just her."

"But you love her."

Will stared at him. "Of course I do," he said finally. "I had come to think I would never love anyone, but I love her."

"Is this curse supposed to be some business about taking away your ability to love? Because that's nonsense if I've ever heard it. Jem's your *parabatai*. I've seen you with him. You love him, don't you?"

"Jem is my great sin," said Will. "Don't talk to me about Jem."

"Don't talk to you about Jem, don't talk to you about Tessa. You want me to open a portal to the demon worlds for you, and you won't talk to me or tell me why? I won't do it, Will." Magnus crossed his arms over his chest.

Will rested a hand on the mantel. He was very still, the flames showing the outlines of him, the clear beautiful profile, the grace of his long slender hands. "I saw my family today," he said, and then amended that quickly. "My sister. I saw my younger sister. Cecily. I knew they lived, but I never thought I would see them again. They cannot be near me."

"Why?" Magnus made his voice soft; he felt he was on the verge of something, some sort of breakthrough with this odd, infuriating, damaged, shattered boy. "What did they do that was so terrible?"

"What did *they* do?" Will's voice rose. "What did *they* do? Nothing. It is me. I am poison. Poison to them. Poison to anyone who loves me."

"Will—"

"I lied to you," Will said, turning suddenly away from the fire.

"Shocking," Magnus murmured, but Will was gone, gone into his memories, which was perhaps for the best. He had begun to pace, scuffing his boots along Camille's lovely Persian carpet.

"You know what I've told you. I was in the library of my parents' house in Wales. It was a rainy day; I was bored, going through my father's old things. He kept a few things from his old life as a Shadowhunter, things he had not wanted, for sentiment I suppose, to give up. An old stele, though I did not know what it was at the time, and a small, engraved box, in a false drawer of his desk. I suppose he assumed that would be enough to keep us out, but nothing is enough to keep out curious children. Of course the first thing I did upon finding the box was open it. A mist poured out of it in a blast, forming almost instantly into a living demon. The moment I saw the creature, I began to scream. I was only twelve. I'd never seen anything like it. Enormous, deadly, all jagged teeth and barbed tail—and I had nothing. No weapons. When it roared, I fell to the carpet. The thing was hovering over me, hissing. Then my sister burst in."

"Cecily?"

"Ella. My elder sister. She had something blazing in her hand. I know what it was now—a seraph blade. I had no idea then. I screamed for her to get out, but she put herself between the creature and me. She had absolutely no fear, my sister. She never had. She was not afraid to climb the tallest tree, to ride the wildest horse—and she had no fear there, in the library. She told the thing to get out. It was hovering there like a great, ugly insect. She said, 'I banish you.' Then it laughed."

It would. Magnus felt a strange stirring of both pity and liking for the girl, brought up to know nothing about demons, their summoning or their banishment, yet standing her ground regardless.

"It laughed, and it swung out with its tail, knocking her to the ground. Then it fixed its eyes on me. They were all red, no whites at all. It said, 'It is your father I would destroy, but as he is not here, you will have to do.' I was so shocked, all I could do was stare. Ella was crawling over the carpet, grabbing for the fallen seraph blade. 'I curse you,' it said. 'All who love you will die. Their love will be their destruction. It may take moments, it may take years, but any who look upon you with love will die of it, unless you remove yourself from them forever. And I shall begin it with *her*.' It snarled in Ella's direction, and vanished."

Magnus was fascinated despite himself. "And did she fall dead?"

"No." Will was still pacing. He took off his jacket, slung it over a chair. His longish dark hair had begun to curl with the heat coming off his body, mixing with the heat of the fire; it stuck to the back of his neck. "She was unharmed. She took me in her arms. *She* comforted *me*. She told me the demon's words meant nothing. She admitted she had read some of the forbidden books in the library, and that was how she knew what a seraph blade was, and how to use it, and that the thing I had opened was called a Pyxis, though she could not imagine why my father would have kept one. She made me promise not to touch anything of my parents' again unless she was there, and then she led me up to bed, and sat reading while I fell asleep. I was exhausted with the shock of it all, I think. I remember hearing her murmur to my mother, something about how I had been taken ill while they had been out, some childish fever. By that point I was enjoying the fuss that was being made over me, and the demon was beginning to seem a rather exciting memory. I recall planning how to tell Cecily about it—without admitting, of course, that Ella had saved me while I had screamed like a child—"

"You *were* a child," Magnus noted.

"I was old enough," said Will. "Old enough to know what it meant when I was woken up the next morning by my mother howling with grief. She was in Ella's room, and Ella was dead in her bed. They did their best to keep me out, but I saw what I needed to see. She was swelled up, greenish-black like something had rotted her from inside. She didn't look like my sister anymore. She didn't look *human* anymore.

"I knew what had happened, even if they didn't. '*All who love you will die. And I shall begin it with her.*' It was my curse at work. I knew then that I had to get away from them—from all my family—before I brought the same horror down on them. I left that night, following the roads to London."

Magnus opened his mouth, then closed it again. For once he didn't know what to say.

"So, you see," said Will, "my curse can hardly be called nonsense. I have seen it at work. And since that day I have striven to be sure that what happened to Ella will happen to no one else in my life. Can you imagine it? Can you?" He raked his hands through his black hair, letting the tangled strands fall back into his eyes. "Never letting anyone near you. Making everyone who might otherwise love you, hate you. I left my family to distance myself from them, and that they might forget me. Each day I must show cruelty to those I have chosen to make my home with, lest they let themselves feel too much affection for me."

"Tessa . . ." Magnus's mind was suddenly full of the serious-faced gray-eyed girl who had looked at Will as if he were a new sun dawning on the horizon. "You think she does not love you?"

"I do not think so. I have been foul enough to her." Will's voice was wretchedness and misery and self-loathing all combined. "I think there was a time when she almost— I thought she was dead, you see, and I showed her—I let her see what I felt. I think she might have returned my feelings after that. But I crushed her, as brutally as I could. I imagine she simply hates me now."

"And Jem," said Magnus, dreading the answer, knowing it.

"Jem is dying anyway," Will said in a choked voice. "Jem is

what I have allowed myself. I tell myself, if he dies, it is not my fault. He is dying anyway, and in pain. Ella's death at least was swift. Perhaps through me he can be given a good death." He looked up miserably, met Magnus's accusing eyes. "No one can live with nothing," he whispered. "Jem is all I have."

"You should have told him," said Magnus. "He would have chosen to be your *parabatai* anyway, even knowing the risks."

"I cannot burden him with that knowledge! He would keep it secret if I asked him to, but it would pain him to know it—and the pain I cause others would only hurt him more. Yet if I were to tell Charlotte, to tell Henry and the rest, that my behavior is a sham—that every cruel thing I have said to them is a lie, that I wander the streets only to give the impression that I have been out drinking and whoring when in reality I have no desire to do either—then I have ceased to push them away."

"And thus you have never told anyone of this curse? No one but myself, since you were twelve years old?"

"I could not," Will said. "How could I be sure they would form no attachment to me, once they knew the truth? A story like that might engender pity, pity could become attachment, and then . . ."

Magnus raised his eyebrows. "Are you not concerned about me?"

"That you might *love* me?" Will sounded genuinely startled. "No, for you hate Nephilim, do you not? And besides, I imagine you warlocks have ways to guard against unwanted emotions. But for those like Charlotte, like Henry, if they knew the persona I presented to them was false, if they knew of my true heart . . . they might come to care for me."

"And then they would die," said Magnus.

***

Charlotte raised her face slowly from her hands. "And you've absolutely no idea where he is?" she asked for the third time. "Will is simply—gone?"

"Charlotte." Jem's voice was soothing. They were in the drawing room, with its wallpaper of flowers and vines. Sophie was by the fire, using the poker to coax more flames from the coal. Henry sat behind the desk, fiddling with a set of copper instruments; Jessamine was on the chaise, and Charlotte was in an armchair by the fire. Tessa and Jem sat somewhat primly side by side on the sofa, which made Tessa feel peculiarly like a guest. She was full of sandwiches that Bridget had brought in on a tray, and tea, its warmth slowly thawing her insides. "It isn't as if this is unusual. When do we ever know where Will is at nighttime?"

"But this is different. He saw his family, or his sister at least. Oh, poor Will." Charlotte's voice shook with anxiety. "I had thought perhaps he was finally beginning to forget about them . . ."

"No one forgets about their family," said Jessamine sharply. She sat on the chaise longue with a watercolor easel and papers propped before her; she had recently made the decision that she had fallen behind in pursuing the maidenly arts, and had begun painting, cutting silhouettes, pressing flowers, and playing on the spinet in the music room, though Will said her singing voice made him think of Church when he was in a particularly complaining mood.

"Well, no, of course not," said Charlotte hastily, "but perhaps not to live with the memory constantly, as a sort of dreadful weight on you."

"As if we'd know what to do with Will if he didn't have the morbs every day," said Jessamine. "Anyway, he can't have cared about his family that much in the first place or he wouldn't have left them."

Tessa gave a little gasp. "How can you say that? You don't know why he left. You didn't see his face at Ravenscar Manor—"

"Ravenscar Manor." Charlotte was staring blindly at the fireplace. "Of all the places I thought they'd go . . ."

"Pish and tosh," said Jessamine, looking angrily at Tessa. "At least his family's alive. Besides, I'll wager he wasn't sad at all; I'll wager you he was shamming. He always is."

Tessa glanced toward Jem for support, but he was looking at Charlotte, and his look was as hard as a silver coin. "What do you mean," he said, "of all the places you thought they'd go? Did you know that Will's family had moved?"

Charlotte started, and sighed. "Jem . . ."

"It's important, Charlotte."

Charlotte glanced over at the tin on her desk that held her favorite lemon drops. "After Will's parents came here to see him, when he was twelve, and he sent them away . . . I begged him to speak to them, just for a moment, but he wouldn't. I tried to make him understand that if they left, then he could never see them again, and I could never tell him news of them. He took my hand, and he said, 'Please just promise me you'll tell me if they die, Charlotte. Promise me.'" She looked down, her fingers knotting in the material of her dress. "It was such an odd request for a little boy to make. I—I had to say yes."

"So you've been looking into the welfare of Will's family?" Jem asked.

"I hired Ragnor Fell to do it," Charlotte said. "For the first three years. The fourth year he came back to me and told me that the Herondales had moved. Edmund Herondale—that's Will's father—had lost their house gambling. That was all Ragnor was able to glean. The Herondales had been forced to move. He could find no further trace of them."

"Did you ever tell Will?" Tessa said.

"No." Charlotte shook her head. "He had made me promise to tell him if they died, that was all. Why add to his unhappiness with the knowledge that they had lost their home? He never mentioned them. I had grown to hope he might have forgotten—"

"He has never forgotten." There was a force in Jem's words that stopped the nervous movement of Charlotte's fingers.

"I should not have done it," Charlotte said. "I should never have made that promise. It was a contravention of the Law—"

"When Will truly wants something," said Jem quietly, "when he *feels* something, he can break your heart."

There was a silence. Charlotte's lips were tight, her eyes suspiciously bright. "Did he say anything about where he was going when he left Kings Cross?"

"No," said Tessa. "We arrived, and he just up and dusted—sorry, got up and ran," she corrected herself, their blank looks alerting her to the fact that she was using American slang.

"'Up and dusted,'" said Jem. "I like that. Makes it sound like he left a cloud of dust spinning in his wake. He didn't say anything, no—just elbowed his way through the crowd and was gone. Nearly knocked down Cyril coming to get us."

"None of it makes any sense," Charlotte moaned. "Why on earth would Will's family be living in a house that used to belong to Mortmain? In Yorkshire of all places? This is not where I thought this road would lead. We sought Mortmain and we found the Shades; we sought him again and found Will's family. He encircles us, like that cursed *ouroboros* that is his symbol."

"You had Ragnor Fell look into Will's family's welfare before," said Jem. "Can you do it again? If Mortmain is somehow entangled with them . . . for whatever reason . . ."

"Yes, yes, of course," said Charlotte. "I will write to him immediately."

"There is a part of this I do not understand," Tessa said. "The reparations demand was filed in 1825, and the complainant's age was listed as twenty-two. If he was twenty-two then, he'd be seventy-five now, and he doesn't look that old. Maybe forty . . ."

"There are ways," Charlotte said slowly, "for mundanes who dabble in dark magic to prolong their lives. Just the sort of spell, by the way, that one might find in the Book of the White. Which is why possession of the Book by anyone other than the Clave is considered a crime."

"All that newspaper business about Mortmain inheriting a shipping company from his father," Jem said. "Do you think he pulled the vampire trick?"

"The vampire trick?" echoed Tessa, trying in vain to remember such a thing from the *Codex*.

"It's a way vampires have of keeping their money over time," said Charlotte. "When they have been too long in one place, long enough that people have started to notice that they never age, they fake their own death and leave their inheritance to a long-lost son or nephew. Voila—the nephew shows up, bears an uncanny resemblance to his father or uncle, but there he is and he gets the money. And they go on like that for generations sometimes. Mortmain could easily have left the company to himself to disguise the fact that he wasn't aging."

"So he pretended to be his own son," said Tessa. "Which would also have given him a reason to be seen changing the direction of the company—to return to Britain and begin interesting himself in mechanisms, that sort of thing."

"And is probably also why he left the house in Yorkshire," said Henry.

"Though that does not explain why it is being inhabited by Will's family," mused Jem.

"Or where Will is," added Tessa.

"Or where *Mortmain* is," put in Jessamine, with a sort of dark glee. "Only nine more days, Charlotte."

Charlotte put her head back into her hands. "Tessa," she said, "I hate to ask this of you, but it is, after all, why we sent you to Yorkshire, and we must leave no stone unturned. You still have the button from Starkweather's coat?"

Wordlessly Tessa took the button from her pocket. It was round, pearl and silver, strangely cold in her hand. "You want me to Change into him?"

"Tessa," Jem said quickly. "If you do not want to do this, Charlotte—*we*—would never require it."

"I know," Tessa said. "But I offered, and I would not go back on my word."

"Thank you, Tessa." Charlotte looked relieved. "We must know if there is anything he is hiding from us—if he was lying to you about any part of this business. His involvement in what happened to the Shades . . ."

Henry frowned. "It will be a dark day when you cannot trust your fellow Shadowhunters, Lottie."

"It is a dark day already, Henry dear," Charlotte replied without looking at him.

"You won't help me, then," Will said in a flat voice. Using magic, Magnus had built the fire up in the grate. In the glow of the leaping flames, the warlock could see more of the details of Will—the dark hair curling close at the nape of his neck, the delicate cheekbones and strong jaw, the shadow cast by his lashes. He reminded Magnus of someone; the memory tickled at the back of his mind, refusing to come clear. After so many years, it was hard sometimes to pick out individual memories, even of those you had loved. He could no longer remember his mother's face, though he knew she had looked like him, a mixture of his Dutch grandfather and his Indonesian grandmother.

"If your definition of 'help' involves dropping you into the demon realms like a rat into a pit full of terriers, then no, I won't help you," said Magnus. "This is madness, you know. Go home. Sleep it off."

"I'm not drunk."

"You might as well be." Magnus ran both hands through his thick hair and thought, suddenly and irrationally, of Camille. And was pleased. Here in this room, with Will, he had gone nearly two hours without thinking of her at all. Progress. "You think you're the only person who's ever lost anyone?"

Will's face twisted. "Don't make it sound like that. Like some ordinary sort of grief. It's not like that. They say time heals all wounds, but that presumes the source of the grief is finite. Over. This is a fresh wound every day."

"Yes," said Magnus, leaning back against the cushions. "That is the genius of curses, isn't it."

"It would be one thing if I had been cursed so that everyone I loved would die," said Will. "I could keep myself from loving. To keep others from caring for me—it is an odd, exhausting procedure." He *sounded* exhausted, Magnus thought, and dramatic in that way that only seventeen-year-olds could be. He also doubted the truth of Will's statement that he could have kept himself from loving, but understood why the boy would want to tell himself such a story. "I must play the part of another person all day, each day—bitter and vicious and cruel—"

"I rather liked you that way. And don't tell me you don't enjoy yourself at least a little, playing the devil, Will Herondale."

"They say it runs in our blood, that sort of bitter humor," said Will, looking at the flames. "Ella had it. So did Cecily. I never thought I did until I found I needed it. I have learned good lessons in how to be hateful over all these years. But I feel myself losing myself—" He groped for words. "I feel myself diminished, parts of me spiraling away into the darkness, that which is good and honest and true— If you hold it away from yourself long enough, do you lose it entirely? If no one cares for you at all, do you even really exist?"

He said this last so softly that Magnus had to strain to hear him. "What was that?"

"Nothing. Something I read somewhere once." Will turned to him. "You would be doing me a mercy, sending me to the demon realms. I might find what I am looking for. It is my only chance—and without that chance my life is worthless to me anyway."

"Easy enough to say at seventeen," said Magnus, with no small amount of coldness. "You are in love and you think that is all there is in the world. But the world is bigger than you, Will, and may have need of you. You are a Shadowhunter. You serve a greater cause. Your life is not yours to throw away."

"Then nothing is mine," said Will, and pushed himself away from the mantel, staggering a little as if he really were drunk. "If I don't even own my own life—"

"Who ever said we were owed happiness?" Magnus said softly, and in his mind he saw the house of his childhood, and his mother flinching away from him with frightened eyes, and her husband, who was not his father, burning. "What about what we owe to others?"

"I've given them everything I have already," said Will, seizing his coat off the back of the chair. "They've had enough out of me, and if this is what you have to say to me, then so have you—*warlock*."

He spat the last word like a curse. Regretting his harshness, Magnus began to rise to his feet, but Will pushed past him toward the door. It slammed behind him. Moments later Magnus saw him pass by the front window, struggling into his coat as he walked, his head bent down against the wind.

Tessa sat before her vanity table, wrapped in her dressing gown and rolling the small button back and forth in her palm. She had asked to be left alone to do what Charlotte had requested of her. It was not the first time she had transformed into a man; the Dark Sisters had forced her to do it, more than once, and while it was a peculiar feeling, it was not what fueled her reluctance. It was the darkness she had seen in Starkweather's eyes, the slight sheen of madness to his tone when he spoke of the spoils he had taken. It was not a mind she wanted to acquaint herself with further.

She did not have to do it, she thought. She could walk out there and tell them she had tried and it had not worked. But she knew even as the thought flickered through her mind, she could not do that. Somehow she had come to think of herself as bound with loyalty to the Institute's Shadowhunters. They had protected her, shown her kindness, taught her much of the truth of what she was, and they had the same goal she did—find Mortmain and destroy him. She thought of Jem's kind eyes on her, steady and silver and full of faith. With a deep breath she closed her fingers around the button.

The darkness came and enveloped her, wrapping her in its cool silence. The faint sound of the fire crackling in the grate, the wind against the panes of the window, vanished. Blackness and silence. She felt her body Change: Her hands felt large and swollen, shot through with the pains of arthritis. Her back ached, her head felt heavy, her feet were throbbing and painful, and there was a bitter taste in her mouth. Rotting teeth, she thought, and felt ill, so ill that she had to force her mind back to the darkness surrounding her, looking for the light, the connection.

It came, but not as the light usually did, as steady as a beacon. It came in shattered fragments, as if she were watching a mirror break into pieces. Each piece held an image that whipped by her, some at terrifying speed. She saw the image of a horse rearing back, a dark hill covered in snow, the black basalt Council room of the Clave, a cracked headstone. She struggled to seize and catch at a single image. Here was one, a memory: Starkweather dancing at a ball with a laughing woman in an empire-waisted ball gown. Tessa discarded it, reaching for another:

The house was small, nestled in the shadows between one hill and another. Starkweather watched from the darkness of a copse of trees as the front door opened and out came a man. Even in memory Tessa felt Starkweather's heart begin to beat more quickly. The man was tall, broad-shouldered—and as green-skinned as a lizard. His hair was black. The child he held by the hand, by contrast, seemed as normal as a child could be—small, chubby-fisted, pink-skinned.

Tessa knew the man's name, because Starkweather knew it.

John Shade.

Shade hoisted the child up onto his shoulders as through the door of the house spilled a number of odd-looking metal creatures, like a child's jointed dolls, but human-size, and with skin made of shining metal. The creatures were featureless. Though, oddly, they wore clothes—the rough workman's coveralls of a Yorkshire farmer on some, and on others plain muslin dresses. The automatons joined hands and began to sway as if they were at a country dance. The child laughed and clapped his hands.

"Look well on this, my son," said the green-skinned man, "for one day I shall rule a clockwork kingdom of such beings, and you shall be its prince."

"John!" came a voice from inside the house; a woman leaned through the window. She had long hair the color of a cloudless sky. "John, come in. Someone will see! And you'll frighten the boy!"

"He's not frightened at all, Anne." The man laughed, and

set the boy down on the ground, ruffling his hair. "My little clockwork prince . . ."

A swell of hatred rose in Starkweather's heart at the memory, so violent that it ripped Tessa free, sending her spinning through the darkness again. She began to realize what was happening. Starkweather was becoming senile, losing the thread that connected thought and memory. What came and went in his mind was seemingly random. With an effort she tried to visualize the Shade family again, and caught the brief edge of a memory—a room torn apart, cogs and cams and gears and ripped metal everywhere, fluid leaking as black as blood, and the green-skinned man and blue-haired woman lying dead among the ruins. Then that, too, was gone, and she saw, again and again, the face of the girl from the portrait on the stairwell—the child with the fair hair and stubborn expression—saw her riding a small pony, her face set determinedly, saw her hair blowing in the wind off the moors—saw her screaming and writhing in pain as a stele was set to her skin and black Marks stained its whiteness. And last, Tessa saw her own face, appearing out of the shadowy gloom of the York Institute's nave, and she felt the wave of his shock ripple through her, so strong that it threw her out of his body and back into her own.

There was a faint thump as the button fell out of her hand and struck the floor. Tessa raised her head and looked into the mirror over her vanity. She was herself again, and the bitter taste in her mouth now was blood where she had bitten her lip.

She rose to her feet, feeling ill, and went over to the window, throwing it open to feel the cool night air on her sweaty skin. The night outside was heavy with shadow; there was little wind, and the black gates of the Institute seemed to loom before her, their motto speaking more than ever of mortality and death. A glimmer of movement caught her eye. She looked down and saw a white shape gazing up at her from the stony courtyard below. A face, twisted but recognizable. Mrs. Dark.

She gasped and jerked back reflexively, out of sight of the window. A wave of dizziness came over her. She shook it off fiercely, her hands gripping the sill, and pulled herself forward again, gazing down with dread—

But the courtyard was empty, nothing moving inside it but shadows. She closed her eyes, then opened them again slowly, and put her hand to the ticking angel at her throat. There had been nothing there, she told herself, just the rags of her wild imagination. Telling herself she'd better rein in her daydreaming or she'd end up as mad as old Starkweather, she slid the window shut.

8

A Shadow on the Soul

Oh, just, subtle, and mighty opium! that to the hearts of poor and rich alike, for the wounds that will never heal, and for "the pangs that tempt the spirit to rebel," bringest an assuaging balm; eloquent opium! that with thy potent rhetoric stealest away the purposes of wrath; and to the guilty man for one night givest back the hopes of his youth, and hands washed pure from blood.

—Thomas De Quincey, *Confessions of an English Opium-Eater*

In the morning when Tessa went down for breakfast, she found to her surprise that Will was not there. She had not realized how completely she had expected him to return during the night, and she found herself pausing in the doorway, scanning the seats around the table as if somehow she had accidentally glanced past him. It was not until her gaze came to rest on Jem, who returned her look with a rueful and worried expression of his own, that she knew that it was true. Will was still gone.

"Oh, he'll be back, for goodness' sake," said Jessamine crossly, banging her teacup down in its saucer. "He always does come crawling home. Look at the two of you. Like you've lost a favorite puppy."

Tessa shot Jem an almost guilty, conspiratorial look as she sat down across from him and took a slice of bread from the toast rack. Henry was absent; Charlotte, at the head of the table, was very clearly trying not to look nervous and worried, and failing. "Of course he will," she said. "Will can take care of himself."

"Do you think he might have gone back to Yorkshire?" said Tessa. "To warn his family?"

"I . . . don't think so," Charlotte responded. "Will has avoided his family for years. And he knows the Law. He knows he cannot speak to them. He knows what he would lose." Her eyes rested briefly on Jem, who was playing industriously with his spoon.

"When he saw Cecily, at the manor, he attempted to rush to her—" Jem said.

"In the heat of the moment," said Charlotte. "But he returned with you to London; I am confident he will return to the Institute as well. He knows you obtained that button, Tessa. He'll want to discover what Starkweather knew."

"Precious little, really," said Tessa. She still felt obscurely guilty that she had not found more useful information in Starkweather's memories. She had tried to explain what it was like to be in the mind of someone whose brain was decaying, but it had been hard to find the words, and she remembered mainly the look of disappointment on Charlotte's face when she'd said she had discovered nothing useful about Ravenscar Manor. She had told them all of Starkweather's memories of the Shade family, and that indeed if their deaths had been the impetus for Mortmain's desire for justice and vengeance, it did seem as if it would be a powerful one. She had kept his shock at seeing her to herself—it was baffling still, and seemed somehow private.

"What if Will chooses to leave the Clave forever?" Tessa said. "Would he return to his family to protect them?"

"No," Charlotte replied a little sharply. "No. I don't think he will do that." *She would miss Will if he were gone,* Tessa thought with surprise. Will was always so unpleasant—and often so to Charlotte—that Tessa sometimes forgot the stubborn love Charlotte seemed to feel for all her charges.

"But if they're in danger—," Tessa protested, then fell silent as Sophie entered the room carrying a pot of hot water, and set it down. Charlotte brightened at the sight of her.

"Tessa, Sophie, Jessamine," she said. "Lest you forget, you all have training this morning with Gabriel and Gideon Lightwood."

"I cannot do it," Jessamine said immediately.

"Why not? I thought you had recovered from your headache—"

"Yes, but I don't want it to come *back*, do I?" Jessamine stood up hurriedly. "I'd prefer to help you, Charlotte."

"I don't need your assistance writing to Ragnor Fell, Jessie. I'd really rather you took advantage of the training—"

"But there's dozens of replies piling up in the library from the Downworlders we've queried about Mortmain's whereabouts," Jessamine argued. "I could help you sort through those."

Charlotte sighed. "Very well." She turned to Tessa and Sophie. "In the meantime you won't say anything to the

Lightwood boys about Yorkshire, or about Will? I could do without having them in the Institute right now myself, but there's no help for it. It's a show of good faith and confidence to continue the training. You must behave in all ways as if nothing is wrong. Can you do that, girls?"

"Of course we can, Mrs. Branwell," said Sophie immediately. Her eyes were bright and she was smiling. Tessa sighed inwardly, not sure how to feel. Sophie adored Charlotte, and would do anything to please her. She also detested Will and was unlikely to be worried about his absence. Tessa looked across the table at Jem. She felt a hollowness in her stomach, the ache of not knowing where Will was, and wondered if he felt it too. His normally expressive face was still and unreadable, though when he caught her glance, he smiled a gentle, encouraging smile. Jem was Will's *parabatai*, his blood brother; surely if there were truly something to be concerned about where Will was involved, Jem would not be able to hide it—would he?

From the kitchen Bridget's voice rolled out in a sweet high warble:

"Must I go bound while you go free
Must I love a man who doesn't love me
Must I be born with so little art
As to love a man who'll break my heart?"

Tessa pushed her chair back from the table. "I think I had better go and get dressed."

Having changed from her day dress into gear, Tessa sat down on the edge of her bed and picked up the copy of *Vathek* Will had given her. It did not bring the thought of Will smiling to her mind, but other images of Will—Will bending over her in the Sanctuary, covered in blood; Will squinting into the sun on the roof of the Institute; Will rolling down the hill in Yorkshire with Jem, splattering himself with mud and not caring; Will falling off the table in the dining room; Will holding her in the dark. *Will, Will, Will.*

She threw the book. It struck the fireplace mantel and bounced off, landing on the floor. If only there were some way to scrape Will out of her mind, like scraping the mud off your shoe. If only she knew where he was. Worry made it worse, and she could not stop herself from worrying. She could not forget the look on his face as he had gazed at his sister.

Distraction made her late to the training room; fortunately, when she arrived, the door was open and there was no one there but Sophie, holding a long knife in her hand and examining it thoughtfully as she might examine a dust mop to decide if there was still use in it or if it was time for it to be thrown away.

She looked up as Tessa came into the room. "Well, you look like a wet weekend, miss," she said with a smile. "Is everything all right?" She cocked her head to the side as Tessa nodded. "Is it Master Will? He's gone off missing for a day or two before. He'll be back, don't you fear."

"That's kind of you to say, Sophie, especially as I know you are not overfond of him."

"I rather thought you weren't either," said Sophie, "least-ways not any*more* . . ."

Tessa looked at her sharply. She had not had a real conversation with Sophie about Will since the roof incident, she thought, and besides, Sophie had warned her off him, comparing him to a poisonous snake. Before Tessa could say anything in reply, the door opened and Gabriel and Gideon Lightwood came in, followed by Jem. He winked at Tessa before disappearing, closing the door behind him.

Gideon went straight over to Sophie. "A good choice of blade," he said, faint surprise underlining his words. She blushed, looking pleased.

"So," said Gabriel, who had somehow managed to get behind Tessa without her noticing. After examining the racks of weapons along the walls, he drew down a knife and handed it to her. "Feel the weight of the blade there."

Tessa tried to feel the weight of it, struggling to remember what he had told her about where and how it should balance in her palm.

"What do you think?" Gabriel asked. She looked up at him. Of the two boys he certainly looked more like his father, with his aquiline features and the faint shading of arrogance to his expression. His slim mouth curled up at the corners. "Or are you too busy worrying about Herondale's whereabouts to practice today?"

Tessa nearly dropped the knife. "What?"

"I heard you and Miss Collins when I was coming up the stairs. Disappeared, has he? Not surprising, considering I don't think Will Herondale and a sense of responsibility are even on speaking terms."

Tessa set her chin. Conflicted as she was about Will, there was something about someone *outside* the Institute's small family criticizing him that set her teeth on edge. "It's quite a common occurrence, nothing to fuss about," she said. "Will is a—free spirit. He'll return soon enough."

"I hope not," said Gabriel. "I hope he's dead."

Tessa's hand tightened around the knife. "You mean that, don't you? What did he do to your sister to make you hate him so much?"

"Why don't you ask him?"

"Gabriel." Gideon's voice was sharp. "Shall we get to the instruction, please, and cease wasting time?"

Gabriel glared at his older brother, who was standing quite peaceably with Sophie, but obediently turned his attention from Will to the day's training. They were practicing how to hold blades today, and how to balance them as they swept them through the air without the blade point drooping forward or the handle slipping from the hand. It was harder than it looked, and today Gabriel wasn't patient. She envied Sophie, being taught by Gideon, who was always a careful, methodical instructor, though he did have a habit of slipping into Spanish whenever Sophie did something wrong. "*Ay Dios mio,*" he would say, pulling the blade from where it had stuck, point down, in the floor. "Shall we try that again?"

"Stand up straight," Gabriel was saying to Tessa meanwhile, impatiently. "No, *straight.* Like this." He demonstrated. She wanted to snap at him that she, unlike him, had not had a lifetime of being taught how to stand and move; that Shadowhunters were natural acrobats, and she was nothing of the sort.

"Hmph," she said. "I'd like to see *you* learn how to manage sitting and standing up straight in stays and petticoats and a dress with a foot's worth of train!"

"So would I," said Gideon from across the room.

"Oh, by the Angel," said Gabriel, and he took her by the

shoulders, flipping her around so she stood with her back to him. He put his arms around her, straightening her spine, arranging the knife in her hand. She could feel his breath on the back of her neck, and it made her shiver—and filled her with annoyance. If he was touching her, it was only because he presumed he could, without asking, and because he thought it would irritate Will.

"Let me go," she said, under her breath.

"This is part of your training," said Gabriel in a bored voice. "Besides, look at my brother and Miss Collins. She isn't complaining."

She glanced across the room at Sophie, who seemed earnestly engaged in her lesson with Gideon. He was standing behind her, one arm around her from the back, showing her how to hold a needle-tipped throwing knife. His hand was gently cupped around hers, and he appeared to be speaking to the back of her neck, where her dark hair had escaped from its tight chignon and curled becomingly. When he saw Tessa looking at them, he flushed.

Tessa was amazed. Gideon Lightwood, blushing! Had he been *admiring* Sophie? Apart from her scar, which Tessa barely noticed anymore, she *was* lovely, but she was a mundane, and a servant, and the Lightwoods were awful snobs. Tessa's insides felt suddenly tight. Sophie had been treated abominably by her previous employer. The last thing she needed was some pretty Shadowhunter boy taking advantage of her.

Tessa looked around, about to say something to the boy with his arms around her—and stopped. She had forgotten that it was Gabriel beside her, not Jem. She had grown so used to Jem's presence, the ease with which she could converse with him, the comfort of his hand on her arm when they walked, the fact that he was the only person in the world now she felt she could say absolutely anything to. She realized with surprise that though she had just seen him at breakfast, she missed him, with what felt almost like an ache inside.

She was so caught up in this mixture of feelings—missing Jem, and a sense of passionate protectiveness over Sophie—that her next throw went wide by several feet, flying by Gideon's head and bouncing off the windowsill.

Gideon looked calmly from the fallen knife to his brother. Nothing seemed to bother him, not even his own near decapitation. "Gabriel, what is the problem, exactly?"

Gabriel turned his gaze on Tessa. "She won't listen to me," he said spitefully. "I can't instruct someone who won't listen."

"Maybe if you were a better instructor, she'd be a better listener."

"And maybe you would have seen the knife coming," said Gabriel, "if you paid more attention to what's going on around you and less to the back of Miss Collins's head."

So even Gabriel had noticed, Tessa thought, as Sophie blushed. Gideon gave his brother a long, steady look—she sensed there would be words between the two of them at home—then turned to Sophie and said something in a low voice, too low for Tessa to hear.

"What's happened to you?" she said under her breath to Gabriel, and felt him stiffen.

"What do you mean?"

"You're usually patient," she said. "You're a good teacher,

Gabriel, most of the time, but today you're snappish and impatient and . . ." She looked down at his hand on her arm. "Improper."

He had the good grace to release her, looking ashamed of himself. "A thousand pardons. I should not have touched you like that."

"No, you shouldn't. And after the way you criticize Will—"

He flushed along his high cheekbones. "I've apologized, Miss Gray. What more do you want of me?"

"A change in behavior, perhaps. An explanation of your dislike of Will—"

"I've told you! If you wish to know why I dislike him, you can ask him yourself!" Gabriel whirled and stalked out of the room.

Tessa looked at the knives stuck into the wall and sighed. "So ends my lesson."

"Try not to be too put out," said Gideon, approaching her with Sophie by his side. It was very odd, Tessa thought; Sophie usually seemed uneasy around men, any men, even gentle Henry. With Will she was like a scalded cat, and with Jem, blushing and watchful, but beside Gideon she seemed . . .

Well, it was hard to define. But it was most peculiar.

"It is not your fault he is like this today," Gideon went on. His eyes on Tessa were steady. This close up she could see that they were not precisely the same color as his brother's. They were more of a gray-green, like the ocean under a cloudy sky. "Things have been . . . difficult for us at home with Father, and Gabriel is taking it out on you, or, really, anyone who happens to be nearby."

"I'm most sorry to hear that. I hope your father is well," murmured Tessa, praying she would not be stricken down on the spot for this blatant falsehood.

"I suppose I had better go after my brother," said Gideon without answering her question. "If I do not, he will take the carriage and leave me stranded. I hope to have him back to you at our next session in a better humor." He bowed to Sophie, then Tessa. "Miss Collins, Miss Gray."

And he was gone, leaving both girls looking after him in mingled confusion and surprise.

With the training session mercifully over, Tessa found herself hurrying to change back into her ordinary clothes, and then to lunch, eager to see if Will had returned. He hadn't. His chair, between Jessamine and Henry, still sat empty—but there was someone new in the room, someone who made Tessa stop short at the doorway, trying not to stare. A tall man, he sat near the head of the table beside Charlotte, and was green. Not a very dark green—his skin had a faint greenish sheen to it, like light reflecting off the ocean, and his hair was snowy white. From his forehead curled two small elegant horns.

"Miss Tessa Gray," said Charlotte, making the introductions, "this is the High Warlock of London, Ragnor Fell. Mr. Fell, Miss Gray."

After murmuring that she was delighted to meet him, Tessa sat down at the table beside Jem, diagonally from Fell, and tried not to stare at him out of the corner of her eye. As Magnus's cat's eyes were his warlock's mark, Fell's would be his horns and tinted skin. She couldn't help being fascinated by Downworlders still, warlocks in particular. Why were they marked and she wasn't?

"What's on the carpet, then, Charlotte?" Ragnor was saying. "Did you really call me out here to discuss dark doings on the Yorkshire moors? I was under the impression that nothing of great interest ever happened in Yorkshire. In fact, I was under the impression that there *was* nothing in Yorkshire except sheep and mining."

"So you never knew the Shades?" Charlotte inquired. "The warlock population of Britain is not so large . . ."

"I knew them." As Fell sawed into the ham on his plate, Tessa saw that he had an extra joint to each finger. She thought of Mrs. Black, with her elongated taloned hands, and repressed a shudder. "Shade was a little mad, with his obsession with clockwork and mechanisms. Their death was a shock to Downworld. The ripples of it went through the community, and there was even some discussion of vengeance, though none, I believe, was ever taken."

Charlotte leaned forward. "Do you remember their son? Their adopted child?"

"I knew of him. A married warlock couple is rare. One who adopts a human child from an orphanage is rarer still. But I never saw the boy. Warlocks—we live forever. A gap of thirty, even fifty, years between meetings is not unusual. Of course now that I know what the boy grew up to be, I wish I had met him. Do you think there is value in attempting to discover who his true parents were?"

"Certainly, if it can be discovered. Whatever information we can glean about Mortmain could be useful."

"I can tell you he gave himself that name," said Fell. "It sounds like a Shadowhunter name. It is the sort of name someone with a grudge against Nephilim, and a dark sense of humor, would take. *Mort main*—"

"Hand of death," supplied Jessamine, who was proud of her French.

"It does make one wonder," said Tessa. "If the Clave had simply given Mortmain what he wanted—reparations—would he still have become what he did? Would there ever have been a Pandemonium Club at all?"

"Tessa—," Charlotte began, but Ragnor Fell waved her silent. He gazed amusedly down the table at Tessa. "You're the shape-changer, aren't you?" he said. "Magnus Bane told me about you. No mark on you at all, they say."

Tessa swallowed and looked him straight in the eye. They were discordantly human eyes, ordinary in his extraordinary face. "No. No mark."

He grinned around his fork. "I do suppose they've looked *everywhere*?"

"I'm sure Will's tried," said Jessamine in a bored tone. Tessa's silverware clattered to her plate. Jessamine, who had been mashing her peas flat with the side of her knife, looked up when Charlotte let out an aghast, *"Jessamine!"*

Jessamine shrugged. "Well, he's like that."

Fell turned back to his plate with a faint smile on his face. "I remember Will's father. Quite the ladies' man, he was. They couldn't resist him. Until he met Will's mother, of course. Then he threw it all in and went to live in Wales just to be with her. What a case he was."

"He fell in love," said Jem. "It isn't that peculiar."

"'Fell' into it," said the warlock, still with the same faint smile. "Hurtled into it is more like. Headlong-crashed into it.

Still, there are always some men like that—just one woman for them, and only she will do, or nothing."

Charlotte looked over at Henry, but he appeared completely lost in thought, counting something—though who knew what—off on his fingers. He was wearing a pink and violet waistcoat today, and had gravy on his sleeve. Charlotte's shoulders slumped visibly, and she sighed. "Well," she said. "By all accounts they were very happy together—"

"Until they lost two of their three children and Edmund Herondale gambled away everything they had," said Fell. "But I imagine you never told young Will about that."

Tessa exchanged a glance with Jem. *My sister is dead*, Will had said. "They had three children, then?" she said. "Will had two sisters?"

"Tessa. Please." Charlotte looked uneasy. "Ragnor . . . I never hired you to invade the privacy of the Herondales, or Will. I did it because I had promised Will I would tell him if harm came to his family."

Tessa thought of Will—a twelve-year-old Will, clinging to Charlotte's hand, begging to be told if his family died. *Why run?* she thought for the hundredth time. *Why put them behind you?* She had thought perhaps he did not care, but clearly he had cared. Cared still. She could not stop the tightening at her heart as she thought of him calling out for his sister. If he loved Cecily as she had once loved Nate . . .

Mortmain had done something to his family, she thought. As he had to hers. That bound them to each other in a peculiar way, she and Will. Whether he knew it or not.

"Whatever it is that Mortmain has been planning," she heard herself say, "he has been planning it a long time. Since before I was born, when he tricked or coerced my parents into 'making' me. And now we know that years ago he involved himself with Will's family and moved them to Ravenscar Manor. I fear we are like chess pieces he slides about a board, and the outcome of the game is already known to him."

"That is what he desires us to think, Tessa," said Jem. "But he is only a man. And each discovery we make about him makes him more vulnerable. If we were no threat, he would not have sent that automaton to warn us off."

"He knew exactly where we would *be*—"

"There is nothing more dangerous than a man bent on revenge," said Ragnor. "A man who has been bent on it for nearly three score years, who has nurtured it from a tiny, poisonous seed to a living, choking flower. He will see it through, unless you end him first."

"Then, we will end him," said Jem shortly. It was as close to a threat as Tessa had ever heard him make.

Tessa looked down at her hands. They were a paler white than they had been when she lived in New York, but they were her hands, familiar, the index finger slightly longer than the middle one, the half-moons of her nails pronounced. *I could Change them*, she thought. *I could become anything, anyone.* She had never felt more mutable, more fluid, or more lost.

"Indeed." Charlotte's tone was firm. "Ragnor, I want to know why the Herondale family is in that house—that house that belonged to Mortmain—and I want to see to it that they are safe. And I want to do it without Benedict Lightwood or the rest of the Clave hearing about it."

"I understand. You want me to look out for them as quietly as possible while also making inquiries regarding Mortmain in the area. If he moved them there, it must have been for a purpose."

Charlotte exhaled. "Yes."

Ragnor twirled his fork. "That will be expensive."

"Yes," Charlotte said. "I am prepared to pay."

Fell grinned. "Then, I am prepared to endure the sheep."

The rest of the lunch passed in awkward conversation, with Jessamine moodily destroying her food without eating it, Jem unusually quiet, Henry muttering equations to himself, and Charlotte and Fell finalizing their plans for the protection of Will's family. As much as Tessa approved of the idea—and she did—there was something about the warlock that made her uncomfortable in a way Magnus never had, and she was glad when lunch was over and she could escape to her room with a copy of *The Tenant of Wildfell Hall*.

It was not her favorite of the Brontë sisters' books—that honor went to *Jane Eyre*, and then *Wuthering Heights*, with *Tenant* a distant third—but she had read the other two so many times that no surprises lay between the pages, only phrases so familiar to her they had become like old friends. What she really wanted to read was *A Tale of Two Cities*, but Will had quoted Sydney Carton to her enough times that she was afraid that picking it up would make her think of him, and make the weight of her nervousness greater. After all, it was never Darnay he quoted, only Sydney, drunk and wrecked and dissipated. Sydney, who died for love.

It was dark out, and the wind was blowing gusts of light rain against the windowpanes when the knock came at her door. It was Sophie, carrying a letter on a silver tray. "A letter for you, miss."

Tessa put the book down in astonishment. "Mail for *me*?"

Sophie nodded and came closer, holding out the tray. "Yes, but it doesn't say who it's from. Miss Lovelace almost snatched it, but I managed to keep it from her, nosy thing."

Tessa took the envelope. It was addressed to her, indeed, in a slanting, unfamiliar hand, printed on heavy cream-colored paper. She turned it over once, began to open it, and caught sight of Sophie's wide-eyed curious gaze reflected in the window. She turned and smiled at her. "That will be all, Sophie," she said. It was the way she had read heroines dismissing servants in novels, and it seemed to be correct. With a disappointed look Sophie took her salver and retired from the room.

Tessa unfolded the letter and spread it out on her lap.

Dear sensible Miss Gray,

I write to you on behalf of a mutual friend, one William Herondale. I know that it is his habit to come and go—most often go—from the Institute as he pleases, and that therefore it may be some time before any alarm is raised at his absence. But I ask you, as one who holds your good sense in esteem, not to assume this absence to be of the ordinary sort. I saw him myself last night, and he was, to say the least, distraught when he left my residence. I have reason for concern that he might do himself an injury, and therefore I suggest that his whereabouts be sought and his safety ascertained. He is a difficult young man to like, but I believe you see the good in him, as I do, Miss Gray, and that is why I humbly address my letter to you—

Your servant,

Magnus Bane

Postscript: If I were you, I would not share the contents of this letter with Mrs. Branwell. Just a suggestion.

M.B.

Though reading Magnus's letter made her feel as if her veins were full of fire, somehow Tessa survived the rest of the afternoon, and dinner as well, without—she thought—betraying any outward sign of her distress. It seemed to take Sophie an agonizingly long time to help her out of her dress, brush her hair, stoke the fire, and tell her the day's gossip. (Cyril's cousin worked in the Lightwoods' house and had reported that Tatiana—Gabriel and Gideon's sister—was due to return from her honeymoon on the Continent with her new husband any day now. The household was in an uproar as she was rumored to have a most unpleasant disposition.)

Tessa muttered something about how she must take after her father that way. Impatience made her voice a croak, and Sophie was only just prevented from rushing out to get her a tisane of mint by Tessa's insistence that she was exhausted, and needed sleep more than she needed tea.

The moment the door shut behind Sophie, Tessa was on her feet, shimmying out of her nightclothes and into a dress, lacing herself up as best she could and throwing a short jacket on over the top. After a cautious glance out into the corridor, she slipped out of her room and across the hall to Jem's door, where she knocked as quietly as she could. For a moment nothing happened, and she had the fleeting worry that he had already gone to sleep, but then the door flew open and Jem stood on the threshold.

She had clearly caught him in the middle of readying

himself for bed; his shoes and jacket were off, his shirt open at the collar, his hair an adorable rumpled mess of silver. She wanted to reach out and smooth it down. He blinked at her. "Tessa?"

Without a word she handed him the note. He glanced up and down the corridor, then gestured her inside the room. She shut the door behind him as he read Magnus's scrawl once, and then again, before balling it up in his hand, the crackling paper loud in the room. "I *knew* it," he said.

It was Tessa's turn to blink. "Knew what?"

"That this wasn't an ordinary sort of absence." He sat down on the trunk at the foot of his bed and shoved his feet into his shoes. "I felt it. Here." He put his hand over his chest. "I knew there was something strange. I felt it like a shadow on my soul."

"You don't think he'd really hurt himself, do you?"

"Hurt himself, I don't know. Put himself in a situation where he might be hurt—" Jem stood up. "I should go."

"Don't you mean 'we'? You weren't thinking of going looking for Will without me, were you?" she asked archly, and when he said nothing, she said, "That letter was addressed to me, James. I didn't have to show it to you."

He half-closed his eyes for a moment, and when he opened them, he was smiling crookedly. "*James,*" he said. "Ordinarily only Will calls me that."

"I'm sorry—"

"No. Don't be. I like the sound of it on your lips."

Lips. There was something strangely, delicately indelicate about the word, like a kiss itself. It seemed to hover in the air between them while they both hesitated. *But it's Jem,* Tessa thought in bewilderment. Jem. Not Will, who could make her feel as if he were running his fingers along her bare skin just by looking at her—

"You're right," Jem said, clearing his throat. "Magnus would not have sent the letter to you had he not intended you to be part of searching for Will. Perhaps he thinks your power will be useful. In either case—" He turned from her, going to his wardrobe and flinging it open. "Wait for me in your room. I will be there momentarily."

Tessa wasn't sure if she nodded—she thought she had—and moments later she found herself back in her bedroom, leaning against the door. Her face felt hot, as if she had stood too close to a fire. She looked around. When had she started to think of this room as *her* bedroom? The big, grand space, with its mullioned windows and softly glowing witchlight tapers, was so unlike the tiny box room she had slept in in the flat in New York, with its puddles of wax on the bedside table, caused by her staying up all night reading by candlelight, and the cheap wooden-framed bed with its thin blankets. In the winter the windows, ill-seated, would rattle in their frames when the wind blew.

A soft knock on the door drew her out of her reverie, and she turned, flinging it open to find Jem on the threshold. He was fully dressed in Shadowhunter gear—the tough leather-looking black coat and trousers, the heavy boots. He put a finger to his lips and gestured for her to follow him.

It was probably ten o'clock at night, Tessa guessed, and the witchlight was burning low. They took a curious, winding path through the corridors, not the one she was used to taking to get to the front doors. Her confusion was answered when they reached a door set at the end of a long corridor. There was a rounded look to the space they stood in, and Tessa guessed they were probably inside one of the Gothic towers that stood at each corner of the Institute.

Jem pushed the door open and ushered her in after him; he closed the door firmly behind them, slipping the key he had used back into his pocket. "This," he said, "is Will's room."

"Gracious," Tessa said. "I've never been in here. I was starting to imagine he slept upside down, like a bat."

Jem laughed and went past her, over to a wooden bureau, and began to rummage through the contents on top of it as Tessa glanced around. Her heart was beating fast, as if she were seeing something she wasn't meant to see—some secret, hidden part of Will. She told herself not to be silly, it was just a room, with the same heavy dark furniture as all the other Institute rooms. It was a mess, too—covers kicked down to the foot of the bed; clothes draped over the backs of chairs, teacups half-full of liquid not yet cleared away, balanced precariously on the nightstand. And everywhere books—books on the side tables, books on the bed, books in stacks on the floor, books double-lined in shelves along the walls. As Jem rummaged, Tessa wandered to the shelves and looked curiously at the titles.

She was not surprised to find that they were almost all fiction and poetry. Some were titles in languages she couldn't read. She recognized Latin and the Greek alphabet. There were also books of fairy tales, *The Arabian Nights*, James Payn's work, Anthony Trollope's *Vicar of Bullhampton*, Thomas Hardy's *Desperate Remedies*, a pile of Wilkie Collins—*The New Magdalen*, *The Law and the Lady*, *The Two Destinies*, and a new Jules Verne novel titled *Child of the Cavern* that she itched to get her hands on. And then, there it was—*A Tale of Two Cities*. With a rueful smile she reached to take it from the shelf. As she lifted it, several scrawled-on papers that had been pressed between the covers fluttered to the floor. She knelt to pick them up—and froze. She recognized the handwriting instantly. It was her own.

Her throat tightened as she thumbed through the pages. *Dear Nate*, she read. *I tried to Change today, and failed. It was a coin they gave me, and I could get nothing from it. Either it was never owned by a person, or my power is weakening. I would not care, but that they whipped me—have you ever been whipped before? No, a silly question. Of course you haven't. It feels like fire being laid in lines across your skin. I am ashamed to say I cried, and you know how I hate to cry . . .* And *Dear Nate, I missed you so much today, I thought I would die. If you are gone, there is no one in the world who cares if I am dead or alive. I feel myself dissolving, vanishing into nothingness, for if there is no one in the world who cares for you, do you really exist at all?*

These were the letters she had written her brother from the Dark House, not expecting Nate to read them—not expecting anyone to read them. They were more of a diary than letters, the only place where she could pour forth her horror, her sadness, and her fear. She knew that they had been found, that Charlotte had read them, but what were they doing here in *Will's* room, of all places, hidden between the pages of a book?

"Tessa." It was Jem. She turned quickly, slipping the letters into the pocket of her coat as she did so. Jem stood by the bureau, holding a silver knife in his hand. "By the Angel, this place is such a tip, I wasn't sure I'd be able to find it." He turned it over in his hands. "Will didn't bring much from home when he came here, but he did bring this. It's a dagger his father gave him. It has the Herondale bird markings on the blade. It should have a strong enough imprint of him for us to track him with it."

Despite the encouraging words, he was frowning.

"What's wrong?" Tessa asked, crossing the room to him.

"I found something else," he said. "Will has always been the one to buy my—my medicine for me. He knew I despised the whole transaction, finding Downworlders willing to sell it, paying for the stuff . . ." His chest rose and fell quickly, as if merely talking about it sickened him. "I would give him money, and off he would go. I found a bill, though, for the last transaction. It appears the drugs—the medicine—does not cost what I thought it did."

"You mean Will's been cheating you out of money?" Tessa was surprised. Will could be awful and cruel, she thought, but somehow she had thought his cruelty of a more refined order than that. Less petty. And to do that to Jem, of all people . . .

"Quite the opposite. The drugs cost much more than he said they did. He must have been making up the difference somehow." Still frowning, he slid the dagger into his belt. "I know him better than anyone else in the world," he said matter-of-factly. "And yet still I find that Will has secrets that surprise me."

Tessa thought of the letters stuffed into the Dickens book, and what she intended to say to Will about it when she saw him again. "Indeed," she said. "Though it is not so much a mystery, is it? Will would do anything for you—"

"I'm not sure I would take it quite that far." Jem's tone was wry.

"Of course he would," said Tessa. "Anyone would. You're so kind and so good—"

She broke off, but Jem's eyes had already widened. He looked surprised, as if he were not used to such praise, but surely he must be, Tessa thought in confusion. Surely everyone who knew him knew how lucky they were. She felt her cheeks begin to warm again, and cursed herself. *What* was going on?

A faint rattle came from the window; Jem turned after a moment's pause. "That will be Cyril," he said, and there was a slight, rough undercurrent to his voice. "I—I asked him to bring the carriage around. We had better go."

Tessa nodded, wordless, and followed him from the room.

When Jem and Tessa emerged from the Institute, the wind was still gusting into the courtyard, sending dried leaves skittering in circles like faerie dancers. The sky was heavy with a yellow fog, the moon a gold disk behind it. The Latin words over the Institute's gates seemed to glow, picked out by the moonlight: *We are dust and shadows.*

Cyril, waiting with the carriage and the two horses, Balios and Xanthos, looked relieved to see them; he helped Tessa up into the carriage, Jem following her, and then swung himself up into the driver's seat. Tessa, sitting opposite Jem, watched with fascination as he drew both the dagger and the stele from his belt; holding the dagger in his right hand, he drew a rune on the back of that hand with the tip of his stele. It looked to Tessa like all Marks looked, a ripple of unreadable waving lines, circling around to connect with one another in bold black patterns.

He gazed down at his hand for a long moment, then shut his eyes, his face still with intense concentration. Just as Tessa's nerves began to sing with impatience, his eyes flew open. "Brick Lane, near Whitechapel High Street," he said, half to himself; returning the dagger and stele to his belt, he leaned out the window, and she heard him repeat the words to Cyril. A moment later Jem was back in the carriage, shutting the window against the cold air, and they were sliding and bumping forward over the cobblestones.

Tessa took a deep breath. She had been eager to look for Will all day, worried about him, wondering where he was—but now that they were rolling into the dark heart of London, all she could feel was dread.

9

Fierce Midnight

Fierce midnights and famishing morrows,
And the loves that complete and control
All the joys of the flesh, all the sorrows
That wear out the soul.
—Algernon Charles Swinburne, "Dolores"

Tessa kept the curtain on her side of the carriage pulled back, her eyes on the glass of the window, as they rolled along Fleet Street toward Ludgate Hill. The yellow fog had thickened, and she could make out little through it—the dark shapes of people hurrying to and fro, the hazy words of advertising signs painted on the sides of buildings. Every once in a while the fog would part and she would get a clear glimpse of something—a little girl carrying bunches of wilting lavender, leaning against a wall, exhausted; a knife grinder rolling his cart wearily homeward; a sign for Bryant and May's Lucifer Matches looming suddenly out of the gloom.

"Chuckaways," said Jem. He was leaning back against the seat across from her, his eyes bright in the dimness. She wondered if he had taken some of the drug before they left, and if so, how much.

"Pardon?"

He mimed the act of striking a match, blowing it out, and tossing the remainder over his shoulder. "That's what they call matches here—chuckaways, because you toss them aside after one use. It's also what they call the girls who work at the match factories."

Tessa thought of Sophie, who could easily have become one of those "chuckaways," if Charlotte hadn't found her. "That's cruel."

"It's a cruel part of the city we're going into. The East End. The slums." He sat forward. "I want you to be careful, and to stay close by me."

"Do you know what Will's doing there?" Tessa asked, half-afraid of the answer. They were passing by the great bulk of St. Paul's now, looming up above them like a giant's glimmering marble tombstone.

Jem shook his head. "I don't. I only got a sense—a fleeting image of the street—from the tracking spell. I will say, though, that there are few *harmless* reasons for a gentleman to go 'down to Chapel' after dark."

"He could be gambling . . ."

"He could be," Jem agreed, sounding as if he doubted it.

"You said you would sense it. Here." Tessa touched herself over the heart. "If something had happened to him. Is that because you're *parabatai*?"

"Yes."

"So there's more to being *parabatai* than just swearing to look out for each other. There's something—mystical about it."

Jem smiled at her, that smile that was like a light suddenly being turned on in every room of a house. "We're Nephilim. Every one of our life's passages has some mystical component—our births, our deaths, our marriages, everything has a ceremony. There is one as well if you wish to become someone's *parabatai*. First you must ask them, of course. It's no small commitment—"

"You asked Will," Tessa guessed.

Jem shook his head, still smiling. "He asked me," he said. "Or rather he told me. We were training, up in the training room, with longswords. He asked me and I said no, he deserved someone who was going to live, who could look out for him all his life. He bet me he could get the sword away from me, and if he succeeded, I'd have to agree to be his blood brother."

"And he got it away from you?"

"In nine seconds flat." Jem laughed. "Pinned me to the wall. He must have been training without my knowing about it, because I'd never have agreed if I'd thought he was that good with a longsword. Throwing daggers have always been his weapons." He shrugged. "We were thirteen. They did the ceremony when we were fourteen. Now it's been three years and I can't imagine not having a *parabatai*."

"Why didn't you want to do it?" Tessa asked a little hesitantly. "When he first asked you."

Jem ran a hand through his silvery hair. "The ceremony binds you," he said. "It makes you stronger. You have each other's strength to draw on. It makes you more aware of where the other one is, so you can work seamlessly together in a fight. There are runes you can use if you are part of a pair of *parabatai* that you can't use otherwise. But . . . you can choose only one *parabatai* in your life. You can't have a second, even if the first one dies. I didn't think I was a very good bet, considering."

"That seems a harsh rule."

Jem said something then, in a language she didn't understand. It sounded like "*khalepa ta kala.*"

She frowned at him. "That isn't Latin?"

"Greek," he said. "It has two meanings. It means that that which is worth having—the good, fine, honorable, and noble things—are difficult to attain." He leaned forward, closer to her. She could smell the sweet scent of the drug on him, and the tang of his skin underneath. "It means something else as well."

Tessa swallowed. "What's that?"

"It means 'beauty is harsh.'"

She glanced down at his hands. Slim, fine, capable hands, with blunt-cut nails, and scars across the knuckles. Were any of the Nephilim unscarred? "These words, they have a special appeal to you, don't they?" she asked softly. "These dead languages. Why is that?"

He was leaning close enough to her that she felt his warm breath on her cheek when he exhaled. "I cannot be sure," he said, "though I think it has something to do with the clarity of them. Greek, Latin, Sanskrit, they contain pure truths, before we cluttered our languages with so many useless words."

"But what of your language?" she said softly. "The one you grew up speaking?"

His lips twitched. "I grew up speaking English and Mandarin Chinese," he said. "My father spoke English, and Chinese badly. After we moved to Shanghai, it was even worse. The dialect there is barely intelligible by someone who speaks Mandarin."

"Say something in Mandarin," said Tessa with a smile.

Jem said something rapidly, that sounded like a lot of breathy vowels and consonants run together, his voice rising and falling melodically: *"Ni hen piao liang."*

"What did you say?"

"I said your hair is coming undone. Here," he said, and reached out and tucked an escaping curl back behind her ear. Tessa felt the blood spill hot up into her cheeks, and was glad for the dimness of the carriage. "You have to be careful with it," he said, taking his hand back slowly, his fingers lingering against her cheek. "You don't want to give the enemy anything to grab hold of."

"Oh—yes—of course." Tessa looked quickly toward the window—and stared. The yellow fog hung heavy over the streets, but she could see well enough. They were in a narrow thoroughfare—though broad, perhaps, by London's standards. The air seemed thick and greasy with coal dust and fog, and the streets were lined with people. Filthy, dressed in rags, they slumped against the walls of tipsy-looking buildings, their eyes watching the carriage go by like hungry dogs following the progress of a bone. Tessa saw a woman wrapped in a shawl, a basket of flowers drooping from one hand, a baby folded into a corner of the shawl propped against her shoulder. Its eyes were closed, its skin as pale as curd; it looked sick, or dead. Barefoot children, as dirty as homeless cats, played together in the streets; women sat leaning against one another on the stoops of buildings, obviously drunk. The men were worst of all, slumped against the sides of houses, dressed in dirty, patched topcoats and hats, the looks of hopelessness on their faces like etchings on gravestones.

"Rich Londoners from Mayfair and Chelsea like to take midnight tours of districts like these," said Jem, his voice uncharacteristically bitter. "They call it slumming."

"Do they stop and—and help in some way?"

"Most of them, no. They just want to stare so they can go home and talk at their next tea party about how they saw real 'mug-hunters' or 'dollymops' or 'Shivering Jemmys.' Most of them never get out of their carriages or omnibuses."

"What's a Shivering Jemmy?"

Jem looked at her with flat silver eyes. "A freezing, ragged beggar," he said. "Someone likely to die of the cold."

Tessa thought of the thick paper pasted over the cracks in the windowpanes in her New York apartment. But at least she had had a bedroom, a place to lie down, and Aunt Harriet to make her hot soup or tea over the small range. She had been lucky.

The carriage came to a stop at an unprepossessing corner. Across the street the lights of an open public house spilled out onto the street, along with a steady stream of drunkards, some with women leaning on their arms, the women's brightly colored dresses stained and dirty and their cheeks highly rouged. Somewhere someone was singing "Cruel Lizzie Vickers."

Jem took her hand. "I can't glamour you against the glances of mundanes," he said. "So keep your head down and keep close to me."

Tessa smiled crookedly but didn't take her hand out of his. "You said that already."

He leaned close and whispered into her ear. His breath sent

a shiver racing through her whole body. "It's *very* important."

He reached past her for the door and swung it open. He leaped down onto the pavement and helped her down after him, pulling her close against his side. Tessa looked up and down the street. There were some incurious stares from the crowds, but the two of them were largely ignored. They headed toward a narrow door painted red. There were steps around it, but unlike all the other steps in the area, they were bare. No one was sitting on them. Jem took them quickly, pulling her up after him, and rapped sharply on the door.

It was opened after a moment by a woman in a long red dress, fitted so tightly to her body that Tessa's eyes widened. She had black hair piled on her head, kept in place by a pair of gold chopsticks. Her skin was very pale, her eyes rimmed with kohl—but on closer examination Tessa realized she was white, not foreign. Her mouth was a sulky red bow. It turned down at the corners as her gaze came to rest on Jem.

"No," she said. "No Nephilim."

She moved to shut the door, but Jem had raised his cane; the blade shot out from the base of it, holding the door open wide. "No trouble," he said. "We're not here for the Clave. It's personal."

She narrowed her eyes.

"We're looking for someone," he said. "A friend. Take us to him, and we won't bother you further."

At that, she threw her head back and laughed. "I know who you're looking for," she said. "There's only one of your kind here." She turned away from the door with a shrug of contempt. Jem's blade slid back into its casing with a hiss, and he ducked under the low lintel, drawing Tessa after him.

Beyond the door was a narrow corridor. A heavy sweet smell hung on the air, like the smell that hung about Jem's clothing after he had taken his drug. Her hand tightened involuntarily on his. "This is where Will comes to buy the—to buy what I need," he whispered, inclining his head so that his lips nearly touched her ear. "Although why he would be here now . . ."

The woman who had opened the door for them glanced back over her shoulder as she set off down the hall. There was a slit up the back of her dress, showing much of her legs—and the end of a long, slender forked tail, marked with black and white markings like the scales of a snake. *She's a warlock*, Tessa thought with a dull thud at her heart. Ragnor, the Dark Sisters, this woman—why was it that warlocks always seemed so—sinister? With the exception of Magnus perhaps, but she had the feeling Magnus was an exception to many rules.

The corridor widened out into a large room, its walls painted dark red. Great lamps, their sides carved and painted with delicate traceries that threw patterned light against the walls, hung down from the ceiling. Along the walls were ranged beds, in bunks, like the inside of a ship. A large round table dominated the center of the room. At it sat a number of men, their skin the same blood-red as the walls, their black hair clipped close to their heads. Their hands ended in blue-black talons that had also been clipped, probably to allow them to more easily count and sift and mix the various powders and concoctions they had spread out before them. The powders seemed to glimmer and shine under the lamplight, like pulverized jewels.

"Is this an opium den?" Tessa whispered into Jem's ear.

His eyes were raking the room anxiously. She could sense

the tension in him, a thrum just under the skin, like the fast-beating heart of a hummingbird. "No." He sounded distracted. "Not really—mostly demon drugs and faerie powders. Those men at the table, they're ifrits. Warlocks without powers."

The woman in the red dress was leaning over the shoulder of one of the ifrits. Together they looked up and over at Tessa and Jem, their eyes lingering on Jem. Tessa didn't like the way they were looking at him. The warlock woman was smiling; the ifrit's look was calculating. The woman straightened up and swayed over to them, her hips moving like a metronome under the tight satin of her dress.

"Madran says we have what you want, silver boy," said the warlock woman, raking a blood-red nail across Jem's cheek. "No need for pretense."

Jem flinched back from her touch. Tessa had never seen him look so unnerved. "I told you, we're here for a friend," he snapped. "A Nephilim. Blue eyes, black hair—" His voice rose. "*Ta xian zai zai na li?*"

She looked at him for a moment, then shook her head. "You are foolish," she said. "There is little of the *yin fen* left, and when it is gone, you will die. We struggle to obtain more, but lately the demand—"

"Spare us your attempts to sell your merchandise," said Tessa, suddenly angry. She couldn't bear the look on Jem's face, as if each word were the cut of a knife. No wonder Will bought his poisons for him. "Where is our friend?"

The warlock woman hissed, shrugged, and pointed toward one of the bunk beds bolted to the wall. "There."

Jem whitened as Tessa stared. Their occupants were so still that at first she had thought the beds were empty, but she realized now, looking more closely, that each was taken up by a sprawled figure. Some lay on their sides, arms trailing over the edges of the bed, hands splayed; most were on their backs, eyes open, staring at the ceiling or the bunk above them.

Without another word Jem began to stalk across the room, Tessa on his heels. As they drew closer to the beds, she realized that not all the occupants were human. Blue, violet, red, and green skin flashed past; green hair as long and netted as a web of seaweed brushed restlessly against a dirty pillow; taloned fingers gripped the wooden sides of a bunk as someone moaned. Someone else was giggling softly, hopelessly, a sound sadder than weeping; another voice repeated a children's rhyme over and over and over again:

"Oranges and lemons
Say the bells of St. Clement's
When will ye pay me?
Ring the bells at Old Bailey
When I grow rich
Say the bells of Shoreditch—"

"Will," whispered Jem. He had stopped at a bunk halfway down the wall, and leaned against it, as if his legs threatened to give way.

Lying in the bunk was Will, half-tangled in a dark, ragged blanket. He wore nothing but trousers and a shirt; his weapons belt hung on a nail peg inside the bunk. His feet were bare, his eyes half-lidded, their blue only slightly visible beneath the fringe of his dark lashes. His hair was wet with sweat, pasted to his forehead, his cheeks bright red and feverish. His chest rose and fell raggedly, as if he were having trouble drawing breath.

Tessa reached out and put the back of her hand to his forehead. It was burning. "Jem," she said softly. "Jem, we must get him out of here."

The man in the bunk beside them was still singing. Not that he was quite a man, exactly. His body was short and twisted, his shoeless feet ending in cloven hooves.

"When will that be?
Say the bells of Stepney
I do not know,
Says the great bell of Bow"

Jem was still staring down at Will, motionless. He seemed frozen. His face had gone a patchy white and red color.

"*Jem!*" Tessa whispered. "Please. Help me get him on his feet." When Jem did not move, she reached out, took Will by the shoulder, and shook him. "Will. Will, wake up, please."

Will only groaned and turned away from her, burying his head against his arm. He was a Shadowhunter, she thought, six feet of bone and muscle, far too heavy for her to lift. Unless—

"If you do not help me," Tessa said to Jem, "I swear, I will Change into you, and I will lift him myself. And then everyone here will see what you look like in a dress." She fixed him with a look. "Do you understand?"

Very slowly he raised his eyes to hers. He did not look fazed by the idea of being seen by ifrits in a dress; he did not look as if he saw her at all. It was the first time she could remember seeing those silver eyes without any light behind them. "Do you?" he said, and reached into the bunk, catching Will by the arm and hauling him sideways, taking little care, and bumping Will's head, hard, against the side rail of the bed.

Will groaned and opened his eyes. "Let me go—"

"Help me with him," Jem said without looking at Tessa, and together they wrestled Will out of the bunk. He nearly fell, sliding his arm around Tessa to balance himself as Jem retrieved his weapons belt from the nail it was hanging from.

"Tell me this is not a dream," Will whispered, nuzzling his face into the side of her neck. Tessa jumped. He felt feverishly hot against her skin. His lips grazed her cheekbone; they were as soft as she remembered.

"Jem," Tessa said desperately, and Jem looked over at them; he had been buckling Will's belt over his own, and it seemed clear he hadn't heard a word Will had said. He knelt down to stuff Will's feet into his boots, then rose to take his *parabatai*'s arm. Will seemed delighted by this.

"Oh, good," he said. "Now we're all three together."

"Shut up," said Jem.

Will giggled. "Listen, Carstairs, you haven't any of the needful on you, have you? I'd stump up, but I'm flat out."

"*What* did he say?" Tessa was baffled.

"He wants me to pay for his drugs." Jem's voice was stiff. "Come. We'll get him to the carriage, and I'll come back with the money."

As they struggled toward the door, Tessa heard the voice of the cloven-footed man, following them, thin and as high as music piped through reeds, ending in a high-pitched giggle.

"Here comes a candle to light you to bed,
And here comes a chopper to chop off your head!"

***

Even the dirty Whitechapel air seemed clear and fresh after the cloying incense stench of the faerie drug den. Tessa almost stumbled going down the stairs. The carriage was thankfully still at the curb, and Cyril was swinging himself down out of the seat, heading over to them, concern on his big, open face.

"Is he all right, then?" he said, taking the arm that Will had draped over Tessa's shoulders and draping it over his own. Tessa slipped aside gratefully; her back had begun to ache.

Will predictably, though, did not like this. "Let me go," he said with sudden irritation. "Let me go. I can stand."

Jem and Cyril exchanged glances, then moved apart. Will staggered, but stayed upright. He raised his head, the cold wind lifting the sweaty hair from his neck and forehead, blowing it across his eyes. Tessa thought of him up on the roof of the Institute: *And I behold London, a human awful wonder of God.*

He looked at Jem. His eyes were bluer than blue, his cheeks flushed, his features angelic. He said, "You did not have to come and fetch me like some child. I was having quite a pleasant time."

Jem looked back at him. "God damn you," he said, and hit Will across the face, sending him spinning. Will didn't lose his footing, but fetched up against the side of the carriage, his hand to his cheek. His mouth was bleeding. He looked at Jem with total astonishment.

"Get him into the carriage," Jem said to Cyril, and turned and went back through the red door—to pay for whatever Will had taken, Tessa thought. Will was still staring after him, the blood reddening his mouth.

"James?" he said.

"Come along, then," said Cyril, not unkindly. He really was awfully like Thomas, Tessa thought as he opened the carriage door and helped Will inside, and then Tessa after him. He gave her a handkerchief from his pocket. It was warm and smelled like cheap eau de cologne. She smiled and thanked him as he shut the door.

Will was slumped in the corner of the carriage, his arms around himself, his eyes half-open. Blood had trickled down his chin. She leaned over and pressed the handkerchief to his mouth; he reached up and put his hand over hers, holding it there. "I've made a mess of things," he said. "Haven't I?"

"Dreadfully, I'm afraid," said Tessa, trying not to notice the warmth of his hand over hers. Even in the darkness of the carriage, his eyes were luminously blue. What was it Jem had said, though, about beauty? *Beauty is harsh.* Would people forgive Will the things he did if he were ugly? And did it help him, in the end, to be forgiven? Though, she could not help but feel he did the things he did not because he loved himself too much but because he hated himself. And she did not know why.

He closed his eyes. "I'm so tired, Tess," he said. "I only wanted pleasant dreams for once."

"That is not the way to get them, Will," she said softly. "You cannot buy or drug or dream your way out of pain."

His hand tightened over hers.

The carriage door opened. Tessa drew back from Will hastily. It was Jem, his face like thunder; he spared a cursory glance at Will, threw himself into a seat, and reached up to rap on the roof. "Cyril, drive home," he called, and after a moment the carriage lurched forward into the night. Jem reached out and drew the curtains across the windows. In the dimness Tessa slipped the handkerchief into her sleeve. It was still damp with Will's blood.

Jem said nothing all the way back from Whitechapel, merely stared stonily ahead of him with his arms folded while Will slept, a faint smile on his face, in the corner of the carriage. Tessa, across from them both, could think of nothing to say to break Jem's silence. This was so utterly unlike him—Jem, who was always sweet, always kind, always optimistic. His expression now was worse than blank, his nails digging into the fabric of his gear, his shoulders stiff and angular with rage.

The moment they drew up in front of the Institute, he threw the door open and leaped out. She heard him shout something to Cyril about helping Will to his room, and then he stalked away, up the steps, without another word to her. Tessa was so shocked, she could only stare after him for a moment. She moved to the carriage door; Cyril was already there, his hand up to help her down. Barely had Tessa's shoes hit the cobblestones than she was hurrying after Jem, calling his name, but he was already inside the Institute. He had left the door open for her, and she dashed in after him, after only a brief glance to confirm that Will was being helped by Cyril. She hurried up the stairs, dropping her voice as she realized that, of course, the Institute was asleep, the witchlight torches dimmed to their lowest glow.

She went to Jem's room first and knocked; when there was no answer, she sought a few of his most commonly visited haunts—the music room, the library—but, finding nothing, she returned, disconsolate, to her own room to ready herself for bed. In her nightgown, her dress brushed and hung up, she crawled between the sheets of her bed and stared at the ceiling. She even picked up Will's copy of *Vathek* from her floor, but for the first time the poem in the front failed to make her smile, and she could not concentrate on the story.

She was startled at her own distress. Jem was angry at Will, not at her. Still, she thought, it was perhaps the first time he had lost his temper in front of her. The first time he had been curt with her, or not attended with kindness to her words, had not seemed to think of her first before himself. . . .

She had taken him for granted, she thought with surprise and shame, watching the flickering candlelight. She had assumed his kindness was so natural and so innate, she had never asked herself whether it cost him any effort. Any effort to stand between Will and the world, protecting each of them from the other. Any effort to accept the loss of his family with equanimity. Any effort to remain cheerful and calm in the face of his own dying.

A rending noise, the sound of something being wrenched apart, tore through the room. Tessa sat bolt upright. What *was* that? It seemed to be coming from outside her door—across the hall—

Jem?

She leaped to her feet and caught her dressing gown down from its peg. Hurriedly slipping into it, she darted out the door and into the corridor.

She had been correct—the noise was coming from Jem's room. She remembered the first night she had met him, the lovely violin music that had poured like water through the doorway. This noise sounded nothing like Jem's music. She could hear the saw of bow against string, yet it sounded like screaming, like a person screaming in awful pain. She both longed to go in and felt terrified to do so; finally she took hold of the knob of the door and swung it open, and then ducked inside and pulled the door closed fast after her.

"Jem," she whispered.

The witchlight torches were burning low on the walls. Jem sat on the trunk at the foot of his bed in just his shirtsleeves and trousers, his silver hair tousled, the violin propped against his shoulder. He was sawing at it viciously with the bow, wringing awful sounds out of it, making it scream. As Tessa watched, one of the violin strings snapped with a shriek.

"Jem!" she cried again, and when he did not look up, she strode across the room and wrenched the bow out of his hand. "Jem, *stop*! Your violin—your lovely violin—you'll ruin it."

He looked up at her. His pupils were enormous, the silver of his eyes only a thin ring around the black. He was breathing hard, his shirt open at the neck, sweat standing out on his collarbones. His cheeks were flushed. "What does it matter?" he said in a voice so low it was almost a hiss. "What does any of it matter? I'm dying. I won't outlast the decade. What does it matter if the violin goes before I do?"

Tessa was appalled. He never spoke like this about his illness, never.

He stood up and turned away from her, toward the window. Only a little moonlight found its way into the room through the fog; there seemed to be shapes visible in the white mist pressed against the window—ghosts, shades, mocking faces. "You know it is true."

"Nothing is decided." Her voice shook. "Nothing is inevitable. A cure—"

"There's no cure." He no longer sounded angry, just

detached, which was almost worse. "I will die, and you know it, Tess. Probably within the next year. I am dying, and I have no family in the world, and the one person I trusted more than any other made sport of what is killing me."

"But, Jem, I don't think that's what Will meant to do at all." Tessa leaned the bow against the footboard and moved closer to him, tentatively, as if he were an animal she was fearful of startling. "He was just trying to escape. He is running from something, something dark and awful. You know he is, Jem. You saw how he was after—after Cecily."

She stood just behind him now, close enough to reach out and touch him tentatively on the arm, but she did not. His white shirt was stuck to his shoulder blades with sweat. She could see the Marks on his back through the fabric. He dropped the violin almost carelessly onto the trunk and turned to face her. "He knows what it means to me," he said. "To see him even toy with what has destroyed my life—"

"But he wasn't thinking of you—"

"I know that." His eyes were almost all black now. "I tell myself he's better than he makes himself out to be, but, Tessa, what if he isn't? I have always thought, if I had nothing else, I had Will. If I have done nothing else that made my life matter, I have always stood by him. But perhaps I shouldn't."

His chest was rising and falling so fast, it alarmed her; she put the back of her hand to his forehead and nearly gasped. "You're burning up. You should be resting—"

He flinched away from her, and she dropped her hand, hurt. "Jem, what is it? You don't want me to touch you?"

"Not like that," he flared, and then flushed even darker than before.

"Like what?" She was honestly bewildered; this was behavior she might have expected from Will, but not from Jem—this mysteriousness, this anger.

"As if you were a nurse and I were your patient." His voice was firm but uneven. "You think because I am ill that I am not like—" He drew a ragged breath. "Do you think I do not know," he said, "that when you take my hand, it is only so that you can feel my pulse? Do you think I do not know that when you look into my eyes, it is only to see how much of the drug I have taken? If I were another man, a normal man, I might have hopes, presumptions even; I might—" His words seemed to catch, either because he realized he had said too much or because he had run out of breath; he was gasping, his cheeks flushed.

She shook her head, feeling her plaits tickle her neck. "This is the fever speaking, not you."

His eyes darkened, and he began to turn away from her. "You can't even believe I could want you," he said in a half whisper. "That I am alive enough, healthy enough—"

"No—" Without thinking, she caught at his arm. He stiffened. "James, that isn't at all what I meant—"

He curled his fingers around her hand where it lay on his arm. His own scorched her skin, as hot as fire. And then he turned her and drew her toward him.

They stood face-to-face, chest to chest. His breath stirred her hair. She felt the fever rising off him like mist off the Thames; sensed the pounding of the blood through his skin; saw with a strange clarity the pulse at his throat, the light on the pale curls of his hair where they lay against his paler neck. Prickles of heat ran up and down her skin, bewildering her.

This was Jem—her friend, as steady and reliable as a heartbeat. Jem did not set her skin on fire or make the blood rush fast inside her veins until she was dizzy.

"Tessa," he said. She looked up at him. There was nothing steady or reliable about his expression. His eyes were dark, his cheeks flushed. As she raised her face, he brought his down, his mouth slanting across hers, and even as she froze in surprise, they were kissing. *Jem.* She was kissing Jem. Where Will's kisses were all fire, Jem's were like pure air after a long time of being closed up in the airless dark. His mouth was soft and firm; one of his hands circled the back of her neck gently, guiding her mouth to his. With his other hand he cupped her face, running his thumb gently across her cheekbone. His lips tasted of burned sugar; the sweetness of the drug, she guessed. His touch, his lips, were tentative, and she knew why. Unlike Will, he would *mind* that this was the height of impropriety, that he should not be touching her, kissing her, that she should be pulling away.

But she did not want to pull away. Even as she wondered at the fact that it was Jem she was kissing, Jem making her head swim and her ears ring, she felt her arms rise as if of their own accord, curving around his neck, drawing him closer.

He gasped against her mouth. He must have been so sure she would push him away that for a moment he went still. Her hands glided over his shoulders, urging him with gentle touches, with a murmur against his lips, not to pause. Hesitantly he returned her caress, and then with greater force—kissing her again and again, each time with increasing urgency, cupping her face between his burning hands, his thin violinist's fingers stroking her skin, making her shiver. His hands moved to the small of her back, pressing her against him; her bare feet slipped on the carpet, and they half-stumbled backward onto the bed.

Her fingers wound tightly in his shirt, Tessa drew Jem down onto her, taking the weight of him onto her body with the feeling that she was being given back something that had belonged to her forever, a bit of her that she had missed without knowing she was missing it. Jem was light, hollow-boned like a bird and with the same racing heart; she ran her hands through his hair, and it was as soft as she had always in her most buried dreams thought it would be, like pinfeathers between her fingers. He could not seem to stop running his hands over her in wonder. They traced their way down her body, his breath ragged in her ear as he found the tie of her dressing gown and paused there, with shaking fingers.

His uncertainty made Tessa's heart feel as if it were expanding inside her chest, its tenderness big enough to hold them both inside it. She wanted Jem to *see* her, just as she was, herself, Tessa Gray, with none of the Change on her. She reached down and undid the tie, sliding the dressing gown off her shoulders so that she was revealed before him in only her white batiste nightgown.

She looked up at him, breathless, shaking her loosened hair out of her face. Propping himself over her, he gazed down, and said again, huskily, what he had said in the carriage before, when he had touched her hair. "*Ni hen piao liang.*"

"What does it mean?" she whispered, and this time he smiled and said:

"It means that you are beautiful. I did not want to tell you before. I did not want you to think I was taking liberties."

She reached up and touched his cheek, so close to hers, and then the fragile skin of his throat, where the blood beat hard beneath the surface. His eyelashes fluttered down as he followed the movement of her finger with his eyes, like silvery rain.

"Take them," she whispered.

He bent down to her; their mouths met again, and the shock of sensation was so strong, so overpowering, that she shut her eyes against it as if she could hide in the darkness. He murmured and gathered her against him. They rolled sideways, her legs scissoring around his, their bodies shifting to press each other closer and closer still so it became hard to breathe, and yet they could not stop. She found the buttons on his shirt, but even when she opened her eyes, her hands were shaking almost too hard to undo them. Clumsily she worked them free, tearing the fabric. As he shrugged the shirt free of his shoulders, she saw that his eyes were lightening to a pure silver again. She had only a moment to marvel at that, though; she was too busy marveling at the rest of him. He was so thin, without Will's cording of muscle, but there was something about his fragility that was lovely, like the spare lines of a poem. *Gold to airy thinness beat.* Though a layer of muscle still covered his chest, she could see the shadows between his ribs. The pendant of jade Will had given him lay below his angular collarbones.

"I know," he said, looking down at himself self-consciously. "I am not— I mean, I look—"

"Beautiful," she said, and she meant it. "You are beautiful, James Carstairs."

His eyes went wide as she reached to touch him. Her hands

had stopped shaking. They were exploratory, fascinated now. Her mother had owned a very old copy of a book once, she remembered, its pages so fragile they were liable to turn to dust when you touched them, and she felt that same responsibility of enormous care now as she brushed her fingers over the Marks on his chest, across the hollows between his ribs and the slope of his stomach, which shuddered under her touch; here was something that was as breakable as it was lovely.

He did not seem to be able to stop touching her, either. His skilled musician's hands grazed her sides, skimming up her bare legs beneath her nightdress. He touched her as he usually touched his beloved violin, with a soft and urgent grace that left her breathless. They seemed to share his fever now; their bodies burned, and their hair was wet with sweat, pasted to their foreheads and necks. Tessa didn't care; she wanted this heat, this near-pain. This was not herself, this was some other Tessa, some dream Tessa, who would behave like this, and she remembered her dream of Jem in a bed surrounded by flames. She had just never dreamed she would burn with him. She wanted more of this feeling, she knew, more of this fire, but none of the novels she had read told her what happened now. Did *he* know? Will would know, she thought, but Jem, like her, she sensed, must have been following an instinct that ran as deep as her bones. His fingers slipped into the nonexistent space between them, finding the buttons that held her nightdress closed; he bent to kiss her bared shoulder as the fabric slid aside. No one had ever kissed her bare skin there before, and the feeling was so startling that she put out a hand to brace herself, and knocked a pillow from the bed; it hit the small side table. There was the sound of a crash. A sudden sweet dark scent, as of spices, filled the room.

Jem jerked his hands back, a look of horror on his face. Tessa sat up as well, pulling the front of her nightdress together, suddenly self-conscious. Jem was staring over the side of the bed, and she followed his line of sight. The lacquer box that held his drugs had fallen and broken open. A thick layer of shining powder lay across the floor. A faint silvery mist seemed to rise from it, carrying the sweet, spicy smell.

Jem pulled her back, his arm around her, but there was fear in his grip now rather than passion. "Tess," he said in a low voice. "You can't touch this stuff. To get it on your skin would be—dangerous. Even to breathe it in— Tessa, you must go."

She thought of Will, ordering her out of the attic. Was this how it was always going to be—some boy would kiss her, and then order her away as if she were an unwanted servant? "I *won't* go," she flared. "Jem, I can help you clean it up. I am—"

Your friend, she was about to say. But what they had been doing was not what friends did. What was she to him?

"Please," he said softly. His voice was husky. She recognized the emotion. It was shame. "I do not want you to see me on my knees, grubbing around on the floor for the drug that I need to live. That is not how any man wants the girl he—" He took a shaking breath. "I'm sorry, Tessa."

The girl he what? But she could not ask; she was overwhelmed—with pity, with sympathy, with shock at what they had done. She leaned forward and kissed his cheek. He didn't move as she slipped from the bed, retrieved her dressing gown, and went quietly out of the room.

***

The corridor was the same as it had been when Tessa had crossed it moments—hours—minutes?—before: dim with lowered witchlight stretching far in either direction. She had just slipped into her own bedroom and was about to shut the door when her eye caught a flicker of movement down at the end of the hall. Some instinct held her in place, the door almost shut, her eye pressed to the barely open crack.

The movement was someone walking down the hall. A fair-haired boy, she thought for a moment, in confusion, but no—it was *Jessamine*, Jessamine dressed in boys' clothes. She wore trousers and a jacket open over a waistcoat; a hat was in her hand, and her long fair hair was tied back behind her head. She glanced behind her as she hurried down the hall, as if afraid of being followed. A few moments later she had vanished around the corner, out of sight.

Tessa slid the door shut, her mind racing. What on earth was that about? What was Jessamine doing, wandering the Institute in the dead of night, dressed like a boy? After hanging up her dressing gown, Tessa went to lie down on her bed. She felt tired down in the marrow of her bones, the sort of tired she had felt the night her aunt died, as if she had exhausted her body's capacity to feel emotion. When she closed her eyes, she saw Jem's face, and then Will's, his hand to his bloody mouth. Thoughts of the two of them swirled together in her head until she fell asleep finally, not sure if she was dreaming of kissing one of them, or the other.

10

The Virtue of Angels

The virtue of angels is that they cannot deteriorate; their flaw is that they cannot improve. Man's flaw is that he can deteriorate; and his virtue is that he can improve.

—Hasidic saying

"I suppose you all know by now," Will remarked at breakfast the next morning, "that I went to an opium den last night."

It was a subdued morning. It had dawned rainy and gray, and the Institute felt leadenly weighted down, as if the sky were pressing on it. Sophie passed in and out of the kitchen carrying steaming platters of food, her pale face looking pinched and small; Jessamine slumped tiredly over her tea; Charlotte looked weary and unwell from her night spent in the library; and Will's eyes were red-rimmed, his cheek bruised where Jem had hit him. Only Henry, reading the paper with one hand while he stabbed at his eggs with the other, seemed to have any energy.

Jem was conspicuous mainly by his absence. When Tessa had woken up that morning, she had floated for a moment in a blissful state of forgetfulness, the events of the night before a dim blur. Then she had sat bolt upright, absolute horror crashing over her like a wave of scalding water.

Had she really done all those things with *Jem?* His bed—his hands on her—the spilled drugs. She had raised her hands and touched her hair. It fell free over her shoulders, where Jem had tugged it out of its plaits. *Oh, God,* she thought. *I really did all that; that was me.* She had pressed her hands to her eyes, feeling an overwhelming mix of confusion, terrified happiness—for she could not deny that it had been wonderful in its way—horror at herself, and hideous and total humiliation.

Jem would think she had utterly lost control of herself. No wonder he couldn't face her at breakfast. She could barely face herself in the mirror.

"Did you hear me?" Will said again, clearly disappointed at the reception of his announcement. "I said I went to an opium den last night."

Charlotte looked up from her toast. Slowly she folded her newspaper, set it on the table beside her, and pushed her reading glasses down her upturned nose. "No," she said. "That undoubtedly glorious aspect of your recent activities was unknown to us, in fact."

"So is that where you've been all this time?" Jessamine asked listlessly, taking a sugar cube from the bowl and biting into it. "Are you quite a hopeless addict now? They say it takes only one or two doses."

"It wasn't really an *opium* den," Tessa protested before she could stop herself. "That is to say—they seemed to have more of a trade in magic powders and things like that."

"So perhaps not an opium den precisely," said Will, "but still a den. Of vice!" he added, punctuating this last bit by stabbing his finger into the air.

"Oh, dear, not one of those places that's run by ifrits," sighed Charlotte. "Really, Will—"

"Exactly one of those places," said Jem, coming into the breakfast room and sliding into a chair beside Charlotte—quite as far away from Tessa as it was possible to sit, she noticed, with a pinching feeling in her chest. He didn't look at her either. "Off Whitechapel High Street."

"And how do you and Tessa know so much about it?" asked Jessamine, who appeared revitalized by either her sugar intake or the expectation of some good gossip, or both.

"I used a tracking spell to find Will last night," said Jem. "I was growing concerned at his absence. I thought he might have forgotten the way back to the Institute."

"You worry too much," said Jessamine. "It's silly."

"You're quite right. I won't make that mistake again," said Jem, reaching for the dish of kedgeree. "As it turned out, Will wasn't in need of my assistance at all."

Will looked at Jem thoughtfully. "I seem to have woken up with what they call a Monday mouse," he said, pointing at the bruised skin under his eye. "Any idea where I got it?"

"None." Jem helped himself to some tea.

"Eggs," said Henry dreamily, looking at his plate. "I do love eggs. I could eat them all day."

"Was there really a need to bring Tessa with you to Whitechapel?" Charlotte asked Jem, sliding her glasses off and placing them on the newspaper. Her brown eyes were reproachful.

"Tessa is not made of delicate china," said Jem. "She will not break."

For some reason this statement, though he said it still without looking at her, sent a flood of images through Tessa's mind of the night before—of clinging to Jem in the shadows of his bed, his hands gripping her shoulders, their mouths fierce on each other's. No, he had not treated her as if she were breakable then. A boiling flood of heat seared her cheeks, and she looked down quickly, praying for her blush to go away.

"You might be surprised to know," said Will, "that I saw something rather interesting in the opium den."

"I'm sure you did," said Charlotte with asperity.

"Was it an egg?" Henry inquired.

"Downworlders," said Will. "Almost all werewolves."

"There's nothing interesting about werewolves." Jessamine sounded aggrieved. "We're focusing on finding Mortmain now, Will, if you haven't forgotten, not some drug-addled Downworlders."

"They were buying *yin fen*," said Will. "Buckets of it."

At that Jem's head snapped up and he met Will's eyes.

"They had already begun to change color," said Will. "Quite a few had silver hair, or eyes. Even their skin had started to silver over."

"This is very disturbing." Charlotte frowned. "We should speak to Woolsey Scott as soon as this Mortmain matter is cleared up. If there is an issue of addiction to warlock powders in his pack, he will want to know about it."

"Don't you think he already does?" said Will, sitting back in his chair. He looked pleased to have finally gotten a reaction to his news. "It is his pack, after all."

"His pack is all of London's wolves," objected Jem. "He can't possibly keep real track of them all."

"I'm not sure you want to wait," said Will. "If you can get hold of Scott, I'd speak to him as soon as possible."

Charlotte tilted her head to the side. "And why is that?"

"Because," said Will. "One of the ifrits asked a werewolf why he needed so much *yin fen*. Apparently it works on werewolves as a stimulant. The answer was that it pleased the Magister that the drug kept them working all night long."

Charlotte's teacup crashed into her saucer. "Working on what?"

Will smirked, clearly pleased at the effect he was having. "I've no idea. I lost consciousness about then. I was having a lovely dream about a young woman who had mislaid nearly all her clothes . . ."

Charlotte was white-faced. "Dear God, I hope Scott isn't caught up with the Magister. De Quincey first, now the wolves—all our allies. The Accords . . ."

"I'm sure it will all be all right, Charlotte," said Henry mildly. "Scott doesn't seem the sort to get tangled up with Mortmain's sort."

"Perhaps you should be there when I speak with him," said Charlotte. "Nominally, you *are* the head of the Institute—"

"Oh, no," said Henry with a look of horror. "Darling, you'll be quite all right without me. You're such a genius where these negotiations are concerned, and I'm simply not. And besides, the invention I'm working on now could shatter the whole clockwork army into pieces if I get the formulations right!"

He beamed round the table proudly. Charlotte looked at him for a long moment, then pushed her chair back from the table, stood up, and walked out of the room without another word.

Will regarded Henry from beneath half-lidded eyes. "Nothing ever disturbs your circles, does it, Henry?"

Henry blinked. "What do you mean?"

"Archimedes," Jem said, as usual knowing what Will meant, though not looking at him. "He was drawing a mathematical diagram in the sand when his city was attacked by Romans. He was so intent on what he was doing that he didn't see the soldier coming up behind him. His last words were 'Do not disturb my circles.' Of course, he was an old man by then."

"And he was probably never married," said Will, and he grinned at Jem across the table.

Jem didn't return his grin. Without looking at Will, or Tessa—without looking at any of them—he got to his feet and went out of the room after Charlotte.

"Oh, bother," said Jessamine. "Is this one of those days where we all stalk out in a fury? Because I simply haven't got the energy for it." She put her head down on her arms and closed her eyes.

Henry looked bewilderedly from Will to Tessa. "What is it? What have I done wrong?"

Tessa sighed. "Nothing dreadful, Henry. It's just— I think Charlotte wanted you to come *with* her."

"Then, why didn't she say so?" Henry's eyes were mournful. His joy over his eggs and inventions seemed to have vanished. Perhaps he shouldn't have married Charlotte, Tessa thought, her mood as bleak as the weather. Perhaps, like Archimedes, he would have been happier drawing circles in the sand.

"Because women never say what they think," said Will. His eyes drifted toward the kitchen, where Bridget was clearing up the remains of the meal. Her singing floated lugubriously out into the dining room.

"'I fear you are poisoned, my own pretty boy,
I fear you are poisoned, my comfort and joy!'
'O yes, I am poisoned; mother, make my bed soon,
There's a pain in my heart, and I mean to lie down.'"

"I swear that woman had a previous career as a death-hunter selling tragic ballads down around the Seven Dials," said Will. "And I do wish she wouldn't sing about poisoning just after we've eaten." He looked sideways at Tessa. "Shouldn't you be off putting on your gear? Haven't you training with the lunatic Lightwoods today?"

"Yes, this morning, but I needn't change clothes. We're just practicing knife throwing," said Tessa, somewhat amazed that she was able to have this mild and civil a conversation with Will after the events of last night. Cyril's handkerchief, with Will's blood on it, was still in her dresser drawer; she remembered the warmth of his lips on her fingers, and darted her eyes away from his.

"How fortunate that I am a crack hand at knife throwing." Will got to his feet and held out his arm to her. "Come along; it'll drive Gideon and Gabriel mad if I watch the training, and I could do with a little madness this morning."

Will was correct. His presence during the training session seemed to madden Gabriel at least, though Gideon, as he seemed to do with everything, took this intrusion in a stolid manner. Will sat on a low wooden bench that ran along one of the walls, and ate an apple, his long legs stretched out before him, occasionally calling out bits of advice that Gideon ignored and that Gabriel took like blows to the chest.

"*Must* he be here?" Gabriel growled to Tessa the second time he had nearly dropped a knife while handing it to her. He put a hand on her shoulder, showing her the sight line for the target she was aiming at—a black circle drawn on the wall. She knew how much he would rather she were aiming at Will. "Can't you tell him to go away?"

"Now, why would I do that?" Tessa asked reasonably. "Will is my friend, and you are someone whom I do not even like."

She threw the knife. It missed its target by several feet, striking low in the wall near the floor.

"No, you're still weighting the point too much—and what do you mean, you don't like me?" Gabriel demanded, handing her another knife as if by reflex, but his expression was very surprised indeed.

"Well," Tessa said, sighting along the line of the knife, "you behave as if you dislike *me*. In fact, you behave as if you dislike us all."

"I don't," Gabriel said. "I just dislike *him*." He pointed at Will.

"Dear me," said Will, and he took another bite of his apple. "Is it because I'm better-looking than you?"

"Both of you be quiet," Gideon called from across the room. "We're meant to be working, not snapping at each other over years-old petty disagreements."

"Petty?" Gabriel snarled. "He *broke* my *arm*."

Will took another bite out of his apple. "I can hardly believe you're still upset about that."

Tessa threw the knife. This throw was better. It landed inside the black circle, if not in the center itself. Gabriel looked around for another knife and, not seeing one, let out an exhalation of annoyance. "When *we* run the Institute," he said, pitching his voice loud enough for Will to hear, "this training room will be far better kept up and supplied."

Tessa looked at him angrily. "Amazing that I don't like you, isn't it?"

Gabriel's handsome face crumpled into an ugly look of contempt. "I don't see what this has to do with you, little warlock; this Institute isn't your home. You don't belong in this place. Believe me, you'd be better off with my family running things here; we could find uses for your . . . talent. Employment that would make you rich. You could live where you liked. And Charlotte can go run the Institute in York, where she'll do considerably less harm."

Will was sitting upright now, apple forgotten. Gideon and Sophie had ceased their practicing and were watching the conversation—Gideon wary, Sophie wide-eyed. "If you hadn't noticed," Will said, "someone already runs the York Institute."

"Aloysius Starkweather is a senile old man." Gabriel dismissed him with a wave of his hand. "And he has no descendants he can beg the Consul to appoint in his place. Since the business with his granddaughter, his son and daughter-in-law packed up and went to Idris. They won't come back here for love or money."

"What business with his granddaughter?" Tessa demanded,

flashing back to the portrait of the sickly-looking little girl on the staircase of the York Institute.

"Only lived to be ten or so," said Gabriel. "Never was very healthy, by all accounts, and when they first Marked her—Well, she must have been improperly trained. She went mad, turned Forsaken, and died. The shock killed old Starkweather's wife, and sent his children scurrying to Idris. It wouldn't be much trouble to get him replaced by Charlotte. The Consul must see he's no good—far too married to the old ways."

Tessa looked at Gabriel in disbelief. His voice had retained its cool indifference as he'd told the story of the Starkweathers, as if it were a fairy tale. And she—she didn't want to pity the old man with the sly eyes and the bloody room full of dead Downworlders' remains, but she couldn't help it. She pushed Aloysius Starkweather from her mind. "Charlotte runs *this* Institute," she said. "And your father will not take it from her."

"She deserves to have it taken from her."

Will tossed his apple core into the air, at the same time drawing a knife from his belt and throwing it. The knife and the apple sailed across the room together, somehow managing to stick into the wall just beside Gabriel's head, the knife driven cleanly through the core and into the wood. "Say that again," said Will, "and I'll darken your daylights for you."

Gabriel's face worked. "You have no idea what you're talking about."

Gideon took a step forward, warning in every line of his posture. "Gabriel—"

But his brother ignored him. "You don't even know what your precious Charlotte's father did to mine, do you? I only just learned it myself a few days ago. My father finally broke down and told us. He'd protected the Fairchilds till then."

"Your father?" Will's tone was incredulous. "Protected the *Fairchilds?*"

"He was protecting us as well." Gabriel's words tumbled over themselves. "My mother's brother—my uncle Silas—was one of Granville Fairchild's closest friends. Then Uncle Silas broke the Law—a tiny thing, a minor infraction—and Fairchild discovered it. All he cared about was the Law, not friendship, not loyalty. He went straight to the Clave." Gabriel's voice rose. "My uncle *killed* himself in shame, and my mother died of the grief. The Fairchilds don't care about anyone but themselves and the Law!"

For a moment the room was silent; even Will was speechless, looking utterly taken aback. It was Tessa who spoke at last, "But that is the fault of Charlotte's father. Not of Charlotte."

Gabriel was white with rage, his green eyes standing out against his pale skin. "You don't understand," he said viciously. "You're not a Shadowhunter. We have blood pride. Family pride. Granville Fairchild wanted the Institute to go to his daughter, and the Consul made it happen. But even though Fairchild is dead, we can still take that away from him. He was hated—so hated that no one would have married Charlotte if he hadn't paid off the Branwells to hand Henry over. Everyone knows it. Everyone knows he doesn't really love her. How could he—"

There was a crack, like the sound of a rifle shot, and Gabriel fell silent. Sophie had slapped him across the face. His pale skin was already beginning to redden. Sophie was staring at him, breathing hard, an incredulous look on her face, as if she could not believe what she had done.

Gabriel's hands tightened at his sides, but he didn't move. He couldn't, Tessa knew. He could not strike a girl, a girl who was not even a Shadowhunter or a Downworlder but merely a mundane. He looked to his brother, but Gideon, expressionless, met his eyes and shook his head slowly; with a choked sound Gabriel spun on his heel and stalked from the room.

"Sophie!" Tessa exclaimed, reaching for her. "Are you all right?"

But Sophie was looking anxiously up at Gideon. "I'm so sorry, sir," she said. "There's no excuse—I lost my head, and I—"

"It was a well-placed blow," Gideon said calmly. "I see you've been paying attention to my training."

Will was sitting up on the bench, his blue eyes lively and curious. "Was it true?" he said. "That story Gabriel just told us."

Gideon shrugged. "Gabriel worships our father," he said. "Anything Benedict says is like a pronouncement from on high. I knew my uncle had killed himself, but not the circumstances, until the day after we first came back from training you. Father asked us how the Institute seemed to be run, and I told him it seemed in fine condition, no different from the Institute in Madrid. In fact, I told him I could see no evidence that Charlotte was doing a lax job. That was when he told us this story."

"If you don't mind my asking," said Tessa, "what was it that your uncle had done?"

"Silas? Fell in love with his *parabatai*. Not, actually, as Gabriel says, a minor infraction but a major one. Romantic relationships between *parabatai* are absolutely forbidden. Though even the best-trained Shadowhunter can fall prey to emotion. The Clave would have separated the two of them, though, and that Silas couldn't face. That's why he killed himself. My mother was consumed with rage and grief. I can well believe that her dying wish was that we would take the Institute from the Fairchilds. Gabriel was younger than I when our mother died—only five years old, clinging to her skirts still—and it seems to me his feelings are too overwhelming for him now to quite understand them. Whereas I—I feel that the sins of the fathers should not be visited on the sons."

"Or the daughters," said Will.

Gideon looked at him and gave him a crooked smile. There was no dislike in it; in fact, it was jarringly the look of someone who understood Will, and why he behaved as he did. Even Will looked a bit surprised. "There is the problem that Gabriel will never come back here, of course," said Gideon. "Not after this."

Sophie, whose color had started to return, paled again. "Mrs. Branwell will be furious—"

Tessa waved her back. "I'll go after him and apologize, Sophie. It will be all right."

She heard Gideon call after her, but she was already hurrying from the room. She hated to admit it, but she'd felt a spark of sympathy for Gabriel when Gideon had been telling his story. Losing a mother when you were so young you could barely remember her later was something she had familiarity with. If someone had told her that her mother had had a dying wish, she wasn't sure she wouldn't have done everything in her power to execute it . . . whether it made sense or not.

"Tessa!" She was partway down the corridor when she heard Will calling after her. She spun and saw him striding down the hall in her direction, a half smile on his face.

Her next words wiped his smile away. "*Why* are you following me? Will, you shouldn't have left them alone! You must go back to the training room, right away."

Will planted his feet. "Why?"

Tessa threw up her hands. "Don't men notice anything? Gideon has designs on Sophie—"

"On *Sophie?*"

"She's a very beautiful girl," flared Tessa. "You're an idiot if you haven't noticed the way he looks at her, but I don't want him taking advantage of her. She's had enough such trouble in her life—and besides, if you're with me, Gabriel won't talk to me. You know he won't."

Will muttered something under his breath and seized her wrist. "Here. Come with me."

The warmth of his skin against hers sent a jolt up her arm. He pulled her into the drawing room and across to the great windows that looked down over the courtyard. He released her wrist just in time for her to lean forward and see the Lightwoods' carriage rattling furiously across the stone yard and under the iron gates.

"There," Will said. "Gabriel's gone anyway, unless you want to chase after the carriage. And Sophie's perfectly sensible. She's not going to let Gideon Lightwood have his way with her. Besides, he's about as charming as a postbox."

Tessa, surprising even herself, let out a gasp of laughter. She put her hand up to cover her mouth, but it was too late; she was already laughing, leaning a little against the window.

Will looked at her, his blue eyes quizzical, his mouth just beginning to quirk up in a grin. "I must be more amusing than I thought. Which would make me very amusing indeed."

"I'm not laughing at you," she told him in between giggles.

"Just— Oh! The look on Gabriel's face when Sophie slapped him. My goodness." She pushed her hair out of her face and said, "I really shouldn't be laughing. Half the reason he was so awful was your goading him. I should be angry with you."

"Oh, *should*," said Will, spinning away to drop into a chair near the fire, and stretching out his long legs toward the flames. Like every room in England, Tessa thought, it was chilly in here except just in front of the fire. One roasted in the front and froze in the back, like a badly cooked turkey. "No good sentences ever include the word 'should.' I *should* have paid the tavern bill; now they're coming to break my legs. I *should* never have run off with my best friend's wife; now she devils me constantly. I *should*—"

"You *should*," Tessa said softly, "think about the way the things you do affect Jem."

Will rolled his head back against the leather of the chair and regarded her. He looked drowsy and tired and beautiful. He could have been some Pre-Raphaelite Apollo. "Is this a serious conversation now, Tess?" His voice still held humor but was edged, like a gold blade edged in razored steel.

Tessa came and sat down in the armchair across from his. "Aren't you worried that he's cross with you? He's your *parabatai*. And he's Jem. He's never cross."

"Perhaps it's better that he's cross with me," said Will. "So much saintlike patience cannot be good for anyone."

"Do not mock him." Tessa's tone was sharp.

"Nothing is beyond mockery, Tess."

"Jem is. He has always been good to you. He is nothing but goodness. That he hit you last night, that only shows how capable you are of driving even saints to madness."

"*Jem* hit me?" Will, fingering his cheek, looked amazed. "I must confess, I remember very little of last night. Only that the two of you woke me, though I very much wanted to stay asleep. I remember Jem shouting at me, and you holding me. I knew it was you. You always smell of lavender."

Tessa ignored this. "Well, Jem hit you. And you deserved it."

"You *do* look scornful—rather like Raziel in all those paintings, as if he were looking down on us. So tell me, scornful angel, what did I do to deserve being hit in the face by James?"

Tessa reached for the words, but they eluded her; she turned to the language she and Will shared—poetry. "You know, in that essay of Donne's, what he says—"

"'License my roving hands, and let them go'?" quoted Will, eyeing her.

"I meant the *essay* about how no man is an island. Everything you do touches others. Yet you never think about it. You behave as if you live on some sort of—of Will island, and none of your actions can have any consequences. Yet they do."

"How does my going to a warlock den affect Jem?" Will inquired. "I suppose he had to come and haul me out, but he's done more dangerous things in the past for me. We protect each other—"

"No, you *don't*," Tessa cried in frustration. "Do you think he cares about the danger? Do you? His whole life has been destroyed by this drug, this *yin fen*, and there you go off to a warlock den and drug yourself up as if it doesn't even matter, as if it's just a game to you. He has to take this foul stuff every day just so he can live, but in the meantime it's killing him. He hates to be dependent on it. He can't even bring himself to buy it; he has *you* do that." Will made a sound of protest, but Tessa held up a hand. "And then *you* swan down to Whitechapel and throw your money at the people who make these drugs and addict other people to them, as if it were some sort of holiday on the Continent for you. What were you thinking?"

"But it had nothing to do with Jem at all—"

"You didn't think about him," said Tessa. "But perhaps you should have. Don't you understand he thinks you made a mockery out of what's killing him? And you're supposed to be his brother."

Will had whitened. "He can't think that."

"He does," she said. "He understands you don't care what other people think about you. But I believe he always expected you'd care what he thought. What he felt."

Will leaned forward. The firelight made odd patterns against his skin, darkening the bruise on his cheek to black. "I do care what other people think," he said with a surprising intensity, staring into the flames. "It's all I think about—what others think, what they feel about me, and I about them; it drives me mad. I wanted escape—"

"You can't mean that. Will Herondale, minding what others think of him?" Tessa tried to make her voice as light as possible. The look on his face startled her. It was not closed but open, as if he were caught half-entangled in a thought he desperately wanted to share, but could not bear to. *This is the boy who took my private letters and hid them in his room*, she thought, but she could work up no anger about it. She had thought she would be furious when she saw him again, but she was not, only puzzled and wondering. Surely it showed a curiosity about other people that was quite un-Will-like, to want to read them in the first place?

There was something raw in his face, his voice. "Tess," he said. "That is *all* I think about. I never look at you without thinking about what you feel about me and fearing—"

He broke off as the drawing room door opened and Charlotte came in, followed by a tall man whose bright blond hair shone like a sunflower in the dim light. Will turned away quickly, his face working. Tessa stared at him. *What* had he been going to say?

"Oh!" Charlotte was clearly startled to see them both. "Tessa, Will—I didn't realize you were in here."

Will's hands were in fists at his sides, his face in shadow, but his voice was level when he replied: "We saw the fire going. It's as chill as ice in the rest of the house."

Tessa stood up. "We'll just be on our way—"

"Will Herondale, excellent to see you looking well. And Tessa Gray!" The blond man broke away from Charlotte and came toward Tessa, beaming as if he knew her. "The shape-changer, correct? Enchanted to meet you. What a curiosity."

Charlotte sighed. "Mr. Woolsey Scott, this is Miss Tessa Gray. Tessa, this is Mr. Woolsey Scott, head of the London werewolf pack, and an old friend of the Clave."

"Very well, then," said Gideon as the door shut behind Tessa and Will. He turned toward Sophie, who was suddenly acutely aware of the largeness of the room, and how small she felt inside it. "Shall we continue with the training?"

He held out a knife to her, shining like a silver wand in the room's dimness. His green eyes were steady. *Everything* about Gideon was steady—his gaze, his voice, the way he held himself. She remembered what it felt like to have those steady arms around her, and shivered involuntarily. She had never been alone with him before, and it frightened her. "I don't think my heart would be in it, Mr. Lightwood," she said. "I appreciate the offer all the same, but . . ."

He lowered his arm slowly. "You think that I don't take training you seriously?"

"I think you're being very generous. But I ought to face facts, oughtn't I? This training was never about me or Tessa. It was about your father and the Institute. And now that I've slapped your brother—" She felt her throat tighten. "Mrs. Branwell would be so disappointed in me if she knew."

"Nonsense. He deserved it. And the little matter of the *blood feud* between our families does come to mind." Gideon spun the silver knife carelessly about his finger and thrust it through his belt. "Charlotte would probably give you a rise in salary if she knew."

Sophie shook her head. They were only a few steps from a bench; she sank down onto it, feeling exhausted. "You don't know Charlotte. She'd feel honor-bound to discipline me."

Gideon settled himself on the bench—not beside her, but against the far side of it, as distant from her as he could get. Sophie couldn't decide whether she was pleased about that or not. "Miss Collins," he said. "There is something you ought to know."

She laced her fingers together. "What is that?"

He leaned forward a little, his broad shoulders hunched. She could see the flecks of gray in his green eyes. "When my father called me back from Madrid," he said, "I did not want to come. I had never been happy in London. Our house has been a miserable place since my mother died."

Sophie just stared at him. She could think of no words. He was a Shadowhunter and a gentleman, and yet he seemed to be unburdening his soul to her. Even Jem, for all his gentle kindness, had never done that.

"When I heard about these lessons, I thought they would be a dreadful waste of my time. I pictured two very silly girls uninterested in any sort of instruction. But that describes neither Miss Gray nor yourself. I should tell you, I used to train younger Shadowhunters in Madrid. And there were quite a few of them who didn't have the same native ability that you do. You're a talented student, and it's a pleasure to teach you."

Sophie felt herself flush scarlet. "You can't be serious."

"I am. I was pleasantly surprised the first time I came here, and again so the next time and the next. I found that I was looking forward to it. In fact, it would be fair to say that since my return home, I have hated everything in London except these hours here, with you."

"But you said '*ay Dios mio*' every time I dropped my dagger—"

He grinned. It lit up his face, changed it. Sophie stared at him. He was not beautiful like Jem was, but he was very handsome, especially when he smiled. The smile seemed to reach out and touch her heart, speeding its pace. *He is a Shadowhunter*, she thought. *And a gentleman. This is not the way to think about him. Stop it.* But she could not stop, any more than she had been able to put Jem out of her mind. Though, where with Jem she had felt safe, with Gideon she felt an excitement like lightning that coursed up and down her veins, shocking her. And yet she did not want to let it go.

"I speak Spanish when I'm in a good mood," he said. "You might as well know that about me."

"So it wasn't that you were so weary of my ineptitude that you were wishing to hurl yourself off the roof?"

"Just the opposite." He leaned closer to her. His eyes were the green-gray of a stormy sea. "Sophie? Might I ask you something?"

She knew she should correct him, ask him to call her Miss Collins, but she didn't. "I—yes?"

"Whatever happens with the lessons—might I see you again?"

Will had risen to his feet, but Woolsey Scott was still examining Tessa, his hand under his chin, studying her as if she were something under glass in a natural history exhibit. He was not at all what she would have thought the leader of a pack of werewolves would look like. He was probably in his early twenties, tall but slender to the point of slightness, with blond hair nearly to his shoulders, dressed in a velvet jacket, knee breeches, and a trailing scarf with a paisley print. A tinted monocle obscured one pale green eye. He looked like drawings she'd seen in *Punch* of those who called themselves "aesthetes."

"Adorable," he pronounced finally. "Charlotte, I insist they stay while we talk. What a charming couple they make. See how his dark hair sets off her pale skin—"

"Thank you," said Tessa, her voice shooting several octaves higher than usual, "Mr. Scott, that's very gracious, but there is no attachment between Will and myself. I don't know what you've heard—"

"Nothing!" he declared, throwing himself into a chair and arranging his scarf around him. "Nothing at all, I assure you, though your blushing belies your words. Come along now, everyone, sit down. There's no need to be intimidated by me. Charlotte, ring for some tea. I'm parched."

Tessa looked to Charlotte, who shrugged as if to say there was nothing to be done about it. Slowly Tessa sat back down. Will sat as well. She didn't look at him; she couldn't, with Woolsey Scott grinning at them both as if he knew something she didn't know.

"And where's young Mr. Carstairs?" he inquired. "Adorable boy. Such interesting coloring. And so talented on the violin. Of course, I've heard Garcin himself play at the Paris Opera, and after that, well, everything simply sounds like coal dust scraping the eardrums. Pity about his illness."

Charlotte, who had gone across the room to ring for Bridget, returned and sat down, smoothing her skirts. "In a way, that's what I wanted to speak to you about—"

"Oh, no, no, no." From nowhere Scott had produced a majolica box, which he waved in Charlotte's direction. "No serious discussion, please, until I've had my tea and a smoke. Egyptian cigar?" He offered her the box. "They're the finest available."

"No, thank you." Charlotte looked mildly horrified at the idea of smoking a cigar; indeed, it was hard to picture, and Tessa felt Will, beside her, laugh silently. Scott shrugged and went back to his smoking preparations. The majolica box was a clever little thing with compartments for the cigars, tied in a bundle with a silk ribbon, new matches and old, and a place to tap one's ashes. They watched as the werewolf lit his cigar with evident relish, and the sweet scent of tobacco filled the room.

"Now," he said. "Tell me how you've been, Charlotte, darling. And that abstracted husband of yours. Still wandering around the crypt inventing things that blow up?"

"Sometimes," said Will, "they're even *supposed* to blow up."

There was a rattle, and Bridget arrived with a tea tray, sparing Charlotte the need to answer. She set the tea things down on the inlaid table between the chairs, glancing back and forth anxiously. "I'm sorry, Mrs. Branwell. I thought there was only going to be two for tea—"

"It's quite all right, Bridget," said Charlotte, her tone firmly dismissive. "I will ring for you if we need anything else."

Bridget dropped a curtsy and left, casting a curious eye over her shoulder at Woolsey Scott as she went. He took no notice of her. He had already poured milk into his teacup and was looking reproachfully at his hostess. "Oh, Charlotte."

She looked at him in bewilderment. "Yes?"

"The tongs—the sugar tongs," Scott said sadly, in the voice of someone remarking on the tragic death of an acquaintance. "They're silver."

"Oh!" Charlotte looked startled. Silver, Tessa remembered, was dangerous for werewolves. "I'm so sorry—"

Scott sighed. "It's quite all right. Fortunately, I travel with my own." From another pocket in his velvet jacket—which was buttoned over a silk waistcoat with a print of water lilies that would have put one of Henry's to shame—he produced a rolled-up bit of silk; unrolling it revealed a set of gold tongs and a teaspoon. He set them on the table, took the lid off the teapot, and looked pleased. "Gunpowder tea! From Ceylon, I presume? Have you ever had the tea in Marrakech? They drench it in sugar or honey—"

"Gunpowder?" said Tessa, who had never been able to stop herself from asking questions even when she knew perfectly well it was a bad idea. "There isn't *gunpowder* in the tea, is there?"

Scott laughed and set the lid back down. He sat back while Charlotte, her mouth set in a thin line, poured tea into his cup. "How charming! No, they call it that because the leaves of the tea are rolled into small pellets that resemble gunpowder."

Charlotte said, "Mr. Scott, we really *must* discuss the situation at hand."

"Yes, yes, I read your letter." He sighed. "Downworlder politics. So dull. I don't suppose you'd let me tell you about having my portrait painted by Alma-Tadema? I was dressed as a Roman soldier—"

"Will," said Charlotte firmly. "Perhaps you should share with Mr. Scott what you saw in Whitechapel last night."

Will, somewhat to Tessa's surprise, obediently did as told, keeping the sarcastic observations to a minimum. Scott watched him over the rim of his teacup as Will spoke. His eyes were such a pale green, they were nearly yellow.

"Sorry, my boy," he said when Will was done speaking. "I don't see why this requires an urgent meeting. We're all aware of the existence of these ifrit dens, and I can't be watching every member of my pack at every moment. If some of them choose to partake in vice . . ." He leaned closer. "You do know that your eyes are almost the exact shade of pansy petals? Not quite blue, not quite violet. Extraordinary."

Will widened his extraordinary eyes and smirked. "I think it was the mention of the Magister that concerned Charlotte."

"Ah." Scott turned his gaze on Charlotte. "You're concerned

that I'm betraying you the way you thought de Quincey did. That I'm in league with the Magister—let's just call him by his name, shall we? Mortmain—and I'm letting him use my wolves to do his bidding."

"I had thought," Charlotte said, haltingly, "that perhaps London's Downworlders felt betrayed by the Institute, after what happened with de Quincey. His death—"

Scott adjusted his monocle. As he did, light flashed along the gold band he wore around his index finger. Words gleamed out against it: *L'art pour l'art.* "Was the best surprise I've had since I discovered the Savoy Turkish Baths on Jermyn Street. I despised de Quincey. Loathed him with every fiber of my being."

"Well, the Night Children and the Moon's Children's have never quite—"

"De Quincey had a werewolf killed," Tessa said suddenly, her memories mixing with Camille's, with the recollection of a pair of yellow-green eyes like Scott's. "For his—attachment—to Camille Belcourt."

Woolsey Scott turned a long, curious look on Tessa. "That," he said, "was my brother. My *older* brother. He was pack leader before me, you see, and I inherited the post. Usually one must kill to become pack leader. In my case, it was put to a vote, and the task of avenging my brother in the name of the pack was mine. Only now, you see—" He gestured with an elegant hand. "You've taken care of de Quincey for me. You've no idea how grateful I am." He cocked his head to the side. "Did he die well?"

"He died screaming." Charlotte's bluntness startled Tessa.

"What a beautiful thing to hear." Scott put down his teacup. "For this you have earned a favor. I will tell you what I know, though it isn't much. Mortmain came to me in the early days, wanting me to join with him in the Pandemonium Club. I refused, for de Quincey had already joined, and I would not be part of a club that had him in it. Mortmain let me know there would be a place for me should I change my mind—"

"Did he tell you of his goals?" Will interrupted. "Of the ultimate purpose of the club?"

"The destruction of all Shadowhunters," said Scott. "I rather thought you knew that. It isn't a *gardening* club."

"He has a grudge, we think," said Charlotte. "Against the Clave. Shadowhunters killed his parents some years ago. They were warlocks, deep in the study of the black arts."

"Less of a grudge, more of an idée fixe," said Scott. "An obsession. He would see your kind wiped out, though he seems content to start with England and work his way out from there. A patient, methodical sort of madman. The worst kind." He sat back in his chair and sighed. "News *has* reached me of a group of young wolves, unsworn to any pack, who have been doing some sort of underground work and have been getting paid very well for it. Flashing their tin around among the pack wolves and creating animosities. I did not know about the drug."

"It will keep them working for him, night and day, until they drop from exhaustion or the drug kills them," said Will. "And there is no cure for addiction to it. It is deadly."

The werewolf's yellow-green eyes met his. "This *yin fen*, this silver powder, it is what your friend James Carstairs is addicted to, isn't it? And he's alive."

"Jem survives it because he is a Shadowhunter, and because he uses as little as possible, as infrequently as possible. And even then it will kill him in the end." Will's voice was deadly flat. "As would withdrawing from it."

"Well, well," said the werewolf breezily. "I do hope that the Magister's merrily buying the stuff up doesn't create a shortage, in that case."

Will went white. It was clear the thought hadn't occurred to him. Tessa turned toward Will, but he was already on his feet, moving toward the door. It shut behind him with a bang.

Charlotte frowned. "Lord, he's off to Whitechapel again," she said. "Was that necessary, Woolsey? I think you just terrified the poor boy, and probably for nothing."

"Nothing wrong with a bit of foresight," said Scott. "I took my own brother for granted, until de Quincey killed him."

"De Quincey and the Magister were two of a kind—ruthless," Charlotte said. "If you could help us—"

"The whole situation is certainly beastly," observed Scott. "Unfortunately, lycanthropes who are not members of my pack are not my responsibility."

"If you could simply send out *feelers*, Mr. Scott. Any bit of information about where they are working or what they are doing could be invaluable. The Clave would be grateful."

"Oh, the *Clave*," said Scott, as if deadly bored. "Very well. Now, Charlotte. Let us talk about you."

"Oh, but I am *very* dull," said Charlotte, and she—quite deliberately, Tessa was sure—upset the teapot. It struck the table with a gratifying bang, spilling hot water. Scott jumped up with a cry, flipping his scarf out of the way of danger.

Charlotte rose to her feet, clucking. "Woolsey, dear," she said, placing a hand on his arm, "you've been *such* a help. Let me show you out. There's an antique *keris* that was sent to us from the Bombay Institute I've just been *yearning* to show you. . . ."

11

WILD UNREST

Your woe hath been my anguish; yea, I quail
And perish in your perishing unblest.
And I have searched the highths and depths, the scope
Of all our universe, with desperate hope
To find some solace for your wild unrest.
—James Thomson, "The City of Dreadful Night"

To my dear Mrs. Branwell—

You may be surprised to receive a letter from me so soon after my departure from London, but despite the sleepiness of the countryside, events here have continued apace, and I thought it best to keep you abreast of developments.

The weather continues fine here, allowing me much time for exploring the countryside, especially the area around Ravenscar Manor, which is indeed a fine old building. The Herondale family appears to live alone there: only the father, Edmund; the mother; and the youngest daughter, Cecily, who is near to fifteen and very like her brother in restlessness, in manner, and in looks. I will arrive at how I know all that in a moment.

Ravenscar itself is near a small village. I set myself up at the local inn, the Black Swan, and posed as a gentleman interested in buying property in the area. The locals have been most forthcoming with information, and when they were not, a persuasion spell or two helped them to see the matter from my point of view.

It seems the Herondales mix very little with local society. Despite—or perhaps because of—this tendency, rumor about them abounds. It seems they do not own Ravenscar Manor but are indeed, by way of its custodians, watching over it for its true owner—Axel Mortmain, of course. Mortmain seems no one to these people but a wealthy industrialist who purchased a country manor he rarely visits; I encountered no rumor about any connection of his to the Shades, whose legacy here seems long forgotten. The Herondales themselves are a matter of curious speculation. It is known that they had a child who died, and that Edmund, whom I knew once, turned to drink and to gambling; eventually he gambled away their home in Wales, whereupon, destitute, they were offered the occupation of this house in Yorkshire by its owner. That was two years ago.

I had all this confirmed for me this afternoon when, watching the manor from a distance, I was startled by the appearance of a girl. I knew who she was immediately. I had seen her go in and out of the house, and her resemblance to her brother Will, as I said, is pronounced. She set into me at once, demanding to know why I was spying on her family. She did not seem angry at first but rather hopeful. "Did my brother send you?" she asked. "Have you any word of my brother?"

It was quite heartbreaking, but I know the Law, and could tell her only that her brother was well and wished to know that they were safe. At that she became angry and opined that Will could best ensure his family's safety by returning to them. She also said that it was not the death of her sister (did you know of this sister?) that had undone her father, but rather Will's desertion. I shall leave it up to your discretion whether to pass this on to young Master Herondale, as it seems news that would do more harm than good.

When I spoke to her of Mortmain, she chatted easily to me of him—a family friend, she said, who had stepped in to offer them this home when they had nothing. As she spoke, I began to get a sense of how Mortmain thinks. He knows it is against the Law for Nephilim to interfere with Shadowhunters who have chosen to leave the Clave, and that therefore Ravenscar Manor would be avoided; he knows also that the Herondales' occupancy of it makes the objects in it theirs, and therefore none can be used to track him. And last, he knows that power over the Herondales could translate into power over Will. Does he require power over Will? Not now perhaps, but there may be a time when he desires it, and when he does, it will be to hand. He is a well-prepared man, and men such as that are dangerous.

Were I you, and I am not, I would reassure Master Will that his family is safe and I am watching them; avoid speaking to him of Mortmain until I can gather more information. As far as I can glean from Cecily, the Herondales do not know where Mortmain is. She said that he was in Shanghai, and on occasion they receive correspondence from his company there, all stamped with peculiar stamps. It is my understanding, however, that the Shanghai Institute believes him not to be there.

I told Miss Herondale that her brother missed her; it seemed the least I could do. She appeared gratified. I shall remain in this area a good while longer, I think; I have become myself curious as to how the misfortunes of the Herondales are entwined with Mortmain's plans. There are still secrets to be unearthed here beneath the peaceful green of the Yorkshire countryside, and I aim to discover them.

—Ragnor Fell

Charlotte read the letter over twice, to commit its details to memory, and then, having folded it small, cast it into the drawing room fire. She stood wearily, leaning against the mantel, watching as the flame ate away the paper in lines of black and gold.

She was not sure if she was surprised, or disturbed, or simply made bone-weary by the contents of the letter. Trying to find Mortmain was like reaching to swat a spider, only to realize that you were helplessly entangled in the sticky strands of its web. And Will—she hated to speak of this with him. She looked into the fire with unseeing eyes. Sometimes she thought Will had been sent to her by the Angel specifically to try her patience. He was bitter, he had a tongue like the lash of a whip, and he met her every attempt to show him love and affection with venom or contempt. And still, when she looked at him, she saw the boy he'd been at twelve, curled in the corner of his bedroom with his hands over his ears as his parents called his name from the steps below, entreating him to come out, to come back to them.

She had knelt beside him after the Herondales had gone away. She remembered him lifting his face to her—small and white and set, with those blue eyes and dark lashes; he'd been as pretty as a girl then, thin and delicate, before he had thrown himself into Shadowhunter training with such single-mindedness that within two years all that delicacy had been gone, covered over by muscle and scars and Marks. She'd taken his hand then, and he'd let it lie in hers like a dead thing. He'd bitten his lower lip, though he didn't appear to have noticed, and blood covered his chin and dripped onto his shirt. *Charlotte, you'll tell me, won't you? You'll tell me if anything happens to them?*

Will, I can't—

I know the Law. I just want to know if they live. His eyes had pleaded with her. *Charlotte, please . . .*

"Charlotte?"

She looked up from the fire. Jem stood in the doorway of the drawing room. Charlotte, still half-caught in the web of the past, blinked at him. When he had first arrived from Shanghai, his hair and eyes had been as black as ink. Over time they had silvered, like copper oxidizing to verdigris, as the drugs had worked their way through his blood, changing him, killing him slowly.

"James," she said. "It's late, isn't it?"

"Eleven o'clock." He put his head to the side, studying her. "Are you all right? You look as if your peace of mind has been rather cut up."

"No, I just—" She gestured vaguely. "It is all this business with Mortmain."

"I have a question," Jem said, moving farther into the drawing room and lowering his voice. "Not wholly unrelated. Gabriel said something today, during training—"

"You were there?"

He shook his head. "Sophie told it to me. She didn't like to carry tales, but she was troubled, and I can't blame her. Gabriel asserted that his uncle had committed suicide and that his mother had died of grief because—well, because of your father."

"My father?" Charlotte said blankly.

"Apparently Gabriel's uncle, Silas, committed some infraction of the Law, and your father discovered it. Your father went to the Clave. The uncle killed himself out of shame, and Mrs. Lightwood died of grief. According to Gabriel, 'The Fairchilds don't care about anyone but themselves and the Law.'"

"And you are telling me this because . . . ?"

"I wondered if it was true," said Jem. "And if it is, perhaps it might be useful to communicate to the Consul that Benedict's motive for wanting the Institute is revenge, not selfless desire to see it run better."

"It's not true. It can't be." Charlotte shook her head. "Silas Lightwood did kill himself—because he was in love with his *parabatai*—but not because my father told the Clave about it. The first the Clave knew of it was from Silas's suicide note. In fact, Silas's father asked my father for help in writing Silas's eulogy. Does that sound like a man who blamed my father for his son's death?"

Jem's eyes darkened. "That's interesting."

"Do you think Gabriel's simply being nasty, or do you think his father lied to him to—"

Charlotte never finished her sentence. Jem doubled up suddenly, as if he had been punched in the stomach, with a fit of coughing so severe that his thin shoulders shook. A spray of red blood spattered the sleeve of his jacket as he raised his arm to cover his face.

"Jem—" Charlotte started forward with her arms out, but he staggered upright and away from her, holding his hand out as if to ward her off.

"I'm all right," he gasped. "I'm fine." He wiped blood from his face with the sleeve of his jacket. "Please, Charlotte," he added in a defeated voice as she moved toward him. "Don't."

Charlotte stopped herself, her heart aching. "Is there nothing—"

"You know there's nothing." He lowered his arm, the blood on his sleeve like an accusation, and gave her the sweetest smile. "Dear Charlotte," he said. "You have always been like the best sort of older sister I could have hoped for. You do know that, don't you?"

Charlotte just looked at him, openmouthed. It sounded so much like a good-bye, she could not bear to reply. He turned with his usual light tread and made his way out of the room. She watched him go, telling herself it meant nothing, that he was no worse than he had been, that he still had time. She loved Jem, as she loved Will—as she could not help loving them all—and the thought of losing him shattered her heart. Not only for her own loss, but for Will's. If Jem died, she could not help but feel, he would take all that was still human about Will with him when he went.

***

It was nearly midnight when Will returned to the Institute. It had begun raining on him when he'd been halfway down Threadneedle Street. He had ducked under the awning of Dean and Son Publishers to button his jacket and pull his scarf tight, but the rain had already gotten into his mouth—great, icy drops that tasted of charcoal and silt. He had hunched his shoulders against the needlelike sting of it as he'd left the shelter of the awning and headed past the Bank, toward the Institute.

Even after years in London, rain made him think of home. He still remembered the way it had rained in the countryside, in Wales, the green fresh taste of it, the way it felt to roll over and over down a damp hillside, getting grass in your hair and clothes. If he shut his eyes, he could hear his sisters' laughter echo in his ears. *Will, you'll ruin your clothes; Will, Mother will be furious . . .*

Will wondered if you could ever really be a Londoner if you had that in your blood—the memory of great open spaces, the wideness of the sky, the clear air. Not these narrow streets choked with people, the London dust that got everywhere—in your clothes, a thin powdering on your hair and down the back of your neck—the smell of the filthy river.

He had reached Fleet Street. Temple Bar was visible through the mist in the distance; the street was slick with rain. A carriage rattled by as he ducked into an alley between two buildings, the wheels splashing dirty water up against the curb.

He could see the spire of the Institute in the distance now. They had certainly already finished supper, Will thought. Everything would be put away. Bridget would be asleep; he could duck into the kitchen and cobble together a meal from bread and cheese and cold pie. He had been missing a great many meals lately, and if he was truthful with himself, there was only one reason for it: He was avoiding Tessa.

He did not want to avoid her—indeed, he had failed miserably at it that afternoon, accompanying her not just to training but also to the drawing room afterward. Sometimes he wondered if he did these things just to test himself. To see if the feelings had gone. But they had not. When he saw her, he wanted to be with her; when he was with her, he ached to touch her; when he touched even her hand, he wanted to embrace her. He wanted to feel her against him the way he had in the attic. He wanted to know the taste of her skin and the smell of her hair. He wanted to make her laugh. He wanted to sit and listen to her talk about books until his ears fell off. But all these were things he could not want, because they were things he could not have, and wanting what you could not have led to misery and madness.

He had reached home. The door of the Institute swung open under his touch, opening onto a vestibule full of flickering torchlight. He thought of the blur the drugs had brought to him in the den on Whitechapel High Street. A blissful release from wanting or needing anything. He had dreamed he was lying on a hill in Wales with the sky high and blue overhead, and that Tessa had come walking up the hill to him and had sat down beside him. *I love you,* he had said to her, and kissed her, as if it were the most natural thing in the world. *Do you love me?*

She had smiled at him. *You will always come first in my heart,* she had said.

Tell me this is not a dream, he had whispered to her as she'd put her arms around him, and then he'd no longer known what was waking and what was sleeping.

He shrugged out of his coat as he went up the stairs, shaking out his wet hair. Cold water was trickling down the back of his shirt, dampening his spine, making him shiver. The precious packet he had bought from the ifrits was in his trousers pocket. He slipped his hand in, touching his fingers to it, just to be sure.

The corridors burned with low witchlight; he was halfway down the first one when he paused. Tessa's door was here, he knew, across from Jem's. And there, in front of her door, stood Jem—though "stood" was perhaps not the right word. He was pacing back and forth, "wearing a path in the carpet," as Charlotte would have said.

"James," Will said, more surprised than anything else.

Jem's head jerked up, and he backed away from Tessa's door instantly, retreating toward his own. His face went blank. "I suppose I shouldn't be surprised to find you wandering the halls at all hours."

"I think we can agree that the reverse is more out of character," said Will. "Why are you awake? Are you all right?"

Jem cast a last glance at Tessa's door, and then turned to face Will. "I was going to apologize to Tessa," he said. "I think my violin playing was keeping her awake. Where have you been? Assignation with Six-Fingered Nigel again?"

Will grinned, but Jem didn't return the smile. "I've something for you, actually. Come along, let me into your room. I don't want to spend all night standing about in the hall."

After a moment's hesitation Jem shrugged and opened his door. He went in, Will following; Will shut and bolted the door behind them as Jem threw himself into an armchair. There was a fire in the grate, but it had burned down to pale red-gold coals. He looked at Will. "What is it, then—," he began, and bent almost double, convulsed by a hard cough. It passed quickly, before Will could move or speak, but when Jem straightened, and brushed the back of his hand across his mouth, it came away smeared with red. He looked at the blood expressionlessly.

Will felt sick. He approached his *parabatai*, producing a handkerchief, which Jem took, and then the silver powder he'd bought in Whitechapel. "Here," he said, feeling awkward. He hadn't felt awkward around Jem in five years, but there it was. "I went back to Whitechapel, got this for you."

Jem, having cleaned the blood from his hand with Will's handkerchief, took the packet and stared down at the *yin fen*. "I have enough of this," he said. "For at least another month." He looked up then, a sudden flicker in his eyes. "Or did Tessa tell you—"

"Did she tell me what?"

"Nothing. I spilled some of the powder the other day. I managed to retrieve most of it." Jem set the packet down on the table beside him. "This wasn't necessary."

Will sat down on the trunk at the foot of Jem's bed. He hated sitting there—his legs were so long, he always felt like an adult trying to squeeze behind a schoolroom desk—but he wanted to bring his eyes level with Jem's. "Mortmain's minions have been buying up the *yin fen* supply in the East End," he said. "I confirmed it. If you had run out and he was the only one with a supply . . ."

"We would have been put in his power," said Jem. "Unless

you were willing to let me die, of course, which would be the sensible course of action."

"I would *not* be willing." Will sounded sharp. "You're my blood brother. I've sworn an oath not to let any harm come to you—"

"Leaving aside oaths," said Jem, "and power plays, did any of this have to do with me?"

"I don't know what you mean—"

"I had begun to wonder if you were capable of the desire to spare anyone suffering."

Will rocked back slightly, as if Jem had pushed him. "I . . ." He swallowed, looking for the words. It had been so long since he had searched for words that would earn him forgiveness and not hatred, so long since he had sought to present himself in anything but the worst light, that he wondered for a panicked moment if it were even something he was still able to do. "I spoke to Tessa today," he said finally, not noticing that Jem's face paled even more markedly. "She made me understand—that what I did last night was unforgivable. Though," he added hastily, "I do still hope that you will forgive me." *By the Angel, I'm bad at this.*

Jem raised an eyebrow. "For what?"

"I went to that den because I could not stop thinking about my family, and I wanted—I needed—to stop thinking," said Will. "It did not cross my mind that it would look to you as if I were making a mockery out of your sickness. I suppose I am asking your forgiveness for my lack of consideration." His voice dropped. "Everyone makes mistakes, Jem."

"Yes," said Jem. "You just make more of them than most people."

"I—"

"You hurt everyone," said Jem. "Everyone whose life you touch."

"Not you," Will whispered. "I hurt everyone but you. I never meant to hurt you."

Jem put his hands up, pressing his palms against his eyes. "Will—"

"You can't never forgive me," Will said, hearing the panic tinging his own voice. "I'd be—"

"Alone?" Jem lowered his hands, but he was smiling now, crookedly. "And whose fault is that?" He leaned back against the seat, his eyes half-lidded with tiredness. "I would always have forgiven you," he said. "I would have forgiven you if you hadn't apologized. In fact, I wasn't expecting you would. Tessa's influence, I can only guess."

"I am not here at her request. James, you are all the family I have." Will's voice shook. "I would die for you. You know that. I would die *without* you. If it were not for you, I would be dead a hundred times over these past five years. I owe you everything, and if you cannot believe I have empathy, perhaps you might at least believe I know honor—honor, and debt—"

Jem looked actually alarmed now. "Will, your discomposure is greater than my anger warranted. My temper has cooled; you know I have never had much of one."

His tone was soothing, but something in Will could not be soothed. "I went to get you that medicine because I cannot bear the thought of you dying or in pain, certainly not when I could have done something to prevent it. And I did it because I was afraid. If Mortmain came to us and said he was the only one who had the drug that would save your life, you must know

I would give him whatever he wanted so that I could get it for you. I have failed my family before, James. I would not fail you—"

"*Will.*" Jem rose to his feet; he came across the room to Will and knelt down, looking up into his friend's face. "You begin to concern me. Your regret does you admirable credit, but you must know . . ."

Will looked down at him. He remembered Jem as he had been when he had just come from Shanghai, and had seemed to be all great dark eyes in a pinched white face. It had not been easy to make him laugh then, but Will had set himself to trying. "Know what?"

"That I will die," Jem said. His eyes were wide, and fever-bright; there was a trace of blood, still, at the corner of his mouth. The shadows under his eyes were nearly blue.

Will dug his fingers into Jem's wrist, denting the material of his shirt. Jem did not wince.

"You swore to stay with me," he said. "When we made our oath, as *parabatai*. Our souls are knit. We are one person, James."

"We are two people," said Jem. "Two people with a covenant between us."

Will knew he sounded like a child, but he could not help it. "A covenant that says you must not go where I cannot come with you."

"Until death," Jem replied gently. "Those are the words of the oath. 'Until aught but death part thee and me.' Someday, Will, I will go where none can follow me, and I think it will be sooner rather than later. Have you ever asked yourself why I agreed to be your *parabatai*?"

"No better offers forthcoming?" Will tried for humor, but his voice cracked like glass.

"I thought you needed me," Jem said. "There is a wall you have built about yourself, Will, and I have never asked you why. But no one should shoulder every burden alone. I thought you would let me inside if I became your *parabatai*, and then you would have at least someone to lean upon. I did wonder what my death would mean for you. I used to fear it, for your sake. I feared you would be left alone inside that wall. But now . . . something has changed. I do not know why. But I know that it is true."

"That what is true?" Will's fingers were still digging into Jem's wrist.

"That the wall is coming down."

Tessa could not get to sleep. She lay unmoving on her back, staring up at the ceiling. There was a crack across the plaster of it that looked sometimes like a cloud and sometimes like a razor, depending on the shift of the candlelight.

Dinner had been tense. Apparently Gabriel had told Charlotte that he refused to return and partake in the training anymore, so it was going to be only Gideon working with her and Sophie from now on. Gabriel had refused to say why, but it was clear Charlotte blamed Will; Tessa, seeing how exhausted Charlotte looked at the prospect of more conflict with Benedict, had felt heavy with guilt for having brought Will with her to the training, and for having laughed at Gabriel.

It did not help that Jem had not been at dinner. She had wanted so badly to speak to him today. After he had avoided her eyes at breakfast and then been "ill" at dinner, panic had twisted her stomach. Was he horrified by what had happened between them the night before—or worse, sickened? Maybe in his secret heart of hearts, he felt as Will did, that warlocks were beneath him. Or maybe it had nothing to do with what she was. Maybe he was simply repelled by her wantonness; she had welcomed his embraces, not pushed him away, and hadn't Aunt Harriet always said that men were weak where desire was concerned, and that women were the ones who had to exercise restraint?

She hadn't exercised much last night. She remembered lying beside Jem, his gentle hands on her. She knew with a painful inner honesty that if things had continued, she would have done whatever he wanted. Even now, thinking about it, her body felt hot and restless; she shifted in bed, punching one of the pillows. If she had destroyed the closeness she shared with Jem by allowing what had happened last night, she would never forgive herself.

She was about to bury her face in the pillow, when she heard the noise. A soft rapping at the door. She froze. It came again, insistently. *Jem.* Her hands shaking, she leaped from the bed, ran to the door, and threw it open.

On the threshold stood Sophie. She wore her black housemaid's dress, but her white cap had come askew and her dark curls were tumbling down. Her face was very white and there was a spot of blood on her collar; she looked horrified and almost sick.

"Sophie." Tessa's voice betrayed her surprise. "Are you all right?"

Sophie looked around fearfully. "May I come in, miss?"

Tessa nodded and held the door open for her. When they

were both safely inside, she bolted it and sat down on the edge of her bed, apprehension like a lead weight in her chest. Sophie remained standing, twisting her hands in front of her.

"Sophie, please, what is it?"

"It's Miss Jessamine," Sophie burst out.

"What about Jessamine?"

"She . . . It's just to say, I've seen her . . ." She broke off, looking wretched. "She's been slipping away in the nights, miss."

"Has she? I saw her last night, in the corridor, dressed as a boy and looking quite furtive. . . ."

Sophie looked relieved. She didn't like Jessamine, Tessa knew that well enough, but she was a well-trained maid, and a well-trained maid did not tattle on her mistress. "Yes," she said eagerly. "I've been noticing it for days now. Her bed sometimes not slept in at all, mud on the rugs in the mornings when it weren't there the night before. I would've told Mrs. Branwell, but she's had so dreadful much on her mind, I couldn't bear to."

"So why are you telling me?" Tessa asked. "It sounds as if Jessamine's found herself a suitor. I can't say I approve of her behavior, but"—she swallowed, thinking of her own behavior the night before—"neither of us is responsible for it. And perhaps there is some harmless explanation. . . ."

"Oh, but, miss." Sophie plunged her hand into the pocket of her dress and drew it out with a stiff cream-colored card clamped between her fingers. "Tonight I found this. In the pocket of her new velvet jacket. You know, the one with the ecru stripe."

Tessa did not care about the ecru stripe. Her eyes were fixed on the card. Slowly she reached out and took it, turning it over in her hand. It was an invitation to a ball.

July 20, 1878

Mr. BENEDICT LIGHTWOOD
presents his compliments
to MISS JESSAMINE LOVELACE,
and requests the honor of her company
at a masquerade ball given on Tuesday next,
the 27th of July. RSVP.

The invitation went on to give details of the address and the time the ball would begin, but it was what was written on the back of the invitation that froze Tessa's blood. In a casual hand, as familiar to her as her own, were scrawled the words: *My Jessie. My very heart is bursting at the thought of seeing you tomorrow night at the "great affair." However great it may be, I shall have eyes for nothing and no one but you. Do wear the white dress, darling, as you know how I like it—"in gloss of satin and glimmer of pearls," as the poet said. Yours always, N.G.*

"Nate," Tessa said numbly, staring down at the letter. "*Nate* wrote this. And quoted *Tennyson.*"

Sophie drew her breath in sharply. "I feared—but I thought it couldn't be. Not after all he did."

"I know my brother's handwriting." Tessa's voice was grim. "He's planning to meet her tonight at this—this secret ball. Sophie, where is Jessamine? I must speak to her this instant."

Sophie's hands began to twist more rapidly. "See, that's the thing, miss—"

"Oh, God, has she gone already? We'll have to get Charlotte. I don't see another way—"

"She hasn't gone. She's in her room," Sophie interrupted.

"So she doesn't know you found this?" Tessa flapped the card.

Sophie swallowed visibly. "I—she found me with it in my hand, miss. I tried to hide it, but she'd already seen it. She had such a menacing look on her face when she came reaching for it, I couldn't help myself. All the training sessions I've done with Master Gideon, they just took over and, well—"

"Well, *what*? Sophie—"

"I hit her on the head with a mirror," Sophie said hopelessly. "One of those silver-backed ones, so it was quite heavy. She went down just like a stone, miss. So I . . . I tied her to the bed and I came looking for you."

"Let me see if I have this quite correct," said Tessa after a pause. "Jessamine found you with the invitation in your hand, so you struck her over the head with a mirror and tied her to her bed?"

Sophie nodded.

"Good Lord," said Tessa. "Sophie, we're going to need to fetch someone. This ball cannot remain a secret, and Jessamine . . ."

"Not Mrs. Branwell," Sophie moaned. "She'll sack me. She'll have to."

"Jem—"

"No!" Sophie's hand flew to her collar, where the spot of blood was. Jessamine's blood, Tessa realized with a jolt. "I couldn't bear if he thought I could do such a thing—he's so gentle. Please don't make me tell him, miss."

Of course, Tessa thought. Sophie loved Jem. In all the mess of the past few days, she had nearly forgotten. A wave of shame swamped her as she thought of the night before; she fought it back, and said determinedly, "There is only one person, then, Sophie, whom we can go to. You do understand that?"

"Master Will," said Sophie with loathing, and sighed. "Very well, miss. I suppose I don't care what he thinks of me."

Tessa rose and reached for her dressing gown, and wrapped it around herself. "Look upon the bright side, Sophie. At least Will won't be shocked. I doubt Jessamine's the first unconscious female he's ever dealt with, or that she'll be the last either."

Tessa had been wrong about at least one thing: Will *was* shocked.

"*Sophie* did this?" he said, not for the first time. They were standing at the foot of Jessamine's bed. She lay flung upon it, her chest rising and falling slowly like the famous Sleeping Beauty waxwork of Madame du Barry. Her fair hair was scattered on the pillow, and a large, bloody welt ran across her forehead. Each of her wrists was tied to a post of the bed. "*Our* Sophie?"

Tessa glanced over at Sophie, who was sitting in a chair by the door. Her head was down, and she was staring at her hands. She studiously avoided looking at Tessa or Will.

"Yes," Tessa said, "and do stop repeating it."

"I think I may be in love with you, Sophie," said Will. "Marriage could be on the cards."

Sophie whimpered.

"Stop it," Tessa hissed. "I think you're frightening the poor girl more than she's already frightened."

"What's to be frightened of? Jessamine? It looks like Sophie won that little altercation easily." Will was having trouble repressing a grin. "Sophie, my dear, there is nothing to worry about. Many's the time I have wanted to hit Jessamine over the head myself. No one could blame you."

"She's afraid Charlotte will sack her," said Tessa.

"For hitting Jessamine?" Will relented. "Tess, if this invitation is what it looks like, and Jessamine is truly meeting your brother in secret, she may have betrayed us all. Not to mention, what is Benedict Lightwood doing, throwing parties that none of us know about? Parties to which Nate is invited? What Sophie did was heroic. Charlotte will thank her."

At that, Sophie lifted her head. "Do you think so?"

"I know it," said Will. For a moment he and Sophie looked at each other steadily across the room. Sophie looked away first, but if Tessa was not mistaken, there had been—for the first time—no dislike in her eyes when she'd gazed at Will.

From his belt Will drew his stele. He sat down on the bed beside Jessamine and gently brushed aside her hair. Tessa bit her lip, restraining the impulse to ask him what he was doing.

He laid his stele against Jessamine's throat and quickly sketched two runes. "An *iratze*," he said, without Tessa's having to ask. "That is, a healing rune, and a Sleep Now rune. This should keep her quiet at least until morning. Your skill with a hand mirror is to be admired, Sophie, but your knot making could be improved."

Sophie muttered something under her breath in response. The suspension of her dislike of Will appeared to be over.

"The question," said Will, "is what to do now."

"We must tell Charlotte—"

"No," Will said firmly. "We must not."

Tessa looked at him in astonishment. "Why not?"

"Two reasons," said Will. "First, she would be duty-bound

to tell the Clave, and if Benedict Lightwood is hosting this ball, I would make a fair guess that some of his followers will be there. But they might not all be. If the Clave is warned, they may be able to get word to him before anyone can arrive to observe what is truly going on. Second, the ball began an hour ago. We do not know when Nate will arrive, seeking Jessamine, and if he does not see her, he may well depart. He is the best connection to Mortmain we have. We do not have any time to lose or waste, and waking Charlotte to tell her of this will do both."

"Jem, then?"

Something flickered in Will's eyes. "No. Not tonight. Jem is not well enough, but he will say he is. After last night I owe it to him to leave him out of this."

Tessa looked at him hard. "Then what do you propose to do?"

Will's mouth quirked up at both corners. "Miss Gray," he said, "would you be amenable to attending a ball with me?"

"Do you remember the *last* party we went to?" Tessa inquired.

Will's smile remained. He had that look of heightened intensity that he wore when he was strategizing a plan. "Don't tell me that you weren't thinking the same thing I was, Tessa."

Tessa sighed. "Yes," she said. "I shall Change into Jessamine and go in her place. It is the only plan that makes sense." She turned to Sophie. "Do you know the dress Nate spoke of? A white dress of Jessamine's?"

Sophie nodded.

"Get it brushed and ready to be worn," said Tessa. "You will have to do my hair as well, Sophie. Are you calm enough?"

"Yes, miss." Sophie got to her feet and scurried across the room to the wardrobe, which she threw open. Will was still looking at Tessa; his smile widened.

Tessa lowered her voice. "Will, has it crossed your mind that Mortmain might be there?"

The smile vanished from Will's face. "You will go nowhere near him if he is."

"You cannot tell me what to do."

Will frowned. He was not reacting at all in the way Tessa felt he should. When Capitola in *The Hidden Hand* dressed up as a boy and took on the marauding Black Donald to prove her bravery, no one snapped at *her*.

"Your power is impressive, Tessa, but you are in no position to capture a powerful adult magic user like Mortmain. You will leave that to me," he said.

She scowled at him. "And how do *you* plan not to be recognized at this ball? Benedict knows your face, as do—"

Will seized the invitation out of her hand and waved it at her. "It's a *masked* ball."

"And I suppose you just happen to have a mask."

"As a matter of fact I do," said Will. "Our last Christmas party was themed along the lines of the Venetian Carnevale." He smirked. "Tell her, Sophie."

Sophie, who was busy with what looked like a concoction of spiderwebs and moonbeams on the brushing tray, sighed. "It's true, miss. And you let him deal with Mortmain, you hear? It's too dangerous otherwise. And you'll be all the way in Chiswick!"

Will looked at Tessa with triumph. "If even Sophie agrees with me, you can't very well say no."

"I could," Tessa said mutinously, "but I won't. Very well. But you must stay out of Nate's way while I speak with him. He isn't an idiot; if he sees us together, he's quite capable of putting two and two together. I get no sense from his note that he expects Jessamine to be accompanied."

"I get no sense from his note at all," said Will, bounding to his feet, "except that he can quote Tennyson's lesser poetry. Sophie, how quickly can you have Tessa ready?"

"Half an hour," said Sophie, not looking up from the dress.

"Meet me in the courtyard in half an hour, then," said Will. "I'll wake Cyril. And be prepared to swoon at my finery."

The night was a cool one, and Tessa shivered as she passed through the doors of the Institute and stood at the head of the steps outside. This was where she had sat, she thought, that night she and Jem had walked to Blackfriars Bridge together, the night the clockwork creatures had attacked them. It was a clearer night tonight, despite the day of rain; the moon chased stray wisps of cloud across an otherwise unmarked black sky.

The carriage was there, at the foot of the steps, Will waiting in front of it. He glanced up as the doors of the Institute closed behind her. For a moment they simply stood and looked at each other. Tessa knew what he was seeing—she had seen it herself, in the mirror in Jessamine's room. She was Jessamine down to the last inch, clothed in a delicate ivory silk dress. It was low-cut, revealing a great deal of Jessamine's white bosom, with a silk ribbon at the collar to emphasize the shape of her throat. The sleeves were short, leaving her arms vulnerable to the night air. Even if the neckline hadn't been so low, Tessa would have felt naked without her angel, but she couldn't wear it:

Nate would have been sure to notice it. The skirt, with a waterfall train, belled out behind her from a laced, slender waist; her hair was dressed high, with a length of pearls held in place by pearl pins, and she wore a gold domino half mask that set off Jessamine's pale, fair hair to perfection. *I look so delicate*, she had thought with detachment, staring at the mirror's silvered surface as Sophie had fussed about her. *Like a faerie princess.* It was easy to think such thoughts when the reflection was not truly your own.

But Will—Will. He had said she should be ready to swoon at his finery, and she had rolled her eyes, but in his black and white evening dress, he looked more beautiful than she had imagined. The stark and simple colors brought out the angular perfection of his features. His dark hair tumbled over a black half mask that emphasized the blueness of the eyes behind it. She felt her heart contract, and hated herself instantly for it. She looked away from him, at Cyril, in the driver's seat of the carriage. His eyes narrowed in confusion as he saw her; he looked from her to Will, and back again, and shrugged. Tessa wondered what on earth Will had told him they were doing to explain the fact that he was taking Jessamine to Chiswick in the middle of the night. It must have been quite a story.

"Ah," was all Will said as she descended the steps and drew her wrap around herself. She hoped he would put down to the cold the involuntary shiver that went over her as he took her hand. "I see now why your brother quoted that execrable poetry. You are meant to *be* Maud, aren't you? 'Queen rose of the rosebud garden of girls'?"

"You know," Tessa said as he helped her up into the carriage, "I don't care for that poem either."

He swung himself up after her and slammed the carriage door shut. "Jessamine adores it."

The carriage began to rumble across the cobblestones, and through the open doors of the gate. Tessa found that her heart was beating very fast. Fear of being caught by Charlotte and Henry, she told herself. Nothing to do with being alone with Will in the carriage. "I am not Jessamine."

He looked at her levelly. There was something in his eyes, a sort of quizzical admiration; she wondered if it was simply admiration of Jessamine's looks. "No," he said. "No, even though you are the perfect picture of Jessamine, I can see Tessa through it somehow—as if, if I were to scrape away a layer of paint, there would be my Tessa underneath."

"I am not *your* Tessa either."

The light sparkling in his eyes dimmed. "Fair enough," he said. "I suppose you are not. What is it like, being Jessamine, then? Can you sense her thoughts? Read what she feels?"

Tessa swallowed, and touched the velvet curtain of the carriage with a gloved hand. Outside she could see the gaslights going by in a yellow blur; two children were slumped in a doorway, leaning against each other, asleep. Temple Bar flew by overhead. She said, "I tried. Upstairs in her bedroom. But there's something wrong. I—I couldn't feel anything from her."

"Well, I suppose it's hard to meddle in someone's brains if they've got no brains to start with."

Tessa made a face. "Be flippant about it if you like, but there is something wrong with Jessamine. Trying to touch her mind is like trying to touch—a nest of snakes, or a poisonous cloud. I can feel a little of her emotions. A great deal of rage, and longing, and bitterness. But I cannot pick out the individual thoughts among them. It is like trying to hold water."

"That's curious. Have you ever come across anything like it before?"

Tessa shook her head. "It concerns me. I am afraid Nate will expect me to know something and I will not know it or have the right answer."

Will leaned forward. On wet days, which was nearly every day, his normally straight dark hair would begin to curl. There was something about the vulnerable curling of his damp hair against his temples that made her heart ache. "You are a good actress, and you know your brother," he said. "I have every confidence in you."

She looked at him in surprise. "You do?"

"And," he went on without answering her question, "in the event that something goes awry, I will be there. Even if you don't see me, Tess, I'll be there. Remember that."

"All right." She cocked her head to the side. "Will?"

"Yes?"

"There was a third reason you didn't want to wake up Charlotte and tell her what we were doing, wasn't there?"

He narrowed his blue eyes at her. "And what's that?"

"Because you do not yet know if this is simply a foolish flirtation on Jessamine's part, or something deeper and darker. A true connection to my brother and to Mortmain. And you know that if it is the second, it will break Charlotte's heart."

A muscle jumped at the corner of his mouth. "And what do I care if it does? If she is foolish enough to attach herself to Jessamine—"

"You care," said Tessa. "You are no inhuman block of ice,

Will. I have seen you with Jem—I saw you when you looked at Cecily. And you had another sister, didn't you?"

He looked at her sharply. "What makes you think I had—I have—more than one sister?"

"Jem said he thought your sister was dead," she said. "And you said, 'My sister *is* dead.' But Cecily is clearly very much alive. Which made me think you had a sister who had died. One that wasn't Cecily."

Will let out a long, slow breath. "You're clever."

"But am I clever and right, or clever and wrong?"

Will looked as if he were glad for the mask that hid his expression. "Ella," he said. "Two years older than I. And Cecily, three years younger. My sisters."

"And Ella . . ."

Will looked away, but not before she saw the pain in his eyes. So Ella was dead.

"What was she like?" Tessa asked, remembering how grateful she had been when Jem had asked that of her, about Nate. "Ella? And Cecily, what kind of girl is she?"

"Ella was protective," said Will. "Like a mother. She would have done anything for me. And Cecily was a little mad creature. She was only nine when I left. I can't say if she's still the same, but she was—like Cathy in *Wuthering Heights*. She was afraid of nothing and demanded everything. She could fight like a devil and swear like a Billingsgate fishwife." There was amusement in his voice, and admiration, and . . . love. She had never heard him talk about anyone that way, except perhaps Jem.

"If I might ask—," she began.

Will sighed. "You know you'll ask whether I say it's all right or not."

"You have a younger sister of your own," she said. "So what exactly did you do to *Gabriel's* sister to make him hate you so?"

He straightened. "Are you serious?"

"Yes," she said. "I am forced to spend a great deal of time with the Lightwoods, and Gabriel clearly despises you. And you did break his arm. It would ease my mind if I knew why."

Shaking his head, Will raked his fingers through his hair. "Dear God," he said. "Their sister—her name is Tatiana, by the way; she was named after her mother's dear friend, who was Russian—was twelve years old, I think."

"Twelve?" Tessa was horrified.

Will exhaled. "I see you have already decided for yourself what happened," he said. "Would it ease your mind further to know that I myself was twelve? Tatiana, she . . . fancied herself in love with me. In that way that little girls do. She would follow me around and giggle and duck behind pillars to stare at me."

"One does silly things when one is twelve."

"It was the first Christmas party at the Institute that I attended," he said. "The Lightwoods were there in all their finery. Tatiana in silver hair ribbons. She had a little book she carried around with her everywhere. She must have dropped it that night. I found it shoved down the back of one of the chaise longues. It was her diary. Filled with poems about me—the color of my eyes, the wedding we would have. She had written 'Tatiana Herondale' all over it."

"That sounds rather adorable."

"I had been in the drawing room, but I came back into the ballroom with the diary. Elise Penhallow had just finished playing the spinet. I got up beside her and commenced reading from Tatiana's diary."

"Oh, Will—you didn't!"

"I did," he said. "She had rhymed 'William' with 'million,' as in 'You will never know, sweet William / How many are the million / ways in which I love you.' It had to be stopped."

"What happened?"

"Oh, Tatiana ran out of the room in tears, and Gabriel leaped onto the stage and attempted to strangle me. Gideon simply stood there with his arms crossed. You'll notice that's all he ever does."

"I suppose Gabriel didn't succeed," said Tessa. "In strangling you, I mean."

"Not before I broke his arm," said Will with relish. "So there you are. That's why he hates me. I humiliated his sister in public, and what he won't mention is that I humiliated him, too. He thought he could best me easily. I'd had little formal training, and I'd heard him call me 'very nearly a mundane' behind my back. Instead I beat him hollow—snapped his arm, in fact. It was certainly a more pleasant sound than Elise banging away on the spinet."

Tessa rubbed her gloved hands together to warm them, and sighed. She wasn't sure what to think. It was hardly the story of seduction and betrayal she had expected, but neither did it show Will in an admirable light.

"Sophie says she's married now," she said. "Tatiana. She's just getting back from traveling the Continent with her new husband."

"I am sure she is as dull and stupid now as she was then." Will sounded as if he might fall asleep. He thumbed the curtain closed, and they were in darkness. Tessa could hear his breath, feel the warmth of him sitting across from her. She could see why a proper young lady would never ride in a carriage with a gentleman not related to her. There was something oddly intimate about it. Of course, she had broken the rules for proper young ladies what felt like long ago, now.

"Will," she said again.

"The lady has another question. I can hear it in her tone. Will you never have done asking questions, Tess?"

"Not until I get all the answers I want," she said. "Will, if warlocks are made by having one demon parent and one human parent, what happens if one of those parents is a Shadowhunter?"

"A Shadowhunter would never allow that to happen," said Will flatly.

"But in the *Codex* it says that most warlocks are the result of—of a violation," Tessa said, her voice hitching on the ugly word, "or shape-changer demons taking on the form of a loved one and completing the seduction by a trick. Jem told me Shadowhunter blood is always dominant. The *Codex* says the offspring of Shadowhunters and werewolves, or faeries, are always Shadowhunters. So could not the angel blood in a Shadowhunter cancel out that which was demonic, and produce—"

"What it produces is nothing." Will tugged at the window curtain. "The child would be born dead. They always are. Stillborn, I mean. The offspring of a demon and a Shadowhunter parent is death." In the little light he looked at her. "Why do you want to know these things?"

"I want to know what I am," she said. "I believe I am some . . . combination that has not been seen before. Part faerie, or part—"

"Have you ever thought of transforming yourself into one of your parents?" Will asked. "Your mother, or father? It would give you access to their memories, wouldn't it?"

"I have thought of it. Of course I have. But I have nothing of my father's or mother's. Everything that was packed in my trunks for the voyage here was discarded by the Dark Sisters."

"What about your angel necklace?" Will asked. "Wasn't that your mother's?"

Tessa shook her head. "I tried. I—I could reach nothing of her in it. It has been mine so long, I think, that what made it hers has evaporated, like water."

Will's eyes gleamed in the shadows. "Perhaps you are a clockwork girl. Perhaps Mortmain's warlock father built you, and now Mortmain seeks the secret of how to create such a perfect facsimile of life when all he can build are hideous monstrosities. Perhaps all that beats beneath your chest is a heart made of metal."

Tessa drew in a breath, feeling momentarily dizzy. His soft voice was so convincing, and yet— "No," she said sharply. "You forget, I remember my childhood. Mechanical creatures do not change or grow. Nor would that explain my ability."

"I know," said Will with a grin that flashed white in the darkness. "I only wanted to see if I could convince *you*."

Tessa looked at him steadily. "I am not the one who has no heart."

It was too dark in the carriage for her to tell, but she sensed that he flushed, darkly. Before he could say anything in response, the wheels came to a jerking halt. They had arrived.

12

Masquerade

So now I have sworn to bury
All this dead body of hate,
I feel so free and so clear
By the loss of that dead weight,
That I should grow light-headed, I fear,
Fantastically merry;
But that her brother comes, like a blight
On my fresh hope, to the Hall to-night.
—Alfred, Lord Tennyson, "Maud"

Cyril had paused the carriage outside the gates of the property, under the shade of a leafy oak tree. The Lightwoods' country house in Chiswick, just outside London proper, was massive, built in the Palladian style, with soaring pillars and multiple staircases. The radiance of the moon made everything pearlescent like the inside of an oyster shell. The stone of the house seemed to gleam silver, while the gate that ran around the property had the sheen of black oil. None of the lights in the house seemed to be illuminated—the place was as dark as pitch and grave-silent, the vast grounds stretching all around it, down to the edge of a meander in the Thames River, unlit and deserted. Tessa began to wonder if they had made a mistake in coming here.

As Will left the carriage, helping her down after him, his head turned, his fine mouth hardening. "Do you smell that? Demonic witchcraft. Its stink is on the air."

Tessa made a face. She could smell nothing unusual—in fact, this far out of the city center, the air seemed cleaner than it had near the Institute. She could smell wet leaves and dirt. She looked over at Will, his face raised to the moonlight, and wondered what weapons lay concealed under his closely fitted frock coat. His hands were sheathed in white gloves, his starched shirtfront immaculate. With the mask, he could have been an illustration of a handsome highwayman in a penny dreadful.

Tessa bit her lip. "Are you certain? The house looks deadly quiet. As if no one were home. Could we be wrong?"

He shook his head. "There is powerful magic at work here. Something stronger than a glamour. A true ward. Someone very much does not want us to know what is happening here tonight." He glanced down at the invitation in her hand, shrugged, and went up to the gate. There was a bell there, and he rang it, the noise jangling Tessa's already stretched nerves. She glared at him. He grinned. "*Caelum denique*, angel," he said, and melted away into the shadows, just as the gate before her opened.

A hooded figure stood before her. Her first thought was of the Silent Brothers, but their robes were the color of parchment, and the figure that stood before her was robed in the color of black smoke. The hood hid its face completely. Wordlessly she held out her invitation.

The hand that took it from her was gloved. For a moment the hidden face regarded the invitation. Tessa could not help but fidget. In any ordinary circumstance, a young lady attending a ball alone would be so improper as to be scandalous. But this was no ordinary circumstance. At last, a voice issued from beneath the hood:

"Welcome, Miss Lovelace."

It was a gritty voice, a voice like skin being scraped over a rough, tearing surface. Tessa's spine prickled, and she was glad she could not see beneath the hood. The figure returned the invitation to her and stepped back, gesturing her inside; she followed, forcing herself not to look around to see if Will was following.

She was led around the side of the house, down a narrow garden path. The gardens extended for a good distance out around the house, silvery-green in the moonlight. There was a circular black ornamental pond, with a white marble bench beside it, and low hedges, carefully clipped, running alongside neat paths. The path she was on ended at a tall and narrow entrance set into the house's side. A strange symbol was carved into the door. It seemed to shift and change as Tessa looked at it, making her eyes hurt. She looked away as her hooded companion opened the door and gestured for her to go inside.

She entered the house, and the door slammed behind her. She turned just as it shut, catching a glimpse, she thought, of the face beneath the hood. She thought she had seen something very like a cluster of red eyes in the center of a dark oval, like the eyes of a spider. She caught her breath as the door clicked shut and she was plunged into darkness.

As she reached, blindly, for the handle of the door, light sprang up all around her. She was standing at the foot of a long, narrow staircase that led upward. Torches burning with a greenish flame—not witchlight—ran up the sides of the stairs.

At the top of the stairs was a door. Another symbol was painted on this one. Tessa felt her mouth go even dryer. It was the *ouroboros*, the double serpent. The symbol of the Pandemonium Club.

For a moment she felt frozen with fear. The symbol brought bleak memories rushing back: the Dark House; the Sisters torturing her, trying to force her to Change; Nate's betrayal. She wondered what Will had said to her in Latin before he had vanished. "Courage," no doubt, or some variant of that. She thought of Jane Eyre, bravely facing down the angry Mr. Rochester; Catherine Earnshaw, who when mauled by a savage dog "did not yell out—no! she would have scorned to do it." And lastly she thought of Boadicea, who Will had told her was "braver than any man."

It's just a ball, Tessa, she told herself, and reached for the knob. *Just a party.*

She had never been to a ball before, of course. She knew only a little of what to expect, and all of that was from books. In Jane Austen's books the characters were constantly waiting for there to be a ball, or arranging a ball, and often an entire village seemed to be involved in the planning and location of the ball. Whereas in other books, such as *Vanity Fair*, they were grand backdrops against which scheming and plotting occurred. She knew that there would be a dressing room for the ladies, where she could leave her shawl, and one for the men, where they could safely dispose of hats, overcoats, and walking sticks. There ought to be a dance card for her, where the names of the men who had asked her to dance could be marked down. It was rude to dance more than a few dances in a row with the same gentleman. There should be a grand, beautifully decorated ballroom, and a smaller refreshment room, where there would be iced drinks and sandwiches and biscuits and tipsy cake . . .

But it was not quite like that. As the door closed behind her, Tessa found no servants hurrying to greet her, to guide her to the ladies' dressing room and offer to take her shawl or assist her with a missing button. Instead a wash of noise and music and light struck her like a wave. She stood at the entrance to a room so grand, it was hard to believe that it fit somehow into the Lightwoods' house. A great crystal chandelier hung from the ceiling; it was only after looking at it for several moments that Tessa realized it was shaped like a spider, with eight dangling "legs," each of which held a collection of massive tapers. The walls, what she could see of them, were a very dark blue, and running all along the side that faced the river were French windows, some propped open to catch the breeze, for the room, despite the cool weather outside, was stifling. Beyond the windows were curved stone balconies, looking out over a view of the city. The walls were largely obscured by great swathes of shimmering fabric, loops and whorls of it hanging over the windows and moving in the faint breeze. The fabric was figured with all manner of patterns, woven in gold; the same shimmering, shifting patterns that had hurt Tessa's eyes downstairs.

The room was crowded with people. Well, not quite *people*,

exactly. The majority looked human enough. She caught sight also of the dead white faces of vampires, and a few of the violet and red-hued ifrits, all dressed in the height of fashion. Most, though not all, of the attendees wore masks—elaborate contraptions of gold and black, beaked Plague Doctor masks with tiny spectacles, red devil masks complete with horns. Some were bare-faced, though, including a group of women whose hair was muted tints of lavender, green, and violet. Tessa did not think they were dyes, either, and they wore their hair loose, like nymphs in paintings. Their clothes were scandalously loose as well. They were clearly uncorseted, dressed in flowing fabrics of velvet, tulle, and satin.

In and among the human guests darted figures of all sizes and shapes. There was a man, far too tall and thin to *be* a man, dressed in topcoat and tails, looming over a young woman in a green cloak whose red hair shone like a copper penny. Creatures that looked like great dogs roamed among the guests, their yellow eyes wide and watchful. They had rows of spikes along their backs, like drawings of exotic animals she had seen in books. A dozen or so little goblin creatures screeched and chattered to one another in an incomprehensible language. They appeared to be fighting over some foodstuff—what looked like a torn-apart frog. Tessa swallowed down bile and turned—

And saw them, where she had not before. Her mind had perhaps dismissed them as decorations, suits of armor, but they were not. Automatons lined the walls, silent and motionless. They were human in shape, like the coachman who had belonged to the Dark Sisters, and wore the livery of the Lightwood household, each with a patterned *ouroboros* over its left breast. Their faces were blank and featureless, like children's sketches that had not been filled in.

Someone caught her by the shoulders. Her heart gave a great leap of fear— *She had been discovered!* As every muscle in her body tightened, a light, familiar voice said:

"I thought you'd never get here, Jessie dear."

She turned and looked up into the face of her brother.

The last time Tessa had seen Nate, he had been bruised and bloodied, snarling at her in a corridor of the Institute, a knife in his hand. He had been a terrible mixture of frightening and pathetic and horrifying all at once.

This Nate was quite different. He smiled down at her—Jessamine was so much shorter than she was; it was odd not to reach to her brother's chin, but rather to his chest—with vivid blue eyes. His fair hair was brushed and clean, his skin unmarked by bruises. He wore an elegant dress coat and a black shirtfront that set off his fair good looks. His gloves were spotlessly white.

This was Nate as he had always dreamed of being—rich-looking, elegant, and sophisticated. A sense of contentment oozed from him—less contentment, Tessa had to admit, than self-satisfaction. He looked like Church did after he had killed a mouse.

Nate chuckled. "What is it, Jess? You look as if you've seen a ghost."

I have. The ghost of the brother I once cared about. Tessa reached for Jessamine, for the imprint of Jessamine in her mind. Again it felt as if she were passing her hands through poisonous water, unable to grasp anything solid. "I—a sudden fear came over me, that you would not be here," she said.

This time his laugh was tender. "And miss a chance to see you? Don't be a foolish girl." He glanced around, smiling. "Lightwood should lay himself out to impress the Magister more often." He held out a hand to her. "Would you do me the honor of favoring me with a dance, Jessie?"

Jessie. Not "Miss Lovelace." Any doubt Tessa might have had that their attachment was serious indeed was gone. She forced her lips into a smile. "Of course."

The orchestra—a collection of small purple-skinned men dressed in silvery netting—was playing a waltz. Nate took her hand and drew her out onto the floor.

Thank God, Tessa thought. Thank God she'd had years of her brother swinging her around the living room of their tiny flat in New York. She knew exactly how he danced, how to fit her movements to his, even in this smaller, unfamiliar body. Of course, he had never looked down at her like this—tenderly, with lips slightly parted. Dear God, what if he *kissed* her? She had not thought of the possibility. She would be sick all over his shoes if he did. *Oh, God,* she prayed. *Let him not try.*

She spoke rapidly, "I had dreadful trouble sneaking out of the Institute tonight," she said. "That little wretch Sophie nearly found the invitation."

Nate's grip tightened on her. "But she didn't, did she?"

There was a warning in his voice. Tessa sensed she was already close to a serious gaffe. She tried a quick glance around the room— Oh, *where* was Will? What had he said? *Even if you don't see me, I'll be there?* But she had never felt so much on her own.

With a deep breath she tossed her head in her best imitation of Jessamine. "Do you take me for a fool? Of course not. I rapped her skinny wrist with my mirror, and she dropped it immediately. Besides, she probably can't even read."

"Truly," said Nate, relaxing visibly, "they could have found you a lady's maid who more befits a lady. One who speaks French, can sew . . ."

"Sophie can sew," Tessa said automatically, and could have slapped herself. "Passably," she amended, and batted her eyelashes up at Nate. "And how have you been keeping since the last time we saw each other?" *Not that I have the slightest idea when that might have been.*

"Very well. The Magister continues to favor me."

"He is wise," Tessa breathed. "He recognizes an invaluable treasure when he sees one."

Nate touched her face lightly with a gloved hand. Tessa willed herself not to stiffen. "All down to you, my darling. My veritable little mine of information." He moved closer to her. "I see you wore the dress I asked you to," he whispered. "Ever since you described how you wore it to your last Christmas ball, I have yearned to see you in it. And may I say that you dazzle the eyes?"

Tessa's stomach felt as if it were trying to force its way up into her throat. Her eyes darted around the room again. With a lurch of recognition, she saw Gideon Lightwood, cutting a fine figure in his evening dress, though he stood stiffly against one of the walls as if plastered there. Only his eyes moved around the room. Gabriel was wandering to and fro, a glass of what looked like lemonade in his hand, his eyes glowing with curiosity. She saw him go up to one of the girls with long lavender hair and begin a conversation. *So much for any hope that the boys did not know what their father was up to,* she thought, glancing away from Gabriel in irritation. And then she saw Will.

He was leaning against the wall opposite her, between two empty chairs. Despite his mask she felt as if she could see directly into his eyes. As if he were standing close enough to touch. She would have half-expected him to look amused at her predicament, but he did not; he looked tense, and furious, and . . .

"God, I'm jealous of every other man who looks at you," Nate said. "You should be looked at only by me."

Good Lord, Tessa thought. Did this line of talk really work on most women? If her brother had come to her with the aim of asking her advice on these pearls, she would have told him straight off that he sounded like an idiot. Though perhaps she only thought he sounded like an idiot because he was her brother. And despicable. Information, she thought. I must get information and then get away from him, before I really am sick.

She looked for Will again, but he was gone, as if he had never been there. Still, she believed him now that he was *somewhere*, watching her, even if she couldn't see him. She plucked up her nerve, and said, "Really, Nate? Sometimes I fear you value me only for the information I can give you."

For a moment he stopped and was stock-still, almost jerking her out of the dance. "Jessie! How can you even think such a thing? You know how I adore you." He looked at her reproachfully as they began to move to the music again. "It is true that your connection to the Nephilim of the Institute has been invaluable. Without you we would never have known they were going to York, for instance. But I thought you knew that you were helping me because we are working toward a future together. When I have become the Magister's right hand, darling, think how I will be able to provide for you."

Tessa laughed nervously. "You're right, Nate. It's only that I get frightened sometimes. What if Charlotte were to find out I was spying for you? What would they do to me?"

Nate swung her around easily. "Oh, nothing, darling; you've said it yourself, they're cowards." He looked past her and raised an eyebrow. "Benedict, up to his old tricks," he said. "Rather disgusting."

Tessa looked around and saw Benedict Lightwood leaning back on a scarlet velvet sofa near the orchestra. He was coatless, a glass of red wine in one hand, his eyes half-lidded. Sprawled across his chest, Tessa saw to her shock, was a woman—or at least it had the form of a woman. Long black hair worn loose, a low-cut black velvet gown—and the heads of little serpents poking out from her eyes, hissing. As Tessa watched, one of them extended a long, forked tongue and licked the side of Benedict Lightwood's face.

"That's a demon," Tessa breathed, forgetting for a moment to be Jessamine. "Isn't it?"

Fortunately Nate seemed to find nothing odd about the question. "Of course it is, silly bunny. That's what Benedict fancies. Demon women."

Will's voice echoed in Tessa's ears, *I would be surprised if some of the elder Lightwood's nocturnal visits to certain houses in Shadwell haven't left him with a nasty case of demon pox.* "Oh, ugh," she said.

"Indeed," said Nate. "Ironic, considering the high-and-mighty manner in which the Nephilim conduct themselves.

I ask myself often why Mortmain favors him so and wishes to see him installed in the Institute so badly." Nate sounded peevish.

Tessa had already guessed as much, but the knowledge that Mortmain was most assuredly behind Benedict's fierce determination to take the Institute from Charlotte still felt like a blow. "I just don't see," she said, trying her best to adopt Jessie's lightly peevish demeanor, "what *use* it will be to the Magister. It's just a big stuffy old building. . . ."

Nate laughed indulgently. "It's not the building, silly thing. It's the position. The head of the London Institute is one of the most powerful Shadowhunters in England, and the Magister controls Benedict as if he were a puppet. Using him, he can destroy the Council from within, while the automaton army destroys them from without." He spun her expertly as the dance required; only Tessa's years of practice dancing with Nate kept her from falling over, so distracted was she by shock. "Besides, it's not *quite* true that the Institute contains nothing of value. Access to the Great Library alone will be invaluable for the Magister. Not to mention the weapons room . . ."

"And Tessa." She clamped down on her voice so it wouldn't tremble.

"Tessa?"

"Your sister. The Magister still wants her, doesn't he?"

For the first time Nate looked at her with a puzzled surprise. "We've been over this, Jessamine," he said. "Tessa will be arrested for illegal possession of articles of dark magic, and sent to the Silent City. Benedict will bring her forth from there and deliver her to the Magister. It is all part of whatever bargain they struck, though what Benedict is getting from it is not clear to me yet. It must be something quite significant, or he would not be so willing to turn on his own."

Arrested? Possession of articles of dark magic? Tessa's head spun.

Nate's hand slipped around the back of her neck. He was wearing gloves, but Tessa couldn't rid herself of the feeling that something slimy was touching her skin. "My little Jessie," he murmured. "You behave almost as if you've forgotten your own part in this. You *did* hide the Book of the White in my sister's room as we asked you to, did you not?"

"Of—of course I did. I was only joking, Nate."

"That's my good girl." He was leaning closer. He was definitely going to kiss her. It was most improper, but then nothing about this place could be considered proper. In a state of absolute horror, Tessa sputtered:

"Nate—I feel dizzy—as if I might faint. I think it's the heat. If you could fetch me a lemonade?"

He looked down at her for a moment, his mouth tight with bottled annoyance, but Tessa knew he could not refuse. No gentleman would. He straightened up, brushed off his cuffs, and smiled. "Of course," he said with a bow. "Let me help you to a seat first."

She protested, but his hand was already on her elbow, guiding her toward one of the chairs lined up along the walls. He settled her into it and vanished into the crowd. She watched him go, trembling all over. *Dark magic.* She felt sick, and angry. She wanted to slap her brother, shake him till he told her the rest of the truth, but she knew she couldn't.

"You must be Tessa Gray," said a soft voice at her elbow. "You look just like your mother."

Tessa nearly jumped out of her skin. At her side stood a tall slender woman with long, unbound hair the color of lavender petals. Her skin was a pale blue, her dress a long and floating confection of gossamer and tulle. Her feet were bare, and in between her toes were thin webs like a spider's, a darker blue than her skin. Tessa's hands went to her face in sudden horror—was she losing her disguise?—but the blue woman laughed.

"I didn't mean to make you fearful of your illusion, little one. It is still in place. It is just that my kind can see through it. All this"—she gestured vaguely at Tessa's blond hair, her white dress and pearls—"is like the vapor of a cloud, and you the sky beyond it. Did you know your mother had eyes just like yours, gray sometimes and blue at others?"

Tessa found her voice. "Who are you?"

"Oh, my kind doesn't like to give our names, but you can call me whatever you like. You can invent a lovely name for me. Your mother used to call me Hyacinth."

"The blue flower," Tessa said faintly. "How did you know my mother? You don't look any older than me—"

"After our youth, my kind does not age or die. Nor will you. Lucky girl! I hope you appreciate the service done you."

Tessa shook her head in bewilderment. "Service? What service? Are you speaking of Mortmain? *Do you know what I am?*"

"Do you know what *I* am?"

Tessa thought of the *Codex*. "A faerie?" she guessed.

"And do you know what a changeling is?"

Tessa shook her head.

"Sometimes," Hyacinth confided, dropping her voice to a whisper, "when our faerie blood has grown weak and thin, we will find our way into a human home, and take the best, the prettiest, and the plumpest child—and, quick as a wink, replace the babe with a sickly one of our own. While the human child grows tall and strong in our lands, the human family will find itself burdened with a dying creature fearful of cold iron. Our bloodline is strengthened—"

"Why bother?" Tessa demanded. "Why not just steal the human child and leave nothing in its place?"

Hyacinth's dark blue eyes widened. "Why, because that would not be *fair*," she said. "And it would breed suspicion among the mundanes. They are stupid, but there are many of them. It does not do to rouse their ire. That is when they come with iron and torches." She shuddered.

"Just a moment," Tessa said. "Are you telling me I'm a *changeling*?"

Hyacinth bubbled over with giggles. "Of course not! What a ridiculous thought!" She held her hands to her heart as she laughed, and Tessa saw that her fingers, too, were bound together with blue webbing. Suddenly she smiled, showing glittering teeth. "There's a very good-looking boy staring over here," she said. "As handsome as a faerie lord! I should leave you to your business." She winked, and before Tessa could protest, Hyacinth melted back into the crowd.

Shaken, Tessa turned, expecting the "good-looking boy" to be Nate—but it was Will, leaning against the wall beside her. The moment her eyes found him, he turned and began studiously examining the dance floor. "What did that faerie woman want?"

"I don't know," Tessa said, exasperated. "To tell me I'm *not* a changeling, apparently."

"Well, that's good. Process of elimination." Tessa had to

admit, Will was doing a good job of somehow blending in with the dark curtains behind him, as if he were not there at all. It must have been a Shadowhunter talent. "And what news from your brother?"

She gripped her hands together, looking at the floor while she spoke. "Jessamine's been spying for Nate all this time. I don't know how long exactly. She's been telling him everything. She thinks he's in love with her."

Will looked unsurprised. "Do *you* think he's in love with her?"

"I think Nate cares only about himself," said Tessa. "There's worse, too. Benedict Lightwood is working for Mortmain. That is why he is scheming to get the Institute. So the Magister can have it. And have *me*. Nate knows all about it, of course. He doesn't care." Tessa looked at her hands again. Jessamine's hands. Small and delicate in their fine white kid gloves. *Oh, Nate*, she thought. *Aunt Harriet used to call him her blue-eyed boy.*

"I expect that was before he killed her," said Will. Only then did Tessa realize she had spoken aloud. "And there he is again," he added, in a mutter, under his breath. Tessa glanced out at the crowd and saw Nate, his fair hair like a beacon, coming toward her. In his hand was a glass of sparkling golden liquid. She turned to tell Will to hurry away, but he had already vanished.

"Fizzy lemonade," said Nate, coming up to her and thrusting the glass into her hand. The ice-cold sides felt good against the heat of her skin. She took a sip; despite everything, it was delicious.

Nate stroked her hair back from her forehead. "Now, you were saying," he said. "You *did* hide the book in my sister's room . . ."

"Yes, just as you told me to do," Tessa fibbed. "She suspects nothing, of course."

"I should hope not."

"Nate . . ."

"Yes?"

"Do you know what the Magister intends to do with your sister?"

"I've told you, she isn't my sister." Nate's voice was clipped. "And I've no idea what he plans to do with her, nor any interest. *My* plans are all for my—*our* future together. I should hope that you are as dedicated?" Tessa thought of Jessamine, sitting sullenly in the room with the other Shadowhunters while they shuffled through papers about Mortmain; Jessamine falling asleep at the table rather than leave when they were discussing plans with Ragnor Fell. And Tessa pitied her even as she hated Nate, hated him so much it felt like fire in her throat. *I've told you, she isn't my sister.*

Tessa let her eyes widen, her lip tremble. "I'm doing the best I can, Nate," she said. "Don't you believe me?"

She felt a faint sense of triumph as she watched him visibly beat back his annoyance. "Of course, darling. Of course." He examined her face. "Are you feeling better? Shall we dance again?"

She clutched the glass in her hand. "Oh, I don't know . . ."

"Of course," Nate chuckled, "they do say a gentleman should dance only the first set or two with his wife."

Tessa froze. It was as if time had stopped: Everything in the room seemed to freeze along with her, even the smirk on Nate's face.

Wife?

He and Jessamine were *married?*

"Angel?" said Nate, his voice sounding as if it were coming from far away. "Are you all right? You've gone white as a sheet."

"Mr. Gray." A dull, mechanical voice spoke from behind Nate's shoulder. It was one of the blank-faced automatons, holding out a silver tray on which was a folded piece of paper. "A message for you."

Nate turned in surprise and plucked the paper from the tray; Tessa watched as he unfolded it, read it, cursed, and stuffed it into his coat pocket. "My, my," he said. "A note from himself." *He must mean the Magister*, Tessa thought. "I'm needed apparently. A dreadful bore, but what can you do?" He took her hand and raised her to her feet, then leaned in for a chaste kiss on the cheek. "Speak to Benedict; he'll make sure you're escorted back out to the carriage, *Mrs. Gray*." He spoke the last two words in a whisper.

Tessa nodded numbly.

"Good girl," Nate said. Then he turned and vanished into the crowd, followed by the automaton. Tessa stared after them both dizzily. It must be the shock, she thought, but everything in the room had begun to look a little—peculiar. It was as if she could see each individual ray of light sparking off the crystals of the chandelier. The effect was beautiful, if strange and a little dizzying.

"Tessa." It was Will, evolving effortlessly into the space beside her. She turned to look at him. He looked flushed, as if he had been running—another beautiful, strange effect, she thought, the black hair and mask, the blue eyes and fair skin, and the flush across his high cheekbones. It was like looking at a painting. "I see your brother got the note."

"Ah." Everything clicked into place. "You sent it."

"I did." Looking pleased with himself, Will plucked the glass of lemonade out of her hand, drained the remainder, and set it on a windowsill. "I had to get him out of here. And we should probably follow suit, before he realizes the note is a falsity and he returns. Though I did direct him to Vauxhall; it'll take him ages to get there and back, so we're likely safe—" He broke off, and she could hear sudden alarm in his voice. "Tess—Tessa? Are you all right?"

"Why do you ask?" Her voice echoed in her own ears.

"Look." He reached out and caught a swinging tendril of her hair, pulling it forward so she could see it. She stared. Dark brown, not fair. Her own hair. Not Jessamine's.

"Oh, God." She put a hand to her face, recognizing the familiar tingles of the Change as they began to wash over her. "How long—"

"Not long. You were Jessamine when I sat down." He caught hold of her hand. "Come along. Quickly." He began to stride toward the exit, but it was a long way across the ballroom, and Tessa's whole body was twitching and shivering with the Change. She gasped as it bit into her like teeth. She saw Will whip his head around, alarmed; felt him catch her as she stumbled, and half-carry her forward. The room swung around her. *I can't faint. Don't let me faint.*

A wash of cool air struck her face. She realized distantly that Will had swung them through a pair of French doors and they were out on a small stone balcony, one of many overlooking the gardens. She moved away from him, tearing the gold mask from her face, and nearly collapsed against the stone balustrade. After slamming the doors behind them, Will turned and hurried over to her, laying a hand lightly on her back. "Tessa?"

"I'm all right." She was glad for the stone railing beneath her hands, its solidity and hardness inexpressibly reassuring. The chilly air was lessening her dizziness too. Glancing down at herself, she could see she had become fully Tessa again. The white dress was now a full few inches too short, and the lacing so tight that her décolletage spilled up and over the low neckline. She knew some women laced themselves tight just to get this effect, but it was rather shocking seeing so much of her own skin on display.

She looked sideways at Will, glad for the cold air keeping her cheeks from flaming. "I just—I don't know what happened. That's never happened to me before, losing the Change without noticing like that. It must have been the surprise of it all. They're married, did you know that? Nate and Jessamine. Married. Nate was never the marrying sort. And he doesn't love her. I can tell. He doesn't love anyone but himself. He never has."

"Tess," Will said again, gently this time. He was leaning against the railing too, facing her. They were only a very little distance apart. Above them the moon swam through the clouds, a white boat on a still, black sea.

She closed her mouth, aware that she had been babbling. "I'm sorry," she said softly, looking away.

Almost hesitantly he laid his hand against her cheek, turning her to face him. He had stripped off his glove, and his skin was bare against hers. "There's nothing to be sorry about," he said. "You were brilliant in there, Tessa. Not a step out of place." She felt her face warm beneath his cool fingers, and was amazed. Was this Will speaking? *Will*, who had spoken to her on the roof of the Institute as if she were so much rubbish? "You did love your brother once, didn't you? I could see your face as he was speaking to you, and I wanted to kill him for breaking your heart."

You broke my heart, she wanted to say. Instead she said, "Some part of me misses him as—as you miss your sister. Even though I know what he is, I miss the brother I thought I had. He was my only family."

"The Institute is your family now." His voice was incredibly gentle. Tessa looked at him in amazement. Gentleness was not something she would ever have associated with Will. But it was there, in the touch of his hand on her cheek, in the softness of his voice, in his eyes when he looked at her. It was the way she had always dreamed a boy would look at her. But she had never dreamed up someone as beautiful as Will, not in all her imaginings. In the moonlight the curve of his mouth looked pure and perfect, his eyes behind the mask nearly black.

"We should go back inside," she said, in a half whisper. She did not want to go back inside. She wanted to stay here, with Will achingly close, almost leaning into her. She could feel the heat that radiated from his body. His dark hair fell around the mask, into his eyes, tangling with his long eyelashes. "We have only a little time—"

She took a step forward—and stumbled into Will, who caught her. She froze—and then her arms crept around him, her fingers lacing themselves behind his neck. Her face was pressed against his throat, his soft hair under her fingers. She closed her eyes, shutting out the dizzying world, the light beyond the French windows, the glow of the sky. She wanted to be here with Will, cocooned in this moment, inhaling the clean sharp scent of him, feeling the beat of his heart against hers, as steady and strong as the pulse of the ocean.

She felt him inhale. "Tess," he said. "Tess, look at me."

She raised her eyes to his, slow and unwilling, braced for anger or coldness—but his gaze was fixed on hers, his dark blue eyes somber beneath their thick black lashes, and they were stripped of all their usual cool, aloof distance. They were as clear as glass and full of desire. And more than desire—a tenderness she had never seen in them before, had never even associated with Will Herondale. That, more than anything else, stopped her protest as he raised his hands and methodically began to take the pins from her hair, one by one.

This is madness, she thought, as the first pin rattled to the ground. They should be running, fleeing this place. Instead she stood, wordless, as Will cast Jessamine's pearl clasps aside as if they were so much paste jewelry. Her own long, curling dark hair fell down around her shoulders, and Will slid his hands into it. She heard him exhale as he did so, as if he had been holding his breath for months and had only just let it out. She stood as if mesmerized as he gathered her hair in his hands, draping it over one of her shoulders, winding her curls between his fingers. "My Tessa," he said, and this time she did not tell him that she was not his.

"Will," she whispered as he reached up and unlocked her hands from around his neck. He drew her gloves off, and they joined her mask and Jessie's pins on the stone floor of the balcony. He pulled off his own mask next and cast it aside, running his hands through his damp black hair, pushing it back from his forehead. The lower edge of the mask had left marks across his high cheekbones, like light scars, but when she reached to touch them, he gently caught at her hands and pressed them down.

"No," he said. "Let me touch you first. I have wanted . . ."

She did not say no. Instead she stood, wide-eyed, gazing up at him as his fingertips traced her temples, then her cheekbones, then—softly despite their rough calluses—outlined the shape of her mouth as if he meant to commit it to memory. The gesture made her heart spin like a top inside her chest. His eyes remained fixed on her, as dark as the bottom of the ocean, wondering, dazed with discovery.

She stood still as his fingertips left her mouth and trailed a path down her throat, stopping at her pulse, slipping to the silk ribbon at her collar and pulling at one end of it; her eyelids fluttered half-closed as the bow came apart and his warm hand covered her bare collarbone. She remembered once, on the *Main*, how the ship had passed through a patch of strangely shining ocean, and how the *Main* had carved a path of fire through the water, trailing sparks in its wake. It was as if Will's hands did the same to her skin. She burned where he touched her, and could feel where his fingers had been even when they had moved on. His hands moved lightly but lower, over the bodice of her dress, following the curves of her breasts. Tessa gasped, even as his hands slid to grip her waist and draw her toward him, pulling their bodies together until there was not a millimeter of space between them.

He bent to put his cheek against hers. His breath against her ear made her shudder with each deliberately spoken word. "I have wanted to do this," he said, "every moment of every hour of every day that I have been with you since the day I met you. But you know that. You *must* know. Don't you?"

She looked up at him, lips parted in bewilderment. "Know what?" she said, and Will, with a sigh of something like defeat, kissed her.

His lips were soft, so soft. He had kissed her before, wildly and desperately and tasting of blood, but this was different. This was deliberate and unhurried, as if he were speaking to her silently, saying with the brush of his lips on hers what he could not say in words. He traced slow, glancing butterfly kisses across her mouth, each as measured as the beat of a heart, each saying she was precious, irreplaceable, wanted. Tessa could no longer keep her hands at her sides. She reached to cup the back of his neck, to tangle her fingers in the dark silky waves of his hair, to feel his pulse hammering against her palms.

His grip on her was firm as he explored her mouth thoroughly with his. He tasted of the sparkling lemonade, sweet and tingling. The movement of his tongue as he flicked it lightly across her lips sent delicious shudders through her whole body; her bones melted and her nerves seared. She yearned to pull him against her—but he was being so gentle with her, so unbelievably gentle, though she could feel how much he wanted her in the trembling of his hands, the hammering of his heart against hers. Surely someone who did not care even a little could not behave with such gentleness. All the pieces inside her that had felt broken and jagged when she had looked at Will these past few weeks began to knit together and heal. She felt light, as if she could float.

"Will," she whispered against his mouth. She wanted him closer to her so badly, it was like an ache, a painful hot ache that spread out from her stomach to speed her heart and knot her hands in his hair and set her skin to burning. "Will, you need not be so careful. I will not break."

"Tessa," he groaned against her mouth, but she could hear the hesitation in his voice. She nipped gently at his lips, teasing him, and his breath caught. His hands flattened against the small of her back, pressing her to him, as his self-control slipped and his gentleness began to blossom into a more demanding urgency. Their kisses grew deeper and deeper still, as if they could breathe each other, consume each other, devour each other whole. Tessa knew she was making whimpering sounds in the back of her throat; that Will was pushing her back, back against the railing in a way that should have hurt but oddly did not; that his hands were at the bodice of Jessamine's dress, crushing the delicate fabric roses. Distantly Tessa heard the knob of the French doors rattle; they opened, and still she and Will clung together, as if nothing else mattered.

There was a murmur of voices, and someone said, "I told you, Edith. That's what happens when you drink the pink drinks," in a disapproving tone. The doors shut again, and Tessa heard footsteps going away. She broke away from Will.

"Oh, my heavens," she said, breathless. "How humiliating—"

"I don't care." He pulled her back to him, nuzzled the side of her neck, his face hot against her cold skin. His mouth glanced across hers. "Tess—"

"You keep saying my name," she murmured. She had one hand on his chest, holding him a little bit away, but had no idea how long she could keep it there. Her body ached for him. Time had snapped and lost its meaning. There was only this moment, only Will. She had never felt anything like it, and she wondered if this was what it was like for Nate when he was drunk.

"I love your name. I love the sound of it." He sounded drunk too, his mouth on hers as he spoke so she could feel the delicious movement of his lips. She breathed his breath, inhaling him. Their bodies fit together perfectly, she couldn't help noticing; in Jessie's white satin heeled shoes, she was but a little shorter than he was, and had only to tilt her head back slightly to kiss him. "I have to ask you something. I have to know—"

"So *there* you two are," came a voice from the doorway. "And quite a spectacular display you're making, if I do say so."

They sprang apart. There, standing in the doorway—though Tessa could not remember the sound of the doors having opened—a long cigar held between his thin brown fingers, was Magnus Bane.

"Let me guess," Magnus said, exhaling smoke. It made a white cloud in the shape of a heart that distorted as it drifted away from his mouth, expanding and twisting until it was no longer recognizable. "You had the lemonade."

Tessa and Will, now standing side by side, glanced at each other. It was Tessa who spoke first. "I—yes. Nate brought me some."

"It has a bit of a warlock powder mixed into it," said Magnus. He was wearing all black, with no other ornamentation save on his hands. Each finger bore a ring set with a huge stone of a different color—lemon yellow citrine, green jade, red ruby, blue topaz. "The kind that lowers your inhibitions and makes you do things you would"—he coughed delicately—"not otherwise do."

"Oh," said Will. And then: "Oh." His voice was low. He

turned away, leaning his hands on the balustrade. Tessa felt her face begin to burn.

"Gracious, that's a lot of bosom you're showing," Magnus went on blithely, gesturing toward Tessa with the burning tip of his cigar. "*Tout le monde sur le balcon*, as they say in French," he added, miming a vast terrace jutting out from his chest. "Especially apt, as we are now, in fact, on a balcony."

"Let her alone," said Will. Tessa couldn't see his face; he had his head down. "She didn't know what she was drinking."

Tessa crossed her arms, realized this only intensified the severity of the bosom problem, and dropped them. "This is Jessamine's dress, and she's half my size," she snapped. "I would never go out like this under ordinary circumstances."

Magnus raised his eyebrows. "Changed back into yourself, did you? When the lemonade took effect?"

Tessa scowled. She felt obscurely humiliated—to have been caught kissing Will; to be standing in front of Magnus in something her aunt would have dropped dead to see her in—yet part of her wished Magnus would go away so she could kiss Will again. "What are you doing here, yourself, if I might ask?" she snapped ungraciously. "How did you know *we* were here?"

"I have sources," said Magnus, trailing smoke airily. "I thought you two might be up against it. Benedict Lightwood's parties have a reputation for danger. When I heard you were here—"

"We're well equipped to handle danger," Tessa said.

Magnus eyed her bosom openly. "I can see that," he said. "Armed to the teeth, as it were." Done with his cigar, he flicked it over the balcony railing. "One of Camille's human subjugates was here and recognized Will. He got a message to me, but if one of you was recognized already, what's the chance it could happen again? It's time to make yourselves scarce."

"What do you care if we get out or not?" It was Will, his head still down, his voice muffled.

"You owe me," Magnus said, his voice steely. "I mean to collect."

Will turned on him. Tessa was startled to see the expression on his face. He looked sick and ill. "I should have known that was it."

"You may choose your friends, but not your unlikely saviors," Magnus said cheerfully. "Shall we go, then? Or would you rather stay here and take your chances? You can start up with the kissing where you left off when you get back to the Institute."

Will scowled. "Get us out of here."

Magnus's cat eyes gleamed. He snapped his fingers, and a shower of blue sparks fell around them in a sudden, startling rain. Tessa tensed, expecting them to burn her skin, but she felt only wind rushing past her face. Her hair lifted as a strange energy crackled through her nerves. She heard Will gasp—and then they were standing on one of the stone paths in the garden, near the ornamental pond, the great Lightwood manor rising, silent and dark, above them.

"There," said Magnus in a bored tone. "That wasn't so difficult, was it?"

Will looked at him with no gratitude. "Magic," he muttered.

Magnus threw his hands up. They still crackled with blue energy, like heat lightning. "And just what do you think your precious runes are? *Not* magic?"

"Shush," Tessa said. She was bone-weary suddenly. She

ached where the corset crushed her ribs, and her feet, in Jessamine's too-small shoes, were in agony. "Stop spouting off, the both of you. I think someone's coming."

They all paused, just as a chattering group rounded the corner of the house. Tessa froze. Even in the cloudy moonlight, she could see they were not human. They were not Downworlders, either. It was a group of demons—one a shambling corpse-like figure with black holes for eyes; another half again the size of a man, blue-skinned and dressed in a waistcoat and trousers, but with a barbed tail, lizard's features, and a flat snakelike snout; and another that seemed to be a spinning wheel covered in wet red mouths.

Several things happened at once.

Tessa jammed the back of her hand against her mouth before she could scream. There was no point in running. The demons had already seen them and had come to a dead stop on the path. The smell of rot wafted from them, blotting out the scent of the trees.

Magnus raised his hand, blue fire circling his fingers. He was muttering words under his breath. He looked as discomposed as Tessa had ever seen him.

And Will—Will, whom Tessa had expected to reach for his seraph blades—did something entirely unexpected. He raised a trembling finger, pointed at the blue-skinned demon, and breathed, "*You.*"

The blue-skinned demon blinked. All the demons stood stock-still, looking at one another. There must have been some agreement in place, Tessa thought, to keep them from attacking the humans at the party, but she did not like the way the wet red mouths were licking their lips. "Er," the demon Will had addressed said, in a surprisingly ordinary voice. "I don't recall— That is, I don't think I've had the pleasure of your acquaintance?"

"*Liar!*" Will staggered forward and charged; as Tessa watched in amazement, he barreled past the other demons and threw himself onto the blue demon. It let out a high-pitched shriek. Magnus was watching what was going on with his mouth open. Tessa cried, "Will! *Will!*" but he was rolling over and over on the grass with the blue-skinned creature, which was surprisingly nimble. He had it by the back of its waistcoat, but it tore free and dashed away, streaking across the gardens, Will in hot pursuit.

Tessa took a few steps after them, but her feet were a white-hot agony. Kicking off Jessamine's shoes, she was about to race after Will when she realized the remaining demons were making an angry buzzing noise. They seemed to be addressing Magnus.

"Ah, well, you know," he said, having regained his composure, and he gestured in the direction Will had disappeared in. "Disagreement. Over a woman. It happens."

The buzzing noise increased. It was clear the demons did not believe him.

"Gambling debt?" Magnus suggested. He snapped his fingers, and flame burst up from his palm, bathing the garden in a stark glow. "I suggest you not concern yourselves overmuch with it, gentlemen. Festivities and merriment await you inside." He gestured toward the narrow door that led to the ballroom. "Much more pleasant than what will await you out here if you continue to linger."

That seemed to convince them. The demons moved off,

buzzing and muttering, taking their stench of garbage with them.

Tessa spun around. "Quickly, we have to go after them—"

Magnus reached down and scooped her shoes up off the path. Holding them by their satin ribbons, he said, "Not so quickly, Cinderella. Will's a Shadowhunter. He runs fast. You'll never catch him."

"But you—there must be some magic—"

"*Magic,*" Magnus said, mimicking Will's disgusted tone. "Will's where he has to be, doing what he has to do. His purpose is killing demons, Tessa."

"Do you—not like him?" Tessa asked; it was an odd question, perhaps, but there was something in the way Magnus looked at Will, spoke to Will, that she could not put her finger on.

To her surprise, Magnus took the question seriously. "I do like him," he said, "though rather despite myself. I thought him a pretty bit of poison to start with, but I have come around. There is a soul under all that bravado. And he is really *alive*, one of the most alive people I have ever met. When he feels something, it is as bright and sharp as lightning."

"We all *feel*," Tessa said, thoroughly surprised. Will, feeling more strongly than everyone else? Madder than everyone else, perhaps.

"Not like that," said Magnus. "Trust me, I have lived a long time, and I do know." His look was not without sympathy. "And you will find that feelings fade too, the longer you live. The oldest warlock I ever met had been alive nearly a thousand years and told me he could no longer even remember what love felt like, or hatred, either. I asked him why he did not end his life, and he said he still felt one thing, and that was fear—fear of what lies after death. 'The undiscover'd country from whose bourne no traveller returns.'"

"Hamlet," said Tessa automatically. She was trying to push back thoughts of her own possible immortality. The concept of it was too grand and terrifying to truly encompass, and besides . . . it might not even be true.

"We who are immortal, we are chained to this life by a chain of gold, and we dare not sever it for fear of what lies beyond the drop," said Magnus. "Now come along, and don't begrudge Will his moral duties." He started off down the path, Tessa limping quickly after him in an effort to keep up.

"But he behaved as if he knew that demon—"

"Probably tried to kill it before," said Magnus. "Sometimes they get away."

"But how will he get back to the Institute?" Tessa wailed.

"He's a clever boy. He'll find a way. I'm more concerned with getting *you* back to the Institute before someone notices you're missing and there's the devil of a row." They'd reached the front gates, where the carriage awaited, Cyril resting peacefully in the driver's seat, his hat pulled down over his eyes.

She glared mutinously at Magnus as he swung the carriage door open and reached out a hand to help her up into it. "How do you know Will and I didn't have Charlotte's permission to be here tonight?"

"Do give me more credit than that, darling," he said, and grinned in such an infectious manner that Tessa, with a sigh, gave him her hand. "Now," he said, "I'll take you back to the Institute, and on the way you can tell me all about it."

13

THE MORTAL SWORD

"Take my share of a fickle heart,
Mine of a paltry love:
Take it or leave it as you will,
I wash my hands thereof."
–Christina Rosetti, "Maude Clare"

"Oh, my dear merciful heavens!" said Sophie, starting up from her chair as Tessa opened the door to Jessamine's bedroom. "Miss Tessa, what *happened*?"

"Sophie! Shh!" Tessa waved a warning hand as she shut the door behind her. The room was as she had left it. Her nightgown and dressing gown were folded neatly on a chair, the cracked silver mirror was on the vanity table, and Jessamine—Jessamine was still soundly unconscious, her wrists rope-bound to the posts of the bed. Sophie, seated in a chair by the wardrobe, had clearly been there since Will and Tessa had left; she clutched a hairbrush in one hand (to hit Jessamine with, should she awaken again, Tessa wondered?), and her hazel eyes were huge.

"But miss . . ." Sophie's voice trailed off as Tessa's gaze went to her reflection in the looking glass. Tessa could not help but stare. Her hair had come down, of course, in a tangled mess all over her shoulders, Jessamine's pearl pins gone where Will had flung them; she was shoeless and limping, her white stockings filthy, her gloves gone, and her dress obviously nearly choking her to death. "Was it very dreadful?"

Tessa's mind went suddenly back to the balcony, and Will's arms around her. *Oh, God.* She pushed the thought away and glanced over at Jessamine, still sleeping peacefully. "Sophie, we are going to have to wake Charlotte. We have no choice."

Sophie looked at her with round eyes. Tessa could not blame her; she dreaded rousing Charlotte. Tessa had even pleaded with Magnus to come in with her to help break the news, but he had refused, on the grounds that internecine Shadowhunter dramas had nothing to do with him, and he had a novel to get back to besides.

"Miss—," Sophie protested.

"We must." As quickly as she could, Tessa told Sophie the gist of what had happened that night, leaving out the part with Will on the balcony. No one needed to know about that. "This is beyond us now. We cannot come in over Charlotte's head any longer."

Sophie made no more sound of protest. She laid the hairbrush down on the vanity, stood up, smoothed her skirts, and said, "I will fetch Mrs. Branwell, miss."

Tessa sank into the chair by the bed, wincing as Jessamine's dress pinched her. "I wish you would call me Tessa."

"I know, miss." Sophie left, closing the door quietly behind her.

Magnus was lying on the sofa in the drawing room with his boots up when he heard the commotion. He grinned without moving at the sound of Archer protesting, and Will protesting. Footsteps neared the door. Magnus flipped a page in his poetry book as the door swung open and Will stalked in.

He was barely recognizable. His elegant evening clothes were torn and stained with mud, his coat ripped lengthwise, his boots encrusted with mud. His hair stood up wildly, and his face was raked by dozens of scratches, as if he had been attacked by a dozen cats simultaneously.

"I'm sorry, sir," said Archer despairingly. "He pushed past me."

"Magnus," Will said. He was grinning. Magnus had seen him grin before, but there was real joy in it this time. It transformed Will's face, took it from beautiful but cold to incandescent. "Tell him to let me in."

Magnus waved a hand. "Let him in, Archer."

The human subjugate's gray face twisted, and the door slammed behind Will. "Magnus!" He half-staggered, half-stalked over to the fireplace, where he leaned against the mantel. "You won't believe—"

"Shh," said Magnus, his book still open on his knees. "Listen to this:

I am tired of tears and laughter,
And men that laugh and weep
Of what may come hereafter

For men that sow to reap:
I am weary of days and hours,
Blown buds of barren flowers,
Desires and dreams and powers
And everything but sleep."

"Swinburne," said Will, leaning against the mantel. "Sentimental and overrated."

"*You* don't know what it is to be immortal." Magnus tossed the book aside and sat up. "So what is it you want?"

Will pulled up his sleeve. Magnus swallowed a sound of surprise. Will's forearm bore a long, deep, and bloody gash. Blood braceleted his wrist and dripped from his fingers. Embedded in the gash, like a crystal sunk into the wall of a cave, was a single white tooth.

"What the—," Magnus began.

"Demon tooth," Will said, his breath a little short. "I chased that blue bastard all around Chiswick, but it got away from me—not before it bit me, though. It left this tooth in me. You can use it, right? To summon the demon?" He took hold of the tooth and yanked it free. Even more blood welled up and spilled down his arm, splattering onto the ground.

"Camille's carpet," Magnus protested.

"It's blood," said Will. "She ought to be thrilled."

"Are you all right?" Magnus looked at Will in fascination. "You're bleeding a great deal. Haven't you a stele on your person somewhere? A healing rune—"

"I don't care about healing runes. I care about this." Will dropped the bloody tooth into Magnus's hand. "Find the demon for me. I know you can do it."

Magnus glanced down with a moue of distaste. "I most likely can, but . . ."

The light in Will's face flickered. "But?"

"But not tonight," said Magnus. "It may take me a few days. You'll have to be patient."

Will took a ragged breath. "I can't be patient. Not after tonight. You don't understand—" He staggered then, and caught himself by seizing the mantel. Alarmed, Magnus rose from the sofa.

"Are you all right?"

The color was coming and going in Will's face. His collar was dark with sweat. "I don't know—," he gasped. "The tooth. It might have been poisonous . . ."

His voice trailed off. He slid forward, his eyes rolling up. With an epithet of surprise Magnus caught Will before he could hit the bloody carpet and, hoisting the boy in his arms, carried him carefully over to the sofa.

Tessa, seated in the chair beside Jessamine's bed, massaged her aching ribs and sighed. The corset was still biting into her, and she had no idea when she'd get a chance to remove it; her feet ached, and she hurt down deep in her soul. Seeing Nate had been like having a knife twisted in a fresh wound. He had danced with "Jessamine"—flirted with her—and had casually discussed the fate of Tessa, his sister, as if it meant nothing to him at all.

She supposed it should not surprise her, that she should be beyond surprise where Nate was concerned. But it hurt just the same.

And Will—those few moments out on the balcony with Will had been the most confusing of her life. After the way

Will had spoken to her on the roof, she had sworn never to entertain romantic thoughts of him again. He was no dark, brooding Heathcliff nursing a secret passion, she had told herself, merely a boy who thought himself too good for her. But the way he had looked at her on the terrace, the way he had smoothed her hair back from her face, even the faint tremble in his hands when he'd touched her—surely those things could not be the product of falsehood.

But then, she had touched him back the same way. In that moment she had wanted nothing but Will. Had felt nothing but Will. Yet just the night before she had touched and kissed Jem; she had felt that she loved him; she had let him see her as no one had ever seen her before. And when she thought of him now, thought of his silence this morning, his absence from dinner, she missed him again, with a physical pain that could not be a lie.

Could you really love two different people at once? Could you split your heart in half? Or was it just that the time with Will on the balcony had been a madness induced by warlock drugs? Would it have been the same with *anyone*? The thought haunted her like a ghost.

"Tessa."

Tessa nearly leaped out of her seat. The voice was almost a whisper. It was Jessamine. Her eyes were half-open, the reflected firelight flickering in their brown depths.

Tessa sat up straight. "Jessamine. Are you . . ."

"What happened?" Jessamine's head rolled fretfully from side to side. "I don't remember." She tried to sit up and gasped, finding her hands bound. "Tessa! Why on earth—"

"It's for your own good, Jessamine." Tessa's voice shook. "Charlotte—she has questions she has to ask you. It would be so much better if you were willing to answer them—"

"The party." Jessamine's eyes flicked back and forth, as if she were watching something Tessa couldn't see. "Sophie, that little monkey, was going through my things. I found her with the invitation in her hands—"

"Yes, the party," said Tessa. "At Benedict Lightwood's. Where you were meeting Nate."

"You read his note?" Jessamine's head whipped to the side. "Don't you know how rude and improper it is to read another person's private correspondence?" She tried to sit up again, and fell back once more against the pillows. "Anyway, he didn't sign it. You can't prove—"

"Jessamine, there is little advantage in falsehood now. I can prove it, for I went to the party, and I spoke with my brother there."

Jessamine's mouth opened in a pink O. For the first time she seemed to note what Tessa was wearing. "My dress," she breathed. "You disguised yourself as me?"

Tessa nodded.

Jessamine's eyes darkened. "Unnatural," she breathed. "Disgusting creature! What did you do to Nate? What did you say to him?"

"He made it very clear you have been spying for Mortmain," said Tessa, wishing that Sophie and Charlotte would return. What on earth was taking them so long? "That you have betrayed us, reporting on all our activities, carrying out Mortmain's commands—"

"Us?" Jessamine screamed, struggling upright as much as the ropes would allow her. "You are not a Shadowhunter! You owe them no loyalty! They do not care about you, any more than they care about me. Only Nate cares for me—"

"My brother," Tessa said in a barely controlled voice, "is a lying murderer, incapable of feeling. He may have married you, Jessamine, but he does not love you. The Shadowhunters have helped and protected me, as they have done for you. And yet you turn on them like a dog the moment my brother snaps his fingers. He will abandon you, if he does not kill you first."

"Liar!" Jessamine screamed. "You don't understand him. You never did! His soul is pure and fine—"

"Pure as ditch water," Tessa said. "I understand him better than you do; you are blinded by his charm. He cares nothing for you."

"Liar—"

"I saw it in his eyes. *I saw the way he looks at you.*"

Jessamine gasped. "How can you be so cruel?"

Tessa shook her head. "You can't see it, can you?" she said wonderingly. "For you it is all play, like those dolls in your dollhouse—moving them about, making them kiss and marry. You wanted a mundane husband, and Nate was good enough. You cannot see what your traitorous behavior has cost those who have always cared for you."

Jessamine bared her teeth; in that moment she looked enough like a trapped, cornered animal that Tessa almost shrank back. "I love Nate," she said. "And he loves me. You are the one who does not understand love. 'Oh, I cannot decide between Will and Jem. Whatever shall I do?'" she said in a high-pitched voice, and Tessa flushed hotly. "So what if Mortmain wants to destroy the Shadowhunters of Britain. I say let them burn."

Tessa gaped at her, just as the door behind her was flung

open, and Charlotte marched in. She looked drawn and hollow with exhaustion, in a gray dress that matched the shadows beneath her eyes, but her carriage was erect, her eyes clear. Behind her came Sophie, scuttling as if frightened—and a moment later Tessa saw why, for bringing up the rear of the party was an apparition in parchment-colored robes, his face hidden beneath the shadow of his hood, and a deadly bright blade in his hand. It was Brother Enoch, of the Silent Brothers, carrying the Mortal Sword.

"Let us burn? Is that what you said, Jessamine?" said Charlotte in a bright, hard voice so unlike her that Tessa stared.

Jessamine gasped. Her eyes were fixed on the blade in Brother Enoch's hand. Its great hilt was carved in the shape of an angel with outspread wings.

Brother Enoch flicked the Sword toward Jessamine, who flinched back, and the ropes binding her wrists to the bedposts unraveled. Her hands fell limply into her lap. She stared at them, and then at Charlotte. "Charlotte, Tessa's a liar. She's a lying Downworlder—"

Charlotte paused at the side of the bed and looked down at Jessamine dispassionately. "That has not been my experience of her, Jessamine. And what of Sophie? She has always been a most honest servant."

"She struck me! With a mirror!" Jessamine's face was red.

"Because she found this." Charlotte drew the invitation, which Tessa had given over to Sophie, from her pocket. "Can you explain this, Jessamine?"

"There's nothing against the Law about going to a party." Jessamine sounded equal parts sulky and frightened. "Benedict Lightwood is a Shadowhunter—"

"This is Nathaniel Gray's writing." Charlotte's voice never seemed to lose its even edge, Tessa thought. There was something about that fact that made it seem even more inexorable. "He is a spy, wanted by the Clave, and you have been meeting with him in secret. Why is that?"

Jessamine's mouth opened slightly. Tessa waited for excuses—*It's all lies, Sophie invented the invitation, I was only meeting Nate to gain his confidence*—but instead tears came. "I love him," she said. "And he loves me."

"So you betrayed us to him," said Charlotte.

"I didn't!" Jessamine's voice rose. "Whatever Tessa says, it isn't true! She's lying. She's always been jealous of me, and she's lying!"

Charlotte gave Tessa a measured look. "Is she, now. And Sophie?"

"Sophie hates me," Jessamine sobbed. This at least was true. "She ought to be put out on the street—without references—"

"Do cease turning on the taps, Jessamine. It accomplishes nothing." Charlotte's voice cut through Jessamine's sobs like a blade. She turned to Enoch. "The true story will be easy enough to get. The Mortal Sword, please, Brother Enoch."

The Silent Brother stepped forward, the Mortal Sword leveled at Jessamine. Tessa stared in horror. Was he going to *torture* Jessamine in her own bed, in front of them all?

Jessamine cried out. "No! No! Get him away from me! *Charlotte!*" Her voice rose to a terrible wailing scream that seemed to go on and on, splitting Tessa's ears, her head.

"Put out your hands, Jessamine," said Charlotte coldly.

Jessamine shook her head wildly, her fair hair flying.

"Charlotte, no," Tessa said. "Don't hurt her."

"Don't interfere in what you don't understand, Tessa," said Charlotte in a clipped voice. "Put your hands out, Jessamine, or it will go very badly for you."

With tears running down her face, Jessamine thrust her hands forward, palms up. Tessa tensed all over. She felt suddenly sick and sorry she had had anything to do with this plan. If Jessamine had been fooled by Nate, then so had she. Jessie did not deserve this—

"It's all right," said a soft voice at her shoulder. It was Sophie. "He won't hurt her with it. The Mortal Sword makes Nephilim tell the truth."

Brother Enoch laid the blade of the Mortal Sword flat across Jessamine's palms. He did it without either force or gentleness, as if he were hardly aware of her as a person at all. He let the blade go and stepped back; even Jessamine's eyes rounded in surprise; the blade seemed to balance perfectly across her hands, utterly immobile.

"It is not a torture device, Jessamine," said Charlotte, her hands folded in front of her. "We must employ it only because you cannot be trusted to tell the truth otherwise." She held up the invitation. "This is yours, is it not?"

Jessamine did not answer. She was looking at Brother Enoch, her eyes wide and black with terror, her chest rising and falling fast. "I cannot think, not with that monster in the room—" Her voice trembled.

Charlotte's mouth thinned, but she turned to Enoch and spoke a few words. He nodded, then glided silently from the room. As the door shut behind him, Charlotte said, "There. He is waiting in the corridor. Do not think he will not catch you should you try to run, Jessamine."

Jessamine nodded. She seemed to droop, broken like a toy doll.

Charlotte fluttered the invitation in her hand. "This is yours, yes? And it was sent to you by Nathaniel Gray. This writing is his."

"Y-yes." The word seemed pulled from Jessamine against her will.

"How long have you been meeting him in secret?"

Jessamine set her mouth, but her lips were trembling. A moment later a torrent of words burst from her mouth. Her eyes darted round in shock as if she could not believe she was speaking. "He sent me a message only a few days after Mortmain invaded the Institute. He apologized for his behavior toward me. He said he was grateful for my nursing of him and that he had not been able to forget my graciousness or my beauty. I—I wanted to ignore him. But a second letter came, and a third. . . . I agreed to meet him. I left the Institute in the middle of the night and we met in Hyde Park. He kissed me—"

"Enough of that," said Charlotte. "How long did it take him to convince you to spy on us?"

"He said that he was only working for Mortmain until he could put together enough of a fortune to live comfortably. I said we could live together on my fortune, but he wouldn't have it. It had to be his money. He said he would not live off his wife. Is that not noble?"

"So by this point he had already proposed?"

"He proposed the second time we met." Jessamine sounded breathy. "He said he knew there would never be another woman for him. And he promised that once he had enough money, I would have just the life I had always wanted, that we would never worry about money, and that there would be ch-children." She sniffled.

"Oh, Jessamine." Charlotte sounded almost sad.

Jessamine flushed. "It was true! He loved me! He has more than proved it. We are married! It was done most properly in a church with a minister—"

"Probably a deconsecrated church and some flunky dressed to look like a minister," said Charlotte. "What do you know of mundane weddings, Jessie? How would you know what a proper wedding *was*? I give you my word that Nathaniel Gray does not consider you his wife."

"He does, he does, he *does*!" Jessamine shrieked, and tried to pull away from the Sword. It stuck to her hands as if it had been nailed there. Her wails went up an octave. "I am Jessamine Gray!"

"You are a traitor to the Clave. What else did you tell Nathaniel?"

"Everything," Jessamine gasped. "Where you were looking for Mortmain, which Downworlders you had contacted in your attempt to find him. That was why he was never anywhere you searched. I warned him about the trip to York. That is why he sent the automatons to Will's family's home. Mortmain wanted to terrify you into ceasing the search. He considers you all pestilential annoyances. But he is not afraid of you." Her chest was heaving up and down. "He will win out over you all. He knows it. So do I."

Charlotte leaned forward, her hands on her hips. "But he did not succeed in terrifying us into ceasing the search," she said. "The automatons he sent tried to snatch Tessa but failed—"

"They weren't sent to try to snatch Tessa. Oh, he still plans to take her, but not like that, not yet. His plan is close to realization, and that is when he will move to take the Institute, to take Tessa—"

"How close is he? Has he managed to open the Pyxis?" Charlotte snapped.

"I—I don't know. I don't think so."

"So you told Nate everything and he told you nothing. What of Benedict? Why has he agreed to work hand in glove with Mortmain? I always knew he was an unpleasant man, but it seems unlike him to betray the Clave."

Jessamine shook her head. She was sweating, her fair hair stuck to her temples. "Mortmain is holding something over him, something he wants. I don't know what it is. But he will do anything to get it."

"Including handing me over to Mortmain," said Tessa. Charlotte looked at her in surprise when she spoke, and seemed about to interrupt her, but Tessa hurtled on. "What is this about having me falsely accused of possessing articles of dark magic? How was that to be accomplished?"

"The Book of the White," Jessamine gasped. "I—took it from the locked case in the library. Hid it in your room while you were out."

"Where in my room?"

"Loose floorboard—near the fireplace." Jessamine's pupils were enormous. "Charlotte . . . please . . ."

But Charlotte was relentless. "Where is Mortmain? Has he spoken to Nate of his plans for the Pyxis, for his automatons?"

"I—" Jessamine took a shuddering gasp. Her face was dark red. "I can't—"

"Nate wouldn't have told her," said Tessa. "He would have

known she might have been caught, and he would have thought she'd crack under torture and spill everything. *He* would."

Jessamine gave her a venomous look. "He hates you, you know," she said. "He says that all his life you looked down on him, you and your aunt with your silly provincial morality, judging him for everything he did. Always telling him what to do, never wanting him to get ahead. Do you know what he calls you? He—"

"I don't care," Tessa lied; her voice shook slightly. Despite everything, hearing that her brother hated her hurt more than she had thought it could. "Did he say what I am? Why I have the power I do?"

"He said that your father was a demon." Jessamine's lips twitched. "And that your mother was a Shadowhunter."

The door opened softly, so softly that had Magnus not already been drifting in and out of sleep, the noise would not have woken him.

He looked up. He was sitting in an armchair near the fire, as his favorite place on the sofa was taken up by Will. Will, in bloody shirtsleeves, was sleeping the heavy sleep of the drugged and healing. His forearm was bandaged to the elbow, his cheeks flushed, his head pillowed on his unhurt arm. The tooth Will had pulled from his arm sat on the side table beside him, gleaming like ivory.

The door to the drawing room stood open behind him. And there, framed in the archway, was Camille.

She wore a black velvet traveling cloak open over a brilliant green dress that matched her eyes. Her hair was dressed high on her head with emerald combs, and as he watched, she drew off her white kid gloves, deliberately slowly, one by one, and laid them on the table by the door.

"Magnus," she said, and her voice, as always, sounded like silvery bells. "Did you miss me?"

Magnus sat up straight. The firelight played over Camille's shining hair, her poreless white skin. She was extraordinarily beautiful. "I did not realize you would be favoring me with your presence tonight."

She looked at Will, asleep on the sofa. Her lips curled upward. "Clearly."

"You sent no message. In fact, you have sent me no messages at all since you left London."

"Are you reproaching me, Magnus?" Camille sounded amused. Gliding behind the sofa, she leaned over the back, looking down into Will's face. "Will Herondale," she said. "He is lovely, isn't he? Is he your newest amusement?"

Instead of answering, Magnus crossed his long legs in front of him. "Where have you been?"

Camille leaned forward farther; if she had had breath, it would have stirred the curling dark hair on Will's forehead. "Can I kiss him?"

"No," said Magnus. "Where have you been, Camille? Every night I lay here on your sofa and I waited to hear your step in the hall, and I wondered where you were. You might at least tell me."

She straightened, rolling her eyes. "Oh, very well. I was in Paris, having some new dresses fitted. A much-needed holiday from the dramas of London."

There was a long silence. Then, "You're lying," Magnus said.

Her eyes widened. "Why would you say such a thing?"

"Because it's the truth." He took a crumpled letter from his pocket and threw it onto the floor between them. "You cannot track a vampire, but you can track a vampire's subjugate. You took Walker with you. It was easy enough for me to track him to Saint Petersburg. I have informants there. They let me know that you were living there with a human lover."

Camille watched him, a little smile playing about her mouth. "And that made you jealous?"

"Did you want me to be?"

"*Ça m'est égal,*" said Camille, dropping into the French she used when she truly wanted to annoy him. "It's all the same to me. He had nothing to do with you. He was a diversion while I was in Russia, nothing more."

"And now he is . . ."

"Dead. So he hardly represents competition for you. You must let me have my little diversions, Magnus."

"Otherwise?"

"Otherwise I shall become extremely cross."

"As you became cross with your human lover, and murdered him?" Magnus inquired. "What of pity? Compassion? Love? Or do you not feel that emotion?"

"I *love,*" Camille said indignantly. "You and I, Magnus, who endure forever, love in such a manner as cannot be conceived of by mortals—a dark constant flame to their brief, sputtering light. What do they matter to you? Fidelity is a human concept, based upon the idea that we are here but for a short time. You cannot demand my faithfulness for *eternity.*"

"How foolish of me. I thought I could. I thought I could at least expect you not to lie to me."

"You are being ridiculous," she said. "A child. You expect me to have the morals of some mundane when I am not human, and neither are you. Regardless, there is precious little you can do about it. I will not be dictated to, certainly not by some half-breed." It was the Downworlders' own insulting term for warlocks. "You are devoted to me; you have said so yourself. Your devotion will simply have to suffer my diversions, and then we shall rub along quite pleasantly. If not, I shall drop you. I cannot imagine you want *that*."

There was a little sneer in her voice as she spoke, and it snapped something inside Magnus. He recalled the sick feeling in his throat when the letter had come from Saint Petersburg. And yet he had waited for her return, hoping she had an explanation. That she would apologize. Ask him to love her again. Now that he realized he was not worth that to her—that he never had been—a red mist passed before his eyes; he seemed to go mad momentarily, for it was the only explanation for what he did next.

"It doesn't matter." He rose to his feet. "I have Will now."

Her mouth opened. "You can't be serious. A *Shadowhunter*?"

"You may be immortal, Camille, but your feelings are vapid and shallow. Will's are not. He understands what it is to love." Magnus, having delivered this insane speech with great dignity, stepped across the room and shook Will's shoulder. "Will. William. Wake up."

Will's hazy blue eyes opened. He was lying on his back, looking upward, and the first thing he saw was Camille's face as she bent over the back of the sofa, regarding him. He jerked upright. "By the Angel—"

"Oh, shush," said Camille lazily, smiling just enough to

show the tips of baby fangs. "I won't hurt you, Nephilim."

Magnus hauled Will to his feet. "The lady of the house," he said, "has returned."

"I see that." Will was flushed, the collar of his shirt dark with sweat. "Delightful," he said to no one in particular, and Magnus wasn't sure whether he meant he was delighted to see Camille, delighted with the effects of the painkilling spell Magnus had used on him—certainly a possibility—or simply rambling.

"And therefore," said Magnus, squeezing Will's arm with a meaning pressure, "we must go."

Will blinked at him. "Go where?"

"Don't worry about that right now, my love."

Will blinked again. "Pardon?" He glanced around, as if he half-expected people to be watching. "I—where's my coat?"

"Ruined with blood," said Magnus. "Archer disposed of it." He nodded toward Camille. "Will's been hunting demons all night. So brave."

Camille's expression was a mixture of amazement and annoyance.

"I *am* brave," Will said. He looked pleased with himself. The painkilling tonics had enlarged his pupils, and his eyes looked very dark.

"Yes, you are," Magnus said, and kissed him. It wasn't the most dramatic kiss, but Will flailed his free arm as if a bee had landed on him; Magnus had to hope Camille would assume this was passion. When they broke apart, Will looked stunned. So did Camille, for that matter.

"*Now,*" Magnus said, hoping that Will would recollect that he was indebted to him. "We must go."

"I—but—" Will swung sideways. "The tooth!" He dashed across the room, retrieved it, and tucked it into Magnus's waistcoat pocket. Then, with a wink at Camille that, Magnus thought, God alone knew how she would interpret, he sauntered out of the room.

"Camille," Magnus began.

She had her arms crossed over her chest and was looking at him venomously. "Carrying on with Shadowhunters behind my back," she said icily, and with no apparent regard for the hypocrisy of her position. "And in my own house! Really, Magnus." She pointed toward the door. "Please leave my residence and do not return. I trust I shall not have to ask you twice."

Magnus was only too pleased to oblige. A few moments later he had joined Will on the pavement outside the house, shrugging on his coat—all he now owned in the world besides what was in his pockets—and fastening the buttons against the chilly air. It would not be long, Magnus thought, before the first gray flush of morning lightened the sky.

"Did you just kiss me?" Will inquired.

Magnus made a split-second decision. "No."

"I thought—"

"On occasion the aftereffects of the painkilling spells can result in hallucinations of the most bizarre sort."

"Oh," Will said. "How peculiar." He looked back at Camille's house. Magnus could see the window of the drawing room, the red velvet curtains drawn tight. "What are we going to do now? About summoning the demon? Have we somewhere to go?"

"*I've* got somewhere to go," said Magnus, saying a prayer of silent thanks for Will's single-minded fixation on demon summoning. "I have a friend I can stop with. You go along back to the Institute. I'll get to work on your blasted demon tooth as soon as I possibly can. I'll send a message to you when I know anything."

Will nodded slowly, then looked up at the black sky. "The stars," he said. "I have never seen them so bright. The wind has blown off the fog, I think."

Magnus thought of the joy on Will's face as he had stood bleeding in Camille's living room, clutching the demon tooth in his hand. *Somehow, I don't think it's the stars that have changed.*

"A *Shadowhunter?*" Tessa gasped. "That's not possible." She whirled around and looked at Charlotte, whose face mirrored her own shock. "It isn't possible, is it? Will told me that the offspring of Shadowhunters and demons are stillborn."

Charlotte was shaking her head. "No. No, it isn't possible."

"But if Jessamine has to tell the truth—" Tessa's voice wavered.

"She has to tell the truth as she believes it," said Charlotte. "If your brother lied to her but she believed him, she will speak it as if it were the truth."

"Nate would never lie to me," Jessamine spat.

"If Tessa's mother was a Shadowhunter," said Charlotte coldly, "then Nate is also a Shadowhunter. Shadowhunter blood breeds true. Did he ever mention *that* to you? That he was a Shadowhunter?"

Jessamine looked revolted. "*Nate* isn't a Shadowhunter!" she cried. "I would have known! I would never have married—" She broke off, biting down on her lip.

"Well, it's one or the other, Jessamine," said Charlotte.

"Either you married a Shadowhunter, a truly supreme irony, or, more likely, you married a liar who used and discarded you. He must have known you'd be caught eventually. And what did he think would happen to you then?"

"Nothing." Jessamine looked shaken. "He said you were weak. That you would not punish me. That you could not bring yourself to truly harm me."

"He was wrong," said Charlotte. "You are a traitor to the Clave. So is Benedict Lightwood. When the Consul hears of all this—"

Jessamine laughed, a thin, broken sound. "Tell him," she said. "That's *exactly* what Mortmain wants." She sputtered. "D-don't bother asking me why. I don't know. But I know he wants it. So tattle all you like, Charlotte. It will only put you in his power."

Charlotte gripped the footboard of the bed, her hands whitening. "Where is Mortmain?"

Jessamine shuddered, shaking her head, her hair whipping back and forth. "No . . ."

"Where is Mortmain?"

"H-he," she gasped. "He—" Jessamine's face was almost purple, her eyes bugging out of her head. She was clutching the Sword so tightly that blood welled around her fingers. Tessa looked at Charlotte in horror. *"Idris,"* Jessamine gasped at last, and slumped back against the pillow.

Charlotte's face froze. "Idris?" she echoed. "Mortmain is in Idris, our homeland?"

Jessamine's eyelids fluttered. "No. He is not there."

"Jessamine!" Charlotte looked as if she were going to leap on the girl and shake her till her teeth rattled. "How can he be in Idris and not be? Save yourself, you stupid girl. Tell us where he is!"

"Stop!" Jessamine cried out. "Stop, it hurts. . . ."

Charlotte gave her a long, hard look. Then she went to the door of the room; when she returned, it was with Brother Enoch in tow. She crossed her arms over her chest and indicated Jessamine with a jerk of her chin. "There is something wrong, Brother. I asked her where Mortmain was; she said Idris. When I asked again, she denied it." Her voice hardened. "Jessamine! Has Mortmain breached the wards of Idris?"

Jessamine made a choking sound; her breath wheezed in and out of her chest. "No, he has not. . . . I swear . . . Charlotte, please . . ."

Charlotte. Brother Enoch spoke firmly, his words echoing in Tessa's mind. *Enough. There is some sort of block in the girl's mind, something placed there by Mortmain. He taunts us with the idea of Idris, yet she confesses he is not there. These blocks are strong. Continue to question her in this manner, and her heart may well fail her.*

Charlotte sagged back. "Then what . . ."

Let me take her to the Silent City. We have our ways of seeking out the secrets locked in the mind, secrets even the girl herself may not be aware she knows.

Brother Enoch withdrew the Sword from Jessamine's grasp. She seemed barely to notice. Her gaze was on Charlotte, her eyes wide and panicked. "The City of Bones?" she whispered. "Where the dead lie? No! I will not go there! I cannot bear that place!"

"Then tell us where Mortmain is," said Charlotte, her voice like ice.

Jessamine only began to sob. Charlotte ignored her. Brother

Enoch lifted the girl to her feet; Jessamine struggled, but the Silent Brother held her in an iron grip, his other hand on the hilt of the Mortal Sword.

"Charlotte!" Jessamine shrieked piteously. "Charlotte, please, not the Silent City! Lock me in the crypt, give me to the Council, but please do not send me alone to that—that graveyard! I shall die of fear!"

"You should have thought of that before you betrayed us," said Charlotte. "Brother Enoch, take her, please."

Jessamine was still shrieking as the Silent Brother lifted her and threw her over his shoulder. As Tessa stared, wide-eyed, he strode from the room carrying her. Her cries and gasps echoed down the corridor long after the door closed behind them—and then were cut off suddenly.

"Jessamine—," Tessa began.

"She is quite all right. He has probably put a Rune of Quietude on her. That is all. There is nothing to worry about," said Charlotte, and she sat down on the edge of the bed. She looked down at her own hands, wonderingly, as if they did not belong to her. "Henry . . ."

"Shall I rouse him for you, Mrs. Branwell?" Sophie asked gently.

"He is in the crypt, working. . . . I could not bear to get him." Charlotte's voice was distant. "Jessamine has been with us since she was a little girl. It would have been too much for him, too much. He does not have it in him to be cruel."

"Charlotte." Tessa touched her shoulder gently. "Charlotte, you are not cruel either."

"I do what I must. There is nothing to worry about," Charlotte said again, and burst into tears.

14

The Silent City

She howl'd aloud, "I am on fire within.
There comes no murmur of reply.
What is it that will take away my sin,
And save me lest I die?"
–Alfred, Lord Tennyson, "The Palace of Art"

"Jessamine," Henry said again, for what must have been the fifth or sixth time. "I still can't believe it. Our Jessamine?"

Every time he said it, Tessa noticed, Charlotte's mouth grew a little tighter. "Yes," she said again. "Jessamine. She has been spying on us and reporting our every move to Nate, who has been passing the information to Mortmain. Must I say it again?"

Henry blinked at her. "I'm sorry, darling. I have been listening. It is only that—" He sighed. "I knew she was unhappy here. But I did not think Jessamine hated us."

"I don't think she did—or does." This was Jem, who was

standing near the fire in the drawing room, one arm upon the mantel. They had not gathered for breakfast as they usually did; there had been no formal announcement as to why, but Tessa guessed that the idea of going on with breakfast, with Jessamine's place empty, as if nothing had happened, had been too dreadful for Charlotte to bear.

Charlotte had wept for only a short time that night before she had regained her composure; she had waved away Sophie's and Tessa's attempts to help with cold cloths or tea, shaking her head stiffly and saying over and over that she should not allow herself to break down like this, that now was the time for planning, for strategy. She had marched to Tessa's room, with Sophie and Tessa hurrying at her heels, and pried feverishly at the floorboards until she'd turned up a small chapbook, like a family Bible, bound in white leather and wrapped in velvet. She had slipped it into her pocket with a determined expression, waving away Tessa's questions, and risen to her feet. The sky outside the windows had already begun to brighten with the wan light of dawn. Looking exhausted, she had told Sophie to instruct Bridget to serve a simple cold breakfast in the drawing room, and to let Cyril know so that the menfolk might be informed. Then she had left.

With Sophie's help Tessa had finally and gratefully fought her way free of Jessamine's dress; she had bathed, and put on her yellow dress, the one Jessamine had bought her. She thought the color might brighten her mood, but she still felt wan and tired.

She found the same look reflected on Jem's face when she came into the drawing room. His eyes were shadowed, and he looked quickly away from her. It hurt. It also made her think of the night before, with Will, on the balcony. But that had been different, she told herself. That had been a result of warlock powders, a temporary madness. Nothing like what had happened between her and Jem.

"I don't think she hates us," Jem said again now, correcting his use of the past tense. "She has always been someone so full of *wanting*. She has always been so desperate."

"It is my fault," Charlotte said softly. "I should not have tried to force being a Shadowhunter upon her when it was something she so clearly despised."

"No. No!" Henry hurried to reassure his wife. "You were never anything but kind to her. You did everything you could. There are some mechanisms that are so—so broken that they cannot be repaired."

"Jessamine is not a watch, Henry," Charlotte said, her tone remote. Tessa wondered if she were still angry with Henry for not seeing Woolsey Scott with her, or if she were simply angry at the world. "Perhaps I should just parcel up the Institute with a bow and give it to Benedict Lightwood. This is the second time that we have had a spy under our roof and not known about it until significant damage was done. Clearly I am incompetent."

"In a way it was really just the one spy," Henry began, but fell silent as Charlotte gave him a look that could have melted glass.

"If Benedict Lightwood is working for Mortmain, he cannot be allowed to have custody of the Institute," said Tessa. "In fact, that ball he threw last night ought to be enough to disqualify him."

"The problem will be proving it," said Jem. "Benedict will

deny everything, and it will be his word against yours—and you are a Downworlder—"

"There's Will," said Charlotte, and frowned. "Speaking of, where *is* Will?"

"Having a lie-in, no doubt," said Jem, "and as for him being a witness, well, everyone thinks Will is a lunatic as it is—"

"Ah," said a voice from the doorway, "having your annual everyone-thinks-Will-is-a-lunatic meeting, are you?"

"It's biannual," said Jem. "And no, this is not that meeting."

Will's eyes sought Tessa across the room. "They know about Jessamine?" he said. He looked tired, but not as tired as Tessa would have thought; he was pale, but there was a suppressed excitement about him that was almost like—happiness. She felt her stomach drop as memories of the previous night—the stars, the balcony, the *kissing*—swept over her.

When had he gotten home last night? she thought. How had he? And why did he look so—excited? Was he horrified by what had happened on the balcony between them last night, or did he find it amusing? And dear God, had he told *Jem?* Warlock powders, she told herself desperately. She had not been herself, acting of her own will. Surely Jem would understand that. It would break her heart to hurt him. If he even cared . . .

"Yes, they know all about Jessamine," she said hastily. "She was questioned with the Mortal Sword and taken to the Silent City, and right now we're having a meeting about what to do next, and it's dreadfully important. Charlotte's very upset."

Charlotte looked at her in puzzlement.

"Well, you *are*," Tessa said, nearly out of breath from speaking so quickly. "And you were asking for Will—"

"And here I am," said Will, throwing himself down into a

chair near Jem. One of his arms had been bandaged, his sleeve pulled down partway over it. The nails of his hand were crusted with dried blood. "Glad to hear Jessamine's in the Silent City. Best place for her. What's the next step?"

"*That's* the meeting we were trying to have," said Jem.

"Well, who knows she's there?" Will asked practically.

"Just us," said Charlotte, "and Brother Enoch, but he's agreed not to inform the Clave for another day or so. Until we decide what to do. Which reminds me, I shall have some choice words for you, Will, haring off to Benedict Lightwood's without informing me, and dragging Tessa with you."

"There was no time to lose," said Will. "By the time we'd have roused you and made you agree to the plan, Nathaniel could have been and gone. And you can't say it was a dreadful idea. We've learned a great deal about Nathaniel and Benedict Lightwood—"

"Nathaniel Gray and Benedict Lightwood aren't Mortmain."

Will traced a pattern on the air with his long, elegant fingers. "Mortmain is the spider at the heart of the web," he said. "The more we learn, the more we know how far his reach extends. Before last night we had no clue he had any connection to Lightwood; now we know the man is his puppet. I say we go to the Clave and report Benedict and Jessamine. Let Wayland take care of them. See what Benedict spills under the Mortal Sword."

Charlotte shook her head. "No, I—I don't think we can do that."

Will tilted his head back. "Why not?"

"Jessamine said it was exactly what Mortmain wanted us to do. And she said it under the influence of the Mortal Sword. She wasn't lying."

"But she could have been *wrong*," said Will. "Mortmain could have foreseen just this circumstance and have had Nate plant the thought in her head for us to discover."

"D'you think he would have thought ahead like that?" said Henry.

"Assuredly," said Will. "The man's a strategist." He tapped his temple. "Like me."

"So you think we should go to the Clave?" asked Jem.

"Bloody hell, no," said Will. "What if it is the truth? Then we'll feel like right fools."

Charlotte threw her hands up. "But you said—"

"I know what I *said*," said Will. "But you have to look at consequences. If we go to the Clave and we're wrong, then we've played into Mortmain's hands. We still have a few days before the deadline is up. Going to the Clave early gains us nothing. If we investigate, and can proceed on a surer footing . . ."

"And how do you propose to investigate?" Tessa inquired.

Will swiveled his head to look at her. There was nothing in his cool blue eyes to recall the Will of the night before, who had touched her with such tenderness, who had whispered her name like a secret. "The problem with questioning Jessamine is that even when forced to tell the truth, there is a limit to her knowledge. We do, however, have one more connection to the Magister. Someone who is likely to know a great deal more. That is your brother, Nate, through Jessamine. He still trusts her. If she summons him to a meeting, then we will be able to capture him there."

"Jessamine would never agree to do it," said Charlotte. "Not now—"

Will gave her a dark look. "You *are* all in a lather, aren't you?" he said. "Of course she wouldn't. We will be asking Tessa to reprise her starring role as Jessamine, A Traitorous Young Lady of Fashion."

"That sounds dangerous," Jem said in a subdued voice. "For Tessa."

Tessa looked at him quickly, and caught a flash of his silvery eyes. It was the first time he had looked at her since she had left his room that night. Was she imagining the concern in his voice when he spoke of danger to her, or was it simply the concern Jem had for *everyone*? Not wishing for her horrible demise was mere kindness, not—not what it was she hoped he felt.

Whatever that might be. Let him at least not despise her. . . .

"Tessa is fearless," said Will. "And there will be little danger to her. We will send him a note arranging a meeting in a place where we might fall upon him easily and immediately. The Silent Brothers can torture him until he gives up the information that we need."

"Torture?" said Jem. "This is Tessa's brother—"

"Torture him," said Tessa. "If that is what is necessary. I give you my permission."

Charlotte looked up at her, shocked. "You can't mean that."

"You said there was a way to dig through his mind for secrets," Tessa said. "I asked you not to do that, and you didn't. I thank you for that, but I will not hold you to that promise. Dig through his mind if you must. There is more to all of this for me than there is for you, you know. For you this is about the Institute and the safety of Shadowhunters. I care about those things too, Charlotte. But Nate—he is working with Mortmain. Mortmain, who wants to trap me and use me, and for what we still do not know. Mortmain, who may know *what I am*. Nate told Jessamine my father was a demon and my mother was a Shadowhunter—"

Will sat up straight. "That's impossible," he said. "Shadowhunters and demons—they cannot procreate. They cannot produce living offspring."

"Then maybe it was a lie, like the lie about Mortmain being in Idris," said Tessa. "That doesn't mean *Mortmain* doesn't know the truth. I must know what I am. If nothing else, I believe it is the key to why he wants me."

There was sadness in Jem's eyes as he looked at her, and then away. "Very well," he said. "Will, how do you propose we lure him to a meeting? Don't you think he knows Jessamine's handwriting? Isn't it likely they have some secret signal between them?"

"Jessamine must be convinced," said Will. "To help us."

"Please don't suggest we torture her," said Jem irritably. "The Mortal Sword has already been used. She has told us all she can—"

"The Mortal Sword did not give us their meeting places or any codes or pet names they might have used," said Will. "Don't you understand? This is Jessamine's last chance. Her last chance to cooperate. To get leniency from the Clave. To be forgiven. Even if Charlotte keeps the Institute, do you think they will leave Jessamine's fate in our hands? No, it will be left to the Consul and the Inquisitor. And they will not be kind. If she does this for us, it could mean her life."

"I am not sure she cares about her life," said Tessa softly.

"Everyone cares," said Will. "Everyone wants to live."

Jem turned away from him abruptly, and stared into the fire.

"The question is, who can we send to persuade her?" said Charlotte. "I cannot go. She hates and blames me most of all."

"I could go," Henry said, his gentle face troubled. "I could perhaps reason with the poor girl, speak with her of the folly of young love, how swiftly it fades in the face of life's harsh reality—"

"No." Charlotte's tone was final.

"Well, I highly doubt she wishes to see *me*," said Will. "It will have to be Jem. He's impossible to hate. Even that devil cat likes him."

Jem exhaled, still staring into the fire. "I will go to the Silent City," he said. "But Tessa should come with me."

Tessa looked up, startled. "Oh, no," she said. "I do not think Jessamine likes me much. She feels I have betrayed her terribly by disguising myself as her, and I cannot say I blame her."

"Yes," said Jem. "But you are Nate's sister. If she loves him as you say she does . . ." His eyes met hers across the room. "You know Nate. You can speak of him with authority. You may be able to make her believe what I cannot."

"Very well," Tessa said. "I will try."

This seemed to signal the end of breakfast; Charlotte darted off to call for a carriage to come for them from the Silent City; it was how the Brothers liked to do things, she explained. Henry returned to his crypt and his inventions, and Jem, after a murmured word to Tessa, went to gather his hat and coat. Only Will remained, staring into the fire, and Tessa, seeing that he was not moving, waited until the door shut behind Jem and came around to stand between Will and the flames.

He raised his eyes to her slowly. He was still wearing the clothes he had been wearing the night before, though his white shirtfront was stained with blood and there was a long, jagged rent in his frock coat. There was a cut along his cheek, too, under his left eye. "Will," she said.

"Aren't you meant to be leaving with Jem?"

"And I shall," she replied. "But I need a promise from you first."

His eyes moved to the fire; she could see the dancing flames reflected in his pupils. "Then tell me what it is quickly. I have important business to get to. I plan to sulk all afternoon, followed, perhaps, by an evening of Byronic brooding and a nighttime of dissipation."

"Dissipate all you like. I only want your assurance that you will tell no one what transpired between us last night on the balcony."

"Oh, that was *you*," said Will, with the air of someone who has just recollected a surprising detail.

"Spare me," she snapped, stung despite herself. "We were under the influence of warlock powders. It meant nothing. Even I do not blame you for what happened, however tedious you are being about it now. But there is no need for anyone else to know, and if you were a gentleman—"

"But I am not."

"But you are a Shadowhunter," she said venomously. "And there is no future for a Shadowhunter who dallies with warlocks."

His eyes danced with fire. He said, "You have become boring to tease, Tess."

"Then give me your word you will tell no one, not even Jem, and I will go away and cease to bore you."

"You have my word on the Angel," he said. "It was not

something I had planned to brag of in the first place. Though why you are so keen that no one here suspect you of a lack of virtue, I do not know."

Jem's face flashed across her inner eye. "No," she said. "You truly don't." And with that she turned on her heel and stalked from the room, leaving him staring after her in confusion.

Sophie hurried down Piccadilly, her head bent, her eyes on the pavement beneath her feet. She was used to hushed murmurs and the occasional stare when she went out and eyes fell upon her scar; she had perfected a way of walking that hid her face beneath the shadow of her hat. She was not ashamed of the scar, but she hated the pity in the eyes of those who saw it.

She was wearing one of Jessamine's old dresses. It was not out of fashion yet, but Jessamine was one of those girls who dubbed any dress she had worn more than three times "historical" and either cast it off or had it made over. It was a striped watered silk in green and white, and there were waxy white flowers and green leaves on her hat. All together, she thought, she could pass for a girl of good breeding—if she were not out on her own, that was—especially with her work-roughened hands covered in a pair of white kid gloves.

She saw Gideon before he saw her. He was leaning against a lamppost outside the great pale-green porte cochere of Fortnum & Mason. Her heart skipped a little beat as she looked at him, so handsome in his dark clothes, checking the time on a gold watch affixed to his waistcoat pocket by a thin chain. She paused for a moment, watching the people stream around him, the busy life of London roaring around him, and Gideon as calm as a rock in the middle of a churning river. All Shadowhunters had something of that to them, she thought, that stillness, that dark aura of separateness that set them apart from the current of mundane life.

He looked up then, and saw her, and smiled that smile that changed his whole face. "Miss Collins," he said, coming forward, and she moved forward to meet him as well, feeling as she did so as if she were stepping into the circle of his separateness. The steady noise of city traffic, pedestrian and otherwise, seemed to dim, and it was just her and Gideon, facing each other on the street.

"Mr. Lightwood," she said.

His face changed, only a little, but she saw it. She saw too that he was holding something in his left hand, a woven picnic basket. She looked at it, and then at him.

"One of Fortnum & Mason's famous hampers," he said with a sideways smile. "Stilton cheese, quails' eggs, rose petal jam—"

"Mr. Lightwood," she said again, interrupting him, to her own amazement. A servant *never* interrupted a gentleman. "I have been most distressed—most distressed in my own mind, you understand, as to whether I should come here at all. I finally decided that I should, if only to tell you to your own face that I cannot see you. I thought you deserved that much, though I am not sure of it."

He looked at her, stunned, and in that moment she saw not a Shadowhunter but an ordinary boy, like Thomas or Cyril, clutching a picnic basket and unable to hide the surprise and hurt on his face. "Miss Collins, if there is something I have done to offend—"

"I cannot see you. That is all," Sophie said, and turned

away, meaning to hurry back the way she had come. If she was quick, she could catch the next omnibus back to the City—

"Miss Collins. Please." It was Gideon, at her elbow. He did not touch her, but he was walking alongside her, his expression distraught. "Tell me what I've done."

She shook her head mutely. The look on his face—perhaps it had been a mistake to come. They were passing Hatchards bookshop, and she considered ducking inside; surely he would not follow her, not into a place where they'd likely be overheard. But then again, perhaps he would.

"I know what it is," he said abruptly. "Will. He told you, didn't he?"

"The fact that you say that informs me that there was something to tell."

"Miss Collins, I can explain. Just come with me—this way." He turned, and she found herself following him, warily. They were in front of St. James's Church; he led her around the side and down a narrow street that bridged the gap between Piccadilly and Jermyn Street. It was quieter here, though not deserted; several passing pedestrians gave them curious looks—the scarred girl and the handsome boy with the pale face, carefully setting his hamper down at his feet.

"This is about last night," he said. "The ball at my father's house in Chiswick. I thought I saw Will. I had wondered if he would tell the rest of you."

"You confess it, then? That you were there, at that depraved—that unsuitable—"

"Unsuitable? It was a sight more than unsuitable," said Gideon, with more force than she had ever heard him use. Behind them the bell of the church tolled the hour; he seemed not to hear it. "Miss Collins, all I can do is swear to you that until last night I had no idea with what low company, what destructive habits, my father had engaged himself. I have been in Spain this past half-year—"

"And he was not like this before that?" Sophie asked, disbelieving.

"Not quite. It is difficult to explain." His eyes strayed past her, their gray-green stormier than ever. "My father has always been one to flout convention. To bend the Law, if not to break it. He has always taught us that this is the way that everyone goes along, that all Shadowhunters do it. And we—Gabriel and I—having lost our mother so young, had no better example to follow. It was not until I arrived in Madrid that I began to understand the full extent of my father's . . . incorrectness. Everyone does not flout the Law and bend the rules, and I was treated as if I were some monstrous creature for believing it to be so, until I changed my ways. Research and observation led me to believe I had been given poor principles to follow, and that it had been done with deliberation. I could think only of Gabriel and how I might save him from the same realization, or at least from having it delivered so shockingly."

"And your sister—Miss Lightwood?"

Gideon shook his head. "She has been sheltered from it all. My father thinks that women have no business with the darker aspects of Downworld. No, it is I who he believes must know of his involvements, for I am the heir to the Lightwood estate. It was with an eye to that that my father brought me with him to the event last night, at which, I assume, Will saw me."

"You knew he was there?"

"I was so disgusted by what I saw inside that room that I

eventually fought my way free and went out into the gardens for some fresh air. The stench of demons had made me nauseated. Out there, I saw someone familiar chasing a blue demon across the parkland with an air of determination."

"Mr. Herondale?"

Gideon shrugged. "I had no idea what he was doing there; I knew he could not have been invited, but could not fathom how he had found out about it, or if his pursuit of the demon was unrelated. I wasn't sure until I saw the look on your face when you beheld me, just now . . ."

Sophie's voice rose and sharpened. "But did you tell your father, or Gabriel? Do they know? About Master Will?"

Gideon shook his head slowly. "I told them nothing. I do not think they expected Will there in any capacity. The Shadowhunters of the Institute are meant to be in pursuit of Mortmain."

"They are," said Sophie slowly, and when his only look was one of incomprehension, she said: "Those clockwork creatures at your father's party—where did you think they came from?"

"I didn't—I assumed they were demon playthings of some sort—"

"They can only have come from Mortmain," said Sophie. "You haven't seen his automatons before, but Mr. Herondale and Miss Gray, they have, and they were sure."

"But why would my father have anything of Mortmain's?"

Sophie shook her head. "It may be that you should not ask me questions you don't want the answer to, Mr. Lightwood."

"Miss Collins." His hair fell forward over his eyes; he tossed it back with an impatient gesture. "Miss Collins, I know that whatever you tell me, it will be the truth. In many ways, of all those I have met in London, I find you the most trustworthy—more so than my own family."

"That seems to me a great misfortune, Mr. Lightwood, for we have known each other only a little time indeed."

"I hope to change that. At least walk to the park with me, Soph—Miss Collins. Tell me this truth of which you speak. If then you still desire no further connection with me, I will respect your wishes. I ask only for an hour or so of your time." His eyes pleaded with her. "Please?"

Sophie felt, almost against her will, a rush of sympathy for this boy with his sea-storm eyes, who seemed so alone. "Very well," she said. "I will come to the park with you."

An entire carriage ride alone with Jem, Tessa thought, her stomach clenching as she drew on her gloves and cast a last glance at herself in the pier glass in her bedroom. Just two nights ago the prospect had precipitated in her no new or unusual feelings; she had been worried about Will, and curious about Whitechapel, and Jem had gently distracted her as they'd rolled along, speaking of Latin and Greek and *parabatai*.

And now? Now she felt like a net of butterflies was loose in her stomach at the prospect of being shut up in a small, close space alone with him. She glanced at her pale face in the mirror, pinched her cheeks and bit her lips to bring color into them, and reached for her hat on the stand beside the vanity. Settling it on her brown hair, she caught herself wishing she had golden curls like Jessamine, and thought—Could I? Would it be possible to Change just that one small part of herself, give herself shimmering hair, or perhaps a slimmer waist or fuller lips?

She whirled away from the glass, shaking her head. How

had she *not* thought of that before? And yet the mere idea seemed like a betrayal of her own face. Her hunger to know what she was still burned inside her; if even her own features were no longer the ones she'd been born with, how could she justify this demand, this need to know her own nature? *Don't you know there is no Tessa Gray?* Mortmain had said to her. If she used her power to turn her eyes sky blue or to darken her lashes, wouldn't she be proving him right?

She shook her head, trying to cast the thoughts off as she hurried from her room and down the steps to the Institute's entryway. Waiting in the courtyard was a black carriage, unmarked by any coat of arms and driven by a pair of matched horses the color of smoke. In the driver's seat sat a Silent Brother; it was not Brother Enoch but another of his brethren that she didn't recognize. His face was not as scarred as Enoch's, from what she could see beneath the hood.

She started down the steps just as the door opened behind her and Jem came out; it was chilly, and he wore a light gray coat that made his hair and eyes look more silver than ever. He looked up at the equally gray sky, heavy with black-edged clouds, and said, "We'd better get into the carriage before it starts to rain."

It was a perfectly ordinary thing to say, but Tessa was struck speechless all the same. She followed Jem silently to the carriage and allowed him to help her in. As he climbed in after her, and swung the door shut behind them, she noticed he was not carrying his sword-cane.

The carriage started forward with a lurch. Tessa, her hand at the window, gave a cry. "The gates—they're locked! The carriage—"

"Hush." Jem put his hand on her arm. She couldn't help a gasp as the carriage rumbled up to the padlocked iron gates—and passed *through* them, as if they had been made of no more substance than air. She felt the breath go out of her in a whoosh of surprise. "The Silent Brothers have strange magic," said Jem, and dropped his hand.

At that moment it began to rain, the sky opening up like a punctured hot water bottle. Through the sheets of silver Tessa stared as the carriage rolled through pedestrians as if they were ghosts, slipped into the narrowest cracks between buildings, rattled through a courtyard and then a warehouse, boxes all about them, and emerged finally on the Embankment, itself slick and wet with rain beside the heaving gray water of the Thames.

"Oh, dear God," Tessa said, and drew the curtain shut. "Tell me we aren't going to roll into the river."

Jem laughed. Even through her shock, it was a welcome sound. "No. The carriages of the Silent City travel only on land, as far as I know, though that travel *is* peculiar. It's a bit sickening the first time or two, but you get used to it."

"Do you?" She looked at him directly. This was the moment. She had to say it, before their friendship suffered further. Before there could be more awkwardness. "Jem," she said.

"Yes?"

"I—you must know—how very much your friendship means to me," she began, awkwardly. "And—"

A look of pain flashed across his face. "Please don't."

Thrown off her stride, Tessa could only blink. "What do you mean?"

"Every time you say that word, 'friendship,' it goes into me like a knife," he said. "To be friends is a beautiful thing, Tessa, and I do not scorn it, but I have hoped for a long time now that we might be more than friends. And then I had thought after the other night that perhaps my hopes were not in vain. But now—"

"Now I have ruined everything," she whispered. "I am so sorry."

He looked toward the window; she could sense that he was fighting some strong emotion. "You should not have to apologize for not returning my feelings."

"But *Jem*." She was bewildered, and could think only of taking his pain away, of making him feel less hurt. "I was apologizing for my behavior that other night. It was forward and inexcusable. What you must think of me . . ."

He looked up in surprise. "Tessa, you can't think that, can you? It is I who have behaved inexcusably. I have barely been able to look at you since, thinking how much you must despise me—"

"I could never despise you," she said. "I have never met anyone as kind and good as you are. I thought it was you who were dismayed by me. That you despised me."

Jem looked shocked. "How could I despise you when it was my own distraction that led to what happened between us? If I had not been in such a desperate state, I would have shown more restraint."

He means he would have had enough restraint to stop me, Tessa thought. *He does not expect propriety of me. He assumes it would not be in my nature.* She stared fixedly at the window again, or the bit of it she could see. The river was visible, black boats bobbing on the tide, the rain mixing with the river.

"Tessa." He scrambled across the carriage so that he was sitting beside her rather than across from her, his anxious, beautiful face close to hers. "I know that mundane girls are taught that it is their responsibility not to tempt men. That men are weak and women must restrain them. I assure you, Shadowhunter mores are different. More equal. It was our equal choice to do—what we did."

She stared at him. He was so kind, she thought. He seemed to read the fears in her heart and move to dispel them before she could speak them aloud.

She thought then of Will. Of what had transpired between them the previous evening. She pushed away the memory of the cold air all around them, the heat between their bodies as they clung together. She had been drugged, as had he. Nothing they had said or done meant anything more than an opium addict's babbling. There was no need to tell anyone; it had meant nothing. Nothing.

"Say something, Tessa." Jem's voice shook. "I fear that you think that I regret that night. I do not." His thumb brushed over her wrist, the bare skin between the cuff of her dress and her glove. "I only regret that it came too soon. I—I would have wanted to—to court you first. To take you driving, with a chaperon."

"A chaperon?" Tessa laughed despite herself.

He went on determinedly. "To *tell* you of my feelings first, before I showed them. To write poetry for you—"

"You don't even like poetry," Tessa said, her voice catching on a half laugh of relief.

"No. But you make me want to write it. Does that not count for anything?"

Tessa's lips curled into a smile. She leaned forward and looked up into his face, so close to hers that she could make out each individual silvery eyelash on his lids, the faint white scars on his pale throat where once there had been Marks. "That sounds almost practiced, James Carstairs. How many girls have you made swoon with that observation?"

"There is only one girl I care to make swoon," he said. "The question is, does she?"

She smiled at him. "She does."

A moment later—she did not know how it had happened—he was kissing her, his lips soft on hers, his hand rising to cup her cheek and chin, holding her face steady. Tessa heard a light crinkling and realized it was the sound of the silk flowers on her hat being crushed against the side of the carriage as his body pressed hers back. She clutched at his coat lapels, as much to keep him close as to stop herself from falling over.

The carriage came to a jerking halt. Jem drew back from her, looking dazed. "By the Angel," he said. "Perhaps we do need a chaperon."

Tessa shook her head. "Jem, I . . ."

Jem still looked stunned. "I think I'd better sit over here," he said, and moved to the seat across from hers. Tessa glanced toward the window. Through the gap in the curtains she saw that the Houses of Parliament loomed above them, towers framed darkly against the lightening sky. It had stopped raining. She was not sure why the carriage had stopped; indeed, it rumbled into life a moment later, rolling directly into what seemed a pit of black shadow that had opened up before them. She knew enough not to gasp in surprise this time; there was darkness, and then they rolled out into the great room of black basalt lit with torches that she remembered from the Council meeting.

The carriage stopped and the door flew open. Several Silent Brothers stood on the other side. Brother Enoch was at their head. Two Brothers flanked him, each holding a burning torch. Their hoods were back. Both were blind, though only one, like Enoch, seemed to have missing eyes; the others had eyes that were shut, with runes scrawled blackly across them. All had their lips stitched shut.

Welcome again to the Silent City, Daughter of Lilith, said Brother Enoch.

For a moment Tessa wanted to reach behind herself for the warm pressure of Jem's hand on hers, let him help her out of the carriage. She thought of Charlotte then. Charlotte, so small and strong, who leaned on no one.

She emerged from the carriage on her own, the heels of her boots ringing on the basalt floor. "Thank you, Brother Enoch," she said. "We are here to see Jessamine Lovelace. Will you take us to her?"

The prisons of the Silent City were beneath its first level, past the pavilion of the Speaking Stars. A dark staircase led down. The Silent Brothers went first, followed by Jem and Tessa, who had not spoken to each other since they'd left the carriage. It was not an awkward silence, though. There was something about the haunting grandeur of the City of Bones, with its great mausoleums and soaring arches, that made her feel as if she were in a museum or a church, where hushed voices were required.

At the bottom of the stairs, a corridor snaked in two

directions; the Silent Brothers turned to the left, and led Jem and Tessa nearly to the end of the hall. As they went, they passed row after row of small chambers, each with a barred, padlocked door. Each contained a bed and washstand, and nothing else. The walls were stone, and the smell was of water and dampness. Tessa wondered if they were under the Thames, or somewhere else altogether.

At last the Brothers stopped at a door, the second to the last on the hall, and Brother Enoch touched the padlock. It clicked open, and the chains holding the door shut fell away.

You are welcome to enter, said Enoch, stepping back. *We will be waiting for you outside.*

Jem put his hand to the door handle and hesitated, looking at Tessa. "Perhaps you should talk to her for a moment alone. Woman to woman."

Tessa was startled. "Are you sure? You know her better than I do—"

"But you know Nate," said Jem, and his eyes flicked away from her briefly. Tessa had the feeling there was something he was not telling her. It was such an unusual feeling when it came to Jem that she was not sure how to react. "I will join you in a moment, once you have put her at ease."

Slowly Tessa nodded. Brother Enoch swung the door open, and she walked inside, flinching a little as the heavy door crashed to behind her.

It was a small room, like the others, stone-bound. There was a washstand and what had probably once been a ceramic jug of water; now it was in pieces on the floor, as if someone had thrown it with great force against the wall. On the narrow bed sat Jessamine in a plain white gown, a rough blanket wrapped around her. Her hair fell around her shoulders in tangled snakes, and her eyes were red.

"Welcome. Nice place to live out of, isn't this?" Jessamine said. Her voice sounded rough, as if her throat were swollen from crying. She looked at Tessa, and her lower lip began to tremble. "Did—did Charlotte send you to bring me back?"

Tessa shook her head. "No."

"But—" Jessamine's eyes began to fill. "She can't *leave* me here. I can hear them, all night." She shuddered, pulling the blanket closer around her.

"You can hear what?"

"The dead," she said. "Whispering in their tombs. If I stay down here long enough, I will join them. I know it."

Tessa sat down on the edge of the bed and carefully touched Jessamine's hair, stroking the snarls lightly. "That won't happen," she said, and Jessamine began to sob. Her shoulders shook. Helplessly Tessa looked around the room, as if something in the miserable cell might give her inspiration. "Jessamine," she said. "I brought you something."

Jessamine very slowly raised her face. "Is it from Nate?"

"No," Tessa answered gently. "It's something of yours." She reached into her pocket and drew it out, extending her hand toward Jessamine. In her palm lay a tiny baby doll that she had taken from its crib inside Jessamine's doll's house. "Baby Jessie."

Jessamine made an "oh" sound low in her throat, and plucked the doll from Tessa's grasp. She held it tightly, against her chest. Her eyes spilled over, her tears making tracks in the grime on her face. She really was a most pitiful sight, Tessa thought. If only . . .

"Jessamine," Tessa said again. She felt as if Jessamine were an animal in need of gentling, and that repeating her name in a kind tone might somehow help. "We need your help."

"In betraying Nate," Jessamine snapped. "But I don't know anything. I don't even know why I'm here."

"Yes, you do." It was Jem, coming into the cell. He was flushed and a little out of breath, as if he had been hurrying. He shot Tessa a conspiratorial glance and closed the door behind him. "You know exactly why you're here, Jessie—"

"Because I fell in love!" Jessamine snapped. "You ought to know what that's like. I see how you look at Tessa." She shot Tessa a poisonous look as Tessa's cheeks flamed. "At least Nate is human."

Jem didn't lose his composure. "I haven't betrayed the Institute for Tessa," he said. "I haven't lied to and endangered those who have cared for me since I was orphaned."

"If you wouldn't," said Jessamine, "you don't really love her."

"If she asked me to," said Jem, "I would know she did not really love *me*."

Jessamine sucked in a breath and turned away from him, as if he had slapped her face. "You," she said in a muffled voice. "I always thought you were the nicest one. But you're horrible. You're all horrible. Charlotte *tortured* me with that Mortal Sword until I told everything. What more could you possibly want from me? You've already forced me to betray the man I love."

At the very corner of Tessa's vision, she saw Jem roll his eyes. There was a certain theatricality to Jessamine's despair, as there was to everything she did, but under it—under the role of wronged woman Jessamine had cast herself in—Tessa felt she was genuinely afraid.

"I know you love Nate," Tessa said. "And I know that I will not be able to convince you that he does not return your sentiment."

"You're jealous—"

"Jessamine, Nate cannot love you. There is something wrong with him—some piece missing from his heart. God knows my aunt and I tried to ignore it, to tell each other it was boyish high-jinks and thoughtlessness. But he murdered our aunt—did he tell you that?—murdered the woman who brought him up, and laughed to me about it later. He has no empathy, no capacity for gratitude. If you shield him now, it will win you nothing in his eyes."

"Nor is it likely you will ever see him again," said Jem. "If you do *not* help us, the Clave will never let you go. It will be you and the dead down here for eternity, if you are not punished with a curse."

"Nate said you would try to frighten me," said Jessamine in a sliver of a voice.

"Nate also said the Clave and Charlotte would do nothing to you because they were weak," said Tessa. "That has not proven true. He said to you only what he had to say, to get you to do what he wanted you to. He is my brother, and I tell you, he is a cheat and a liar."

"We need you to write a letter to him," said Jem. "Telling him you have knowledge of a secret Shadowhunter plot against Mortmain, and to meet you tonight—"

Jessamine shook her head, plucking at the rough blanket. "I will not betray him."

"Jessie." Jem's voice was soft; Tessa did not know how Jessamine could hold out against him. "Please. We are only asking you to save yourself. Send this message; tell us your usual meeting place. That is all we ask."

Jessamine shook her head. "Mortmain," she said. "Mortmain will yet win out over you. Then the Silent Brothers will be defeated and Nate will come to claim me."

"Very well," said Tessa. "Imagine that does happen. You say Nate loves you. Then, he would forgive you anything, wouldn't he? Because when a man loves a woman, he understands that she is weak. That she cannot hold out against, for instance, torture, in the manner in which he could."

Jessamine made a whimpering sound.

"He understands that she is frail and delicate and easily led," Tessa went on, and gently touched Jessamine's arm. "Jessie, you see your choice. If you do not help us, the Clave will know it, and they will not be lenient with you. If you do help us, Nate will understand. If he loves you . . . he has no choice. For love means forgiveness."

"I . . ." Jessamine looked from one of them to the other, like a frightened rabbit. "Would you forgive Tessa, if it were her?"

"I would forgive Tessa anything," Jem said gravely.

Tessa could not see his expression, she was facing Jessamine, but she felt her heart skip a beat. She could not look at Jem, too afraid her expression would betray her feelings.

"Jessie, please," she said instead.

Jessamine was silent for a long time. When she spoke, finally, her voice was as thin as a thread. "You will be meeting him, I suppose, disguised as me."

Tessa nodded.

"You must wear boys' clothes," she said. "When I meet him at night, I am always dressed as a boy. It is safer for me to traverse the streets alone like that. He will expect it." She looked up, pushing her matted hair out of her face. "Have you a pen and paper?" she added. "I will write the note."

She took the proffered items from Jem and began to scribble. "I ought to get something in return for this," she said. "If they will not let me out—"

"They will not," said Jem, "until it is determined that your information is good."

"Then they ought to at least give me better food. It's dreadful here. Just gruel and hard bread." Having finished scribbling the note, she handed it to Tessa. "The boys' clothes I wear are behind the doll's house in my room. Take care moving it," she added, and for a moment again she was Jessamine, her brown eyes haughty. "And if you must borrow some of my clothes, do. You've been wearing the same four dresses I bought you in June over and over. That yellow one is practically ancient. And if you don't want anyone to know you've been kissing in carriages, you should refrain from wearing a hat with easily crushed flowers on it. People aren't blind, you know."

"So it seems," said Jem with great gravity, and when Tessa looked over at him, he smiled, just at her.

15

Thousands More

There is something horrible about a flower;
This, broken in my hand, is one of those
He threw it in just now; it will not live another hour;
There are thousands more; you do not miss a rose.
–Charlotte Mew, "In Nunhead Cemetery"

The rest of the day at the Institute passed in a mood of great tension, as the Shadowhunters prepared for their confrontation with Nate that night. There were no formal meals again, only a great deal of rushing about, as weapons were readied and polished, gear was prepared, and maps consulted while Bridget, warbling mournful ballads, carried trays of sandwiches and tea up and down the halls.

If it hadn't been for Sophie's invitation to "come and have a pickle" Tessa probably wouldn't have eaten anything all day; as it was, her knotted throat would allow only a few bites of sandwich to slide down before she felt as if she were choking.

I'm going to see Nate tonight, she thought, staring at herself in the pier glass as Sophie knelt at her feet, lacing up her boots—boys' boots from Jessamine's hidden trove of male clothing.

And then I am going to betray him.

She thought of the way Nate had lain in her lap in the carriage on the way from de Quincey's, and the way he had shrieked her name and held on to her when Brother Enoch had appeared. She wondered how much of that had been show. Probably at least part of him had been truly terrified—abandoned by Mortmain, hated by de Quincey, in the hands of Shadowhunters he had no reason to trust.

Except that she had told him they were trustworthy. And he had not cared. He had wanted what Mortmain was offering him. More than he had wanted her safety. More than he had cared about anything else. All the years between them, the time that had knitted them together so closely that she had thought them inseparable, had meant nothing to him.

"You can't brood on it, miss," said Sophie, rising to her feet and dusting off her hands. "He aren't—I mean, he isn't worth it."

"Who isn't worth it?"

"Your brother. Wasn't that what you were thinking on?"

Tessa squinted suspiciously. "Can you tell what I'm thinking because you have the Sight?"

Sophie laughed. "Lord, no, miss. I can read it on your face like a book. You always have the same look when you think of Master Nathaniel. But he's a bad hat, miss, not worth your thoughts."

"He's my brother."

"That doesn't mean you're like him," said Sophie decisively. "Some are just born bad, and that's all there is to it."

Some imp of the perverse made Tessa ask: "And what of Will? Do you still think he was born bad? Lovely and poisonous like a snake, you said."

Sophie raised her delicately arched eyebrows. "Master Will is a mystery, no doubt."

Before Tessa could reply the door swung open, and Jem stood in the doorway. "Charlotte sent me to give you—," he began, and broke off, staring at Tessa.

She looked down at herself. Trousers, shoes, shirt, waistcoat, all in order. It was certainly a peculiar feeling, wearing men's clothes—they were tight in places she was not used to clothes being tight, and loose in others, and they itched—but that hardly explained the look on Jem's face.

"I . . ." Jem had flushed all over, red spreading up from his collar to his face. "Charlotte sent me to tell you we're waiting in the drawing room," he said. Then he turned around and left the room hurriedly.

"Goodness," Tessa said, perplexed. "What was that about?"

Sophie chuckled softly. "Well, look at yourself." Tessa looked. She was flushed, she thought, her hair tumbling loose over her shirt and waistcoat. The shirt had clearly been made with something of a feminine figure in mind, since it did not strain over the bosom as much as Tessa had feared it would; still, it was tight, thanks to Jessie's smaller frame. The trousers were tight as well, as was the fashion, molding themselves to her legs. She cocked her head to the side. There *was* something indecent about it, wasn't there? A man was not supposed to be able to see the shape of a lady's upper legs, or so much of the curve of her hips. There was something about the men's clothing that made her look not masculine but . . . undressed.

"My goodness," she said.

"Indeed," said Sophie. "Don't worry. They'll fit better once you Change, and besides . . . he fancies you anyway."

"I—you know—I mean, you think he fancies me?"

"Quite," said Sophie, sounding unperturbed. "You should see the way he looks at you when he doesn't think you see. Or looks up when a door opens, and is always disappointed when it isn't you. Master Jem, he isn't like Master Will. He can't hide what he's thinking."

"And you're not . . ." Tessa searched for words. "Sophie, you're not—put out with me?"

"Why would I be put out with you?" A little of the amusement had gone out of Sophie's voice, and now she sounded carefully neutral.

You're in for it now, Tessa, she thought. "I thought perhaps that there was a time when you looked at Jem with a certain admiration. That is all. I meant nothing improper, Sophie."

Sophie was silent for such a long time that Tessa was sure she was angry, or worse, terribly hurt. Instead she said, finally, "There was a time when I—when I admired him. He was so gentle and so kind, not like any man I'd known. And so lovely to look at, and the music he makes—" She shook her head, and her dark ringlets bounced. "But he never cared for me. Never by a word or a gesture did he lead me to believe he returned my admiration, though he was never unkind."

"Sophie," Tessa said softly. "You have been more than a maidservant since I have come here. You have been a good friend. I would not do anything that might hurt you."

Sophie looked up at her. "Do you care for him?"

"I think," Tessa said with slow caution, "that I do."

"Good." Sophie exhaled. "He deserves that. To be happy. Master Will has always been the brighter burning star, the one to catch attention—but Jem is a steady flame, unwavering and honest. He could make you happy."

"And you would not object?"

"Object?" Sophie shook her head. "Oh, Miss Tessa, it is kind of you to care what I think, but no. I would not object. My fondness for him—and that is all it was, a girlish fondness—has quite cooled into friendship. I wish only his happiness and yours."

Tessa was amazed. All the worrying she had done about Sophie's feelings, and Sophie didn't mind at all. What *had* changed since Sophie had wept over Jem's illness the night of the Blackfriars Bridge debacle? Unless . . . "Have you been walking out with someone? Cyril, or . . ."

Sophie rolled her eyes. "Oh, Lord have mercy on us all. First Thomas, now Cyril. When *will* you stop trying to marry me off to the nearest available man?"

"There must be someone—"

"There's no one," Sophie said firmly, rising to her feet and turning Tessa toward the pier glass. "There you are. Twist up your hair under your hat and you'll be the model of a gentleman."

Tessa did as she was told.

When Tessa came into the library, the small band of Institute Shadowhunters—Jem, Will, Henry, and Charlotte, all in gear now—were grouped around a table on which a small oblong device made of brass was balanced. Henry was gesturing at it animatedly, his voice rising. "This," he was saying, "is what

I have been working on. For just this occasion. It is specifically calibrated to function as a weapon against clockwork assassins."

"As dull as Nate Gray is," Will said, "his head is not actually filled with gears, Henry. He's a human."

"He may bring one of those creatures with him. We don't know he'll be there unaccompanied. If nothing else, that clockwork coachman of Mortmain's—"

"I think Henry is right," said Tessa, and they all whirled to face her. Jem flushed again, though more lightly this time, and offered her a crooked smile; Will's eyes ran up and down her body once, not briskly.

He said, "You don't look like a boy at all. You look like a girl in boys' clothes."

She couldn't tell if he was approving, disapproving, or neutral on the subject. "I'm not trying to fool anyone but a casual observer," she replied crossly. "Nate *knows* Jessamine's a girl. And the clothes will fit me better once I've Changed into her."

"Maybe you should do it now," said Will.

Tessa glared at him, then shut her eyes. It was different, Changing into someone you had been before. She did not need to be holding something of theirs, or to be near them. It was like closing her eyes and reaching into a wardrobe, detecting a familiar garment by touch, and drawing it out. She reached for Jessamine inside herself, and let her free, wrapping the Jessamine disguise around herself, feeling the breath pushed from her lungs as her rib cage contracted, her hair slipping from its twist to fall in light corn silk waves against her face. She pushed it back up under the hat and opened her eyes.

They were all staring at her. Jem was the only one to offer a smile as she blinked in the light.

"Uncanny," said Henry. His hand rested lightly on the object on the table. Tessa, uncomfortable with the eyes on her, moved toward it. "What is that?"

"It's a sort of . . . infernal device that Henry's created," Jem said. "Meant to disrupt the internal mechanisms that keep the clockwork creatures running."

"You twist it, like this"—Henry mimed twisting the bottom half of the thing in one direction and the top half in another—"and then throw it. Try to lodge it into the creature's gears or somewhere that it will stick. It is meant to disrupt the mechanical currents that run through the creature's body, causing them to wrench apart. It could do you some damage too, even if you aren't clockwork, so don't hang on to it once it's activated. I've only two, so . . ."

He handed one to Jem, and another to Charlotte, who took it and hung it from her weapons belt without a word.

"The message has been sent?" Tessa asked.

"Yes. We're only waiting for a reply from your brother now," said Charlotte. She unrolled a paper across the surface of the table, weighting down the corners with copper gears from a stack Henry must have left there. "Here," she said, "is a map that shows where Jessamine claims she and Nate usually meet. It's a warehouse on Mincing Lane, down by Lower Thames Street. It used to be a tea merchant's packing factory until the business went bankrupt."

"Mincing Lane," said Jem. "Center of the tea trade. Also the opium trade. Makes sense Mortmain might keep a warehouse there." He ran a slender finger over the map, tracing the names of the nearby streets: Eastcheap, Gracechurch Street, Lower Thames Street, St. Swithin's Lane. "Such an odd place for Jessamine, though," he said. "She always dreamed of such glamour—of being introduced at Court and putting her hair up for dances. Not of clandestine meetings in some sooty warehouse near the wharves."

"She did do what she set out to do," Tessa said. "She married someone who isn't a Shadowhunter."

Will's mouth quirked into a half smile. "If the marriage were valid, she'd be your sister-in-law."

Tessa shuddered. "I—it's not that I hold a grudge against Jessamine. But she deserves better than my brother."

"Anyone deserves better than that." Will reached under the table and drew out a rolled-up bunch of fabric. He spread it across the table, avoiding the map. Inside were several long, thin weapons, each with a gleaming rune carved into the blade. "I'd nearly forgotten I had Thomas order these for me a few weeks ago. They've only just arrived. Misericords—good for getting in between the jointure of those clockwork creatures."

"The question is," Jem said, lifting one of the misericords and examining the blade, "once we get Tessa inside to meet Nate, how do the rest of us watch their meeting without being noticed? We must be ready to intervene at any moment, especially if it appears that his suspicions have been aroused."

"We must arrive first, and hide ourselves," said Will. "It is the only way. We listen to see if Nate says anything useful."

"I dislike the idea of Tessa being forced to speak with him at all," muttered Jem.

"She can well hold her own; I have seen it. Besides, he is more likely to speak freely if he thinks himself safe. Once captured, even if the Silent Brothers do explore his mind, Mortmain may have thought to put blocks in it to protect his knowledge, which can take time to dismantle."

"I think Mortmain has put in blocks in Jessamine's case," said Tessa. "For whatever it is worth, I cannot touch her thoughts."

"Even more likely he will have done it in Nate's, then," said Will.

"That boy is as weak as a kitten," said Henry. "He will tell us whatever we want to know. And if not, I have a device—"

"Henry!" Charlotte looked seriously alarmed. "Tell me you have not been working on a torture device."

"Not at all. I call it the Confuser. It emits a vibration that directly affects the human brain, rendering it incapable of telling between fiction and fact." Henry, looking proud, reached for his box. "He will simply spill everything that is in his mind, with no attention to the consequences . . ."

Charlotte held up a warning hand. "Not right now, Henry. If we must utilize the . . . Confuser on Nate Gray, we will do so when we have brought him back here. At the moment we must concentrate on reaching the warehouse before Tessa. It is not *that* far; I suggest Cyril takes us there, then returns for Tessa."

"Nate will recognize the Institute's carriage," Tessa objected. "When I saw Jessamine leaving for a meeting with Nate, she was most decidedly going on foot. I shall walk."

"You will get lost," said Will.

"I won't," said Tessa, indicating the map. "It's a simple walk.

I could turn left at Gracechurch Street, go along Eastcheap, and cut through to Mincing Lane."

An argument ensued, with Jem, to Tessa's surprise, siding with Will against the idea of her walking the streets alone. Eventually it was decided that Henry would drive the carriage to Mincing Lane, while Tessa would walk, with Cyril following her at a discreet distance, lest she lose herself in the crowded, dirty, noisy city. With a shrug she agreed; it seemed less trouble than arguing, and she didn't mind Cyril.

"I don't suppose anyone's going to point out," said Will, "that once again we are leaving the Institute without a Shadowhunter to protect it?"

Charlotte rolled up the map with a flick of her wrist. "And which of us would you suggest stay home, then, instead of helping Tessa?"

"I didn't say anything about anyone staying home." Will's voice dropped. "But Cyril will be with Tessa, Sophie's only half-trained, and Bridget . . ."

Tessa glanced over at Sophie, who was sitting quietly in the corner of the library, but the other girl gave no sign of having heard Will. Meanwhile, Bridget's voice was wafting faintly from the kitchen, another miserable ballad:

"So John took out of his pocket
A knife both long and sharp,
And stuck it through his brother's heart,
And the blood came pouring down.
Says John to William, 'Take off thy shirt,
And tear it from gore to gore,

And wrap it round your bleeding heart,
And the blood will pour no more.'"

"By the Angel," said Charlotte, "we really *are* going to have to do something about her before she drives us all to madness, aren't we?"

Before anyone could reply, two things happened at once: Something tapped at the window, startling Tessa so much that she took a step back, and a great, echoing noise sounded through the Institute—the sound of the summoning bell. Charlotte said something to Will—lost in the noise of the bell—and he left the room, while Charlotte crossed it, slid the window up and open, and captured something hovering outside.

She turned away from the window, a fluttering piece of paper in her hand; it looked a bit like a white bird, edges flapping in the breeze. Her hair blew about her face too, and Tessa was reminded how young Charlotte was. "From Nate, I suppose," said Charlotte. "His message for Jessamine." She brought it to Tessa, who tore the creamy parchment lengthwise in her eagerness to get it open.

Tessa glanced up. "It is from Nate," she confirmed. "He has agreed to meet Jessie in the usual place at sundown—" She gave a little gasp as, recognizing itself somehow as having been read, the note burst into quick, heatless flames, consuming itself until it was only a film of black ash on her fingers.

"That gives us only a little time," said Henry. "I will go and tell Cyril to ready the carriage." He looked to Charlotte, as if for approval, but she only nodded without meeting his eyes. With a sigh Henry left the room—nearly bumping into Will, who was on his way back in, followed by a figure in a traveling cloak. For a moment Tessa wondered in confusion if it was a Silent Brother—until the visitor drew his hood back and she saw the familiar sandy-blond curling hair and green eyes.

"Gideon Lightwood?" she said in surprise.

"There." Charlotte slipped the map she was holding into her pocket. "The Institute will not be Shadowhunterless."

Sophie got hastily to her feet—then froze, as if, outside the atmosphere of the training room, she was not sure what to do or say in front of the eldest Lightwood brother.

Gideon glanced around the room. As always his green eyes were calm, unruffled. Will, behind him, seemed to burn with bright energy by contrast, even when he was simply standing still. "You called on me?" Gideon said, and she realized that of course, looking at her, he was seeing Jessamine. "And I am here, though I know not why, or what for."

"To train Sophie, ostensibly," said Charlotte. "And also to look after the Institute while we're gone. We need a Shadowhunter of age to be present, and you qualify. In fact, it was Sophie who suggested you."

"And how long will you be gone?"

"Two hours, three. Not all night."

"All right." Gideon began to unbutton his cloak. There was dust on his boots, and his hair looked as if he had been out in the cold wind, hatless. "My father would say it was good practice for when I run the place."

Will muttered something under his breath that sounded like "bloody cheek." He looked at Charlotte, who shook her head at him minutely.

"It may be that the Institute will be yours one day," she said to Gideon quite mildly. "In any case, we're grateful for your assistance. The Institute is the responsibility of all Shadowhunters, after all. These are our dwelling places—our Idris away from home."

Gideon turned to Sophie. "Are you ready to train?"

She nodded. They left the room together in a group, Gideon and Sophie turning right to make their way to the training room, the rest of them heading for the stairs. Bridget's mournful yowl was even louder out here, and Tessa heard Gideon say something to Sophie about it, and Sophie's soft voice in response, before they were too far away for her to hear them anymore.

It seemed natural to fall into step beside Jem as they went downstairs and through the nave of the cathedral. She was walking close enough to him that though they did not speak, she could feel the warmth of him against her side, the brush of his bare hand against hers as they stepped outside. Sunset was coming. The sky had begun to take on the bronze sheen that came just before twilight. Cyril was waiting on the front stairs, looking so much like Thomas that it hurt one's heart to look at him. He was carrying a long, thin dagger, which he handed off to Will without a word; Will took it and put it through his belt.

Charlotte turned and put her hand against Tessa's cheek. "We shall see you at the warehouse," she said. "You will be perfectly safe, Tessa. And thank you, for doing this for us." Charlotte dropped her hand and went down the steps, Henry following her, and Will just after. Jem hesitated, just for a moment, and Tessa—remembering a night like this one, when he had run up the steps to bid her good-bye—pressed her fingers lightly against his wrist.

"*Mizpah,*" she said.

She heard him suck in his breath. The Shadowhunters were getting into the carriage; he turned and kissed her quickly on the cheek, before spinning and running down the steps after the others; none of them seemed to have noticed, but Tessa put her hand to her face as Jem climbed, last, into the carriage and Henry made his way up to the driver's seat. The gates of the Institute swung open, and the carriage clattered out into the darkening afternoon.

"Shall we go, then, miss?" Cyril inquired. Despite how much he looked like Thomas, Tessa thought, he had a less diffident demeanor. He looked her directly in the eye when he spoke, and the corners of his mouth always seemed to be about to crinkle into a smile. She wondered if there was always one calmer and one more high-strung brother, like Gabriel and Gideon.

"Yes, I think we—" Tessa stopped suddenly, one foot about to descend the steps. It was ridiculous, she knew, and yet—she had taken off the clockwork angel to dress herself in Jessamine's clothes. She had not put it back on. She couldn't *wear* it—Nate would recognize it immediately—but she had meant to put it into her pocket for luck, and she had forgotten. She hesitated now. It was more than silly superstition; twice now the angel had literally saved her life.

She turned. "I have forgotten something. Wait here for me, Cyril. I'll be only a moment."

The door to the Institute was still open; she charged back through it and up the stairs, through the halls and into the corridor that led to Jessamine's room—where she froze.

Jessamine's hall was the same hall that led to the steps to

the training room. She had seen Sophie and Gideon disappear down it minutes ago. Only, they had not disappeared; they were still there. The light was low, and they were only shadows in the dimness, but Tessa could see them plainly: Sophie, standing against the wall, and Gideon pressing her hand.

Tessa took a step backward, her heart jerking inside her chest. Neither of them saw her. They seemed entirely concentrated on each other. Gideon leaned in then, murmuring something to Sophie; gently he brushed a stray strand of hair from her face. Tessa's stomach tensed, and she turned and crept away, as soundlessly as she could.

The sky had turned a shade darker when she came back out onto the steps. Cyril was there, whistling off-key; he broke off abruptly when he saw Tessa's expression. "Is everything all right, miss? Did you get what you wanted?"

Tessa thought of Gideon moving Sophie's hair away from her face. She remembered Will's hands gentle on her waist and the softness of Jem's kiss on her cheek, and felt as if her mind were whirling. Who was she to tell Sophie to be careful, even silently, when she was so lost herself?

"Yes," she lied. "I got what I wanted. Thank you, Cyril."

The warehouse was a great limestone building surrounded by a black wrought iron fence. The windows had been boarded over, and a stout iron padlock held closed the front gates, over which the blackening name of Mortmain and Co. could barely be seen below layers of soot.

The Shadowhunters left the carriage drawn up to the curb, with a glamour on it to prevent it from being stolen or molested by passing mundanes, at least until Cyril arrived to wait with it. A closer inspection of the padlock showed Will that it had been oiled recently and opened; a rune took care of the lack of a key, and he and the others slipped inside, closing the gate behind them.

Another rune unlocked the front door, leading them into a suite of offices. Only one was still furnished, with a desk, a green-shaded lamp, and a floral sofa with a high carved back. "Doubtless where Jessamine and Nate accomplished the majority of their courtship," Will observed cheerfully.

Jem made a noise of disgust and poked at the couch with his cane. Charlotte was bending over the desk, hastily going through the drawers.

"I didn't realize you'd taken up such a strong anti-courtship stance," Will observed to Jem.

"Not on principle. The thought of Nate Gray touching anyone—" Jem made a face. "And Jessamine is so convinced he loves her. If you could see her, I think even you might pity her, Will."

"I would not," said Will. "Unrequited love is a ridiculous state, and it makes those in it behave ridiculously." He tugged at the bandage on his arm as if it were paining him. "Charlotte? The desk?"

"Nothing." She slid the drawers shut. "Some papers listing the prices of tea and the times of tea auctions, but other than that, nothing but dead spiders."

"How romantic," murmured Will. He ducked behind Jem, who had already wandered ahead into the adjacent office, using his cane to sweep away cobwebs as he went. The next few rooms were empty, and the last opened out onto what had once been a warehouse floor. It was a great shadowy cavernous space, its ceiling disappearing up into darkness. Rickety wooden steps led up to a second-floor gallery. Burlap bags were propped against the walls on the first floor, looking for all the world, in the shadows, like slumped bodies. Will raised his witchlight rune-stone in one hand, sending out spokes of light through the room as Henry went to investigate one of the sacks. He was back in a moment, shrugging his shoulders.

"Broken bits of loose-leaf tea," he said. "Orange pekoe, from the looks of it."

But Jem was shaking his head, glancing about. "I am perfectly willing to accept that this was an active tea-trading office at one point, but it's clearly been shuttered for years, ever since Mortmain decided to interest himself in mechanisms instead. And yet the floor is clear of dust." He took Will's wrist, guiding the beam of witchlight over the smooth wooden floor. "There has been activity here—more than simply Jessamine and Nate's meeting in a disused office."

"There are more offices that way," said Henry, pointing to the far end of the room. "Charlotte and I will search them. Will, Jem, you examine the second floor."

It was a rare and novel thrill when Henry gave orders; Will looked at Jem and grinned, and commenced making his way up the rickety wooden stairs. The steps creaked under the pressure, and under Jem's slighter weight behind Will. The witchlight stone in Will's hand threw sharp patterns of light against the wall as he reached the top step.

He found himself on a gallery, a platform where perhaps trunks of tea had been stored, or a foreman had watched the floor below. It was empty now, save for a single figure, lying on the ground. The body of a man, slim and youthful, and as Will came closer, his heart began to pound crazily, because he had seen this before—had had this vision before—the limp body, the silver hair and dark clothes, the closed bruised-looking eyes, fringed with silver lashes.

"Will?" It was Jem, behind him. He looked from Will's silent, stunned face to the body on the floor and pushed past him to kneel down. He took the man by the wrist just as Charlotte reached the top of the steps. Will looked at her in surprise for a moment; her face was sheened with sweat and she looked slightly ill. Jem said, "He has a pulse. Will?"

Will came closer, and knelt down beside his friend. At this distance it was easy to see that the man on the floor was not Jem. He was older, and Caucasian; he had a growth of silver stubble on his chin and cheeks, and his features were broader and less defined. Will's heartbeat slowed as the man's eyes fluttered open.

They were silver discs, like Jem's. And in that moment Will recognized him. He smelled the sweet-sour tang of burning warlock drugs, felt the heat of them in his veins, and knew that he had seen this man before, and knew where.

"You're a werewolf," he said. "One of the packless ones, buying *yin fen* off the ifrits down the Chapel. Aren't you?"

The werewolf's eyes roamed over them both, and fastened on Jem. His lids narrowed, and his hand shot out, grabbing Jem by the lapels. "You," he wheezed. "You're one of us. 'ave you got any of it on you—any of the stuff—"

Jem recoiled. Will seized the werewolf by the wrist and yanked his hand free. It wasn't difficult; there was very little strength in his nerveless fingers. "Don't touch him." Will heard his own voice as if from a distance, clipped and cold. "He doesn't have any of your filthy powder. It doesn't work on us Nephilim like it does on you."

"Will." There was a plea in Jem's voice: *Be kinder.*

"You work for Mortmain," said Will. "Tell us what you do for him. Tell us where he is."

The werewolf laughed. Blood splashed up over his lips and dribbled down his chin. Some of it splattered onto Jem's gear. "As if—I'd know—where the Magister was," he wheezed. "Bloody fools, the pair of you. Bloody useless Nephilim. If I 'ad—me strength—I'd chop yer into bloody rags—"

"But you don't." Will was remorseless. "And maybe we *do* have some *yin fen.*"

"You don't. You think—I don't know?" The werewolf's eyes wandered. "When 'e gave it to me first, I saw things—such things as yer can't imagine—the great crystal city—the towers of Heaven—" Another spasming cough racked him. More blood splattered. It had a silvery sheen to it, like mercury. Will exchanged a look with Jem. *The crystal city.* He couldn't help thinking of Alicante, though he had never been there. "I thought I were going ter live forever—work all night, all day, never get tired. Then we started dying off, one by one. The drug, it kills ya, but 'e never said. I came back here to see if maybe there was still any of it stashed somewhere. But there's none. No point leavin'. I'm dyin' now. Might as well die 'ere as anywhere."

"He knew what he was doing when he gave you that drug," said Jem. "He knew it would kill you. He doesn't deserve your secrecy. Tell us what he was doing—what he was keeping you working on all night and day."

"Putting those *things* together—those metal men. They don't 'arf give you the willies, but the money were good and the drugs were better—"

"And a great deal of good that money will do you now," said Jem, his voice uncharacteristically bitter. "How often did he make you take it? The silver powder?"

"Six, seven times a day."

"No wonder they're running out of it down the Chapel," Will muttered. "Mortmain's controlling the supply."

"You're not supposed to take it like that," said Jem. "The more you take, the faster you die."

The werewolf fixed his gaze on Jem. His eyes were shot through with red veins. "And you," he said. "'Ow much longer 'ave *you* got left?"

Will turned his head. Charlotte was motionless behind him at the top of the stairs, staring. He raised a hand to gesture her over. "Charlotte, if we can get him downstairs, perhaps the Silent Brothers can do something to help him. If you could—"

But Charlotte, to Will's surprise, had turned a pale shade of green. She clapped her hand over her mouth and dashed downstairs.

"Charlotte!" Will hissed; he didn't dare shout. "Oh, bloody hell. All right, Jem. You take his legs, I'll take his shoulders—"

"There's no point, Will." Jem's voice was soft. "He's dead."

Will turned back. Indeed, the silver eyes were wide open, glassy, fixed on the ceiling; the chest had ceased to rise and fall. Jem reached to close his eyelids, but Will caught his friend by the wrist.

"Don't."

"I wasn't going to give him the blessing, Will. Just close his eyes."

"He doesn't deserve that. He was working with the Magister!" Will's whisper was rising to a shout.

"He is like me," said Jem simply. "An addict."

Will looked at him over their joined hands. "He is *not like you*. And you will not die like that."

Jem's lips parted in surprise. "Will . . ."

They both heard the sound of a door opening, and a voice calling out Jessamine's name. Will released Jem's wrist, and both of them dropped flat to the ground, inching to the edge of the gallery to see what was happening on the warehouse floor.

16
Mortal Rage

When I have seen by Time's fell hand defac'd
The rich-proud cost of outworn buried age;
When sometime lofty towers I see down-raz'd,
And brass eternal slave to mortal rage
—Shakespeare, "Sonnet 64"

It was a peculiar experience walking the streets of London as a boy, Tessa thought as she made her way along the crowded pavement of Eastcheap. The men who crossed her path spared her barely a glance, just pushed past her toward the doors of public houses or the next turn in the street. As a girl, walking alone through these streets at night in her fine clothes, she would have been the object of stares and jeers. As a boy she was—invisible. She had never realized what it was like to be invisible before. How light and free she felt—or would have felt, had she not felt like an aristocrat from *A Tale of Two Cities* on his way to the guillotine in a tumbrel.

She caught sight of Cyril only once, slipping between two buildings across the road from 32 Mincing Lane. It was a great stone building, and the black iron fence surrounding it, in the vanishing twilight, looked like rows of jagged black teeth. From the front gates dangled a padlock, but it had been left open; she slipped through, and then up the dusty steps to the front door, which was also unlocked.

Inside she found that the empty offices, their windows looking out onto Mincing Lane, were still and dead; a fly buzzed in one, hurling itself over and over against the plated glass panes until it fell, exhausted, to the sill. Tessa shuddered and hurried on.

In each room she walked into, she tensed, expecting to see Nate; in each room, he was not there. The final room had a door that opened out onto the floor of a warehouse. Dim blue light filtered in through the cracks in the boarded-up windows. She looked around uncertainly. "Nate?" she whispered.

He stepped out of the shadows between two flaking plaster pillars. His blond hair shone in the bluish light, under a silk top hat. He wore a blue tweed frock coat, black trousers, and black boots, but his usually immaculate appearance was disheveled. His hair hung lankly in his eyes, and there was a smear of dirt across his cheek. His clothes were wrinkled and creased as if he had slept in them. "Jessamine," he said, relief evident in his tone. "My darling." He opened his arms.

She came forward slowly, her whole body tensed. She did not want Nate touching her, but she could see no way to avoid his embrace. His arms went around her. His hand caught the brim of her hat and pulled it free, letting her fair curls tumble down her back. She thought of Will pulling the pins from her hair, and her stomach involuntarily tightened.

"I need to know where the Magister is," she began in a shaking voice. "It's terribly important. I overheard some of the Shadowhunters' plans, you see. I know you didn't wish to tell me, but . . ."

He pushed her hair back, ignoring her words. "I see," he said, and his voice was deep and husky. "But first—" He tipped her head up with a finger under her chin. "Come and kiss me, sweet-and-twenty."

Tessa wished he wouldn't quote Shakespeare. She'd never be able to hear that sonnet again without wanting to be sick. Every nerve in her body wanted to leap screaming through her skin in revulsion as he leaned toward her. She prayed for the others to burst in as she let him tilt her head up, up—

Nate began to laugh. With a jerk of his wrist, he sent her hat sailing into the shadows; his fingers tightened on her chin, the nails digging in. "My apologies for my impetuous behavior," he said. "I couldn't help but be curious to see how far you'd go to protect your Shadowhunter friends . . . little sister."

"*Nate.*" Tessa tried to jerk backward, out of his grasp, but his grip on her was too strong. His other hand shot out like a snake, spinning her around, pinning her against him with his forearm across her throat. His breath was hot against her ear. He smelled sour, like old gin and sweat.

"Did you really think I didn't know?" he spat. "After that note arrived at Benedict's ball, sending me off on that wild goose chase to Vauxhall, I realized. It all made sense. I should have known it was you from the beginning. Stupid little girl."

"Stupid?" she hissed. "I got you to spill your secrets, Nate. You told me everything. Did Mortmain find out? Is that why you look like you haven't slept in days?"

He jerked his arm tighter around her, making her gasp with pain. "You couldn't leave well enough alone. You had to pry into my business. Delighted to see me brought low, are you? What kind of sister does that make you, Tessie?"

"You would have killed me if you had the chance. There is no game you can play, nothing you can say to make me think I've betrayed you, Nate. You earned every bit of it. Allying yourself with Mortmain—"

He shook her, hard enough to make her teeth rattle. "As if my alliances are any of your business. I was doing well for myself until you and your Nephilim friends came and meddled. Now the Magister wants my head on a block. Your fault. All your fault. I was almost in despair, till I got that ridiculous note from Jessamine. I knew you were behind it, of course. All the trouble you must have gone through too, torturing her to get her to write me that ridiculous missive—"

"We didn't torture her," Tessa ground out. She struggled, but Nate only held her more tightly, the buttons on his waistcoat digging into her back. "She wanted to do it. She wanted to save her own skin."

"I don't believe you." The hand that wasn't across her throat gripped her chin; his nails dug in, and she yelped with pain. "She loves me."

"No one could love you," Tessa spat. "You're my brother—I loved you—and you have killed even that."

Nate leaned forward and growled, *"I am not your brother."*

"Very well, my half brother, if you must have it—"

"You're not my sister. Not even by half." He said the words with a cruel pleasure. "Your mother and my mother were not the same woman."

"That's not possible," Tessa whispered. "You're lying. Our mother was Elizabeth Gray—"

"*Your* mother was Elizabeth Gray, born Elizabeth Moore," said Nate. "Mine was Harriet Moore."

"Aunt Harriet?"

"She was engaged once. Did you know that? After our parents—your parents—were married. The man died before the wedding could take place. But she was already with child. Your mother raised the baby as hers to spare her sister the shame of the world knowing she had consummated her marriage before it had taken place. That she was a whore." His voice was as bitter as poison. "I'm not your brother, and I never was. Harriet—she never told me she was my mother. I found out from your mother's letters. All those years, and she never said a word. She was too ashamed."

"You killed her," Tessa said numbly. "Your own mother."

"*Because* she was my mother. Because she'd disowned me. Because she was ashamed of me. Because I'll never know who my father was. Because she was a whore." Nate's voice was empty. *Nate* had always been empty. He had never been anything but a pretty shell, and Tessa and her aunt had dreamed into him empathy and compassion and sympathetic weakness because they had wanted to see it there, not because it was.

"Why did you tell Jessamine that my mother was a Shadowhunter?" Tessa demanded. "Even if Aunt Harriet was your mother, she and my mother were sisters. Aunt Harriet would have been a Shadowhunter, too, and so would you. Why tell such a ridiculous lie?"

He smirked. "Wouldn't you like to know?" His grip tightened on her neck, choking her. She gasped and thought suddenly of Gabriel, saying, *Aim your kicks at the kneecaps; the pain is agonizing.*

She kicked up and backward, the heel of her boot colliding with Nate's knee, making a dull cracking sound. Nate yelled, and his leg went out from under him. He kept his grip on Tessa as he fell, rolling so that his elbow jammed into her stomach as they tumbled to the ground together. She gasped, the air punched from her lungs, her eyes filling with tears.

She kicked out at him again, trying to scramble backward, and caught him a glancing blow on the shoulder, but he lunged at her, seizing her by the waistcoat. The buttons popped off it in a rain as he dragged her toward him; his other hand gripped her hair as she flailed out at him, raking her nails down his cheek. The blood that sprang immediately to the surface was a savagely satisfying sight.

"Let me go," she panted. "You can't kill me. The Magister wants me alive—"

"'Alive' is not 'unhurt,'" Nate snarled, blood running down his face and off his chin. He knotted his hand in her hair and dragged her toward him; she screamed at the pain and lashed out with her boots, but he was nimble, dodging her flailing feet. Panting, she sent up a silent call: *Jem, Will, Charlotte, Henry—where are you?*

"Wondering where your friends are?" He hauled her to her

feet, one hand in her hair, the other fisted in the back of her shirt. "Well, here's one of them, at least."

A grinding noise alerted Tessa to a movement in the shadows. Nate dragged her head around by the hair, shaking her. "Look," he spat. "It's time you knew what you are up against."

Tessa stared. The thing that emerged from the shadows was gigantic—twenty feet tall, she guessed, made of iron. There was barely any jointure. It appeared to move as one single fluid mechanism, seamless and almost featureless. Its bottom half did split into legs, each one ending in a foot tipped with metal spikes. Its arms were the same, finishing in clawlike hands, and its head was a smooth oval broken only by a wide jagged-toothed mouth like a crack in an egg. A pair of twisting silvery horns spiraled up from its "head." A thin line of blue fire crackled between them.

In its enormous hands it carried a limp body, dressed in gear. Against the bulk of the gigantic automaton, she looked even smaller than ever.

"Charlotte!" Tessa screamed. She redoubled her attempts to get away from Nate, whipping her head to the side. Some of her hair tore free and fluttered to the ground—Jessamine's fair hair, stained now with blood. Nate retaliated by slapping her hard enough that she saw stars; when she sagged, he caught her around the throat, the buttons on his cuffs digging into her windpipe.

Nate chuckled. "A prototype," he said. "Abandoned by the Magister. Too large and cumbersome for his purposes. But not for mine." He raised his voice. "Drop her."

The automaton's metal hands opened. Charlotte tumbled free and struck the ground with a sickening thump. She lay unmoving. From this distance Tessa could not tell if her chest was rising and falling or not.

"Now crush her," said Nate.

Ponderously the thing raised its spiked metal foot. Tessa clawed at Nate's forearms, ripping his skin with her nails.

"Charlotte!" For a moment Tessa thought the voice screaming was her own, but it was too low-pitched for that. A figure darted out from behind the automaton, a figure all in black, topped by a shock of blazing ginger hair, a thin-bladed misericord in hand.

Henry.

Without even a glance at Tessa and Nate, he launched himself at the automaton, bringing his blade down in a long curving arc. There was the clang of metal on metal. Sparks flew, and the automaton staggered back. Its foot came down, slamming into the floor, inches from Charlotte's supine body. Henry landed, then threw himself at the creature again, slashing out with his blade.

The blade shattered. For a moment Henry simply stood and looked at it with stupid shock. Then the creature's hand whipped forward and seized him by the arm. He shouted out as it lifted him and threw him with incredible force against one of the pillars; he struck it, crumpled, and fell to the floor, where he lay still.

Nate laughed. "*Such* a display of matrimonial devotion," he said. "Who would have thought it? Jessamine always said she thought Branwell couldn't stand his wife."

"You're a pig," Tessa said, struggling in his grasp. "What do you know about the things people do for each other? If Jessamine were burning to death, you wouldn't look up from your card game. You care for nothing but yourself."

"Be quiet, or I'll loosen your teeth for you." Nate shook her again, and called out, "Come! Over here. You must hold her till the Magister arrives."

With a grinding of gears the automaton moved to obey. It was not as swift as its smaller brethren, but its size was such that Tessa could not help but follow its movements with an icy fear. And that was not all. The Magister was coming. Tessa wondered if Nate had summoned him yet, if he was on his way. Mortmain. Even the memory of his cold eyes, his icy, controlling smile, made her stomach turn. "Let me go," she cried, jerking away from her brother. "Let me go to Charlotte—"

Nate shoved her forward, hard, and she sprawled on the ground, her elbows and knees connecting with force with the hard wooden floor. She gasped and rolled sideways, under the shadow of the second-floor gallery, as the automaton lumbered toward her. She cried out—

And they leaped from the gallery above, Will and Jem, each landing on a shoulder of the creature. It roared, a sound like bellows being fed with coal, and staggered back, allowing Tessa to roll out of its path and launch herself to her feet. She glanced from Henry to Charlotte. Henry was pale and still, crumpled beside the pillar, but Charlotte, lying where the automaton had dropped her, was in imminent danger of being crushed by the rampaging machine.

Taking a deep breath, Tessa dashed across the room to Charlotte and knelt down, laying her fingers to Charlotte's throat; there was a pulse there, fluttering weakly. Putting her hands under Charlotte's arms, she began to drag her toward the wall, away from the center of the room, where the automaton was spinning and spitting sparks, reaching up with its pincered hands to claw at Jem and Will.

They were too quick for it, though. Tessa laid Charlotte down among the burlap sacks of tea and gazed across the room, trying to determine a path that might lead her to Henry. Nate was dashing back and forth, shouting and cursing at the mechanical creature; in answer Will sawed off one of its horns and threw it at Tessa's brother. It bounced across the floor, skittering and sparking, and Nate jumped back. Will laughed. Jem meanwhile was clinging on to the creature's neck, doing something that Tessa could not see. The creature itself was turning in circles, but it had been designed for reaching out and grabbing what was in front of it, and its "arms" did not bend properly. It could not reach what clung to the back of its neck and head.

Tessa almost wanted to laugh. Will and Jem were like mice scurrying up and down the body of a cat, driving it to distraction. But hack and slash as they might at the metal creature with their blades, they were inflicting few injuries. Their blades, which she had seen shear through iron and steel as if they were paper, were leaving only dents and scratches on the surface of the mechanical creature's body.

Nate, meanwhile, was screaming and cursing. "Shake them off!" he yelled at the automaton. "Shake them off, you great metal bastard!"

The automaton paused, then shook itself violently. Will slipped, catching on to the creature's neck at the last moment to keep himself from falling. Jem was not so lucky; he stabbed forward with his sword-cane, as if he meant to drive it into the creature's body to arrest his fall, but the blade merely skidded down the creature's back. Jem fell, gracelessly, his weapon clattering, his leg bent under him.

"James!" Will shouted.

Jem dragged himself painfully to his feet. He reached for the stele at his belt, but the creature, sensing weakness, was already on him, reaching out its clawed hands. Jem took several staggering steps backward and fumbled something out of his pocket. It was smooth, oblong, metallic—the object Henry had given him in the library.

He reached back a hand to throw it—and Nate was behind him suddenly, kicking out at his injured, likely broken, leg. Jem didn't make a sound, but the leg went out from under him with a snapping noise and he hit the ground for a second time, the object rolling from his hand.

Tessa scrambled to her feet and ran for it just as Nate did the same. They collided, his greater weight and height bearing her to the floor. She rolled as she fell, as Gabriel had taught her to, to absorb the impact, though the shock still left her breathless. She reached for the device with shaking fingers, but it skittered away from her. She could hear Will screaming her name, calling to her to throw it to him. She stretched her hand out farther, her fingers closing around the device—and then Nate seized her by one leg and dragged her back toward him, mercilessly.

He is bigger than I am, she thought. *Stronger than I am. More ruthless than I am. But there is one thing I can do that he cannot.*

She Changed.

She reached out with her mind for the grip of his hand on her ankle, his skin touching her own. She reached out for the intrinsic, inborn *Nate* that she had always known, that spark inside him that flickered the way it did inside everyone, like a candle in a dark room. She heard him suck in his breath, and then the Change took her, rippling her skin, melting her bones. The buttons at her collar and cuffs snapped as she grew in size, convulsions thrashing through her limbs, ripping her leg free of Nate's grasp. She rolled away from her brother, staggering to her feet, and saw his eyes widen as he looked at her.

She was now, other than her clothes, an exact mirror image of himself.

She whirled on the automaton. It was frozen, waiting for instructions, Will still clinging to its back. He raised his hand, and Tessa threw the device, silently thanking Gabriel and Gideon for the hours of knife throwing instruction. It flew through the air in a perfect arc, and Will caught it out of the sky.

Nate was on his feet. "Tessa," he snarled. "What in the bloody hell do you possibly think you're—"

"Seize him!" she shouted at the automaton, pointing at Nate. "Catch him and hold him!"

The creature did not move. Tessa could hear nothing but Nate's harsh breathing beside her, and the sound of clanking from the metal creature; Will had vanished behind it and was doing something, though she could not see what.

"Tessa, you're a fool," Nate hissed. "This cannot work. The creature is obedient only to—"

"I am Nathaniel Gray!" Tessa shouted up at the metal giant. "And I order you in the name of the Magister to *seize this man and hold him!*"

Nate whirled on her. "Enough of your games, you stupid little—"

His words were cut off suddenly as the automaton bent and seized him in its pincered grasp. It lifted him up, up, level with its slash of a mouth clicking and whirring inquisitively. Nate began to scream, and kept screaming, witlessly, his arms flailing as Will, finished with whatever he was doing, dropped to the ground in a crouch. He shouted something at Tessa, his blue eyes wide and wild, but she couldn't hear him over her brother's screams. Her heart was slamming against her chest; she felt her hair tumble down, hitting her shoulders with a soft, heavy weight. She was herself again, the shock of what was happening too great for her to hold on to the Change. Nate was still screaming—the thing had him in a terrible pincer grip. Will had begun to run, just as the creature, staring at Tessa, reared up with a roar—and Will struck her, knocking her to the ground and covering her with his body as the automaton blew apart like an exploding star.

The cacaphony of bursting, clattering metal was incredible. Tessa tried to cover her ears, but Will's body was pinning her firmly to the ground. His elbows dug into the floor on either side of her head. She felt his breath on the back of her neck, the pounding of his heart against her spine. She heard her brother cry out, a terrible gurgling cry. She turned her head, pressing her face into Will's shoulder as his body jerked against hers; the floor shuddered beneath them—

And it was over. Slowly Tessa opened her eyes. The air was cloudy with plaster dust and floating splinters and tea from torn burlap sacks. Huge chunks of metal lay scattered haphazardly about the floor, and several of the windows had burst open, letting in foggy evening light. Tessa's glance darted about the room. She saw Henry, cradling Charlotte, kissing her pale face as she gazed up at him; Jem, struggling to his feet, stele in hand and plaster dust coating his clothes and hair—and Nate.

At first she thought he was leaning against one of the pillars. Then she saw the spreading red stain across his shirt, and realized. A jagged chunk of metal had gone through him like a spear, pinning him upright to the pillar. His head was down, his hands clawing weakly at his chest.

"*Nate!*" she screamed. Will rolled sideways, freeing her, and she was on her feet in seconds, racing across the room to her brother. Her hands were shaking with horror and revulsion, but she managed to close them around the metal spear in his chest and pull it free. She threw it aside and barely succeeded in catching him as he slumped forward, his sudden dead weight bearing her to the ground. Somehow she found herself on the ground, Nate's limp body stretched awkwardly across her lap.

A memory rose in her mind—her crouching on the floor at de Quincey's town house, holding Nate in her arms. She had loved him then. Trusted him. Now, as she held him and his blood soaked into her shirt and trousers, she felt as if she were watching actors on a stage, playing parts, acting out grief.

"Nate," she whispered.

His eyes fluttered open. A pang of shock went through her. She had thought he was already dead.

"Tessie . . ." His voice sounded thick, as if it were coming through layers of water. His eyes roamed her face, then the blood on her clothes, and then, finally, came to rest on his own chest, where blood pumped steadily through a massive rent in his shirt. Tessa shrugged off her jacket, wadded it up, and pressed it hard against the wound, praying it would be enough to make the blood stop.

It wasn't. The jacket was soaked through instantly, thin wet streams of blood running down Nate's sides. "Oh, God," Tessa whispered. She raised her voice. "Will—"

"Don't." Nate's hand seized her wrist, his nails digging in.

"But, Nate—"

"I'm dying. I know." He coughed, a loose, wet, rattling sound. "Don't you understand? I've failed the Magister. He'll kill me anyway. And he'll make it slow." He made a hoarse, impatient noise. "Leave it, Tessie. I'm not being noble. You know I'm not that."

She took a ragged breath. "I should leave you here to die alone in your own blood. That's what you'd do if it were me."

"Tessie—" A stream of blood spilled from the corner of his mouth. "The Magister was never going to hurt you."

"Mortmain," she whispered. "Nate, where is he? Please. Tell me where he is."

"He—" Nate choked, heaving in a breath. A bubble of blood appeared on his lips. The jacket in Tessa's hand was a sodden rag. His eyes went wide, starkly terrified. "Tessie . . . I—I'm dying. I'm really dying—"

Questions still exploded through her head. *Where is Mortmain? How could my mother be a Shadowhunter? If my father was a demon, how is it that I am still alive when all the offspring of Shadowhunters and demons are stillborn?* But the terror in Nate's eyes silenced her; despite everything, she found her hand slipping into his. "There's nothing to be afraid of, Nate."

"Not for you, maybe. You were always—the good one. I'm going to burn, Tessie. Tessie, where's your angel?"

She put her hand to her throat, a reflexive gesture. "I couldn't wear it. I was pretending to be Jessamine."

"You—must—wear it." He coughed. More blood. "Wear it always. You swear?"

She shook her head. "Nate . . ." *I can't trust you, Nate.*

"I know." His voice was a bare rattle. "There's no forgiveness for—the kinds of things I've had to do."

She tightened her grip on his hand, her fingers slippery with his blood. "I forgive you," she whispered, not knowing, or caring, if it was true.

His blue eyes widened. His face had gone the color of old yellow parchment, his lips almost white. "*You don't know everything I've done, Tessie.*"

She leaned over him anxiously. "Nate?"

But there was no reply. His face went slack, his eyes wide, half-rolled-back in his head. His hand slid out of hers and struck the floor.

"Nate," she said again, and put her fingers to the place where his pulse should have beat in his throat, already knowing what she would find.

There was nothing. He was dead.

Tessa stood up. Her torn waistcoat, her trousers, her shirt, even the ends of her hair, were soaked with Nate's blood. She felt as numb as if she had been dipped in ice-cold water. She turned, slowly, only now, and for the first time, wondering if the others had been watching her, overhearing her conversation with Nate, wondering—

They weren't even looking in her direction. They were kneeling—Charlotte, Jem, and Henry—in a loose circle around a dark shape on the floor, just where she had been lying before, with Will on top of her.

Will.

Tessa had had dreams before in which she'd been walking down a long, darkened corridor toward something dreadful—something she could not see but knew was terrifying and deadly. In the dreams, with each step, the corridor had gotten longer, stretching farther into darkness and horror. That same feeling of dread and helplessness overwhelmed her now as she moved forward, each step feeling like a mile, until she had joined the circle of kneeling Shadowhunters and was looking down at Will.

He lay on his side. His face was white, his breathing shallow. Jem had one hand on his shoulder and was speaking to him in a low, soothing voice, but Will gave no sign of being able to hear him. Blood had pooled under him, smearing the floor, and for a moment Tessa just stared, unable to fathom where it had come from. Then she moved closer and saw his back. His gear had been shredded all along his spine and shoulder blades, the thick material torn by flying shards of razored metal. His skin swam with blood; his hair was soaked with it.

"Will," Tessa whispered. She felt peculiarly dizzy, as if she were floating.

Charlotte looked up. "Tessa," she said. "Your brother . . ."

"He's dead," Tessa said through her daze. "But Will—?"

"He knocked you down and covered you to protect you from the explosion," Jem said. There was no blame in his voice. "But there was nothing to protect him. You two were the closest to the blast. The metal fragments shredded his back. He's losing blood quickly."

"But isn't there anything you can do?" Tessa's voice rose, even as dizziness threatened to envelop her. "What about your healing runes? The *iratzes?*"

"We used an *amissio*, a rune that slows blood loss, but if we attempt a healing rune, his skin will heal over the metal, driving it farther into the soft tissue," said Henry flatly. "We need to get him back home to the infirmary. The metal must be removed before he can be healed."

"Then, we must go." Tessa's voice was shaking. "We must—"

"Tessa," said Jem. He still had his hand on Will's shoulder, but he was looking at her, his eyes wide. "Did you know you're hurt?"

She gestured impatiently at her shirt. "This isn't my blood. This is Nate's. Now we must— Can he be carried? Is there anything—"

"No," Jem interrupted, sharply enough to surprise her. "Not the blood on your clothes. You've a gash on your head. Here." He touched his temple.

"Don't be ridiculous," Tessa said. "I'm perfectly all right." She put her hand up to touch her temple—and felt her hair, thick and stiff with blood, and the side of her face sticky with it, before her fingertips touched the ragged flap of torn skin that ran from the corner of her cheek to her temple. A searing bolt of pain shot through her head.

It was the last straw. Already weak from blood loss and dizzy from repeated shocks, she felt herself begin to crumple. She barely felt Jem's arms go around her as she fell into the darkness.

17

In Dreams

Come to me in my dreams, and then
By day I shall be well again.
For then the night will more than pay
The hopeless longing of the day.
—Matthew Arnold, "Longing"

Consciousness came and went in a hypnotic rhythm, like the sea appearing and disappearing on the deck of a boat in a storm. Tessa knew she lay in a bed with crisp white sheets in the center of a long room; that there were other beds, all the same, in the room; and that there were windows high above her letting in shadows and then the bloody light of dawn. She closed her eyes against it, and the darkness came again.

She woke to whispering voices, and faces hovering over her, anxious. Charlotte, her hair knotted back neatly, still in her gear, and beside her Brother Enoch. His scarred face was no longer a terror. She could hear his voice in her mind. *The wound to her head is superficial.*

"But she fainted," said Charlotte. To Tessa's surprise there was real fear in her voice, real anxiety. "With a blow to the head—"

She fainted from repeated shocks. Her brother died in her arms, you said? And she may have thought Will was dead as well. You said he covered her with his body when the explosion occurred. If he had died, he would have given his life for her. That is quite a burden to bear.

"But you do think she'll be well again?"

When her body and spirit have rested, she will wake. I cannot say when that will be.

"My poor Tessa." Charlotte touched Tessa's face lightly. Her hands smelled of lemon soap. "She has no one in the world at all now. . . ."

The darkness returned, and Tessa fell into it, grateful for the respite from light and thought. She wrapped herself in it like a blanket and let herself float, like the icebergs off the coast of Labrador, cradled in the moonlight by icy black water.

A guttural cry of pain cut through her dream of darkness. She was curled on her side in a tangle of sheets, and a few beds away from her lay Will, on his stomach. She realized, though in her state of numbness it was only a faint shock, that he was probably naked; the sheets had been drawn up to his waist, but his back and chest were bare. His arms were folded on the pillows in front of him, his head resting on them, his body tensed like a bowstring. Blood spotted the white sheets beneath him.

Brother Enoch stood at one side of his bed, and beside him Jem, at Will's head, wearing an anxious expression. "Will," Jem said urgently. "Will, are you sure you won't have another pain-killing rune?"

"No—more," Will ground out, between his teeth. "Just—get it over with."

Brother Enoch raised what looked like a wickedly sharp pair of silver tweezers. Will gulped and buried his head in his arms, his dark hair startling against the white of the sheets. Jem shuddered as if the pain were his own as the tweezers dug deep into Will's back and his body tautened on the bed, muscles tensing under the skin, his cry of agony short and muffled. Brother Enoch drew back the tool, a blood-smeared shard of metal gripped in its teeth.

Jem slid his hand into Will's. "Grip my fingers. It will help the pain. There are only a few more."

"Easy—for you to say," Will gasped, but the touch of his *parabatai*'s hand seemed to relax him slightly. He was arched up off the bed, his elbows digging into the mattress, his breath coming in short pants. Tessa knew she ought to look away, but she couldn't. She realized she had never seen so much of a boy's body before, not even Jem's. She found herself fascinated by the way the lean muscle slid under Will's smooth skin, the flex and swell of his arms, the hard, flat stomach convulsing as he breathed.

The tweezers flashed again, and Will's hand bore down on Jem's, both their fingers whitening. Blood welled and spilled down his bare side. He made no sound, though Jem looked sick and pale. He moved his hand as if to touch Will's shoulder, then drew it back, biting down on his lip.

All this because Will covered my body with his to protect me, Tessa thought. As Brother Enoch had said, it was a burden to bear indeed.

She lay on her narrow bed in her old room in the New York flat. Through the window she could see gray sky, the rooftops of Manhattan. One of her aunt's colorful patchwork quilts was on the bed, and she clutched it to her as the door opened and her aunt herself came in.

Knowing what she knew now, Tessa could see the resemblance. Aunt Harriet had blue eyes, faded fair hair; even the shape of her face was like Nate's. With a smile she came and bent over Tessa, putting a hand on her forehead, cool against Tessa's hot skin.

"I'm so sorry," Tessa whispered. "About Nate. It's my fault he's dead."

"Hush," her aunt said. "It isn't your fault. It is his and mine. I always felt such guilt, you see, Tessa. Knowing I was his mother but not being able to bear telling him. I let him get away with anything he wanted, until he was spoiled beyond saving. If I had told him that I was really his mother, he would not have felt so betrayed when he discovered the truth, and would not have turned against us. Lies and secrets, Tessa, they are like a cancer in the soul. They eat away what is good and leave only destruction behind."

"I miss you so much," Tessa said. "I have no family now. . . ."

Her aunt leaned forward to kiss her on the forehead. "You have more family than you think."

"We will almost certainly forfeit the Institute now," said Charlotte. She did not sound brokenhearted, but distant and detached. Tessa was hovering like a ghost over the infirmary, looking down at where Charlotte stood with Jem at the foot of Tessa's own bed. Tessa could see herself, asleep, her dark hair spread like a fan across her pillows. Will lay asleep a few beds over, his back striped with bandages, an *iratze* black against the back of his neck. Sophie, in her white cap and dark dress, was dusting the windowsills. "We have lost Nathaniel Gray as a source, one of our own has turned out to be a spy, and we are no closer to finding Mortmain than we were a fortnight ago."

"After all that we have done, have learned? The Clave will understand—"

"They will not. They are already at the end of their tether where I am concerned. I might as well march over to Benedict Lightwood's house and make over the Institute paperwork in his name. Have done with it."

"What does Henry say about all this?" asked Jem. He was no longer in gear, and neither was Charlotte; he wore a white shirt and brown cloth trousers, and Charlotte was in one of her drab dark dresses. As Jem turned his hand over, though, Tessa saw that it was still spotted with Will's dried blood.

Charlotte snorted in an unladylike manner. "Oh, Henry," she said, sounding exhausted. "I think he's just so shocked that one of his devices actually worked that he doesn't know what to do with himself. And he can't bear to come in here. He thinks it's his fault that Will and Tessa are hurt."

"Without that device we might all be dead, and Tessa in the hands of the Magister."

"You are welcome to explain that to Henry. I have given up the attempt."

"Charlotte . . ." Jem's voice was soft. "I know what people say. I know you've heard the cruel gossip. But Henry does love you. When he thought you were hurt, at the tea warehouse, he went almost mad. He threw himself against that machine—"

"James." Charlotte clumsily patted Jem's shoulder. "I do appreciate your attempt to console me, but falsehoods never do anyone any good in the end. I long ago accepted that Henry loves his inventions first, and me second—if at all."

"Charlotte," Jem said wearily, but before he could say another word, Sophie had moved to stand beside them, dust cloth in hand.

"Mrs. Branwell," she said in a low voice. "If I might speak to you for just a moment."

Charlotte looked surprised. "Sophie . . ."

"Please, ma'am."

Charlotte placed a hand on Jem's shoulder, said something softly into his ear, and then nodded toward Sophie. "Very well. Come with me to the drawing room."

As Charlotte left the room with Sophie, Tessa realized to her surprise that Sophie was actually taller than her mistress. Charlotte's presence was such that one often forgot how very small she was. And Sophie was as tall as Tessa herself, as slender as a willow. Tessa saw her again in her mind with Gideon Lightwood, pressed up against the corridor wall, and Tessa worried.

As the door closed behind the two women, Jem leaned forward, his arms crossed over the foot of Tessa's brass bed. He was looking at her, smiling a little, though crookedly, his hands hanging loose—dried blood across the knuckles, and under the nails.

"Tessa, my Tessa," he said in his soft voice, as lulling as his violin. "I know you cannot hear me. Brother Enoch says you're not hurt badly. I can't say I find that enough to comfort me. It's rather like when Will assures me that we're only a little bit lost somewhere. I know it means we won't be seeing a familiar street again for hours."

He dropped his voice, so low that Tessa wasn't sure if what he said next was real or part of the dream darkness rising to claim her, though she fought against it.

"I've never minded it," he went on. "Being lost, that is. I had always thought one could not be truly lost if one knew one's own heart. But I fear I may be lost without knowing yours." He closed his eyes as if he were bone-weary, and she saw how thin his eyelids were, like parchment paper, and how tired he looked. "*Wo ai ni*, Tessa," he whispered. "*Wo bu xiang shi qu ni.*"

She knew, without knowing how she knew, what the words meant.

I love you.

And I don't want to lose you.

I don't want to lose you, either, she wanted to say, but the words wouldn't come. Lassitude rose up instead, in a dark wave, and covered her in silence.

Darkness.

It was dark in the cell, and Tessa was conscious first of a feeling of great loneliness and terror. Jessamine lay in the narrow bed, her fair hair hanging in lank ropes over her shoulders. Tessa both hovered over her and felt somehow as if she were touching her mind. She could feel a great aching sense of loss. Somehow Jessamine knew that Nate was dead. Before, when Tessa had tried to touch the other girl's mind, she had met resistance, but now she felt only a growing sadness, like the stain of a drop of black ink spreading through water.

Jessie's brown eyes were open, staring up into the darkness. I have nothing. *The words were as clear as a bell in Tessa's mind.* I chose Nate over the Shadowhunters, and now he is dead, and Mortmain will want me dead as well, and Charlotte despises me. I have gambled and lost everything.

As Tessa watched, Jessamine reached up and drew a small cord from her neck over her head. At the end of the cord was a gold ring with a glittering white stone—a diamond. Clasping it between her fingers, she began to use the diamond to scratch letters into the stone wall.

JG.

Jessamine Gray.

There might have been more to the message, but Tessa would never find out; as Jessamine pressed down on the gemstone, it shattered, and her hand slammed against the wall, scraping her knuckles.

Tessa did not need to touch Jessamine's mind to know what she was thinking. Even the diamond had not been real. With a low cry Jessamine rolled over and buried her face in the rough blankets of the bed.

When Tessa woke again, it was dark. Faint starlight streamed through the high infirmary windows, and there was a witch-light lamp lit on the table near her bed. Beside it was a cup of tisane, steam rising from it, and a small plate of biscuits. She rose to a sitting position, about to reach for the cup—and froze.

Will was seated on the bed beside hers, wearing a loose shirt and trousers and a black dressing gown. His skin was pale in the starlight, but even the light's dimness couldn't wash out the blue of his eyes. "Will," she said, startled, "what are you doing awake?" Had he been watching her *sleep*, she wondered? But what an odd and un-Will-like thing to do.

"I brought you a tisane," he said, a little stiffly. "But you sounded as if you were having a nightmare."

"Did I? I don't even remember what I dreamed." She drew the covers up over herself, though her modest nightgown more than covered her. "I thought I had been escaping into sleep—that real life was the nightmare and that sleep was where I could find peace."

Will picked up the mug and moved to sit beside her on the bed. "Here. Drink this."

She took the cup from him obediently. The tisane had a bitter but appealing taste, like the zest of a lemon. "What will it do?" she asked.

"Calm you," said Will.

She looked at him, the taste of lemon in her mouth. There seemed a haze across her vision; seen through it, Will looked like something out of a dream. "How are your injuries? Are you in pain?"

He shook his head. "Once all the metal was out, they were able to use an *iratze* on me," he said. "The wounds are not completely healed, but they are healing. By tomorrow they will be scars."

"I am jealous." She took another sip of the tisane. It was beginning to make her feel light-headed. She touched the bandage across her forehead. "I believe it will be a good while before this comes off."

"In the meantime you can enjoy looking like a pirate."

She laughed, but it was shaky. Will was close enough to her that she could feel the heat emanating from his body. He was furnace-hot. "Do you have a fever?" she asked before she could stop herself.

"The *iratze* raises our body temperatures. It's part of the healing process."

"Oh," she said. Having him so close to her was sending little shivers through her nerves, but she felt too light-headed to draw away.

"I am sorry about your brother," he said softly, his breath stirring her hair.

"You couldn't be." She spoke bitterly. "I know you think he deserved what he got. He probably did."

"My sister died. She died, and there was nothing I could do about it," he said, and there was raw grief in his voice. "I *am* sorry about your brother."

She looked up at him. His eyes, wide and blue, that perfect face, the bow-shape of his mouth, turned down at the corners in concern. Concern for *her*. Her skin felt hot and tight, her head light and airy, as if she were floating. "Will," she whispered. "Will, I feel very odd."

Will leaned across her to put the mug down on the table, and his shoulder brushed hers. "Do you want me to get Charlotte?"

She shook her head. She was dreaming. She was nearly sure of it now; she had the same feeling of being in her body and yet not in it as she had had when she was dreaming of Jessamine. The knowledge that it was a dream made her bolder. Will was still leaning forward, his arm extended; she curled against him, her head on his shoulder, closing her eyes. She felt him jerk with surprise.

"Did I hurt you?" she whispered, belatedly remembering his back.

"I don't care," he said fervently. "I don't care." His arms went around her, and he held her; she rested her cheek against the warm juncture of his neck and shoulder. She heard the echo of his pulse and smelled the scent of him, blood and sweat and soap and magic. It was not like it had been on the balcony, all fire and desire. He held her carefully, laying his cheek against her hair. He was shaking, even as his chest rose and fell, even as he hesitantly slid his fingers beneath her chin, lifting her face . . .

"Will," Tessa said. "It's all right. It doesn't matter what you do. We're dreaming, you know."

"Tess?" Will sounded alarmed. His arms tightened about her. She felt warm and soft and dizzy. If only Will really were like this, she thought, not just in dreams. The bed rolled under her like a boat set adrift on the sea. She closed her eyes and let the darkness take her.

The night air was cold, the fog thick and yellowish-green under the intermittent pools of gaslight as Will made his way down King's Road. The address Magnus had given him was on Cheyne Walk, down near the Chelsea Embankment, and Will could already smell the familiar scent of the river, silt and water and dirt and rot.

He had been trying to keep his heart from beating its way out of his chest ever since he had found Magnus's note, neatly folded on a tray on the table beside his bed. It had said nothing beyond a curtly scrawled address: *16 Cheyne Walk*. Will was familiar with the Walk and the area around it. Chelsea, near the river, was a popular haunt for artists and literary types, and the windows of the public houses he passed glowed with welcoming yellow light.

He drew his coat around him as he turned a corner, making

his way south. His back and legs still ached from the injuries he had sustained, despite the *iratzes*; he was sore, as if he'd been stung by dozens of bees. And yet he hardly felt it. His mind was full of possibilities. What had Magnus discovered? Surely he would not summon Will if there were no reason? And his body was full of Tessa, the feel and scent of her. Strangely, what pierced his heart and mind most sharply was not the memory of her lips under his at the ball, but the way she had leaned into him tonight, her head on his shoulder, her breath soft against his neck, as if she trusted him utterly. He would have given everything he had in the world and everything he would ever have, just to lie beside her in the narrow infirmary bed and hold her while she slept. Pulling away from her had been like pulling his own skin off, but he'd had to do it.

The way he always had to. The way he always had to deny himself what he wanted.

But maybe—after tonight—

He cut the thought off before it bloomed in his mind. Better not to think about it; better not to hope and be disappointed. He looked around. He was on Cheyne Walk now, with its fine houses with their Georgian fronts. He stopped in front of number 16. It was tall, with a wrought iron fence about it and a prominent bay window. Set into the fence was an ornately worked gate; it was open, and he slipped inside and made his way up to the front door, where he rang the bell.

To his great surprise it was opened not by a footman but by Woolsey Scott, his blond hair in tangles to his shoulders. He wore a dark green dressing gown of Chinese brocade over a pair of dark trousers and a bare chest. A gold-rimmed monocle perched in one eye. He carried a pipe in his left hand, and as he examined Will at his leisure, he exhaled, sending out a cloud of sweet-smelling, cough-inducing smoke. "Finally broken down and admitted you're in love with me, have you?" he inquired of Will. "I do enjoy these surprise midnight declarations." He leaned against the door frame and waved a languid ringed hand. "Go along, have at it."

For once Will was speechless. It was not a position he found himself in often, and he was forced to admit that he did not like it.

"Oh, leave him be, Woolsey," said a familiar voice from inside the house—Magnus, hurrying along the corridor. He was fastening his shirt cuffs as he came forward, and his hair was a thicket of mussed black tangles. "I told you Will would be coming by."

Will looked from Magnus to Woolsey. Magnus was barefoot; so was the werewolf. Woolsey had a glimmering gold chain around his neck. From it hung a pendant that said *Beati Bellicosi*, "Blessed Are the Warriors." Beneath it was an imprint of a wolf's paw. Scott noticed Will staring at it and grinned. "Like what you see?" he inquired.

"*Woolsey*," said Magnus.

"Your note to me *did* have something to do with demon summoning, didn't it?" Will asked, looking at Magnus. "This isn't you . . . calling in your favor, is it?"

Magnus shook his rumpled head. "No. This is business, nothing else. Woolsey's been kind enough to let me lodge with him while I decide what to do next."

"I say we go to Rome," said Scott. "I adore Rome."

"All well and fine, but first I need the use of a room. Preferably one with little or nothing in it."

Scott removed his monocle and stared at Magnus. "And you're going to do *what* in this room?" His tone was more than suggestive.

"Summon the demon Marbas," said Magnus, flashing a grin.

Scott choked on his pipe smoke. "I suppose we all have our ideas about what constitutes an enjoyable evening . . ."

"Woolsey." Magnus ran his hands through his rough black hair. "I hate to bring this up, but you do owe me. Hamburg? 1863?"

Scott threw his hands up. "Oh, very well. You may utilize my brother's room. No one's used it since he died. Enjoy. I'll be in the drawing room with a glass of sherry and some rather naughty woodcuts I had imported from Romania."

With that, he turned and padded off down the hall. Magnus gestured Will inside, and he entered gladly, the warmth of the house enveloping him like a blanket. Since there was no footman, he slid off his blue wool frock coat and draped it over his arm as Magnus watched him with a curious gaze. "Will," he said. "I see you wasted no time after you got my note. I wasn't expecting you until tomorrow."

"You know what this means to me," said Will. "Did you really think I'd delay?"

Magnus's eyes searched his face. "You are prepared," he said. "For this to fail? For the demon to be the incorrect one? For the summoning not to work?"

For a long moment Will could not move. He could see his own face in the mirror that hung by the door. He was horrified to see how raw he looked—as if there were no longer any wall between the world and his own heart's desires. "No," he said. "I am not prepared."

Magnus shook his head. "Will . . ." He sighed. "Come with me."

He turned with catlike grace and made his way down the hall and up the curving wooden steps. Will followed, up through the shadowed staircase, the thick Persian stair runner muffling his footsteps. Niches set back in the walls contained polished marble statues of entwined bodies. Will looked away from them hastily, and then back. It wasn't as if Magnus seemed to be paying attention to what Will was doing, and he'd honestly never imagined two people could *get* themselves into a position like that, much less make it look artistic.

They reached the second landing, and Magnus padded off down the corridor, opening doors as he went and muttering to himself. Finally finding the correct room, he threw the door open and gestured for Will to follow him.

The bedroom of Woolsey Scott's dead brother was dark and cold, and the air smelled of dust. Automatically Will fumbled for his witchlight, but Magnus waved a dismissing hand at him, blue fire sparking from his fingertips. A fire roared up suddenly in the grate, lighting the room. It *was* furnished, though everything had been draped with white cloths—the bed, the wardrobe and dressers. As Magnus stalked through the room, rolling up his shirtsleeves and gesturing with his hands, the furniture began to slide back from the center of the room. The bed swung around and lay flat against the wall; the chairs and bureaus and washstand flew into the corners of the room.

Will whistled. Magnus grinned. "Easily impressed," Magnus said, though he sounded slightly out of breath. He knelt down in the now denuded center of the room and hastily drew a pentagram. In each point of the occult symbol, he scrawled a rune, though none were runes Will knew from the Gray Book. Magnus raised his arms and held them out over the star; he began to chant, and gashes opened up in his wrists, spilling blood into the pentagram's center. Will tensed as the blood struck the floor and began to burn with an eerie blue glow. Magnus backed out of the pentagram, still chanting, reached into his pocket, and produced the demon's tooth. As Will watched, Magnus tossed it into the now flaming center of the star.

For a moment nothing happened. Then, out of the burning heart of the fire, a dark shape began to take form. Magnus had stopped chanting; he stood, his narrowed eyes focused on the pentagram and what was happening within it, the gashes on his arms closing swiftly. There was little sound in the room, just the crackle of the fire and Will's harsh breathing, loud in his own ears, as the dark shape grew in size—coalesced, and, finally, took a solid, recognizable shape.

It was the blue demon from the party, no longer dressed in evening wear. Its body was covered in overlapping blue scales, and a long yellowish tail with a stinger on the end switched back and forth behind it. The demon looked from Magnus to Will, its scarlet eyes narrowed.

"Who summons the demon Marbas?" it demanded in a voice that sounded as if its words were echoing from the bottom of a well.

Magnus jerked his chin toward the pentagram. The message was clear: This was Will's business now.

Will took a step forward. "You don't remember me?"

"I remember you," the demon growled. *"You chased me through the grounds of the Lightwood country house. You tore out one of my*

teeth." It opened its mouth, showing the gap. *"I tasted your blood."* Its voice was a hiss. *"When I escape this pentagram, I will taste it again, Nephilim."*

"No." Will stood his ground. "I'm asking you *if you remember me.*"

The demon was silent. Its eyes, dancing with fire, were unreadable.

"Five years ago," said Will. "A box. A Pyxis. I opened it, and you emerged. We were in my father's library. You attacked, but my sister fended you off with a seraph blade. *Do you recollect me now?*"

There was a long, long silence. Magnus kept his cat's eyes fixed on the demon. There was an implied threat in them, one that Will couldn't read. "Speak the truth," Magnus said finally. "Or it will go badly for you, Marbas."

The demon's head swung toward Will. *"You,"* it said reluctantly. *"You are that boy. Edmund Herondale's son."*

Will sucked in a breath. He felt suddenly light-headed, as if he were going to pass out. He dug his nails into his palms, hard, gashing the skin, letting the pain clear his head. "You remember."

"I had been trapped for twenty years in that thing," Marbas snarled. *"Of course I remember being freed. Imagine it, if you can, idiot mortal, years of blackness, darkness, no light or movement—and then the break, the opening. And the face of the man who imprisoned you hovering just above your gaze."*

"I am not the man who imprisoned you—"

"No. That was your father. But you look just like him to my eyes." The demon smirked. *"I remember your sister. Brave girl, fending me off with that blade she could hardly use."*

"She used it well enough to keep you away from us. That's why you cursed us. Cursed *me*. Do you remember that?"

The demon chuckled. "'*All who love you will find only death. Their love will be their destruction. It may take moments, it may take years, but any who look upon you with love will die of it. And I shall begin it with her.*'"

Will felt as if he were breathing fire. His whole chest burned. "Yes."

The demon cocked its head to the side. "*And you summoned me that we might reminisce about this shared event in our past?*"

"I called you up, you blue-skinned bastard, to get you to take the curse off me. My sister—Ella—she died that night. I left my family to keep them safe. It's been five years. It's enough. *Enough!*"

"*Do not try to engage my pity, mortal,*" said Marbas. "*I was twenty years tortured in that box. Perhaps you too should suffer for twenty years. Or two hundred—*"

Will's whole body tensed. Before he could fling himself toward the pentagram, Magnus said, in a calm tone, "Something about this story strikes me as odd, Marbas."

The demon's eyes flicked toward him. "*And what is that?*"

"A demon, upon being let out of a Pyxis, is usually at its weakest, having been starved for as long as it was imprisoned. Too weak to cast a curse as subtle and strong as the one you claim to have cast on Will."

The demon hissed something in a language Will didn't know, one of the more uncommon demon languages, not Cthonic or Purgatic. Magnus's eyes narrowed.

"But she died," Will said. "Marbas said my sister would die, and she did. That night."

Magnus's eyes were still fixed on the demon's. Some kind of battle of wills was taking place silently, outside Will's range of understanding. Finally Magnus said, softly, "Do you really wish to disobey me, Marbas? Do you wish to anger my father?"

Marbas spat a curse, and turned to Will. Its snout twitched. *"The half-caste is correct. The curse was false. Your sister died because I struck her with my stinger."* It swished its yellowish tail back and forth, and Will remembered Ella knocked to the ground by that tail, the blade skittering from her hand. *"There has never been a curse on you, Will Herondale. Not one put there by me."*

"No," Will said softly. "No, it isn't possible." He felt as if a great storm were blowing through his head; he remembered Jem's voice saying *the wall is coming down*, and he envisioned a great wall that had surrounded him, isolated him, for years, crumbling away into sand. He was free—and he was alone, and the icy wind cut through him like a knife. "No." His voice had taken on a low, keening note. *"Magnus . . ."*

"Are you lying, Marbas?" Magnus snapped. "Do you swear on Baal that you are telling the truth?"

"I swear," said Marbas, red eyes rolling. *"What benefit would it be to me to lie?"*

Will slid to his knees. His hands were locked across his stomach as if they were keeping his guts from spilling out. *Five years*, he thought. Five years wasted. He heard his family screaming and pounding on the doors of the Institute and himself ordering Charlotte to send them away. And they had never known why. They had lost a daughter and a son in a matter of days, and they had never known why. And the others—Henry and Charlotte and Jem—and Tessa—and the things he had done—

Jem is my great sin.

"Will is right," said Magnus. "Marbas, you *are* a blue-skinned bastard. *Burn and die!*"

Somewhere at the edge of Will's vision, dark red flame soared toward the ceiling; Marbas screamed, a howl of agony cut off as swiftly as it had begun. The stench of burning demon flesh filled the room. And still Will crouched on his knees, his breath sawing in and out of his lungs. *Oh God, oh God, oh God.*

Gentle hands touched his shoulders. "Will," Magnus said, and there was no humor in his voice, only a surprising kindness. "Will, I am sorry."

"Everything I've done," Will said. His lungs felt as if he couldn't get enough air. "All the lying, the pushing people away, the abandonment of my family, the unforgivable things I said to Tessa—a waste. A bloody waste, and all because of a lie I was stupid enough to believe."

"You were twelve years old. Your sister was dead. Marbas was a cunning creature. He has fooled powerful magicians, never mind a child who had no knowledge of the Shadow World."

Will stared down at his hands. "My whole life wrecked, destroyed . . ."

"You're seventeen," Magnus said. "You can't have wrecked a life you've barely lived. And don't you understand what this means, Will? You've spent the last five years convinced that no one could possibly love you, because if they did, they would be dead. The mere fact of their continued survival proved their indifference to you. But you were wrong. Charlotte, Henry, Jem—your family—"

Will took a deep breath, and let it out. The storm in his head was ebbing slowly.

"Tessa," he said.

"Well." Now there was a touch of humor to Magnus's voice. Will realized the warlock was kneeling beside him. *I am in a werewolf's house,* Will thought, *with a warlock comforting me, and the ashes of a dead demon mere feet away. Who could ever have imagined?* "I can give you no assurance of what Tessa feels. If you have not noticed, she is a decidedly independent girl. But you have as much a chance to win her love as any man does, Will, and isn't that what you wanted?" He patted Will on the shoulder and withdrew his hand, standing up, a thin dark shadow looming over Will. "If it's any consolation, from what I observed on the balcony the other night, I do believe she rather likes you."

Magnus watched as Will made his way down the front walk of the house. Reaching the gate, he paused, his hand on the latch, as if hesitating on the threshold of the beginning of a long and difficult journey. The moon had come out from behind the clouds and shone on his thick dark hair, the pale white of his hands.

"Very curious," said Woolsey, appearing behind Magnus in the doorway. The warm lights of the house turned Woolsey's dark blond hair into a pale gold tangle. He looked as if he'd been sleeping. "If I didn't know better, I'd say you were fond of that boy."

"Know better in what sense, Woolsey?" Magnus asked, absently, still watching Will, and the light sparking off the Thames behind him.

"He's Nephilim," said Woolsey. "And you've never cared for them. How much did he pay you to summon Marbas for him?"

"Nothing," said Magnus, and now he was not seeing anything that was there, not the river, not Will, only a wash of memories—eyes, faces, lips, receding into memory, love that he could no longer put a name to. "He did me a favor. One he doesn't even remember."

"He's very pretty," said Woolsey. "For a human."

"He's very broken," said Magnus. "Like a lovely vase that someone has smashed. Only luck and skill can put it back together the way it was before."

"Or magic."

"I've done what I can," Magnus said softly as Will pushed the latch, at last, and the gate swung open. He stepped out onto the Walk.

"He doesn't look very happy," Woolsey observed. "Whatever it was you did for him . . ."

"At the moment he is in shock," said Magnus. "He has believed one thing for five years, and now he has realized that all this time he has been looking at the world through a faulty mechanism—that all the things he sacrificed in the name of what he thought was good and noble have been a waste, and that he has only hurt what he loved."

"Good God," said Woolsey. "Are you quite sure you've helped him?"

Will stepped through the gate, and it swung shut behind him. "Quite sure," said Magnus. "It is always better to live the truth than to live a lie. And that lie would have kept him alone forever. He may have had nearly nothing for five years, but now he can have everything. A boy who looks like that . . ."

Woolsey chuckled.

"Though he had already given his heart away," Magnus

said. "Perhaps it is for the best. What he needs now is to love and have that love returned. He has not had an easy life for one so young. I only hope she understands."

Even from this distance Magnus could see Will take a deep breath, square his shoulders, and set off down the Walk. And—Magnus was quite sure he was not imagining it—there seemed to be almost a spring in his step.

"You cannot save every fallen bird," said Woolsey, leaning back against the wall and crossing his arms. "Even the handsome ones."

"One will do," said Magnus, and, as Will was no longer within his sight, he let the front door fall shut.

18

Until I Die

My whole life long I learn'd to love.
This hour my utmost art I prove
And speak my passion–heaven or hell?
She will not give me heaven? 'Tis well!
–Robert Browning, "One Way of Love"

"Miss. Miss!" Tessa woke slowly, Sophie shaking her shoulder. Sunlight was streaming through the windows high above. Sophie was smiling, her eyes alight. "Mrs. Branwell's sent me to bring you back to your room. You can't stay here forever."

"Ugh. I wouldn't want to!" Tessa sat up, then closed her eyes as dizziness washed through her. "You might have to help me up, Sophie," she said in an apologetic voice. "I'm not as steady as I could be."

"Of course, miss." Sophie reached down and briskly helped Tessa out of the bed. Despite her slenderness, she was quite strong. She'd have to be, wouldn't she, Tessa thought, from years of carrying heavy laundry up and down stairs, and coal from the coal scuttle to the grates. Tessa winced a bit as her feet struck the cold floor, and couldn't help glancing over to see if Will was in his infirmary bed.

He wasn't.

"Is Will all right?" she asked as Sophie helped her slide her feet into slippers. "I woke for a bit yesterday and saw them taking the metal out of his back. It looked dreadful."

Sophie snorted. "Looked worse than it was, then. Mr. Herondale barely let them *iratze* him before he left. Off into the night to do the devil knows what."

"*Was* he? I could have sworn I spoke to him last night." They were in the corridor now, Sophie guiding Tessa with a gentle hand on her back. Images were starting to take shape in Tessa's head. Images of Will in the moonlight, of herself telling him that nothing mattered, it was only a dream—and it had been, hadn't it?

"You must have dreamed it, miss." They had reached Tessa's room, and Sophie was distracted, trying to get the doorknob turned without letting go of Tessa.

"It's all right, Sophie. I can stand on my own."

Sophie protested, but Tessa insisted firmly enough that Sophie soon had the door open and was stoking the fire in the grate while Tessa sank into an armchair. There was a pot of tea and a plate of sandwiches on the table beside the bed, and she helped herself to it gratefully. She no longer felt dizzy, but she did feel tired, with a weariness that was more spiritual than physical. She remembered the bitter taste of the tisane she'd drunk, and the way it had felt to be held by Will—but that had been a dream. She wondered how much else of what she'd seen last night had been a dream—Jem whispering at the foot of her bed, Jessamine sobbing into her blankets in the Silent City . . .

"I was sorry to hear about your brother, miss." Sophie was on her knees by the fire, the rekindling flames playing over her lovely face. Her head was bent, and Tessa could not see her scar.

"You don't have to say that, Sophie. I know it was his fault, really, about Agatha—and Thomas—"

"But he was your brother." Sophie's voice was firm. "Blood mourns blood." She bent farther over the coals, and there was something about the kindness in her voice, and the way her hair curled, dark and vulnerable, against the nape of her neck, that made Tessa say:

"Sophie, I saw you with Gideon the other day."

Sophie stiffened immediately, all over, without turning to look at Tessa. "What do you mean, miss?"

"I came back to get my necklace," Tessa said. "My clockwork angel. For luck. And I saw you with Gideon in the corridor." She swallowed. "He was . . . pressing your hand. Like a suitor."

There was a long, long silence, while Sophie stared into the flickering fire. At last she said, "Are you going to tell Mrs. Branwell?"

Tessa recoiled. "What? Sophie, no! I just—wanted to warn you."

Sophie's voice was flat. "Warn me against what?"

"The Lightwoods . . ." Tessa swallowed. "They are not nice people. When I was at their house—with Will—I saw dreadful things, awful—"

"That's Mr. Lightwood, not his sons!" The sharpness in Sophie's voice made Tessa flinch. "They're not like him!"

"How different could they be?"

Sophie stood up, the poker clattering into the fire. "You think I'm such a fool that I'd let some half-hour gentleman make a mockery of me after all I been through? After all Mrs. Branwell's taught me? Gideon's a good man—"

"It's a question of upbringing, Sophie! Can you picture him going to Benedict Lightwood and saying he wants to marry a mundane, and a parlor maid to boot? Can you see him doing that?"

Sophie's face twisted. "You don't know anything," she said. "You don't know what he'd do for us—"

"You mean the *training*?" Tessa was incredulous. "Sophie, really—"

But Sophie, shaking her head, had gathered up her skirts and stalked from the room, letting the door slam shut behind her.

Charlotte, her elbows on the desk in the drawing room, sighed and balled up her fourteenth piece of paper, and tossed it into the fireplace. The fire sparked up for a moment, consuming the paper as it turned black and fell to ashes.

She picked up her pen, dipped it into the inkwell, and began again.

I, Charlotte Mary Branwell, daughter of Nephilim, do hereby and on this date tender my resignation as the director of the London Institute, on behalf of myself and of my husband, Henry Jocelyn Branwell—

"Charlotte?"

Her hand jerked, sending a blot of ink sprawling across the page, ruining her careful lettering. She looked up and saw Henry hovering by the desk, a worried look on his thin, freckled face. She set her pen down. She was conscious, as she always was with Henry and rarely at any other times, of her physical appearance—that her hair was escaping from its chignon, that her dress was not new and had an ink blot on the sleeve, and that her eyes were tired and puffy from weeping.

"What is it, Henry?"

Henry hesitated. "It's just that I've been— Darling, what are you writing?" He came around the desk, glancing over her shoulder. *"Charlotte!"* He snatched the paper off the desk; though ink had smeared through the letters, enough of what she had written was left for him to get the gist. "Resigning from the Institute? How can you?"

"Better to resign than to have Consul Wayland come in over my head and force me out," Charlotte said quietly.

"Don't you mean 'us'?" Henry looked hurt. "Should I have at least a say in this decision?"

"You've never taken an interest in the running of the Institute before. Why would you now?"

Henry looked as if she had slapped him, and it was all Charlotte could do not to get up and put her arms around him and kiss his freckled cheek. She remembered, when she had fallen in love with him, how she had thought he reminded her of an adorable puppy, with his hands just a bit too large for the rest of him, his wide hazel eyes, his eager demeanor. That the mind behind those eyes was as sharp and intelligent as her own was something she had always believed, even when others had laughed at Henry's eccentricities. She had always thought it would be enough just to be near him always, and love him whether he loved her or not. But that had been before.

"Charlotte," he said now. "I know why you're angry with me."

Her chin jerked up in surprise. Could he truly be that perceptive? Despite her conversation with Brother Enoch, she had thought no one had noticed. She had barely been able to think about it herself, much less how Henry would react when he knew. "You do?"

"I wouldn't go with you to meet with Woolsey Scott."

Relief and disappointment warred in Charlotte's breast. "Henry," she sighed. "That is hardly—"

"I didn't realize," he said. "Sometimes I get so caught up in my ideas. You've always known that about me, Lottie."

Charlotte flushed. He so rarely called her that.

"I would change it if I could. Of all the people in the world, I did think you understood. You know—you know it isn't just tinkering for me. You know I want to create something that will make the world better, that will make things better for the Nephilim. Just as you do, in directing the Institute. And though I know I will always come second for you—"

"Second for *me*?" Charlotte's voice shot up to an incredulous squeak. "*You* come second for *me*?"

"It's all right, Lottie," Henry said with incredible gentleness. "I knew when you agreed to marry me that it was because you needed to be married to run the Institute, that no one would accept a woman alone in the position of director—"

"Henry." Charlotte rose to her feet, trembling. "How can you say such terrible things to me?"

Henry looked baffled. "I thought that was just the way it was—"

"Do you think I don't know why you married me?" Charlotte cried. "Do you think I don't know about the money your father owed my father, or that my father promised to forgive the debt if you'd marry me? He always wanted a boy, someone to run the Institute after him, and if he couldn't have that, well, why not *pay* to marry his unmarriageable daughter—too plain, too headstrong—off to some poor boy who was just doing his duty by his family—"

"CHARLOTTE." Henry had turned brick red. She had never seen him so angry. "WHAT ON EARTH ARE YOU TALKING ABOUT?"

Charlotte braced herself against the desk. "You know very well," she said. "It is why you married me, isn't it?"

"You've never said a word about this to me before today!"

"Why would I? It's nothing you didn't know."

"It is, actually." Henry's eyes were blazing. "I know nothing of my father's owing yours anything. I went to your father in good faith and asked him if he would do me the honor of allowing me to ask for your hand in marriage. There was never any discussion of money!"

Charlotte caught her breath. In the years they had been married, she had never said a word about the circumstances of her betrothal to Henry; there had never seemed a reason, and she had never before wanted to hear any stammered denials of what she knew was true. Hadn't her father said it to her when he had told her of Henry's proposal? *He is a good enough man, better than his father, and you need some sort of a husband, Charlotte, if you are going to direct the Institute. I've forgiven his father's debts, so that matter is closed between our families.*

Of course, he had never said, not in so many words, that that was *why* Henry had asked to marry her. She had assumed . . .

"You are not plain," Henry said, his face still blazing. "You are beautiful. And I didn't ask your father if I could marry you out of duty; I did it because I loved you. I've always loved you. I'm your *husband*."

"I didn't think you wanted to be," she whispered.

Henry was shaking his head. "I know people call me eccentric. Peculiar. Even mad. All of those things. I've never minded. But for you to think I'd be so weak-willed— Do you even love me at all?"

"Of course I love you!" Charlotte cried. "That was never in question."

"Wasn't it? Do you think I don't hear what people say? They speak about me as if I weren't there, as if I were some sort of half-wit. I've heard Benedict Lightwood say enough times that you married me only so that you could pretend a man was running the Institute—"

Now it was Charlotte's turn to be angry. "And you criticize me for thinking you weak-willed! Henry, I'd never marry you for that reason, never in a thousand years. I'd give up the Institute in a moment before I'd give up . . ."

Henry was staring at her, his hazel eyes wide, his ginger hair bristling as if he had run his hands madly through it so many times that he was in danger of pulling it out in chunks. "Before you'd give up what?"

"Before I'd give *you* up," she said. "Don't you know that?"

And then she said nothing else, for Henry put his arms around her and kissed her. Kissed her in such a way that she no longer felt plain, or conscious of her hair or the ink spot on her dress or anything but Henry, whom she had always loved. Tears welled up and spilled down her cheeks, and when he drew away, he touched her wet face wonderingly.

"Really," he said. "You love me, too, Lottie?"

"Of course I do. I didn't marry you so I'd have someone to run the Institute with, Henry. I married you because—because I knew I wouldn't mind how difficult directing this place was, or how badly the Clave treated me, if I knew yours would be the last face I saw every night before I went to sleep." She hit him lightly on the shoulder. "We've been married for years, Henry. What did you *think* I felt about you?"

He shrugged his thin shoulders and kissed the top of her head. "I thought you were fond of me," he said gruffly. "I thought you might come to love me, in time."

"That's what I thought about you," she said wonderingly. "Could we really both have been so stupid?"

"Well, I'm not surprised about *me*," said Henry. "But honestly, Charlotte, you ought to have known better."

She choked back a laugh. "Henry!" She squeezed his arms. "There's something else I have to tell you, something very important—"

The door to the drawing room banged open. It was Will. Henry and Charlotte drew apart and stared at him. He looked exhausted—pale, with dark rings about his eyes—but there was a clarity in his face Charlotte had never seen before, a sort of brilliance in his expression. She braced herself for a sarcastic remark or cold observation, but instead he just smiled happily at them.

"Henry, Charlotte," he said. "You haven't seen Tessa, have you?"

"She's likely in her room," said Charlotte, bewildered. "Will, is something the matter? Oughtn't you be resting? After the injuries you sustained—"

Will waved this away. "Your excellent *iratzes* did their

work. I don't require rest. I only wish to see Tessa, and to ask you—" He broke off, staring at the letter on Charlotte's desk. With a few strides of his long legs, he had reached the desk and snatched it up, and read it with the same look of dismay Henry had worn. "Charlotte—no, you can't give up the Institute!"

"The Clave will find you another place to live," Charlotte said. "Or you may stay here until you turn eighteen, though the Lightwoods—"

"I wouldn't want to live here without you and Henry. What d'you think I stay for? The ambiance?" Will shook the piece of paper till it crackled. "I even bloody miss Jessamine— Well, a bit. And the Lightwoods will sack our servants and replace them with their own. Charlotte, you can't let it happen. This is our home. It's Jem's home, Sophie's home."

Charlotte stared. "Will, are you sure you haven't a fever?"

"Charlotte." Will slammed the paper back down onto the desk. "I *forbid* you to resign your directorship. Do you understand? Over all these years you've done everything for me as if I were your own blood, and I've never told you I was grateful. That goes for you as well, Henry. But I am grateful, and because of it I shall not let you make this mistake."

"Will," said Charlotte. "It is over. We have only three days to find Mortmain, and we cannot possibly do so. There simply is not time."

"Hang Mortmain," said Will. "And I mean that literally, of course, but also figuratively. The two-week limit on finding Mortmain was in essence set by Benedict Lightwood as a ridiculous test. A test that, as it turns out, was a cheat. He is working for Mortmain. This test was his attempt to leverage the Institute out from under you. If we but expose Benedict for what he is—Mortmain's puppet—the Institute is yours again, and the search for Mortmain can continue."

"We have Jessamine's word that to expose Benedict is to play into Mortmain's hands—"

"We cannot do nothing," Will said firmly. "It is worth at least a conversation, don't you think?" Charlotte couldn't think of a word to say. This Will was not a Will she knew. He was firm, straightforward, intensity shining in his eyes. If Henry's silence was anything to go by, he was just as surprised. Will nodded as if taking this for agreement.

"Excellent," he said. "I'll tell Sophie to round up the others." And he darted from the room.

Charlotte stared up at her husband, all thoughts of the news she had wished to tell him driven from her mind. "Was that *Will?*" she said finally.

Henry arched one ginger eyebrow. "Perhaps he's been kidnapped and replaced by an automaton," he suggested. "It seems possible . . ."

For once Charlotte could only find herself in agreement.

Glumly Tessa finished the sandwiches and the rest of the tea, cursing her inability to keep her nose out of other people's business. Once she was done, she put on her blue dress, finding the task difficult without Sophie's assistance. *Look at yourself,* she thought, *spoiled after just a few weeks of having a lady's maid. Can't dress yourself, can't stop nosing about where you're not wanted. Soon you'll be needing someone to spoon gruel into your mouth or you'll starve.* She made a horrible face at herself in the mirror and sat down at her vanity table, picking up the silver-backed hairbrush and pulling the bristles through her long brown hair.

A knock came at the door. *Sophie*, Tessa thought hopefully, back for an apology. Well, she would get one. Tessa dropped the hairbrush and rushed to throw the door open.

Just as once before she had expected Jem and been disappointed to find Sophie on her threshold, now, in expecting Sophie, she was surprised to find Jem at her door. He wore a gray wool jacket and trousers, against which his silvery hair looked nearly white.

"Jem," she said, startled. "Is everything all right?"

His gray eyes searched her face, her long, loose hair. "You look as if you were waiting for someone else."

"Sophie." Tessa sighed, and tucked a stray curl behind her ear. "I fear I have offended her. My habit of speaking before I think has caught me out again."

"Oh," said Jem, with an uncharacteristic lack of interest. Usually he would have asked Tessa what she had said to Sophie, and either reassured her or helped her plot a course of action to win Sophie's forgiveness. His customary vivid interest in everything seemed oddly missing, Tessa thought with alarm; he was quite pale as well, and seemed to be glancing behind her as if checking to see whether she was quite alone. "Is now—that is, I would like to speak to you in private, Tessa. Are you feeling well enough?"

"That depends on what you have to tell me," she said with a laugh, but when her laugh brought no answering smile, apprehension rose inside her. "Jem—you promise everything's all right? Will—"

"This is not about Will," he said. "Will is out wandering and no doubt perfectly all right. This is about— Well, I suppose you might say it's about me." He glanced up and down the corridor. "Might I come in?"

Tessa briefly thought about what Aunt Harriet would say about a girl who allowed a boy she was not related to into her bedroom when there was no one else there. But then Aunt Harriet herself had been in love once, Tessa thought. Enough in love to let her fiancé do—well, whatever it was exactly that left one with child. Aunt Harriet, had she been alive, would have been in no position to talk. And besides, etiquette was different for Shadowhunters.

She opened the door wide. "Yes, come in."

Jem came into the room, and shut the door firmly behind him. He walked over to the grate and leaned an arm against the mantel; then, seeming to decide that this position was unsatisfactory, he came over to where Tessa was, in the middle of the room, and stood in front of her.

"Tessa," he said.

"Jem," she replied, mimicking his serious tone, but again he did not smile. "Jem," she said again, more quietly. "If this is about your health, your—illness, please tell me. I will do whatever I can to help you."

"It is not," he said, "about my illness." He took a deep breath. "You know we have not found Mortmain," he said. "In a few days, the Institute may be given to Benedict Lightwood. He would doubtless allow Will and me to remain here, but not you, and I have no desire to live in a house that he runs. And Will and Gabriel would kill each other inside a minute. It would be the end of our little group; Charlotte and Henry would find a house, I have no doubt, and Will and I perhaps would go to Idris until we were eighteen, and Jessie—I suppose it depends what sentence the Clave passes on her. But we could not bring you to Idris with us. You are not a Shadowhunter."

Tessa's heart had begun to beat very fast. She sat down, rather suddenly, on the edge of her bed. She felt faintly sick. She remembered Gabriel's sneering jibe about the Lightwoods' finding "employment" for her; having been to the ball at their house, she could imagine little worse. "I see," she said. "But where should I go— No, do not answer that. You hold no responsibility toward me. Thank you for telling me, at least."

"Tessa—"

"You all have already been as kind as propriety has allowed," she said, "given that allowing me to live here has done none of you any good in the eyes of the Clave. I shall find a place—"

"Your place is with me," Jem said. "It always will be."

"What do you mean?"

He flushed, the color dark against his pale skin. "I mean," he said, "Tessa Gray, will you do me the honor of becoming my wife?"

Tessa sat bolt upright. "*Jem!*"

They stared at each other for a moment. At last he said, trying for lightness, though his voice cracked, "That was not a no, I suppose, though neither was it a yes."

"You can't mean it."

"I do mean it."

"You can't—I'm not a Shadowhunter. They'll expel you from the Clave—"

He took a step closer to her, his eyes eager. "You may not be precisely a Shadowhunter. But you are not a mundane either, nor provably a Downworlder. Your situation is unique, so I do not know what the Clave will do. But they cannot forbid something that is not forbidden by the Law. They will have to take your—our—individual case into consideration, and that could take months. In the meantime they cannot prevent our engagement."

"You *are* serious." Her mouth was dry. "Jem, such a kindness on your part is indeed incredible. It does you credit. But I cannot let you sacrifice yourself in that way for me."

"*Sacrifice?* Tessa, I love you. I *want* to marry you."

"I . . . Jem, it is just that you are kind, so selfless. How can I trust that you are not doing this simply for my sake?"

He reached into the pocket of his waistcoat and drew out something smooth and circular. It was a pendant of whitish-green jade, with Chinese characters carved into it that she could not read. He held it out to her with a hand that trembled ever so slightly.

"I could give you my family ring," he said. "But that is meant to be given back when the engagement is over, exchanged for runes. I want to give you something that will be yours forever."

She shook her head. "I cannot possibly—"

He interrupted her. "This was given to my mother by my father, when they married. The writing is from the I Ching, the Book of Changes. It says, *When two people are at one in their inmost hearts, they shatter even the strength of iron or bronze.*"

"And you think we are?" Tessa asked, shock making her voice small. "At one, that is?"

Jem knelt down at her feet, so that he was gazing up into her face. She saw him as he had been on Blackfriars Bridge, a lovely silver shadow against the darkness. "I cannot explain love," he said. "I could not tell you if I loved you the first moment I saw you, or if it was the second or third or fourth. But I remember the first moment I looked at you walking toward me and realized that somehow the rest of the world seemed to vanish when I was with you. That you were the center of everything I did and felt and thought."

Overwhelmed, Tessa shook her head slowly. "Jem, I never imagined—"

"There is a force and strength in love," he said. "That is what that inscription means. It is in the Shadowhunter wedding ceremony, too. *For love is as strong as death.* Have you not seen how much better I have been these past weeks, Tessa? I have been ill less, coughing less. I feel stronger, I need less of the drug—because of you. Because my love for you sustains me."

Tessa stared. Was such a thing even possible, outside of fairy tales? His thin face glowed with light; it was clear he believed it, absolutely. And he *had* been better.

"You speak of sacrifice, but it is not my sacrifice I offer. It is yours I ask of you," he went on. "I can offer you my life, but it is a short life; I can offer you my heart, though I have no idea how many more beats it shall sustain. But I love you enough to hope that you will not care that I am being selfish in trying to make the rest of my life—whatever its length—happy, by spending it with you. I want to be married to you, Tessa. I want it more than I have ever wanted anything else in my life." He looked up at her through the veil of silvery hair that fell over his eyes. "That is," he said shyly, "if you love me, too."

Tessa looked down at Jem, kneeling before her with the pendant in his hands, and understood at last what people meant when they said someone's heart was in their eyes, for Jem's eyes, his luminous, expressive eyes that she had always found beautiful, were full of love and hope.

And why should he *not* hope? She had given him every reason to believe she loved him. Her friendship, her trust, her confidence, her gratitude, even her passion. And if there was some small locked away part of herself that had not quite given up Will, surely she owed it to herself as much as to Jem to do whatever she could to destroy it.

Very slowly she reached down and took the pendant from Jem. It slipped around her neck on a gold chain, as cool as water, and rested in the hollow of her throat above the spot where the clockwork angel lay. As she lowered her hands from its clasp, she saw the hope in his eyes light to an almost unbearable blaze of disbelieving happiness. She felt as if someone had reached inside her chest and unlocked a box that held her heart, spilling tenderness like new blood through her veins. Never had she felt such an overwhelming urge to fiercely protect another person, to wrap her arms around someone else and curl up tightly with them, alone and away from the rest of the world.

"Then, yes," she said. "Yes, I will marry you, James Carstairs. Yes."

"Oh, thank God," he said, exhaling. "Thank God." And he buried his face in her lap, wrapping his arms around her waist. She bent over him, stroking his shoulders, his back, the silk of his hair. His heart pounded against her knees. Some small inner part of her was reeling with amazement. She had never imagined she had the power to make someone else so happy. And not a magical power either—a purely human one.

A knock came at the door; they sprang apart. Tessa hastily rose to her feet and made her way to the door, pausing to smooth down her hair—and, she hoped, calm her expression—before opening it. This time it really *was* Sophie. Though, her mutinous expression showed she had not come of her own accord. "Charlotte is summoning you to the drawing room, miss," she said. "Master Will has returned, and she wishes to have a meeting." She glanced past Tessa, and her expression soured further. "You, too, Master Jem."

"Sophie—," Tessa began, but Sophie had already turned and was hurrying away, her white cap bobbing. Tessa tightened her grip on the doorknob, looking after her. Sophie had said that she did not mind Jem's feelings for Tessa, and Tessa knew now that Gideon was the reason why. Still . . .

She felt Jem come up behind her and slip his hands into hers. His fingers were slender; she closed her own around them, and let out her held breath. Was this what it meant to love someone? That any burden was a burden shared, that they could give you comfort with a word or a touch? She leaned her head back against his shoulder, and he kissed her temple. "We'll tell Charlotte first, when there's a chance," he said, "and then the others. Once the fate of the Institute is decided . . ."

"You sound as if you don't mind what happens to it," said Tessa. "Won't you miss it here? This place has been your home."

His fingers stroked her wrist lightly, making her shiver. "You are home for me now."

19

If Treason Doth Prosper

Treason doth never prosper: what's the reason?
Why, if it prosper, none dare call it treason.
—Sir John Harrington

Sophie was tending a blazing fire in the drawing room grate, and the room was warm, almost stuffy. Charlotte sat behind her desk, Henry in a chair beside her. Will was sprawled in one of the flowered armchairs beside the fire, a silver tea service at his elbow and a cup in his hand. When Tessa walked in, he sat upright so abruptly that some of the tea spilled on his sleeve; he set the cup down without taking his eyes off her.

He looked exhausted, as if he had been walking all night. He still wore his overcoat, of dark blue wool with a red silk lining, and the legs of his black trousers were splattered with mud. His hair was damp and tangled, his face pale, his jaw dark with the shadow of stubble. But the moment he saw Tessa, his eyes glowed like lanterns at the touch of the lamplighter's match. His whole face changed, and he gazed upon her with such an inexplicable delight that Tessa, astonished, stopped in her tracks, causing Jem to bump into her. For that moment, she could not look away from Will; it was as if he held her gaze to him, and she remembered again the dream she had had the night before, that she was being comforted by him in the infirmary. Could he read the memory of it on her face? Was that why he was staring?

Jem peered around her shoulder. "Hallo, Will. Sure it was a good idea to spend all night out in the rain when you're still healing?"

Will tore his eyes away from Tessa. "I am quite sure," he said firmly. "I had to walk. To clear my head."

"And is your head clear now?"

"Like crystal," Will said, returning his gaze to Tessa, and the same thing happened again. Their gazes seemed to lock together, and she had to tear her eyes away and move across the room to sit on the sofa near the desk, where Will was not in her direct line of sight. Jem came and sat down beside her, but did not reach for her hand. She wondered what would happen if they announced what had just happened now, casually: *The two of us are going to be married.*

But Jem had been correct; it was not the right time for that. Charlotte looked as if, like Will, she had been awake all night; her skin was a sickly yellow color, and there were dark auburn bruises beneath her eyes. Henry sat beside her at the desk, his hand protectively over hers, watching her with a worried expression.

"We are all here, then," Charlotte said briskly, and for a moment Tessa wanted to remark that they were not, for Jessamine was not with them. She stayed silent. "As you probably know, we are near the end of the two-week period granted to us by Consul Wayland. We have not discovered the whereabouts of Mortmain. According to Enoch, the Silent Brothers have examined Nathaniel Gray's body and learned nothing from it, and as he is dead, we can learn nothing from him."

And as he is dead. Tessa thought of Nate as she remembered him, when they had been very young, chasing dragonflies in the park. He had fallen in the pond, and she and Aunt Harriet—his mother—had helped to pull him out; his hand had been slippery with water and green-growing underwater plants. She remembered his hand sliding out of hers in the tea warehouse, slippery with blood. *You don't know everything I've done, Tessie.*

"We can certainly report what we know about Benedict to the Clave," Charlotte was saying when Tessa forcibly snapped her mind back to the conversation at hand. "It would seem to be the sensible course of action."

Tessa swallowed. "What about what Jessamine said? That we'd be playing into Mortmain's hands by doing so."

"But we cannot do nothing," said Will. "We cannot sit back and hand over the keys to the Institute to Benedict Lightwood and his lamentable offspring. They *are* Mortmain. Benedict is his puppet. We must *try*. By the Angel, haven't we enough evidence? Enough to earn him a trial by the Sword, at least."

"When we tried the Sword on Jessamine, there were blocks in her mind put there by Mortmain," Charlotte said wearily. "Do you think Mortmain would be so unwise as to not take the same precaution with Benedict? We will look like fools if the Sword can get nothing out of him."

Will ran his hands through his black hair. "Mortmain expects us to go to the Clave," he said. "It would be his first assumption. He is also used to cutting free associates for whom he no longer has a use. De Quincey, for instance. Lightwood is not irreplaceable to him, and knows it." He drummed his fingers on his knees. "I think that if we went to the Clave, we could certainly get Benedict taken out of the running for leadership of the Institute. But there is a segment of the Clave that follows his lead; some are known to us, but others are not. It is a sad fact, but we do not know whom we can trust beyond ourselves. The Institute is secure with us, and we cannot allow it to be taken away. Where else will Tessa be safe?"

Tessa blinked. "Me?"

Will looked taken aback, as if startled by what he had just said. "Well, you are an integral part of Mortmain's plan. He has always wanted *you*. He has always needed you. We must not let him have you. Clearly you would be a powerful weapon in his hands."

"All of that is true, Will, and of course I will go to the Consul," said Charlotte. "But as an ordinary Shadowhunter, not as head of the Institute."

"But why, Charlotte?" Jem demanded. "You excel at your work—"

"Do I?" she demanded. "For the second time I have not noted a spy under my own roof; Will and Tessa easily evaded my guardianship to attend Benedict's party; our plan to capture Nate, which we never shared with the Consul, went awry, leaving us with a potentially important witness dead—"

"Lottie!" Henry put his hand on his wife's arm.

"I am not fit to run this place," said Charlotte. "Benedict was right. . . . I will of course try to convince the Clave of his guilt. Someone else will run the Institute. It will not be Benedict, I hope, but it will not be me, either—"

There was a clatter. "Mrs. Branwell!" It was Sophie. She had dropped the poker and turned away from the fire. "You can't resign, ma'am. You—you simply can't."

"Sophie," Charlotte said very kindly. "Wherever we go after this, wherever Henry and I set up our household, we will bring you—"

"It isn't that," Sophie said in a small voice. Her eyes darted around the room. "Miss Jessamine— She were—I mean, she was telling the truth. If you go to the Clave like this, you'll be playing into Mortmain's plans."

Charlotte looked at her, perplexed. "What makes you say that?"

"I don't—I don't know exactly." Sophie looked at the floor. "But I know it's true."

"Sophie?" Charlotte's tone was querulous, and Tessa knew what she was thinking: Did they have another spy, another serpent in their garden? Will, too, was leaning forward with narrowed eyes.

"Sophie's not lying," Tessa said abruptly. "She knows because—because we overheard Gideon and Gabriel speaking of it in the training room."

"And you only now decided to mention it?" Will arched his brows.

Suddenly, unreasonably furious with him, Tessa snapped, "Be quiet, Will. If you—"

"I've been stepping out with him," Sophie interrupted loudly. "With Gideon Lightwood. Seeing him on my days off." She was as pale as a ghost. "He told me. He heard his father laughing about it. They knew Jessamine was found out. They were hoping you'd go to the Clave. I should've said something, but it seemed like you didn't want to go to them anyways, so I . . ."

"Stepping out?" said Henry incredulously. "With *Gideon Lightwood?*"

Sophie kept her attention on Charlotte, who was gazing at her, round-eyed. "I know what Mortmain is holding over Mr. Lightwood too," she said. "Gideon only just found out. His father doesn't know he knows."

"Well, dear God, girl, don't just stand there," said Henry, who looked as poleaxed as his wife. "Tell us."

"Demon pox," said Sophie. "Mr. Lightwood's got it, has had for years, and it'll kill him in a right couple of months if he doesn't get the cure. And Mortmain said he can get it for him."

The room exploded in a hubbub. Charlotte raced over to Sophie; Henry called after her; Will leaped from his chair and was dancing in a circle. Tessa stayed where she was, stunned, and Jem remained beside her. Meanwhile, Will appeared to be singing a song about how he had been right about demon pox all along.

"Demon pox, oh, demon pox,
Just how is it acquired?
One must go down to the bad part of town
Until one is very tired.

Demon pox, oh, demon pox
I had it all along—
No, not the pox, you foolish blocks,
I mean this very song—
For I was right, and you were wrong!"

"Will!" Charlotte shouted over the noise. "Have you LOST YOUR MIND? CEASE THAT INFERNAL RACKET! Jem—"

Jem, rising to his feet, clapped his hands over Will's mouth. "Do you promise to be quiet?" he hissed into his friend's ear.

Will nodded, blue eyes blazing. Tessa was staring at him in amazement; they all were. She had seen Will many things—amused, bitter, condescending, angry, pitying—but never *giddy* before.

Jem let him go. "All right, then."

Will slid to the floor, his back against the armchair, and threw his arms up. "A demon pox on all your houses!" he announced, and yawned.

"Oh God, weeks of pox jokes," said Jem. "We're for it now."

"It can't be true," said Charlotte. "It's simply—*demon pox?*"

"How do we know Gideon did not lie to Sophie?" asked Jem, his tone mild. "I am sorry, Sophie. I hate to have to say it, but the Lightwoods are not trustworthy. . . ."

"I've seen Gideon's face when he looks at Sophie," said Will. "It was Tessa who told me first that Gideon fancied our Miss Collins, and I thought back, and I realized it was true. And a man in love—a man in love will tell anything. Betray anyone." He was staring at Tessa as he spoke. She stared back; she could not help it. Her gaze felt pulled to him. The way he looked at her, with those blue eyes like pieces of sky, as if trying to communicate something to her silently. But what on earth . . . ?

She did owe him her life, she realized with a start. Perhaps he had been waiting for her to thank him. But there had been no time, no chance! She resolved to thank him at the first opportunity that presented itself. "Besides, Benedict was holding a demon woman on his lap at that party of his, kissing her," Will went on, glancing away. "She had snakes for eyes. Each man to his own, I suppose. Anyway, the only way you can contract demon pox is by having improper relations with a demon, so . . ."

"Nate told me Mr. Lightwood preferred demon women," said Tessa. "I don't suppose his wife ever knew about *that*."

"Wait." It was Jem, who had suddenly gone very still. "Will—what are the symptoms of demon pox?"

"Quite nasty," said Will with relish. "It begins with a shield-shaped rash on one's back, and spreads over the body, creating cracks and fissures in the skin—"

Jem expelled a gasp of breath. "I—I shall return," he said, "in just a moment. By the Angel—"

And he vanished out the door, leaving the others staring after him.

"You don't think he has demon pox, do you?" Henry inquired of no one in particular.

I hope not, since we just got engaged, Tessa had the urge to say—just to see the looks on their faces—but repressed it.

"Oh, shut up, Henry," said Will, and looked as if he were about to say something else, but the door banged open and Jem was back in the room, panting, and holding a piece of parchment. "I got this," he said, "from the Silent Brothers—when Tessa and I went to see Jessamine." He gave Tessa a slightly guilty look from under his fair hair, and she remembered him leaving Jessamine's cell and returning moments later, looking preoccupied. "It is the report on Barbara Lightwood's death. After Charlotte told us that her father had never turned Silas Lightwood over to the Clave, I thought I would inquire of the Silent Brothers if there was another manner in which Mrs. Lightwood had died. To see if Benedict had also lied that she had died of grief."

"And had he?" Tessa leaned forward, fascinated.

"Yes. In fact, she cut her own wrists. But there was more." He looked down at the paper in his hand. "*A shield-shaped rash, indicative of the heraldic marks of astriola, upon the left shoulder.*" He held it out to Will, who took it and scanned it, his blue eyes widening.

"*Astriola,*" he said. "That *is* demon pox. You had evidence that demon pox existed and you didn't mention it to me! *Et tu, Brute!*" He rolled up the paper and hit Jem over the head with it.

"Ouch!" Jem rubbed his head ruefully. "The words meant nothing to me! I assumed it a minor sort of ailment. It hardly seemed as if it were what killed her. She slit her wrists, but if Benedict wanted to protect his children from the fact that their mother had taken her own life—"

"By the Angel," said Charlotte softly. "No wonder she killed herself. *Because her husband gave her demon pox. And she knew it.*" She whirled on Sophie, who made a little gasping noise. "Does Gideon know of this?"

Sophie shook her head, saucer-eyed. "No."

"But wouldn't the Silent Brothers be obligated to tell

someone if they discovered this?" Henry demanded. "It seems—well, dash it, irresponsible to say the least—"

"Of course they would tell someone. They would tell *her husband.* And no doubt they did, but what of it? Benedict probably already knew," said Will. "There would have been no need to tell the children; the rash appears when one has first contracted the disease, so they were too old for her to have passed it on to them. The Silent Brothers doubtless told Benedict, and he said 'Horrors!' and promptly concealed the whole thing. One cannot prosecute the dead for improper relations with demons, so they burned her body, and that was that."

"So how is it that Benedict is still alive?" Tessa demanded. "Should the disease not have killed him by now?"

"Mortmain," said Sophie. "He's been giving him drugs to slow the progress of the disease all this time."

"Slow it, not stop it?" asked Will.

"No, he's still dying, and faster now," said Sophie. "That's why he's so desperate, and he'll do anything Mortmain wants."

"Demon pox!" Will whispered, and looked at Charlotte. Despite his clear excitement, there was a steady light flickering behind his blue eyes, a light of sharp intelligence, as if he were a chess player examining his next move for potential advantages or drawbacks. "We must contact Benedict immediately," said Will. "Charlotte must play on his vanity. He is too sure of getting the Institute. She must tell him that though the Consul's official decision is not scheduled until Sunday, she has realized that it is he who will come out ahead, and she wishes to meet with him and make peace before it happens."

"Benedict is stubborn—," Charlotte began.

"Not as much as is he is proud," said Jem. "Benedict has always wanted control of the Institute, but he also wants to humiliate you, Charlotte. To prove that a woman cannot run an Institute. He believes that Sunday the Consul will rule to take the Institute away from you, but that does not mean he will be able to pass up a chance to see you grovel in private."

"To what end?" Henry demanded. "Sending Charlotte to confront Benedict accomplishes what, exactly?"

"Blackmail," said Will. His eyes were burning with excitement. "Mortmain may not be in our grasp, but Benedict is, and for now that may be enough."

"You think he will walk away from trying to get the Institute? Won't that simply leave the business for one of his followers to take up?" Jem asked.

"We're not trying to get rid of him. We want him to throw his full support behind Charlotte. To withdraw his challenge and to declare her fit to run the Institute. His followers will be at a loss; the Consul will be satisfied. We hold the Institute. And more than that, we can force Benedict to tell us what he knows of Mortmain—his location, his secrets, everything."

Tessa said dubiously, "But I am almost certain he is more afraid of Mortmain than he is of us, and he certainly needs what Mortmain provides. Otherwise he will die."

"Yes, he will. But what he did—having improper relations with a demon, then infecting his wife, causing her death—is the knowing murder of another Shadowhunter. It would not be considered only murder, either, but murder accomplished through demonic means. That would call down the worst of all punishments."

"What is worse than death?" asked Tessa, and immediately

regretted saying it as she saw Jem's mouth tighten almost imperceptibly.

"The Silent Brothers will remove that which makes him Nephilim. He will become Forsaken," said Will. "His sons will become mundane, their Marks stripped. The name of Lightwood will be stricken from the rolls of Shadowhunters. It will be the end of the Lightwood name among Nephilim. There is no greater shame. It is a punishment even Benedict will fear."

"And if he does not?" said Jem in a low voice.

"Then, we are no worse off, I suppose." It was Charlotte, whose expression had hardened as Will had spoken; Sophie was leaning against the mantel, a dejected figure, and Henry, his hand on his wife's shoulder, looked unusually subdued. "We will call on Benedict. There is no time to send a proper message ahead; it will have to be something of a surprise. Now, where are the calling cards?"

Will sat upright. "You've decided on my plan, then?"

"It's my plan now," said Charlotte firmly. "You may accompany me, Will, but you will follow my lead, and there will be no talk of demon pox until I say so."

"But—but . . ." Will sputtered.

"Oh, leave it," said Jem, kicking Will, not without affection, lightly on the ankle.

"She's *annexed* my plan!"

"Will," Tessa said firmly. "Do you care more about the plan being enacted or about getting credit for it?"

Will pointed a finger at her. "That," he said. "The second one."

Charlotte rolled her eyes skyward. "William, this will be either on my terms or not at all."

Will took a deep breath, and looked at Jem, who grinned at him; Will let the air out of his lungs with a defeated sigh and said, "All right, then, Charlotte. Do you intend for all of us to go?"

"You and Tessa, certainly. We need you as witnesses regarding the party. Jem, Henry, there is no need for you to go, and we require at least one of you to remain and guard the Institute."

"Darling . . ." Henry touched Charlotte's arm with a quizzical look on his face.

She looked up at him in surprise. "Yes?"

"You're sure you don't want me to come with you?"

Charlotte smiled at him, a smile that transformed her tired, pinched face. "Quite sure, Henry; Jem isn't technically an adult, and to leave him here alone—not that he isn't capable—will only add fuel to Benedict's fire of complaints. But thank you."

Tessa looked at Jem; he gave her a regretful smile and, hidden behind the spread of her skirts, pressed her hand with his. His touch sent a warm rush of reassurance through her, and she rose to her feet, amid Will rising to go, while Charlotte sought for a pen to scribble a note to Benedict on the back of a flossed calling card, which Cyril would deliver while they waited in the carriage.

"I'd best fetch my hat and gloves," Tessa whispered to Jem, and made her way to the door. Will was just behind her, and a moment later, the drawing room door swinging shut behind them, they found themselves alone in the corridor. Tessa was about to hurry down the hall toward her room, when she heard Will's footsteps behind her.

"Tessa!" he called, and she swung around. "Tessa, I need to speak with you."

"Now?" she said, surprised. "I gathered from Charlotte that she wanted us to hurry—"

"Damn hurrying," said Will, coming closer to her. "Damn Benedict Lightwood and the Institute and all this business. I want to talk to *you*." He grinned at her. There had always been a reckless energy to him, but this was different—the difference between the recklessness of despair and the abandonment of happiness. But what an odd time to be happy!

"Have you gone quite mad?" she asked him. "You say 'demon pox' the way someone else might say 'massive surprise inheritance.' Are you really that pleased?"

"Vindicated, not happy, and anyway, this isn't about the demon pox. This is about you and me—"

The drawing room door opened, and Henry emerged, Charlotte just behind him. Knowing Jem would be next, Tessa stepped away from Will hastily, though nothing improper had transpired between them at all. *Except in your thoughts*, said a little voice in the back of her mind, which she ignored. "Will, not now," she said under her breath. "I believe I know what it is you want to say, and you're quite right to wish to say it, but this isn't the time or place, is it? Believe me, I am as eager for the talk as you, for it has been weighing heavily on my mind—"

"You are? It has?" Will looked dazed, as if she had hit him with a rock.

"Well—yes," said Tessa, looking up to see Jem coming toward them. "But not *now*."

Will followed her gaze, swallowed, and nodded reluctantly. "Then, when?"

"Later, after we go to the Lightwoods'. Meet me in the drawing room."

"In the drawing room?"

She frowned at him. "Really, Will," she said. "Are you going to repeat everything I say?"

Jem had reached them, and heard this last remark; he grinned. "Tessa, do let poor Will gather his wits about him; he's been out all night and looks as if he can barely remember his own name." He put his hand on his *parabatai*'s arm. "Come along, Herondale. You seem as if you need an energy rune—or two or three."

Will tore his eyes away from Tessa's and let Jem lead him off down the corridor. Tessa watched them, shaking her head. *Boys*, she thought. She would never understand them.

Tessa had gone only a few steps into her bedroom when she stopped in surprise, staring at what was on the bed. A stylish walking suit of cream and gray striped India silk, trimmed with delicate braid and silver buttons. Gray velvet gloves lay beside it, figured with a pattern of leaves in silver thread. At the foot of the bed were bone-colored buttoned boots, and fashionable patterned stockings.

The door opened, and Sophie came in, holding a pale gray hat with trimmings of silver berries. She was very pale, and her eyes were swollen and red. She avoided Tessa's gaze. "New clothing, miss," Sophie said. "The fabric was part of Mrs. Branwell's trousseau, and, well, a few weeks ago she thought of having it made into a dress for you. I think she thought you ought to have some clothes that Miss Jessamine didn't buy for you. She thought it might make you more—comfortable. And these were just delivered this morning. I asked Bridget to lay them out for you."

Tessa felt tears sting the backs of her eyes and sat down hastily on the edge of the bed. The thought that Charlotte, with everything else that was going on, would think of Tessa's comfort at all made her want to cry. But she stifled the urge, as she always did. "Sophie," she said, her voice uneven. "I ought—no, I *wanted*—to apologize to you."

"Apologize to me, miss?" Sophie said tonelessly, laying the hat on the bed. Tessa stared. Charlotte wore such plain clothes herself. She never would have thought of her as having the inclination or taste to choose such lovely things.

"I was entirely wrong to speak to you about Gideon as I did," said Tessa. "I put my nose in where it was decidedly not wanted, and you are quite correct, Sophie. One cannot judge a man for the sins of his family. And I should have told you that, though I saw Gideon at the ball that night, I cannot say he was partaking of the festivities; in fact, I cannot see into his head to determine what he thinks at all, and I should not have behaved as if I could. I am no more experienced than you, Sophie, and where it comes to gentlemen, I am decidedly uninformed. I apologize for acting superior; I shan't do it again, if only you'll forgive me."

Sophie went to the wardrobe and opened it to reveal a second dress—this one of a very dark blue, trimmed with a golden velvet braid, the polonaise slashed down the right side to reveal pale faille flounces beneath. "So lovely," she said a little wistfully, and touched it lightly with her hand. Then she turned to Tessa. "That were—that was a very pretty apology, miss, and I do forgive you. I forgave you in the drawing room, I did, when you lied for me. I don't approve of lying, but I know you meant it out of kindness."

"It was very brave, what you did," said Tessa. "Telling the truth to Charlotte. I know how you feared she'd be angry."

Sophie smiled sadly. "She isn't angry. She's disappointed. I know. She said she couldn't talk to me now but she would later, and I could see it, on her face. It's worse in a way, somehow."

"Oh, Sophie. She's disappointed in Will all the time!"

"Well, who isn't."

"That's not what I meant. I meant she loves you, like you were Will or Jem or—well, you know. Even if she's disappointed, you must stop fearing she'll sack you. She won't. She thinks you're wonderful, and so do I."

Sophie's eyes widened. "Miss Tessa!"

"Well, I do," said Tessa mutinously. "You are brave and selfless and lovely. Like Charlotte."

Sophie's eyes shone. She wiped at them hastily with the edge of her apron. "Now, that's enough of that," she said briskly, still blinking hard. "We must get you dressed and ready, for Cyril's coming round with the carriage, and I know Mrs. Branwell doesn't want to waste any time."

Tessa came forward obediently, and with Sophie's help she changed into the gray and white striped dress. "And do be careful, is all I have to say," said Sophie as she deftly wielded her buttonhook. "The old man is a nasty piece of work, and don't forget it. Very harsh, he is, on those boys."

Those boys. The way she said it made it sound like Sophie had sympathy for Gabriel as well as Gideon. Just what did Gideon think of his younger brother, Tessa wondered, and the sister, too? But she asked nothing as Sophie brushed and curled her hair, and daubed her temples with lavender water.

"Now, don't you look lovely, miss," she said proudly when

she was done at last, and Tessa had to admit that Charlotte had done a fine job in selecting just the right cut to flatter her, and gray suited her well. Her eyes looked bigger and blue, her waist and arms more slender, her bosom fuller. "There's just one other thing . . ."

"What is it, Sophie?"

"Master Jem," said Sophie, startling Tessa. "Please, whatever else you do, miss . . ." The other girl glanced at the chain of the jade pendant tucked down the front of Tessa's dress and bit her lip. "Don't break his heart."

20
The Bitter Root

But now, you are twain, you are cloven apart,
Flesh of his flesh, but heart of my heart;
And deep in one is the bitter root,
And sweet for one is the lifelong flower.
–Algernon Charles Swinburne,
"The Triumph of Time"

Tessa was just drawing on her velvet gloves as she ducked through the front doors of the Institute. A sharp wind had come up off the river and was blowing armfuls of leaves through the courtyard. The sky had gone thunderous and gray. Will stood at the foot of the stairs, hands in his pockets, looking up at the church steeple.

He was hatless, and the wind lifted his black hair and blew it back from his face. He did not seem to see Tessa, and for a moment she stood and looked at him. She knew it was not right to do; Jem was hers, she was his now, and other men might as well not exist. But she could not stop herself from comparing the two—Jem with his odd combination of delicacy and strength, and Will like a storm at sea, slate blue and black with brilliant flashes of temper like heat lightning. She wondered if there would ever be a time when the sight of him didn't move her, make her heart flutter, and if that feeling would subside as she grew used to the idea of being engaged to Jem. It was new enough still that it did not seem real.

There was one thing that was different, though. When she looked at Will now, she no longer felt any pain.

Will saw her then, and smiled through the hair that blew across his face. He reached up to push it back. "That's a new dress, isn't it?" he said as she came down the stairs. "Not one of Jessamine's."

She nodded, and waited resignedly for him to say something sarcastic, about her, Jessamine, the dress, or all three.

"It suits you. Odd that gray would make your eyes look blue, but it does."

She looked at him in astonishment, but before she could do more than open her mouth to ask him if he was feeling all right, the carriage came rattling around the corner of the Institute with Cyril at the reins. He pulled up in front of the steps, and the door of the carriage opened; Charlotte was inside, wearing a wine-colored velvet dress and a hat with a sprig of dried flowers in it. She looked as nervous as Tessa had ever seen her. "Get in quickly," she called, holding her hat on as she leaned out the door. "I think it's going to rain."

To Tessa's surprise, Cyril drove her, Charlotte, and Will not to the manor house in Chiswick but to an elegant house in Pimlico, which was apparently the Lightwoods' weekday residence. It *had* begun to rain, and their wet things—gloves, hats, and coats—were taken from them by a sour-faced footman before they were ushered down many polished corridors and into a large library, where a roaring fire burned in a deep grate.

Behind a massive oak desk sat Benedict Lightwood, his sharp profile made even sharper by the play of light and shadow inside the room. The drapes were pulled across the windows, and the walls were lined with heavy tomes bound in dark leather, gold printing across the spines. On either side of him stood his sons—Gideon at his right, his blond hair falling forward to hide his expression, his arms crossed over his broad chest. On the other side was Gabriel, his green eyes alight with a superior amusement, his hands in the pockets of his trousers. He looked as if he were about to start whistling.

"Charlotte," said Benedict. "Will. Miss Gray. Always a pleasure." He gestured for them to seat themselves in the chairs set before the desk. Gabriel grinned nastily at Will as he sat. Will looked at him, his face a careful blank, and then looked away. *Without a sarcastic remark*, Tessa thought, baffled. Without even a cold glare. *What* was going on?

"Thank you, Benedict." Charlotte, tiny, her spine straight, spoke with perfect poise. "For seeing us on such short notice."

"Of course." He smiled. "You do know that there's nothing you can do that's going to change the outcome of this. It isn't up to me what the Council rules. It is their decision entirely."

Charlotte tilted her head to the side. "Indeed, Benedict. But it is you who are making this happen. If you had not forced Consul Wayland into making a show of disciplining me, there would be no ruling."

Benedict shrugged his narrow shoulders. "Ah, Charlotte.

I remember you when you were Charlotte Fairchild. You were such a delightful little girl, and believe it or not as you will, I am fond of you even now. What I am doing is in the best interests of the Institute and the Clave. A woman cannot run the Institute. It is not in her nature. You'll be thanking me when you're home with Henry raising the next generation of Shadowhunters, as you should be. It might sting your pride, but in your heart you know I'm correct."

Charlotte's chest rose and fell rapidly. "If you abdicated your claim on the Institute before the ruling, do you truly think it would be such a disaster? Me, running the Institute?"

"Well, we'll never find out, will we?"

"Oh, I don't know," Charlotte said. "I think most Council members would choose a woman over a dissolute reprobate who fraternizes not just with Downworlders but with demons."

There was a short silence. Benedict didn't move a muscle. Neither did Gideon.

Finally Benedict spoke, though now there were teeth in the smooth velvet of his voice. "Rumors and innuendo."

"Truth and observation," said Charlotte. "Will and Tessa were at your last gathering, in Chiswick. They observed a great deal."

"That demon woman you were lounging with on the divan," said Will. "Would you call her a friend, or more of a business associate?"

Benedict's dark eyes hardened. "Insolent puppy—"

"Oh, I'd say she was a friend," said Tessa. "One doesn't usually let one's business associates lick one's face. Although I could be wrong. What do I know about these things? I'm only a silly woman."

Will's mouth quirked up at the corner. Gabriel was still staring; Gideon had his eyes on the floor. Charlotte sat perfectly composed, hands in her lap.

"All three of you are quite foolish," said Benedict, gesturing contemptuously toward them. Tessa caught a glimpse of something on his wrist, a shadow, like the coils of a woman's bracelet, before his sleeve fell back to cover it. "That is, if you think the Council will believe any of your lies. You"—he cast a dismissive look at Tessa—"are a Downworlder; your word is worthless. And you"—he flung an arm at Will—"are a certifiable lunatic who fraternizes with warlocks. Not just this chit here but Magnus Bane as well. And when they test me under the Mortal Sword and I refute your claims, who do you think will be believed, you or me?"

Will exchanged a quick look with Charlotte and Tessa. He had been right, Tessa thought, that Benedict did not fear the Sword. "There is other evidence, Benedict," he said.

"Oh?" Lightwood's lip curled upward in a sneer. "And what is that?"

"The evidence of your own poisoned blood," said Charlotte. "Just now, when you gestured at us, I saw your wrist. How far has the corruption spread? It begins on the torso, does it not, and spreads down the arms and legs—"

"What is he talking about?" Gabriel's voice was a mixture of fury and terror. "Father?"

"Demon pox," said Will with the satisfaction of the truly vindicated.

"What a disgusting accusation—," began Benedict.

"Refute it, then," said Charlotte. "Pull up your sleeve. Show us your arm."

The muscle by the side of Benedict's mouth twitched again. Tessa watched him in fascination. He did not terrify her, as Mortmain had, but rather disgusted her, the way the sight of a fat worm wriggling across a garden might. She watched as he whirled on his eldest son.

"You," he snarled. "*You* told them. You betrayed me."

"I did," said Gideon, raising his head and uncurling his arms at last. "And I would again."

"Gideon?" It was Gabriel, sounding bewildered. "Father? What are you talking about?"

"Your brother has betrayed us, Gabriel. He has told our secrets to the Branwells." Benedict spat his words out like poison. "Gideon Arthur Lightwood," Benedict went on. His face looked older, the lines at the sides of his mouth more severe, but his tone was unchanged. "I suggest you think very carefully about what you have done, and what you will do next."

"I *have* been thinking," said Gideon in his soft, low voice. "Ever since you called me back from Spain, I have been thinking. As a child I assumed all Shadowhunters lived as we did. Condemning demons by the light of day, yet fraternizing with them under cover of darkness. I now realize that is not true. It is not our way, Father; it is *your* way. You have brought shame and filth upon the name of Lightwood."

"There is no need to be melodramatic—"

"Melodramatic?" There was terrible contempt in Gideon's normally flat tone. "Father, I fear for the future of the Enclave if you get your hands on the Institute. I am telling you now, I will witness against you at the Council. I will hold the Mortal Sword in my hands and I will tell Consul Wayland why I think Charlotte is a thousand times more fit than you are to run the

Institute. I will reveal what goes on here at night to every member of the Council. I will tell them that you are working for Mortmain. I will tell them *why*."

"Gideon!" It was Gabriel, his voice sharp, cutting across his brother's. "You know our custodianship of the Institute was mother's dying wish. And it is the fault of the Fairchilds that she died—"

"That is a lie," said Charlotte. "She took her own life, but not because of anything my father did." She looked directly at Benedict. "It was, rather, because of something *your* father did."

Gabriel's voice rose. "What do you mean? Why would you say such a thing? Father—"

"Be quiet, Gabriel." Benedict's voice had gone hard and commanding, but for the first time there was fear in his voice, his eyes. "Charlotte, what are you saying?"

"You know very well what I am saying, Benedict," said Charlotte. "The question is whether you wish me to share my knowledge with the Clave. And with your children. You know what it will mean for them."

Benedict sat back. "I know blackmail when I hear it, Charlotte. What do you want from me?"

It was Will who responded, too eager to hold himself back any longer. "Withdraw your claim on the Institute. Speak out for Charlotte in front of the Council. Tell them why you think the Institute should be left in her keeping. You are a well-spoken man. You'll think of something, I'm sure."

Benedict looked from Will to Charlotte. His lip curled. "Those are your terms?"

Before Will could speak, Charlotte said, "Not all our terms.

We need to know how you have been communicating with Mortmain, and where he is."

Benedict chuckled. "I communicated with him through Nathaniel Gray. But, since you've killed him, I doubt he will be a forthcoming source of information."

Charlotte looked appalled. "You mean no one else knew where he was?"

"I certainly don't," said Benedict. "Mortmain is not that stupid, unfortunately for you. He wished me to be able to take the Institute that he might strike at it from its heart. But it was only one of his many plans, a strand of his web. He has been waiting for this a long time. He will have the Clave. And he will have *her*." His eyes rested on Tessa.

"What does he intend to do with me?" Tessa demanded.

"I don't know," Benedict said with a sly smile. "I do know he was consistently asking after your welfare. Such concern, so touching in a potential bridegroom."

"He says he created me," said Tessa. "What does he mean by that?"

"I haven't the vaguest idea. You are mistaken if you think he made me his confidant."

"Yes," said Will, "you two don't seem to have much in common, save a penchant for demon women and evil."

"Will!" snapped Tessa.

"I didn't mean *you*," said Will, looking surprised. "I meant the Pandemonium Club—"

"If you are quite done with your byplay," said Benedict, "I wish to make one thing very clear to my son. Gideon, understand that if you support Charlotte Branwell in this, you will no longer be welcome under my roof. It is not for nothing that they say a man should never hang all his bells on one horse."

In answer Gideon raised his hands in front of him, almost as if he meant to pray. But Shadowhunters did not pray, and Tessa realized quickly what he was doing—slipping the silver ring from his finger. The ring that was like Jem's Carstairs ring, only this one had a pattern of flames about the band. The Lightwood family ring. He set it down on the edge of his father's desk, and turned to his brother.

"Gabriel," he said. "Will you come with me?"

Gabriel's green eyes were brilliant with anger. "You know I cannot."

"Yes, you can." Gideon held his hand out to his brother. Benedict stared between the two of them. He had paled slightly, as if suddenly realizing that he might lose not just one son, but both. His hand gripped the edge of the desk, his knuckles whitening. Tessa could not help staring at the expanse of the wrist that was revealed as his sleeve rose. It was very pale, banded with black circular striations. Something about the sight nauseated her, and she rose from her seat. Will, beside her, was already standing. Only Charlotte was still sitting, as prim and expressionless as ever.

"Gabriel, please," Gideon said. "Come with me."

"Who will take care of father? What will people say about our family if we both abandon him?" Gabriel said, bitterness and desperation coloring his tone. "Who will manage the estates, the Council seat—"

"I don't know," said Gideon. "But it does not need to be you. The Law—"

Gabriel's voice shook. "Family before Law, Gideon." His eyes locked with his brother's for a moment; then he looked away, chewing his lip, and went to stand behind Benedict, his hand on the back of his father's chair.

Benedict smiled; in this one thing, at least, he was triumphant. Charlotte rose to her feet, her chin held high. "I trust we will see you tomorrow, in the Council chamber, Benedict. I trust you will know what to do," she said, and swept from the room, Gideon and Tessa on her heels. Only Will hesitated a moment, in the doorway, his eyes on Gabriel, but when the other boy did not look at him, he shrugged at last and went out after the others, shutting the door behind him.

They rode back to the Institute in silence, rain lashing against the windows of the carriage. Charlotte attempted several times to speak to Gideon, but he was silent, staring at the blurred view of streets as they rolled by. Tessa could not tell if he was angry, or regretted his actions, or might even be relieved. He was as impassive as always, even as Charlotte explained to him that there would always be a room for him at the Institute, and that they could hardly express their gratitude for what he had done. At last, as they rattled down the Strand, he said, "I had really thought Gabriel would come with me. Once he knew about Mortmain . . ."

"He does not understand yet," said Charlotte. "Give him time."

"How did you know?" Will looked at Gideon keenly. "We only just discovered what happened to your mother. And Sophie said you had no idea—"

"I had Cyril deliver two notes," said Charlotte. "One for Benedict and one for Gideon."

"He slipped it into my hand while my father was not looking," Gideon said. "I had only just time to read it before you came in."

"And you chose to believe it?" Tessa said. "So quickly?"

Gideon looked toward the rain-washed window. His jaw was set in a hard line. "Father's story about Mother's death never made sense to me. This made sense."

Crowded into the damp carriage, with Gideon only a few feet from her, Tessa felt the oddest urge to reach out to him, to tell him that she too had had a brother whom she had loved and had lost to what was worse than death, that she understood. She could see now what Sophie liked in him—the vulnerability under the impassive countenance, the solid honesty beneath the handsome bones of his face.

She said nothing, however, sensing it would not be welcome. Will, meanwhile, sat beside her, a bundle of coiled energy. Every once in a while she would catch a flash of blue as he looked at her, or the edge of a smile—a surprisingly *sweet* smile, something like giddiness, which she had never associated with Will before. It was as if he were sharing a private joke with her, only she was not entirely sure she knew what that joke *was*. Still, she felt his tension so keenly that her own calm, or what there was of it, was entirely cut up by the time they finally reached the Institute and Cyril—soaked to the skin, but friendly as always—came around the carriage to open the doors.

He helped Charlotte out first, and then Tessa, and then Will was beside her, having jumped down from the carriage and narrowly skirted a puddle. It had stopped raining. Will glanced up at the sky and took hold of Tessa's arm. "Come along," he whispered, steering her toward the front door of the Institute.

Tessa glanced back over her shoulder, to where Charlotte

stood at the foot of the steps, having succeeded, it seemed, in finally getting Gideon to speak to her. She was gesturing animatedly, using her hands.

"We ought to wait for them, oughtn't we—," Tessa began.

Will shook his dark head determinedly. "Charlotte will be blathering at him for ages about what room he wants to stay in, and how grateful she is for his help, and all I want is to talk to you."

Tessa stared at him as they entered the Institute. Will wanted to talk to her. He had said so before, true, but to speak so straightforwardly was very unlike him.

A thought seized her. Had Jem told him of their engagement? Was he angry, thinking her not worthy of his friend? But when would Jem have had a *chance*? Perhaps while she was dressing—but, then, Will did not *look* angry.

"I can't wait to tell Jem about our meeting," he said as they mounted the stairs. "He'll never believe that scene—for Gideon to turn on his father like that! It's one thing to tell secrets to Sophie, another to renounce your whole allegiance to your family. Yet he cast away his family ring."

"It is as you said," Tessa said as they turned at the top of the stairs and made their way down the corridor. Will's gloved hand was warm on her arm. "Gideon's in love with Sophie. People will do anything for love."

Will looked at her as if her words had jolted him, then smiled, that same maddeningly sweet smile he had given her in the carriage. "Amazing, isn't it?"

Tessa made as if to answer, but they had reached the drawing room. It was bright inside; the witchlight torches were high, and there was a fire in the grate. The curtains were drawn back, showing squares of leaden sky. Tessa took off her hat and gloves and was just laying them on a small Moroccan table when she saw that Will, who had followed her in, was drawing closed the bolt on the door.

Tessa blinked. "Will, why are you locking—"

She never finished her sentence. Covering the space between them in two long strides, Will reached her and caught her up in an embrace. She gasped in surprise as he took her by the arms, walking her backward until they half-collided with the wall, her crinolette protesting.

"*Will,*" she said in surprise, but he was pinning her to the wall with his body, his hands sliding up her shoulders, into her damp hair, his mouth sudden and hot on hers. She fell and spun and drowned in the kiss; his lips were soft and his body was hard against her, and he tasted like rain. Heat spread through the pit of her stomach as his mouth moved urgently on hers, willing her response.

Jem's face flashed against the back of her closed eyelids. She put her hands flat against Will's chest and shoved him away from her, as hard as she could. Her breath came out on a violent exhalation: "*No.*"

Will took a surprised step backward. His voice, when he spoke, was throaty and low. "But last night? In the infirmary? I—you embraced me—"

I did? With an acute shock she realized that what she had taken for a dream had been no dream after all. Or was he lying? But no. There was no manner in which he could have known what she had dreamed.

"I . . ." Her words stumbled over themselves. "I thought I was dreaming . . ."

The hazy look of desire was fast vanishing from his eyes, replaced by hurt and confusion. He almost stammered: "But even today. I thought you—you said you were as eager to be alone with me as I was—"

"I imagined you wanted an apology! You saved my life at the tea warehouse, and I *am* grateful, Will. I thought you wanted me to tell you that—"

Will looked as if she had slapped him. "I didn't save your life so you'd be *grateful*!"

"Then, what?" Her voice rose. "You did it because it's your mandate? Because the Law says—"

"I did it because I love you!" he half-shouted, and then, as if registering the shocked look on her face, he said in a more subdued voice, "I love you, Tessa, and I have loved you, almost since the moment I met you."

Tessa laced her hands together. They were icy cold. "I thought you couldn't be crueler than you were on the roof that day. I was wrong. This is crueler."

Will stood motionless. Then he shook his head slowly, from side to side, like a patient denying the deadly diagnosis of a physician. "You . . . don't believe me?"

"Of course I don't believe you. After the things you said, the way you've treated me—"

"I *had* to," he said. "I had no choice. Tessa, listen." She began to move toward the door; he scrambled to block her way, his blue eyes burning. "Please listen. *Please*."

Tessa hesitated. The way he said "please"—the catch in his voice—this was not like it had been on the roof. Then he had barely been able to look at her. Now he was staring at her desperately, as if he could will her to remain with desire alone.

The voice that cried within her that he would hurt her, that he was not sincere, grew softer, buried under an ever loudening treacherous voice that told her to stay. To hear him out.

"Tessa." Will pushed his hands through his black hair, his slim fingers trembling with agitation. Tessa remembered what it was like to touch that hair, to have her fingers wound through it, like rough silk against her skin. "What I am going to tell you I have never told another living soul but Magnus, and that was only because I needed his help. I have not even told Jem." Will took a deep breath. "When I was twelve, living with my parents in Wales, I found a Pyxis in my father's office."

She was not sure what she had expected Will to say, but this was not it. "A *Pyxis*? But why would your father keep a Pyxis?"

"A memento from his Shadowhunting days? Who can guess? But do you recall the *Codex* discussing curses and how they can be cast? Well, when I opened the box, I released a demon—Marbas—who cursed me. He swore that anyone who loved me was doomed to die. I might not have believed it—I was not well schooled in magic—but my elder sister died that night, horribly. I thought it was the beginning of the curse. I fled my family and came here. It seemed to me the only way to keep them safe, not to bring them death on death. I did not realize at first that I was walking into a second family. Henry, Charlotte, even bloody Jessamine—I had to make sure that no one here could ever love me. To do so, I thought, would be to put them into deadly danger. For years I have held everyone at arm's length—everyone I could not push away entirely."

Tessa stared at him. The words echoed in her head. *Held everyone at arm's length—pushed everyone away—* She thought of his lies, his hiding, the unpleasantness to Charlotte and

Henry, the cruelties that seemed forced, even the story of Tatiana, who had only loved him the way little girls did, and whose affections he had crushed. And then there was . . . "Jem," she whispered.

He looked at her miserably. "Jem is different," he whispered.

"Jem is *dying*. You let Jem in because he was already near death? You thought the curse wouldn't affect him?"

"And with every year that passed, and he survived, that seemed more likely. I thought I could learn to live like this. I thought when Jem was gone, after I turned eighteen, I'd go live by myself, not inflict myself or my curse on anyone—and then everything changed. Because of you."

"Me?" said Tessa in a quiet, stunned voice.

The ghost of a smile touched his mouth. "When I first met you, I thought you were unlike anyone else I had ever known. You made me laugh. No one but Jem has made me laugh in, good God, five years. And you did it like it was nothing, like breathing."

"You did not even know me. Will—"

"Ask Magnus. He'll tell you. After that night on the roof, I went to him. I had pushed you away because I thought you had begun to realize how I felt about you. In the Sanctuary that day, when I thought you were dead, I realized you must have been able to read it on my face. I was terrified. I had to make you hate me, Tessa. So I tried. And then I wanted to die. I had thought I could bear it if you hated me, but I could not. I realized you would be staying in the Institute, and that every time I saw you it would be like standing on that roof all over again, making you despise me and feeling as if I were choking down poison. I went to Magnus and demanded that he help me find the demon who had cursed me in the first place, that the curse might be lifted. If it was, I thought, I could try again. It might be slow and painful and nearly impossible, but I thought I could make you care for me again, if only I could tell you the truth. That I could gain your trust back—build something with you, slowly."

"Are—are you saying the curse is lifted? That it's *gone*?"

"There is no curse on me, Tessa. The demon tricked me. There never was a curse. All these years, I've been a fool. But not so much a fool that I didn't know that the first thing I needed to do once I had learned the truth was tell you how I really felt." He took another step forward, and this time she did not move back. She was staring at him, at the pale, almost translucent skin under his eyes, at the dark hair curling at his temples, the nape of his neck, at the blue of his eyes and the curve of his mouth. Staring at him the way she might stare at a beloved place she was not sure she would ever see again, trying to commit the details to memory, to paint them on the backs of her eyelids that she might see it when she shut her eyes to sleep.

She heard her own voice as if from very far away. "Why me?" she whispered. "Why me, Will?"

He hesitated. "After we brought you back here, after Charlotte found your letters to your brother, I—I read them."

Tessa heard herself say, very calmly, "I know you did. I found them in your room when I was there with Jem."

He looked startled. "You said nothing to me about it."

"At first I was angry," she admitted. "But that was the night we found you in the ifrit den. I felt for you, I suppose. I told myself you had only been curious, or Charlotte had asked you to read them."

"She didn't," he said. "I pulled them out of the fire myself. I read them all. Every word you wrote. You and I, Tess, we're alike. We live and breathe words. It was books that kept me from taking my own life after I thought I could never love anyone, never be loved by anyone again. It was books that made me feel that perhaps I was not completely alone. They could be honest with me, and I with them. Reading your words, what you wrote, how you were lonely sometimes and afraid, but always brave; the way you saw the world, its colors and textures and sounds, I felt—I felt the way you thought, hoped, felt, dreamed. I felt I was dreaming and thinking and feeling *with* you. I dreamed what you dreamed, wanted what you wanted—and then I realized that truly I just wanted *you*. The girl behind the scrawled letters. I loved you from the moment I read them. I love you still."

Tessa had begun to tremble. This was what she had always wanted someone to say. What she had always, in the darkest corner of her heart, wanted *Will* to say. Will, the boy who loved the same books she did, the same poetry she did, who made her laugh even when she was furious. And here he was standing in front of her, telling her he loved the words of her heart, the shape of her soul. Telling her something she had never imagined anyone would ever tell her. Telling her something she would never be told again, not in this way. And not by him.

And it did not matter.

"It's too late," she said.

"Don't say that." His voice was half a whisper. "I love you, Tessa. I love you."

She shook her head. "Will . . . stop."

He took a ragged breath. "I knew you would be reluctant to trust me," he said. "Tessa, please, is it that you do not believe me, or is it that you cannot imagine ever loving me back? Because if it is the second—"

"Will. It doesn't *matter*—"

"Nothing matters more!" His voice grew in strength. "I *know* that if you hate me it is because I forced you to. I *know* that you have no reason to give me a second chance to be regarded by you in a different light. But I am begging you for that chance. I will do anything. *Anything*."

His voice cracked, and she heard the echo of another voice inside it. She saw Jem, looking down at her, all the love and light and hope and expectancy in the world caught up in his eyes.

"No," she whispered. "It isn't possible."

"It is," he said desperately. "It must be. You cannot hate me as much as all that—"

"I don't hate you at all," she said, with great sadness. "I tried to hate you, Will. But I could never manage it."

"Then, there's a chance." Hope flared in his eyes. She should not have spoken so gently—oh, God, was there nothing that would make this less awful? She had to tell him. Now. Quickly. Cleanly. "Tessa, if you don't hate me, then there's a chance that you might—"

"Jem has proposed to me," she blurted out. "And I have said yes."

"*What?*"

"I said that Jem proposed to me," she whispered. "He asked if I would marry him. And I said I would."

Will had gone shockingly white. He said, "Jem. *My* Jem?"

She nodded, without words to say.

Will staggered and put his hand on the back of a chair

for balance. He looked like someone who had been suddenly, viciously kicked in the stomach. "When?"

"This morning. But we have been growing closer, much closer, for a long time."

"You—and Jem?" Will looked as if he were being asked to believe in something impossible—snow in summertime, a London winter without rain.

In answer, Tessa touched with her fingertips the jade pendant Jem had given her. "He gave me this," she said. Her voice was very quiet. "It was his mother's bridal gift."

Will stared at it, at the Chinese characters on it, as if it were a serpent curled about her throat. "He never told me anything. He never said a word about you to me. Not that way." He pushed his hair back from his face, that characteristic gesture she had seen him make a thousand times, only now his hand was visibly shaking. "Do you love him?"

"Yes, I love him," she said, and she saw Will flinch. "Don't you?"

"But he would understand," he said dazedly. "If we explained it to him. If we told him . . . he would understand."

For just a moment Tessa imagined herself drawing the pendant off, going down the hallway, knocking on Jem's door. Giving it back to him. Telling him she had made a mistake, that she could not marry him. She could tell him, tell him everything about herself and about Will—how she was not sure, how she needed time, how she could not promise him all of her heart, how some part of her belonged to Will and always would.

And then she thought of the first words she had ever heard Jem speak, his eyes closed, his back to her, his face to the moonlight. *Will? Will, is that you?* The way Will's voice, his face, softened for Jem as it did for no one else; the way Jem had gripped Will's hands in the infirmary while he'd bled, the way Will had called out *James!* when the warehouse automaton had knocked Jem down.

I cannot sever them, one from the other, she thought. *I cannot be responsible for such a thing.*

I cannot tell either of them the truth.

She imagined Jem's face if she called off the engagement. He would be kind. Jem was always kind. But she would be breaking something precious inside him, something essential. He would not be the same afterward, and there would be no Will to comfort him. And he had so little time.

And Will? What would he do then? Whatever he might think now, she knew that if she broke things off with Jem, even then, he would not touch her, would not be with her, no matter how much he loved her. How could he parade his love for her in front of Jem, knowing his happiness came at the cost of his best friend's pain? Even if Will told himself he could manage it, to him she would always be the girl Jem loved, until the day Jem died. Until the day *she* died. He would not betray Jem, even after death. If it had been anyone else, anyone else in the world—but she did not love anyone else in the world. These were the boys she loved. For better. And for worse.

She made her voice as cold as she could. As calm. "Told him *what?*"

Will only looked at her. There had been light in his eyes on the stairs, as he'd locked the door, when he'd kissed her—a brilliant, joyous light. And it was going now, fading like the last breath of someone dying. She thought of Nate, bleeding to death in her arms. She had been powerless then, to help him.

As she was now. She felt as if she were watching the life bleed out of Will Herondale, and there was nothing she could do to stop it.

"Jem would forgive me," Will said, but there was hopelessness in his face, his voice, already. He had given up, Tessa thought; Will, who never gave up on any fight before it had started. "He . . ."

"He would," she said. "He could never stay angry at you, Will; he loves you too well for that. I do not even think he would hold anger toward me. But this morning he told me he thought he would die without ever loving anyone as his father loved his mother, without ever being loved like that in return. Do you want me to go down the hallway and knock on his door and take that away from him? And would you love me still, if I did?"

Will looked at her for a long moment. Then he seemed to crumple inside, like paper; he sat down in the armchair, and put his face into his hands. "You promise me," he said. "That you love him. Enough to marry him and make him happy."

"Yes," she said.

"Then, if you love him," he said quietly, "please, Tessa, don't tell him what I just told you. Don't tell him that I love you."

"And the curse? He doesn't know—"

"Please don't tell him about that either. Nor Henry, nor Charlotte—no one. I must tell them in my own time, in my own way. Pretend I said nothing to you. If you care about me at all, Tessa . . ."

"I will tell no one," she said. "I swear it. I promise it, on my angel. My mother's angel. And, Will . . ."

He had lowered his hands, but he still could not seem to

look at her. He was gripping the sides of the armchair, his knuckles white. "I think you had better go, Tessa."

But she could not bear to. Not when he was looking like that, like he was dying on the inside. More than anything else, she wanted to go and put her arms around him, to kiss his eyes closed, to make him smile again. "What you have endured," she said, "since you were twelve years old—it would have killed most people. You have always believed that no one loved you, that no one *could* love you, as their continued survival was proof to you that they did not. But Charlotte loves you. And Henry. And Jem. And your family. They all have always loved you, Will Herondale, for you cannot hide what is good about yourself, however hard you try."

He lifted his head and looked at her. She saw the flame of the fire reflected in his blue eyes. "And you? Do you love me?"

Her nails dug into her palms. "Will," she said.

He looked at her, almost through her, blindly. *"Do you love me?"*

"I . . ." She took a deep breath. It hurt. "Jem has been right about you all this time. You were better than I gave you credit for being, and for that I am sorry. Because if this is you, what you are truly like, and I think that it is—then you will have no difficulty finding someone to love you, Will, someone for whom you come first in their heart. But I . . ."

He made a sound halfway between a choking laugh and a gasp. "'First in your heart,'" he said. "Would you believe that is not the only time you have said that to me?"

She shook her head, bewildered. "Will, I have not—"

"You can never love me," he said flatly, and when she did not respond, when she said nothing, he shuddered—a shudder that ran through his whole body—and pushed away from the armchair without looking at her. He stood up stiffly and crossed the room, groping for the bolt on the door; she watched with her hand across her mouth as, after what seemed like an age, he found it, fumbled it open, and went out into the corridor, slamming the door behind him.

Will, she thought. *Will, is that you?* The backs of her eyes ached. Somehow she found that she was sitting on the floor in front of the grate of the fire. She stared at the flames, waiting for the tears to come. Nothing happened. After such a long time of forcing them back, it seemed, she had lost the ability to cry.

She took the poker from the fireplace iron holder and drove the tip of it into the heart of the burning coals, feeling the heat on her face. The jade pendant around her throat warmed, almost burning her skin.

She drew the poker out of the fire. It glowed as red as a heart. She closed her hand around the tip.

For a moment she felt absolutely nothing. And then, as if from a very great distance, she heard herself cry out, and it was like a key turned inside her heart, freeing the tears at last. The poker clattered to the ground.

When Sophie came dashing in, having heard her scream, she found Tessa on her knees by the fire, her burned hand pressed to her chest, sobbing as if her heart would break.

It was Sophie who took Tessa to her room, and Sophie who put her in her nightgown and then in bed, and Sophie who washed her burned hand with a cool flannel and bound it up with a salve that smelled like herbs and spices, the same salve, she told Tessa, that Charlotte had used on Sophie's cheek when she had first come to the Institute.

"Do you think I'll have a scar?" Tessa asked, more out of curiosity than because she cared one way or the other. The burn, and the weeping that had followed it, seemed to have seared and flooded all the emotion out of her. She felt as light and hollow as a shell.

"Probably a bit of a one, not like I've got," said Sophie frankly, securing the bandage around Tessa's hand. "Burns hurt worse than they are, if you catch my meaning, and I got to you quickly with the salve. You'll be all right."

"No, I won't be," said Tessa, looking at her hand, and then over at Sophie. Sophie, lovely as always, calm and patient in her black dress and white cap, her curls clustering around her face. "I'm sorry again, Sophie," she said. "You were right about Gideon, and I was wrong. I should have listened to you. You're the last person on earth inclined to be foolish over men. The next time you say someone is worth trusting, I will believe you."

Sophie's smile flashed out, the smile that made even strangers forget her scar. "I understand why you said it."

"I should have trusted you—"

"I shouldn't have got so angry," Sophie said. "The truth is, I wasn't sure myself what he was going to do. I wasn't sure till he came back in the carriage with you all that he would side with us in the end."

"It must be nice, though," Tessa said, playing with the bedclothes, "that he's going to live here. He'll be so close to you—"

"It will be the worst thing in the world," Sophie said, and suddenly her eyes were full of tears. Tessa froze in horror, wondering what she could have said so wrong. The tears stood in Sophie's eyes, without falling, making their green shimmer. "If he lives here, he'll see me as I really am. A servant." Her voice cracked. "I knew I should never have gone to see him when he asked me. Mrs. Branwell's not the type to punish her servants for having followers and the like, but I knew it was wrong anyway, because he's himself and I'm me, and we don't belong together." She reached up a hand and wiped at her eyes, and then the tears did fall, spilling down both her cheeks, the whole and the scarred one. "I could lose everything if I let myself—and what's he stand to lose? Nothing."

"Gideon's not like that."

"He's his father's son," Sophie said. "Who says that doesn't matter? It's not as if he was going to marry a mundane as it was, but to see me building up his fire, doing the washing-up—"

"If he loves you, he won't mind all that."

"People *always* mind all that. They are not so noble as you think."

Tessa thought of Will with his face in his hands, saying, *If you love him, please, Tessa, don't tell him what I just told you.* "One finds nobility in the oddest places, Soph. Besides, would you really *want* to be a Shadowhunter? Wouldn't you rather—"

"Oh, but I do want it," said Sophie. "More than anything in the world. I always have."

"I never knew," Tessa said, marveling.

"I used to think if I married Master Jem—" Sophie picked at the blanket, then looked up and smiled bleakly. "You haven't broken his heart yet, have you?"

"No," Tessa said. *Just torn my own in two.* "I haven't broken his heart at all."

21

Coals of Fire

O brother, the gods were good to you.
Sleep, and be glad while the world endures.
Be well content as the years wear through;
Give thanks for life, and the loves and lures;
Give thanks for life, O brother, and death,
For the sweet last sound of her feet, her breath,
For gifts she gave you, gracious and few,
Tears and kisses, that lady of yours.
—Algernon Charles Swinburne,
"The Triumph of Time"

Music poured out from under Jem's door, which was partly cracked open. Will stood with his hand on the knob, his shoulder against the wall. He felt profoundly exhausted, more tired than he ever had in his life. A terrible burning energy had kept him alert since he had left Cheyne Walk, but it was gone now, drained away, and there was only an exhausted darkness.

He had waited for Tessa to call after him once he had

slammed the drawing room door, but she had not. He could still see her, looking at him, with her eyes like great gray storm clouds. *Jem has proposed to me, and I have said yes.*

Do you love him?

I love him.

And yet here he was, standing in front of Jem's door. He did not know if he had come here to try to talk Jem out of Tessa—if such a thing could be accomplished—or, more likely, if this was where he had learned to go for comfort and he could not unlearn the habit of years. He pushed the door open; witchlight poured out into the hallway, and he stepped into Jem's room.

Jem was sitting on the trunk at the foot of his bed, his violin balanced on his shoulder. His eyes were closed as the bow sawed over the string, but the corners of his lips quirked up as his *parabatai* came into the room, and he said: "Will? Is that you, Will?"

"Yes," Will said. He was standing just inside the room, feeling as if he could go no farther.

Jem stopped playing and opened his eyes. "Telemann," he said. "Fantasia in E-flat major." He set the violin and bow down. "Well, come in, then. You're making me nervous, standing there."

Will took a few more steps inside. He had spent so much time in this room, he knew it as well as his own. Jem's collection of music books; the case in which his violin lived when he was not playing it; the windows that let in square patches of sunlight. The trunk that had come all the way from Shanghai. The cane with its jade top, leaning against the wall. The box with Kwan Yin on it, that held Jem's drugs. The armchair in which Will had spent countless nights, watching Jem sleep, counting his breaths and praying.

Jem looked up at him. His eyes were luminous; no suspicion colored them, only a simple happiness at seeing his friend. "I am glad you're here."

"So am I," said Will gruffly. He felt awkward, and wondered if Jem could sense it. He had never felt awkward around his *parabatai* before. It was the words, he thought, there on the tip of his tongue, pleading to be said.

You see it, don't you, James? Without Tessa there is nothing for me—no joy, no light, no life. If you loved me, you would let me have her. You can't love her as I do. No one could. If you are truly my brother, you would do this for me.

But the words remained unspoken, and Jem leaned forward, his voice low and confiding. "Will. There was something I wanted to say to you, and not when everyone else was around."

Will braced himself. This was it. Jem was going to tell him about the engagement, and he was going to have to pretend to be happy, and not be sick out the window, which he desperately wanted to be. He stuffed his hands into his pockets. "And what's that?"

The sun glittered off Jem's hair as he ducked his head. "I should have talked to you before. But we never have discussed the subject of love, have we, and with you being such a cynic . . ." He grinned. "I thought you'd mock me for it. And besides, I never thought there was a chance she'd return my feelings."

"Tessa," said Will. Her name was like knives in his mouth.

Jem's smile was luminous, lighting his whole face, and any hope that Will had harbored in some secret chamber of his heart that perhaps Jem did not really love her, was gone, blown away like mist before a hard wind. "You have never shirked your duties," Jem said. "And I know that you would have done what you could to save Tessa in the tea warehouse, whoever she was. But I could not help thinking that perhaps the reason you were so determined to save her was because you knew what she meant to me." He tipped his head back, his smile incandescent. "Did I guess correctly, or am I a thickheaded idiot?"

"You're an idiot," said Will, and swallowed hard, past his dry throat. "But—you are correct. I know what she means to you."

Jem grinned. His happiness was printed all over his face, his eyes, Will thought; he had never seen him look like this. He had always thought of Jem as a calm and peaceful presence, always thought that joy, like anger, was too extreme and human an emotion for him. He realized now that he had been quite wrong; Jem had simply not been happy like this before. Not since his parents had died, Will imagined. But Will had never considered it. He had dwelled on whether Jem was safe, whether he was surviving, but not if he was *happy*.

Jem is my great sin.

Tessa had been right, he thought. He had wanted her to break things off with Jem, whatever the cost; now he realized he did not, could not. *You might at least believe I know honor—honor, and debt,* he had said to Jem, and he had meant it. He owed Jem his life. He could not take from him the one thing Jem wanted more than anything else. Even if it meant Will's own happiness, for Jem was not only someone to whom he owed a debt that could never be repaid, but, as the covenant said, someone he loved as he loved his own soul.

Jem looked not just happier, but stronger, Will thought,

with healthy color in his cheeks, his back straight. "I ought to apologize," Jem said. "I was too severe regarding the ifrits' den. I know you were merely seeking solace."

"No, you were right to have—"

"I wasn't." Jem stood up. "If I was harsh with you, it was because I cannot bear to see you treat yourself as if you are worth nothing. Whatever part you might act to the contrary, I see you as you really are, my blood brother. Not just better than you pretend to be, but better than most people could hope to be." He placed a hand on Will's shoulder, gently. "You are worth everything, Will."

Will closed his eyes. He saw the black basalt Council room, the two circles burning on the ground. Jem stepping from his circle to Will's, so they inhabited the same space, circumscribed by fire. His eyes had still been black then, wide in his pale face. Will remembered the words of the *parabatai* oath. *Whither thou goest, I will go; where thou diest, will I die, and there will I be buried: the Angel do so to me, and more also, if aught but death part thee and me.* That same voice spoke again to him now. "Thank you for what you did for Tessa," said Jem.

Will could not look at Jem; he looked instead toward the wall, where their shadows blended together in relief, so that one could not tell where one boy ended and the other began. "Thank you for watching Brother Enoch pull shards of metal out of my back afterward," he said.

Jem laughed. "What else are *parabatai* for?"

The Council chamber was draped with red banners slashed with black runes; Jem whispered to Tessa that they were runes of decision and judgment.

They took their seats toward the front, in a row that also contained Henry, Gideon, Charlotte, and Will. Tessa had not spoken to Will since the day before; he had not been at breakfast, and had joined them in the courtyard late, still buttoning his coat as he ran down the stairs. His dark hair was disheveled, and he looked as if he had not slept. He seemed to be trying to avoid looking at Tessa, and she, in turn, avoided returning his gaze, though she could feel it flicking over her from time to time, like hot flecks of ash landing on her skin.

Jem was a perfect gentleman; their engagement was still secret, and other than smiling at her every time she looked at him, he behaved in no way out of the ordinary. As they settled themselves in their seats at the Council, she felt him brush her arm with the knuckles of his right hand, gently, before moving his hand away.

She could feel Will watching them, from the end of the row they sat in. She did not look toward him.

In seats on the raised platform at the chamber's center sat Benedict Lightwood, his eagle profile turned away from the mass of the Council, his jaw set. Beside him sat Gabriel, who, like Will, looked exhausted and unshaven. He glanced once at his brother as Gideon entered the room, and then away as Gideon took his seat, deliberately, among the Shadowhunters of the Institute. Gabriel bit his lip and looked down at his shoes, but did not move from where he sat.

She recognized a few more faces in the audience. Charlotte's aunt Callida was there, as was gaunt Aloysius Starkweather—despite, as he had complained, doubtless not being invited. His eyes narrowed as they fell on Tessa, and she turned back quickly to the front of the room.

"We are here," said Consul Wayland when he had taken his place before the lectern with the Inquisitor seated to his left, "to determine to what extent Charlotte and Henry Branwell have been of assistance to the Clave during the past fortnight in the matter of Axel Mortmain, and whether, as Benedict Lightwood has put in a claim, the London Institute would be better off in other hands."

The Inquisitor rose. He was holding something that gleamed silver and black in his hands. "Charlotte Branwell, please come up to the lectern."

Charlotte got to her feet, and climbed up the stairs to the stage. The Inquisitor lowered the Mortal Sword, and Charlotte wrapped her hands around the blade. In a quiet voice she recounted the events of the past two weeks—searching for Mortmain in newspaper clippings and historical accounts, the visit to Yorkshire, the threat against the Herondales, discovering Jessie's betrayal, the fight at the warehouse, Nate's death. She never lied, though Tessa was conscious of when she left out a detail here or there. Apparently the Mortal Sword could be gotten around, if only slightly.

There were several moments during Charlotte's speech when the Council members reacted audibly: breathing in sharply, shuffling their feet, most notably to the revelation of Jessamine's role in the proceedings. "I knew her parents," Tessa heard Charlotte's aunt Callida saying from the back of the room. "Terrible business—terrible!"

"And the girl is where now?" the Inquisitor demanded.

"She is in the cells of the Silent City," said Charlotte, "awaiting punishment for her crime. I informed the Consul of her whereabouts."

The Inquisitor, who had been pacing up and down the platform, stopped and looked Charlotte keenly in the face. "You say this girl was like a daughter to you," he said, "and yet you handed her over to the Brothers willingly? Why would you do something like that?"

"The Law is hard," said Charlotte, "but it is the Law."

Consul Wayland's mouth flicked up at the corner. "And here you said she'd be too soft on wrongdoers, Benedict," he said. "Any comment?"

Benedict rose to his feet; he had clearly decided to shoot his cuffs today, and they protruded, snowy white, from the sleeves of his tailored dark tweed jacket. "I do have a comment," he said. "I wholeheartedly support Charlotte Branwell in her leadership of the Institute, and renounce my claim on a position there."

A murmur of disbelief ran through the crowd.

Benedict smiled pleasantly.

The Inquisitor turned and looked at him in disbelief. "So you are saying," he echoed, "that *despite* the fact that these Shadowhunters killed Nathaniel Gray—or were responsible for his death—our only link to Mortmain, despite the fact that once again they harbored a spy beneath their roof, *despite* the fact that they still don't know where Mortmain is, you would recommend Charlotte and Henry Branwell to run this Institute?"

"They may not know where Mortmain is," said Benedict, "but they know *who* he is. As the great mundane military strategist Sun Tzu said in *The Art of War*, 'If you know your enemies and know yourself, you can win a hundred battles without a single loss.' We know now who Mortmain really is—a mortal man, not a supernatural being; a man afraid of death; a man bent on revenge for what he considers the undeserved murder of his family. Nor does he have compassion for Downworlders. He utilized werewolves to help him build his clockwork army swiftly, feeding them drugs to keep them working around the clock, knowing the drugs would kill the wolves and ensure their silence. Judging by the size of the warehouse he used and the number of workers he employed, his clockwork army will be sizeable. And judging by his motivations and the years over which he has refined his strategies for revenge, he is a man who cannot be reasoned with, cannot be dissuaded, cannot be stopped. We must prepare for a war. And *that* we did not know before."

The Inquisitor looked at Benedict, thin-lipped, as if he suspected that something untoward was going on but could not imagine what it might be. "Prepare for a war? And how do you suggest we do that—building, of course, on all this supposedly valuable information the Branwells have acquired?"

Benedict shrugged. "Well, that of course will be for the Council to decide over time. But Mortmain has tried to recruit powerful Downworlders such as Woolsey Scott and Camille Belcourt to his cause. We may not know where he is, but we now know his ways, and we can trap him in that manner. Perhaps by allying ourselves with some of Downworld's more powerful leaders. Charlotte seems to have them all well in hand, don't you think?"

A faint laugh ran around the Council, but they were not laughing *at* Charlotte; they were smiling with Benedict. Gabriel was watching his father, his green eyes burning.

"And the spy in the Institute? Would you not call that an example of her carelessness?" said the Inquisitor.

"Not at all," said Benedict. "She dealt with the matter swiftly and without compassion." He smiled at Charlotte, a smile like a razor. "I retract my earlier statement about her softheartedness. Clearly she is as able to deal justice without pity as any man."

Charlotte paled, but said nothing. Her small hands were very still on the Sword.

Consul Wayland sighed gustily. "I wish you had come to this conclusion a fortnight ago, Benedict, and saved us all this trouble."

Benedict shrugged elegantly. "I thought she needed to be tested," he said. "Fortunately, she has passed that test."

Wayland shook his head. "Very well. Let us vote on it." He handed what looked like a cloudy glass vessel to the Inquisitor, who stepped down among the crowd and handed the vial to the woman sitting in the first chair of the first row. Tessa watched in fascination as she bent her head and whispered into the vial, then passed it to the man on her left.

As the vial made its way around the room, Tessa felt Jem slip his hands into hers. She jumped, though her voluminous skirts, she suspected, largely hid their hands. She laced her fingers through his slim, delicate ones and closed her eyes. *I love him. I love him. I love him.* And indeed, his touch made her shiver, though it also made her want to weep—with love, with confusion, with heartbreak, remembering the look on Will's face when she had told him she and Jem were engaged, the happiness going out of him like a fire doused by rain.

Jem drew his hand out of hers to take the vial from Gideon on his other side. She heard him whisper, "Charlotte Branwell," before he passed the vial over her, to Henry on her other side.

She looked at him, and he must have misconstrued the unhappiness in her eyes, because he smiled at her encouragingly. "It will be all right," he said. "They'll choose Charlotte."

When the vial finished its travels, it was handed back to the Inquisitor, who presented it with a flourish to the Consul. The Consul took the vial and, placing it on the lectern before him, drew a rune on the glass with his stele.

The vial trembled, like a kettle on the boil. White smoke poured from its open neck—the collected whispers of hundreds of Shadowhunters. They spelled words out across the air.

CHARLOTTE BRANWELL.

Charlotte dropped her hands from the Mortal Sword, almost sagging in relief. Henry made a whooping noise and threw his hat into the air. The room was filled with chatter and confusion. Tessa couldn't stop herself from glancing down the row at Will. He had slumped down in his seat, his head back, his eyes closed. He looked white and drained, as if this last bit of business had taken the remainder of his energy.

A scream pierced the hubbub. Tessa was on her feet in moments, whirling around. It was Charlotte's aunt Callida screaming, her elegant gray head thrown back and her finger pointing Heavenward. Gasps ran around the room as the other Shadowhunters followed her gaze. The air above them was filled with dozens—scores, even—of buzzing black metal creatures, like enormous steel black beetles with coppery wings, zipping back and forth through the air, filling the room with the ugly sound of metallic buzzing.

One of the metal beetles dipped down and hovered in front of Tessa, just at eye level, making a clicking sound. It was eyeless, though there was a circular plate of glass in the flat front of its head. She felt Jem reach for her arm, trying to pull her away from it, but she jerked away impatiently, seized her hat off her head, and slammed it down on top of the thing, trapping it between her hat and the seat of her chair. It immediately set up an enraged, high-pitched buzzing. "Henry!" she called. "Henry, I've got one of the things—"

Henry appeared behind her, pink-faced, and stared down at the hat. A small hole was opening in the side of the elegant gray velvet where the mechanical creature was tearing at it. With a curse Henry brought his fist down hard, crushing the hat and the thing inside it against the seat. It buzzed and went still.

Jem reached around and lifted the smashed hat gingerly. What was left under it was a scatter of parts—a metal wing, a shattered chassis, and broken-off stumps of copper legs. "Ugh," said Tessa. "It's so very—buglike." She glanced up as another cry went through the room. The insectile creatures had come together in a black swirl in the center of the room; as she stared, they swirled faster and faster and then vanished, like black beetles sucked down a drain.

"Sorry about the hat," said Henry. "I'll get you another."

"Bother the hat," said Tessa as the cries of the angry Council echoed through the room. She looked toward the center of the room; the Consul stood with the glowing Mortal Sword in his hand, and behind him was Benedict, stone-faced, with eyes like ice. "Clearly, we have bigger things to worry about."

"It's a sort of camera," Henry said, holding the bits of the smashed metal beetle creature on his lap as the carriage clopped toward home. "Without Jessamine, Nate, or Benedict,

Mortmain must be out of reliable human spies who can report to him. So he sent these things." He poked at a shard; the bits were gathered together in the wreckage of Tessa's hat, held on his lap as they jounced along.

"Benedict didn't look any too pleased to see those things," said Will. "He must realize Mortmain already knows about his defection."

"It was a matter of time," said Charlotte. "Henry, can those things record sound, like a phonautograph, or simply pictures? They were flying around so quickly—"

"I'm not sure." Henry frowned. "I shall have to examine the parts more closely in the crypt. I can find no shutter mechanism, but that does not mean—" He looked up at the uncomprehending faces focused on him, and shrugged. "In any case," he said, "perhaps it is not the worst thing for the Council to get a look at Mortmain's inventions. It is one thing to hear about them, another to *see* what he is doing. Don't you think, Lottie?"

Charlotte murmured an answer, but Tessa didn't hear it. Her mind was caught up in going over a peculiar thing that had occurred just after she'd left the Council chambers and was waiting for the Branwells' carriage. Jem had just turned away from her to speak to Will, when the flap of a black cloak caught her eye, and Aloysius Starkweather stalked up to her, his grizzled face fierce. "Miss Gray," he'd barked. "That clockwork creature—the way it approached you . . ."

Tessa had stood silently, staring—waiting for him to accuse her of something, though she could not imagine what.

"Thee's all right?" he'd said, abruptly and at last, his Yorkshire accent seeming suddenly very pronounced. "It dinna harm thee?"

Slowly Tessa had shaken her head. "No, Mr. Starkweather. Thank you kindly for your inquiry into my welfare, but no."

By then Jem and Will had turned and were staring. As if aware he was drawing attention, Starkweather had nodded once, sharply, turned, and walked off, his ragged cloak blowing behind him.

Tessa could make neither head nor tail of the whole business. She was just thinking of her brief time in Starkweather's head, and the astonishment he'd felt when he'd first seen her, when the carriage came to a jerking halt before the Institute. Relieved to be free of their cramped quarters, the Shadowhunters and Tessa spilled out, onto the drive.

There was a gap in the gray cloud cover over the city, and lemon yellow sunlight poured down, making the front steps glisten. Charlotte started toward them, but Henry stopped her, pulling her close with the arm that wasn't holding Tessa's destroyed hat. Tessa watched them with the first glimmer of happiness she'd felt since yesterday. She had truly come to care for Charlotte and Henry, she realized, and she wanted to see them happy. "What we should remember is that everything went as well as we could have hoped," Henry said, holding her tightly. "I'm so proud of you, darling."

Tessa would have expected a sarcastic comment from Will at this juncture, but he was staring off toward the gates. Gideon looked embarrassed, Jem as if he were pleased.

Charlotte pulled away from Henry, blushing furiously and straightening her hat, but obviously delighted. "Are you really, Henry?"

"Absolutely! Not only is my wife beautiful, she is brilliant, and that brilliance should be recognized!"

"This," said Will, still looking off toward the gates, "is when Jessamine would have told you to stop because you were making her sick."

The smile vanished from Charlotte's face. "Poor Jessie . . ."

But Henry's expression was uncharacteristically hard. "She shouldn't have done what she did, Lottie. It's not your fault. We can only hope the Council deals with her leniently." He cleared his throat. "And let's have no more talk about Jessamine today, shall we? Tonight is for celebration. The Institute is still ours."

Charlotte beamed at him, with so much love in her eyes that Tessa had to look away, toward the Institute. She blinked. High up in the stone wall, her eyes caught a flicker of movement. A curtain twitched away from the corner of a window, and she saw a pale face peering down. Sophie, looking for Gideon? She couldn't be sure—the face was gone as soon as it had appeared.

Tessa dressed with special care that night, in one of the new gowns Charlotte had provided her: blue satin with a heart-shaped basque and a deeply cut, rounded neckline over which was pinned a chemisette of Mechlin lace. The sleeves were short and ruched, showing her long white arms, and she wore her hair in curls, pinned up and back, a coiffure interlaced with dark blue pansies. It was not until after Sophie had carefully fixed them in her hair that Tessa realized they were the color of Will's eyes, and wanted suddenly to pull them out, but of course she did nothing of the sort, only thanked Sophie for her efforts and complimented her sincerely on how prettily her hair had turned out.

Sophie left before she did, to go and help Bridget in the kitchen. Tessa sat down automatically in front of the mirror to bite her lips and pinch her cheeks. She needed the color, she thought. She was unusually pale. The jade pendant was shoved down under the Mechlin lace, where it could not be seen; Sophie had looked at it as Tessa had dressed, but had not commented. She reached for the clockwork angel pendant and fastened it, too, around her throat. It sat below the other pendant, just under her collarbones, and steadied her with its ticking. There was no reason she could not wear both, was there?

When she emerged into the corridor, Jem was waiting for her. His eyes lit up when he saw her, and after a glance up and down the hall, he drew her toward him and kissed her on the mouth.

She willed herself to melt into the kiss, to dissolve against him as she had done before. His mouth was soft on hers and tasted sweet, and his hand when it cupped her neck was strong and gentle. She moved closer to him, wanting to feel the beat of his heart.

He drew back, breathless. "I didn't mean to do that . . ."

She smiled. "I think you did, James."

"Not before I saw you," he said. "I meant only to ask if I could escort you to dinner. But you look so beautiful." He touched her hair. "I'm afraid too much passion could start you shedding petals like a tree in autumn, though."

"Well, you can," she said. "Escort me to dinner, that is."

"Thank you." He ran his fingertips lightly across her cheekbones. "I thought I would wake up this morning and it would have been a dream, you saying yes to me. But it wasn't. Was it?" His eyes searched her face.

She shook her head. She could taste tears in the back of her throat and was glad for the kid gloves that hid the burn on her left hand.

"I'm sorry you're getting such a bad bargain in me, Tessa," he said. "In years, I mean. Shackling yourself to a dying man when you're only sixteen . . ."

"*You're* only seventeen. Plenty of time to find a cure," she whispered. "And we will. Find one. I will be with you. Forever."

"Now, *that* I believe," he said. "When two souls are as one, they stay together on the Wheel. I was born into this world to love you, and I will love you in the next life, and the one after that."

She thought of Magnus. *We are chained to this life by a chain of gold, and we dare not sever it for fear of what lies beyond the drop.*

She knew what he meant now. Immortality was a gift, but not one without its consequences. *For if I am immortal,* she thought, *then I have only this, this one life. I will not turn and change as you do, James. I will not see you in Heaven, or on the banks of the great river, or in whatever life lies beyond this one.*

But she did not say it. It would hurt him, and if there was anything she knew to be true, it was that a fierce unreasoning desire lived in her to protect him from hurt, to stand between him and disappointment, between him and pain, between him and death, and fight them all back as Boadicea had fought back the advancing Romans. She reached up and touched his cheek instead, and he put his face against her hair, her hair full of flowers the color of Will's eyes, and they stood like that, clasped together, until the dinner bell rang a second time.

Bridget, who could be heard singing mournfully in the kitchen, had outdone herself in the dining room, placing candles in silver holders everywhere so the whole place glimmered with light. Cut roses and orchids floated in silver bowls on the white linen tablecloth. Henry and Charlotte presided at the head of the table. Gideon, in evening dress, sat with his eyes fixed on Sophie as she came in and out of the room, though she seemed to be studiously avoiding his glances. And beside him sat Will.

I love Jem. I am marrying Jem. Tessa had repeated it to herself all the way down the hall, but it made little difference; her heart flipped sickeningly in her chest when she saw Will. She had not seen him in evening dress since the night of the ball, and, despite seeming pale and ill, he still looked ridiculously handsome in it.

"Is your cook *always* singing?" Gideon was asking in an awed tone as Jem and Tessa came in. Henry looked up and, on seeing them, smiled all over his friendly, freckled face.

"We were beginning to wonder where you two were—," he began.

"Tessa and I have news," Jem burst out. His hand found Tessa's, and held it; she stood frozen as three curious faces turned toward them—four, if you counted Sophie, who had just walked into the room. Will sat where he was, gazing at the silver bowl in front of him; a white rose was floating in it, and he seemed prepared to stare at it until it went under. In the kitchen Bridget was still singing one of her awful sad songs; the lyrics drifted in through the door:

"'Twas on an evening fair I went to take the air,
I heard a maid making her moan;
Said, 'Saw ye my father? Or saw ye my mother?

Or saw ye my brother John?
Or saw ye the lad that I love best,
And his name it is Sweet William?'"

I may murder her, Tessa thought. Let her make a song about *that.*

"Well, you have to tell us now," said Charlotte, smiling. "Don't leave us dangling in suspense, Jem!"

Jem raised their joined hands and said, "Tessa and I are engaged to be married. I asked her, and—she accepted me."

There was a shocked silence. Gideon looked astonished—Tessa felt rather sorry for him, in a detached sort of way—and Sophie stood holding a pitcher of cream, her mouth open. Both Henry and Charlotte looked startled out of their wits. None of them could have been expecting this, Tessa thought; whatever Jessamine had said about Tessa's mother being a Shadowhunter, she was still a Downworlder, and Shadowhunters did not marry Downworlders. This moment had not occurred to her. She had thought somehow that they would tell everyone separately, carefully, not that Jem would blurt it out in a fever of joyous happiness in the dining room. And she thought, *Oh, please smile. Please congratulate us. Please don't spoil this for him. Please.*

Jem's smile had only just begun to slip, when Will rose to his feet. Tessa drew a deep breath. He *was* beautiful in evening dress, that was true, but he was always beautiful; there was something different about him now, though, a deeper layer to the blue of his eyes, cracks in the hard and perfect armor around himself that let through a blaze of light. This was a new Will, a different Will, a Will she had caught only glimpses of—a Will that perhaps only Jem had ever really known. And now she would never know him. The thought pierced her with a sadness as if she were remembering someone who had died.

He raised his glass of wine. "I do not know two finer people," he said, "and could not imagine better news. May your lives together be happy and long." His eyes sought Tessa's, then slid away from her, fastening on Jem. "Congratulations, brother."

A flood of other voices came after his speech. Sophie set the pitcher down and came to embrace Tessa; Henry and Gideon shook Jem's hand, and Will stood watching it all, still holding the glass. Through the happy babble of voices, only Charlotte was silent, her hand against her chest; Tessa bent worriedly over her. "Charlotte, is everything all right?"

"Yes," Charlotte said, and then more loudly, "*Yes.* It is just—I have news of my own. Good news."

"Yes, darling," said Henry. "We won the Institute back! But everyone does already know—"

"No, not that, Henry. You—" Charlotte made a hiccuping sound, half laughter, half tears. "Henry and I are going to have a child. A boy. Brother Enoch told me. I didn't want to say anything before, but—"

The rest of her words were drowned out by Henry's incredulous whoop of joy. He lifted Charlotte entirely out of her seat and threw his arms around her. "Darling, that's wonderful, wonderful—"

Sophie gave a little shriek and clapped her hands. Gideon looked as if he were so embarrassed that he might conceivably die on the spot, and Will and Jem exchanged bemused smiles. Tessa could not help smiling as well; Henry's delight was infectious. He waltzed Charlotte across the room and then back again before suddenly stopping, horrified that waltzing might be bad for the baby, and sat her down in the nearest chair.

"Henry, I'm perfectly capable of walking," Charlotte said indignantly. "Even of dancing."

"My darling, you are indisposed! You must remain abed for the next eight months. Little Buford—"

"I am *not* naming our child Buford. I don't care if it was your father's name, or if it is a traditional Yorkshire name—," Charlotte began in exasperation, when a knock sounded on the door, and Cyril poked his tousled head in. He stared at the scene of gaiety going on in front of him, and said hesitantly:

"Mr. Branwell, there's someone here to see you all."

Henry blinked. "Someone to see us? But this is a private dinner, Cyril. And I did not hear the bell ring—"

"No, she is Nephilim," said Cyril. "And she says it's very important. She will not wait."

Henry and Charlotte exchanged bewildered glances. "Well, all right, then," said Henry at last. "Let her up, but tell her it will have to be quick."

Cyril vanished. Charlotte rose to her feet, smoothing down her dress and patting her disheveled hair. "Aunt Callida, perhaps?" she said in a puzzled voice. "I can't fathom who else . . ."

The door opened again, and Cyril came in, followed by a young girl of about fifteen. She wore a black traveling cloak over a green dress. Even if Tessa had not seen her before, she would have known who she was instantly—known her by her black hair, by the violet-blue of her eyes, by the graceful curve of her white throat, the delicate angles of her features, the full swoop of her mouth.

She heard Will draw a sudden, violent breath.

"Hello," said the girl, in a voice both surprisingly soft and surprisingly firm. "I apologize for interrupting your dinner hour, but I had nowhere else to go. I am Cecily Herondale, you see. I have come to be trained as a Shadowhunter."

Acknowledgments

Thanks as always to my family: my mother and father; Jim Hill and Kate Connor; Nao, Tim, David, and Ben; Melanie, Jonathan, and Helen Lewis; Florence; and Joyce. Thanks to those who read and critiqued and pointed out anachronisms or inconsistencies: Kelly Link, Clary, Delia Sherman, Holly Black, Sarah Rees Brennan, Justine Larbalestier, Robin Wasserman, Maureen Johnson. Thanks to Lisa Gold, Research Maven (lisagoldresearch.wordpress.com) for her help. Thanks to Joey Yeung and Huan Yu for the Mandarin translations. Thanks to Wayne Miller for Greek and Latin help. My always gratitude to my agent, Barry Goldblatt; my editor, Karen Wojtyla; and the teams at Simon & Schuster and Walker Books for making it all happen. And of course, thanks to my husband, Josh, for keeping Linus and Lucy from eating the manuscript.

A Note on Tessa's England

As in *Clockwork Angel*, the London of *Clockwork Prince* is, as much as I could make it, an admixture of the real and the unreal, the famous and the forgotten. (For instance, there really is a Pyx Chamber in Westminster Abbey.) The geography of real Victorian London is preserved as much as possible, but there were times that wasn't possible.

For those wondering about the Institute: There was indeed a church called All-Hallows-the-Less that burned in the Great Fire of London in 1666; it was located, however, in Upper Thames Street, not where I have placed it, just off Fleet Street. Those familiar with London will recognize the location of the Institute, and the shape of its spire, as that of the famous St. Bride's Church, beloved of newspapermen and journalists, which goes unmentioned in the Infernal Devices as the Institute has taken its place. For those wondering about the Institute in

York, it is based on Holy Trinity Goodramgate, a church you can still find and tour in York.

As for the Lightwoods' house in Chiswick, during the sixteenth and seventeenth centuries it was believed Chiswick was far enough from London to be a healthy refuge from the city's dirt and disease, and wealthy families did have mansions there. The Lightwoods' is based very sketchily on famous Chiswick House. As for Number 16 Cheyne Walk, where Woolsey Scott lives, it was at the time actually rented together by Algernon Charles Swinburne, Dante Gabriel Rossetti, and George Meredith. They were members of the aesthetic movement, and would have appreciated the motto on Woolsey's ring—"*L'art pour l'art*," or "Art for art's sake."

As for the opium den in Whitechapel, much research has been done on the subject but there is no proof that the opium den, much beloved of Sherlock Holmes fans and enthusiasts of the Gothic, ever existed at all. Here it has been replaced by a den of demonic vice. It has never been proved that those existed either, but then, it has never been proved that they didn't.

For those wondering what Will says to Tessa just outside the mansion in Chiswick, *Caelum denique* was the battle cry of the Crusaders and means "Heaven at last!"

Go deeper into the world of
Shadowhunters and Downworlders with

Clockwork Princess

BOOK THREE IN THE INFERNAL DEVICES.

York, 1847.

"I'm afraid," said the little girl sitting on the bed. "Grandfather, can you stay with me?"

Aloysius Starkweather made an impatient noise in the back of his throat as he drew a chair closer to the bedside and seated himself. The impatient noise was only part in earnest. It pleased him that his granddaughter was so trusting of him, that often he was the only one who could calm her. His gruff demeanor had never bothered her, despite her delicate nature.

"There's nothing to be afraid of, Adele," he said. "You'll see."

She looked at him with large eyes. Normally the ceremony of first runing would have been held in one of the grander spaces of the York Institute, but because of Adele's fragile nerves and health, it had been agreed that it could occur in the safety of her bedroom. She was sitting at the edge of her bed, her back very straight. Her ceremonial dress was red, with a red ribbon holding back her fine, fair hair. Her eyes were huge in her thin face, her arms narrow. Everything about her was as fragile as a china cup.

"The Silent Brothers," she said. "What will they do to me?"

"Give me your arm," he said, and she held out her right arm trustingly. He turned it over, seeing the pale blue tracery of veins below the skin. "They will use their steles—you know what a stele is—to draw a Mark upon you. Usually they start with the Voyance rune, which you will know from your studies, but in your case they will begin with Strength."

"Because I am not very strong."

"To build your constitution."

"Like beef broth." Adele wrinkled her nose.

He laughed. "Hopefully not so unpleasant. You will feel a little sting, so you must be brave and not cry out, because Shadowhunters do not cry out in pain. Then the sting will be gone, and you will feel so much stronger and better. And that will be the end of the ceremony, and we will go downstairs and there will be iced cakes to celebrate."

Adele kicked her heels. "And a party!"

"Yes, a party. And presents." He tapped his pocket, where a small box was hidden away—a small box wrapped in fine blue paper, that held an even smaller family ring. "I have one for you right here. You'll get it as soon as the Marking ceremony is over."

"I've never had a party for me before."

"It's because you're becoming a Shadowhunter," said Aloysius. "You know why that's important, don't you? Your first Marks mean you are Nephilim, like me, like your mother and father. They mean you are part of the Clave. Part of our warrior family. Something different and better than everyone else."

"Better than everyone else," she repeated slowly as her bedroom door opened and two Silent Brothers came in. Aloysius saw the flicker of fear in Adele's eyes. She drew her arm back from his grasp. He did not like to see fear in his progeny, though he could not deny that the Brothers were eerie in their silence and their peculiar, gliding motions. They moved around to Adele's side of the bed as the door opened again and Adele's mother and father entered: her father, Aloysius's son, in scarlet gear; his wife in a red dress that belled out at the waist and a golden necklace from which hung an *enkeli* rune. They smiled at their daughter, who gave a tremulous smile back, even as the Silent Brothers surrounded her.

Adele Lucinda Starkweather. It was the voice of the first Silent Brother, Brother Cimon. *You are now of age. It is time for the first of the Angel's Marks to be bestowed on you. Are you aware of the honor being done you, and will you do all in your power to be worthy of it?*

Adele nodded obediently. "Yes."

And do you accept these Marks of the Angel, which will be upon your body forever, a reminder of all that you owe to the Angel, and of your sacred duty to the world?

She nodded again, obediently. Aloysius's heart swelled with pride. "I do accept them," she said.

Then we begin. A stele flashed forth, held in the Silent Brother's long white hand. He took Adele's trembling arm and set the tip of the stele to her skin, and began to draw.

Black lines swirled out from the stele's tip, and Adele stared in wonderment as the symbol for Strength took shape on the pale skin of her inner arm, a delicate design of lines intersecting with each other, crossing her veins, wrapping her arm. Her body was tense, her small teeth sunk into her upper lip. Her eyes flashed upward at Aloysius, and he started at what he saw in them.

Pain. It was normal to feel some pain at the bestowing of a Mark, but what he saw in Adele's eyes—was agony.

Aloysius jerked upright, sending the chair he had been sitting on skittering away behind him. "Stop!" he cried, but it was too late. The rune was complete. The Silent Brother drew back, staring. There was blood on the stele. Adele was whimpering, mindful of her grandfather's admonition that she not cry out—but then her bloody, lacerated skin began to peel back from the bones, blackening and burning under the rune as if it were fire, and she could not help but throw her head back, and scream, and scream . . .

London, 1873.

"Will?" Charlotte Fairchild eased the door of the Institute's training room open. "Will, are you in there?"

A muffled grunt was the only response. The door swung all the way open, revealing the wide, high-ceilinged room on the other side. Charlotte herself had grown up training here, and she knew every warp of the floorboards, the ancient target painted on the north wall, the square-paned windows, so old that they were thicker at the base than the top. In the center of the room stood Will Herondale, a knife held in his right hand.

He turned his head to look at Charlotte, and she thought again what an odd child he was—although at twelve he was barely still a child. He was a very pretty boy, with thick dark hair that waved slightly where it touched his collar—wet now with sweat, and pasted to his forehead. His skin had been tanned by country air and sun when he had first come to the Institute, though six months of city life had drained its color, causing the red flush across his cheekbones to stand out. His eyes were an unusually luminous blue. He would be a handsome man one day, if he could do something about the scowl that perpetually twisted his features.

"What is it, Charlotte?" he snapped.

He still spoke with a slight Welsh accent, a roll to his vowels that would have been charming if his tone hadn't been so sour. He drew his sleeve across his forehead as she came partway through the door, then paused. "I've been looking for you for hours," she said with some asperity, though asperity had little effect on Will. Not much had an effect on Will when he was in a mood, and he was nearly always in a mood. "Didn't you recall what I told you yesterday, that we were welcoming a new arrival to the Institute today?"

"Oh, I remembered." Will threw the knife. It stuck just outside the circle of the target, deepening his scowl. "I just don't care."

The boy behind Charlotte made a stifled noise. A laugh, she would have thought, but certainly he couldn't be laughing? She had been warned the boy coming to the Institute from Shanghai was not well, but she had still been startled when he had stepped from the carriage, pale and swaying like a reed in the wind, his curling dark hair streaked with silver as if he were a man in his eighties, not a boy of twelve. His eyes were wide and silvery-black, strangely beautiful but haunting in such a delicate face. "Will, you *shall* be polite," she said now, and drew the boy out from behind her, ushering him ahead into the room. "Don't mind Will; he's only moody. Will Herondale, may I introduce you to James Carstairs, of the Shanghai Institute."

"Jem," said the boy. "Everyone calls me Jem." He took another step forward into the room, his gaze taking in Will with a friendly curiosity. He spoke without the trace of an accent, to Charlotte's surprise, but then his father was—had been—British. "You can too."

"Well, if everyone calls you that, it's hardly any special favor to me, is it?" Will's tone was acid; for someone so young, he was amazingly capable of unpleasantness. "I think you will find, James Carstairs, that if you keep to yourself and let me alone, it will be the best outcome for both of us."

Charlotte sighed inwardly. She had so hoped that this boy, the same age as Will, would prove a tool to disarm Will of his anger and his viciousness, but it seemed clear that Will had been speaking the truth when he had told her he did not care if another Shadowhunter boy was coming to the Institute. He did not want friends, or want for them. She glanced at Jem, expecting to see him blinking in surprise or hurt, but he was only smiling a little, as if Will were a kitten that had tried to bite him. "I haven't trained since I left Shanghai," he said. "I could use a partner—someone to spar with."

"So could I," said Will. "But I need someone who can keep up with me, not some sickly creature that looks as if he's doddering off to the grave. Although I suppose you might be useful for target practice."

Charlotte, knowing what she did about James Carstairs—a fact she had not shared with Will—felt a sickly horror come over her. *Doddering off to the grave, oh dear Lord.* What was it her father had said? That Jem was dependent on a drug to live, some kind of medicine that would extend his life but not save it. *Oh, Will.*

She made as if to move in between the two boys, as if she could protect Jem from Will's cruelty, more awfully accurate in this instance that even he knew—but then she paused.

Jem had not even changed expression. "If by 'doddering off to the grave' you mean dying, then I am," he said. "I have about two years more to live, three if I am lucky, or so they tell me."

Even Will could not hide his shock; his cheeks flushed red. "I . . ."

But Jem had set his steps toward the target painted on the wall; when he reached it, he yanked the knife free from the wood. Then he turned and walked directly up to Will.

Delicate as he was, they were of the same height, and only inches from each other their eyes met and held. "You may use me for target practice if you wish," said Jem, as casually as if he were talking about the weather. "It seems to me I have little to fear from such an exercise, as you are not a very good shot." He turned, took aim, and let the knife fly. It stuck directly into the heart of the target, quivering slightly. "Or," Jem went on, turning back to Will, "you could allow *me* to teach *you*. For I am a *very* good shot."

Charlotte stared. For half a year she had watched Will push away everyone who'd tried to get near him—tutors; her father; her fiancé, Henry; both the Lightwood brothers—with a combination of hatefulness and precisely accurate cruelty. If it were not that she herself was the only person who had ever seen him cry, she imagined she would have given up hope as well, long ago, that he would ever be any good to anybody. And yet here he was, looking at Jem Carstairs, a boy so fragile-looking that he appeared to be made out of glass, with the hardness of his expression slowly dissolving into a tentative uncertainty. "You are not *really* dying," he said, the oddest tone to his voice, "are you?"

Jem nodded. "So they tell me."

"I am sorry," Will said.

"No," Jem said softly. He drew his jacket aside and took a knife from the belt at his waist. "Don't be ordinary like that. Don't say you're sorry. Say you'll train with me."

He held out the knife to Will, hilt first. Charlotte held her breath, afraid to move. She felt as if she were watching something very important happen, though she could not have said what.

Will reached out and took the knife, his eyes never leaving Jem's face. His fingers brushed the other boy's as he took the weapon from him. It was the first time, Charlotte thought, that she had ever seen him touch any other person willingly.

"I'll train with you," he said.

Is your Institute's edition of *The Shadowhunter's Codex* up-to-date?

Be sure to get the newest edition,
which contains brand-new material and illustrations!
Turn the page to find out more.

THE CLAVE IS PLEASED TO ANNOUNCE

the newest edition of the Nephilim's oldest and most famous training manual: *The Shadowhunter's Codex*. Since the thirteenth century, the *Codex* has been the young Shadowhunter's best friend. When you're being swarmed by demons it can be easy to forget the finer points of obscure demon languages or the fastest way to stop an attack of Raum demons. With the *Codex* by your side, you never have to worry.

Now in its twenty-seventh edition, the *Codex* covers it all: the history and the laws of our world; how to identify, interact with, and, if necessary, kill that world's many colorful denizens; which end of the stele is the end you write with. No more will your attempt to fight off rogue vampires and warlocks be slowed by the need to answer endless questions from your new recruits: What is a Pyxis? Why don't we use guns? If I can't see a warlock's mark, is there a polite way to ask him where it is? Where do we get all our holy water? Geography, history, magic, and zoology textbook all rolled into one, the *Codex* is here to help new Shadowhunters navigate the beautiful but often brutal world that we inhabit.

Do not let it be said that the Clave is outdated or, as the younger Shadowhunters say, "uncool": this new edition of the *Codex* will be available not only in the usual magically sealed demonskin binding, but also in a smart, modern edition using all of today's most exciting printing techniques, including such new features as a sturdy clothbound cover, a protective dust jacket, and information about title, author, publisher, and so on conveniently available right on the cover. You'll be pleased to know that it fits neatly into most satchels, and unlike previous editions, it rarely sets off alarm wards.

The old woodcuts and engravings have been replaced as well: instead, you'll find lavish modern illustrations by some of the brightest luminaries of the fantastic. Creatures, weapons, people, and places have been carefully and accurately rendered by the likes of Rebecca Guay, Charles Vess, Jim Nelson, Theo Black, Elisabeth Alba, and Cassandra Jean. Chapters are beautifully introduced by the drawings of Michael Wm. Kaluta, and along with our condensation of the classic 2,450-page tome *A History of the Nephilim*, you will find a selection of the best of the lovely illustrations of that volume by John Dollar.

This edition of the *Codex* will be available in Institute libraries and what mundanes sometimes call "bookstores."

Hey. Um, Clary Fairchild here. Hi. Look, the Codex *is full of useful information—Simon says it's like a game manual for being a Shadowhunter—and that's great. But it's a little stuffy, for one thing, and for another, you probably know by now that the Clave's versions of things aren't always the most accurate. And then with all the stuff that's been going on lately, it's way out of date now! So this is not just the* Codex*—this is* my *copy of the* Codex. *I've made a ton of notes and tried to fix it when things seem not exactly right in the official story. Jace added some of his notes too. There's also a whole bunch of my drawings and sketches in there—hope you like them!*

Oh, also, it is maybe possible that a certain vampire friend of mine may have taken my Codex *and made his own comments in there too. Just ignore him; he only wants attention.*